Praise for

Heidi Swain

'Brimming with warmth and Christmas cheer'
Sarah Morgan

'Sweet and lovely. I guarantee you will fall in love
with Heidi's wonderful world' **Milly Johnson**

'A little slice of joy' *Heat*

'Grab a hot chocolate and lose yourself in this
heart-warming story of romance, community and secrets.
The perfect story to read by the fire!' **Phillipa Ashley**

'The queen of feel-good' *Woman & Home*

'The most delicious slice of festive fiction: a
true comfort read and the perfect treat to
alleviate all the stress!' **Veronica Henry**

'A story that captures your heart' **Christie Barlow**

'Sparkling and romantic' *My Weekly*

'Sprinkled with Christmas sparkle' **Trisha Ashley**

'Grab a glass of mulled wine and enjoy this sparkling,
snow-filled romance' *Culturefly*

Also by Heidi Swain

The Cherry Tree Café

Summer at Skylark Farm

Mince Pies and Mistletoe at the Christmas Market

Coming Home to Cuckoo Cottage

Sleigh Rides and Silver Bells at the Christmas Fair

Sunshine and Sweet Peas in Nightingale Square

Snowflakes and Cinnamon Swirls
at the Winter Wonderland

Poppy's Recipe for Life

The Christmas Wish List

The Secret Seaside Escape

The Winter Garden

A Taste of Home

Underneath the Christmas Tree

The Summer Fair

A Christmas Celebration

The Book-Lovers' Retreat

That Festive Feeling

The Holiday Escape

Heidi Swain
Home For Christmas

**SIMON &
SCHUSTER**

London · New York · Sydney · Toronto · New Delhi

First published in Great Britain by Simon & Schuster UK Ltd, 2024

Copyright © Heidi-Jo Swain, 2024

The right of Heidi-Jo Swain to be identified as author of this work has been asserted in accordance with the Copyright, Designs and Patents Act, 1988.

3 5 7 9 10 8 6 4

Simon & Schuster UK Ltd
1st Floor
222 Gray's Inn Road
London WC1X 8HB

Simon & Schuster: Celebrating 100 Years of Publishing in 2024

Simon & Schuster Australia,
Sydney

Simon & Schuster India,
New Delhi

www.simonandschuster.co.uk
www.simonandschuster.com.au
www.simonandschuster.co.in

A CIP catalogue record for this book is available from the British Library

Paperback ISBN: 978-1-3985-1960-2
eBook ISBN: 978-1-3985-1961-9
Audio ISBN: 978-1-3985-1962-6

Typeset in Bembo Std by Palimpsest Book Production Ltd, Falkirk, Stirlingshire

Printed and Bound in the UK using 100% Renewable Electricity at
CPI Group (UK) Ltd

MIX
Paper | Supporting
responsible forestry
FSC® C171272

To Clare Marchant,
fellow mermaid and fabulous friend!

Chapter 1

I was certain my heart skipped more than just one happy beat as I stood on the drive with Tink, my beloved King Charles spaniel, and waved off the last of that year's paying guests.

'Come on, then, my love,' I said cheerfully, bending to stroke her silky ears. 'We've got a party to get ready for and some celebrating to do!'

My best friend Jeanie, who, a few months before, had returned to Wynbridge, ostensibly to help her aunt and uncle run the Mermaid pub, but really nursing a broken heart, had spent weeks organising a Hallowe'en party, and I, being more adept with a sewing machine than both her and our other friend Holly, was in charge of costumes.

'Let's go and find your wings,' I said to Tink, and she yipped in response.

Once we were transformed, we set off on foot, rather later than planned. We received more than a few double takes along the way, but that was only to be expected, because it wasn't every day that you saw a lion walking a flying monkey along the pavement in a Fenland market town.

'I was beginning to think I was going to have to send out

a search party,' said Jeanie, looking pointedly at the clock behind the bar as she let us into the spookily decorated pub. 'I thought you'd got waylaid moving back into the house.'

I handed over the bag containing her costume with a smile.

'I haven't even been inside the house yet,' I told her as she locked the pub door behind us. 'I had hoped to be on time, but my mane scuppered the schedule.'

I had triumphantly teased my thick blonde curls into an unruly lion's mane, but it had taken more product than I'd ordinarily use in an entire year to achieve the wild result.

'Well,' said Jeanie, as she cocked her head and looked at me appraisingly, 'I suppose it was worth you being a bit behind time, because you look amazing.'

'Thank you,' I said, twizzling the tail on my costume and hoping my whiskers weren't going to come unstuck, 'and so will you by the time I've finished with you. Let's get you changed before it's time to let everyone in.'

As Jeanie was working behind the bar that evening as well as hosting the party, I'd had to adapt her costume so that she could move freely. The silver lurex catsuit was a somewhat slinky take on the Tin Man, but it achieved the overall impact we'd been hoping for and gave her the ability to walk without the necessity of an oil can.

'Can we tighten the chin strap up a bit?' she requested as she pushed the plastic funnel that I'd sprayed silver further back on her head.

'Here's the third musketeer,' said Jeanie's uncle Jim as he came up the pub stairs ahead of Holly, who was going to complete our ode to Oz. 'Hey,' he then tutted, 'that'd better not be my funnel.'

Thankfully the arrival of the Scarecrow with a flying monkey of her own saved Jeanie from having to confess that it was.

'Oh my god!' Holly laughed as she stepped into the room. 'You two look hilarious.'

'You're pretty amusing yourself,' I couldn't help but giggle.

'The straw's a bit scratchy.' She wriggled as I admired the attention she'd paid to putting the finishing touches on the costume I'd started off for her. 'I hope I'm not allergic.'

Jim shook his head and left us to it, and Holly put her little rescue terrier, Jasper, down to readjust some straw which was poking out of the bottom of her patched trousers. He and Tink greeted each other ecstatically.

'You've got Jasper's wings on upside down,' I pointed out. 'He'll never take to the skies like that.'

'I knew there was something wrong with them,' said Holly, rolling her eyes and scooping him back up again. 'Can you help me sort them? And then we'd better take some photos for me to send to May.'

'Oh yes,' laughed Jeanie. 'She's bound to want to see, isn't she?'

Holly had only moved to the area a few months before Jeanie returned to town, but the three of us had quickly become firm friends. Sometimes, when Jeanie and I were reminiscing over school days, we'd forget that Holly hadn't been around for ever and would have to fill her in on what we were talking about.

Holly's life had changed beyond all recognition since she'd divorced and met her new partner Bear and his flamboyant actress mum, May Madison. May had a great fondness for dressed-up dogs, hence the photocall. Just like me on the work front, Holly was also following her creative passion and her heart's desire. And talking of hearts . . .

'So,' said Jeanie, turning to me with uncanny timing, 'tell me why you assigned us these characters for the party tonight, Bella?'

I could have fobbed her off with the explanation that in Oz, Dorothy had three friends and that the character each of us was portraying was accidental, but I knew she wouldn't believe me. It was time I came clean about the choices I had made.

'Because I thought they genuinely suited us,' I therefore told her. 'As in, they match where we're all at in our lives. Thanks to you two, I've found my courage this year in starting to further expand my business, and Holly has certainly been using her brain to make a success of her work, which ties in with the Scarecrow.'

Holly's debut book, *Tall Tales from Small Dogs*, which she had both written and illustrated, featured a dachshund called Monty and a bull terrier named Queenie, who, in real life, belonged to May and Bear respectively. The book had been a bestseller from practically the moment it hit the shelves.

'Which leaves . . .' I said, biting my lip.

'My heart,' huffed Jeanie, with her hands planted firmly on her hips.

'Your heart,' I echoed softly. 'It's about time it got some exercise.'

The broken heart Jeanie had returned to town with had been carefully glued back together, but she hadn't yet tested it out, even though there was someone wonderful still keenly waiting in the wings to whisk her back off her feet.

'And we know just the man—' Holly began to say, but Jeanie cut her off.

'But what about *your* heart?' she said to me bluntly. 'You could just as easily have been the Tin Man. Your heart could do with a proper workout, too.'

'My colouring's all wrong for silver,' I said lightly, while focusing on fiddling with the rearrangement of Jasper's wings.

'Jeanie does have a point, though . . .' Holly started.

Thankfully, just at that moment, Jeanie's aunt Evelyn stuck her head around the door and cut Holly off, so I didn't have to convince my friends that my own major organ was perfectly healthy. I was genuinely very happy with my single status; that said, I was willing to indulge in a quick dalliance if the right opportunity happened to come along.

Jeanie, on the other hand, had always been more content when she was one half of a pair and, unlike me, had been willing to risk the heartbreak of a committed relationship not working out; therefore she was the one who now needed some encouragement to have a look around the love department again. I was fine staying out of it.

Mum's awful experiences with the two father figures in my life and then losing my decades-long devoted grandparents within weeks of each other ensured that I preferred to keep the few men who entered my life at arm's length. From what I'd witnessed and felt the sting of, it didn't matter how relationships ended – the heart was always compromised in some way and, for me, it simply wasn't worth the risk of putting it on the frontline and getting it broken.

'I take it you're aware of the time, Jeanie?' Evelyn said, having looked over what we were wearing with nothing more than a slight twitch of her lips. 'Ten minutes until opening time, and I can hear there's already quite a crowd outside clamouring to be let in.'

Jeanie looked thrilled. She'd put a lot of effort into promoting the party and had really gone to town on the pumpkin decorations, bloated body balloons and spooky streamers.

'Can you take our picture, please, Evelyn?' Holly politely requested, before the woman who was always on the go disappeared again. 'Then we'll be straight down.'

With the three of us, five if you included the dogs, hamming it up for the photos, I just knew it was going to be a night to remember.

'So, tell me again,' said Holly, her voice raised so I could hear her above the din which had escalated as the pitchers of creepy cocktails had been enthusiastically emptied and refilled, 'when are you moving back into the house?'

We were standing at the end of the bar, which was crowded with mummies and warlocks, vampires and ghouls, because there wasn't a seat to be had. Tink and Jasper, having been admired, had been taken back upstairs so they didn't get trodden on, and I hoped they were having a snooze rather than causing havoc.

'First thing tomorrow,' I said excitedly. 'I'll give the place a quick clean and then move my stuff from the apartment back downstairs and unpack everything else.'

My grandparents had spent their entire married life living in the beautiful house which, thanks to their generosity, now belonged to me, and I adored it. Renting the main part of the property out to visitors for nine months of the year meant I could afford to keep it and also that I generated an income while I properly got my dream business off the ground.

'I daresay you're going to appreciate the space to spread out in now that you need to make so many extra fairies.' Holly smiled.

'Yes,' I said, and swallowed as my heart switched from thumping with excitement about moving back in to trepidation about the extra workload. 'I hope I haven't overcommitted.'

My online business, Away with the Fairies, had recently really taken off and, with Jeanie's and Holly's encouragement, I had signed up to sell a selection of peg and pipe cleaner fairies at various local festive events. I usually stuck to bespoke, one-off commissions sold via an online retailer, but was now branching out.

Unfortunately, however, thanks to some deep-seated teen trauma, I was feeling more nervous than I deserved to be about selling direct to the public. That was also why I was still dithering over whether to accept an offer to lead a workshop at the Cherry Tree Café. I was definitely channelling the Cowardly Lion about that, not that Holly was aware of my mortifying past experience. That was something I hadn't got around to filling her in on.

I felt a pang of envy as I recalled how the café's co-owner Lizzie made teaching crafts look so easy, but I daresay she hadn't been laughed at by classmates during a high school presentation and lost her confidence in front of a crowd as a result.

'You'll manage it all somehow,' Holly said with a sincere smile. 'I know you will.'

Her unshakeable faith in me was both genuine and reassuring.

'Thanks, Holly,' I nodded, trying to sound stoic. 'You're right. I've got this.'

'Cheers to that.' She beamed, clinking her glass against mine.

'Cheers,' I said back. 'And Bear will be back soon,' I reminded her. 'You're in for such a wonderful winter with him staying with you here in Wynbridge.'

As a garden restoration expert, Holly had told me, her partner didn't work during the harshest winter weather. Not outside, anyway.

'I can't wait to see him,' she said, raising her glass again. 'Now I'm properly settled, it's going to be the best Christmas ever, even if it will be a squeeze for the two of us and the dogs in the railway carriages.'

'Christmas!' I sighed dreamily, feeling warmed as the thought of it filled my head and made me forget my former worries. 'I'm so excited for it this year.'

'According to Jeanie,' Holly laughed, 'you're excited for it *every* year.'

'Well, of course I am.' I grinned. 'And I know she's told you why.'

I had so many special memories attached to the festive season. It was the one time of year that Mum could properly stop working, and we'd spend the whole of the holidays staying with her parents in the house which was now mine. I'd always spent the school holidays with my grandparents because of Mum's epic workload, but Christmas was the one time we'd all be there together, and I had loved that.

We embraced every festive tradition, and I had enthusiastically carried them all on. I'd even added a few of my own, and in just a few short weeks the entire house would be transformed into a veritable grotto. Both inside and out.

'Hooray for Christmas!' I cheered, as I pictured myself setting up my advent calendars, decking the halls and snuggling down with Tink under a fleecy blanket with a mug of hot chocolate from the festive station in the kitchen to watch Christmas movies.

Holly and I both jumped as the pub doors crashed open and in marched the Wicked Witch of the West, Glinda and Dorothy, a.k.a. three Wynbridge firefighters who must have just finished their shift. At the sight of what they were wearing, I did a double take.

'I don't believe it!' Holly burst out laughing. 'What are the odds of that?'

I laughed along with her, amused by what an unbelievable coincidence it was that we should have all picked the same film to celebrate the spooky season. That was, until I caught sight of Jeanie's unhappy expression.

'Look out,' I warned Holly, in the hope that we could duck away before Jeanie reached us, but, squeezed in with everyone else, there was no hope of that.

'Which of you two told them?' Jeanie demanded. I was doing an extremely convincing impression of the cowering Lion as she loomed over us. 'Did you let something slip about our costumes, Bella?'

'No,' I insisted, vehemently shaking my head, 'I didn't say a word to anyone.'

'Is that Tim?' Holly giggled, her cocktail hitting its mark at the most inopportune moment. 'Is that Tiny Tim, your high school sweetheart, dressed up as Dorothy, Jeanie?'

'Yes, it's Tim,' I said, confirming what she was witnessing when Jeanie didn't answer and as I tugged at Holly's straw-filled sleeve to try to rein her hilarity in.

'He's not my tiny anything,' Jeanie tutted, which made Holly snort and laugh all the harder. 'Not anymore.'

'I don't know why you're so resistant to our match-making . . .' I started to say, but she quelled me with a look.

'Given that Jeanie and Tim were a couple back in the day' – Holly hiccuped – 'surely we're trying to rekindle rather than matchmake, aren't we?'

'Holly—'

'That was years ago,' Jeanie muttered, firing more daggers in my direction.

Tim spotted Jeanie and attempted to walk through the crowd towards her. He'd only taken a couple of steps in his bright ruby slippers before he turned his ankle over and blurted out a few very un-Dorothy-ish phrases. He tried to regain his composure, but it didn't really work given that he was wearing a dress that was too short for his tall frame.

'Evening,' he said, having firmly yanked down the hem ahead of limping the final few steps. 'Don't we all look grand?'

He leaned heavily on the bar with a pained grimace, and his wig slipped to one side.

'You idiot,' said Jeanie, unable to stop herself from smiling as she leaned over the bar and readjusted his hairdo.

'What do you mean, "idiot"?' Tim grinned back, the pain in his ankle forgotten in the face of Jeanie's reaction to him as he batted his fake lashes. 'I think I'm a dead ringer for Judy G.'

'We need more photos,' said Holly, pulling out her phone as Glinda and the Wicked Witch joined us and, absent monkeys aside, completed the cast.

I gave an involuntary shudder. I'd always been scared of the

Witch, and knowing that it was an annoying lad I had been at school with called Owen under the green face-paint was little consolation.

'It'll have to be later,' said Jeanie, her eyes still on Tim. 'I've got folk to serve. We're swamped back here.'

'Need a hand?' offered Tiny Tim, who was anything but. 'I can still remember how to pull a pint.'

'No, thanks,' Jeanie said lightly, finally looking away. 'I don't trust you not to stand on me in those heels.'

'Wait!' he said, bending down to pull them off and narrowly avoiding his forehead clashing with the bar. 'They're going,' he said, thrusting first one shoe at me and then the other. 'They're gone.'

'I don't want them,' I objected, handing them to his hairy fairy-queen companion.

'Oh, come on, then,' Jeanie relented, looking at Tim again. 'I'll tell you what measures are in the cocktails, and then you can start refilling the empty pitchers.'

Holly and I nudged one another as Tim smoothed down his wig and joined her behind the bar. Everyone in the place knew that he was still the man for Jeanie, except her, but I hoped an evening working together and having a laugh might open her heart a little and help her see what the rest of us could.

As for what she'd said to me earlier about my heart, it really was perfectly fine. Left to my own devices and away with the fairies suited me down to the ground.

Chapter 2

I'd never been much of a drinker, so the following morning I was feeling the impact of every single one of the cocktails I'd downed the night before. Rather than walk home, Tink and I had crashed with Jeanie in her room at the pub, while Holly and Jasper had gone back to the railway carriages at Cuckoo Cottage in a taxi.

'Don't, Tink,' I said, and grimaced, pushing her off as she sat on my chest and licked my face.

'She's offering you hair of the dog,' Jeanie laughed, sounding far too sprightly for my liking.

'Ugh, don't even think that,' I said, pulling a pillow over my head to block out both Tink's unwanted attention and the light. 'Let alone say it.'

'Perhaps you should have stuck to the mocktails,' Jeanie teased.

'I didn't know there *were* mocktails,' I groaned.

'Well, there were, but they're long gone now. How about a bacon sarnie instead?' Jeanie offered. 'I'm having one, with extra brown sauce.'

'I should really get back,' I said, my voice muffled, as I tried not to think about gloopy sauce, brown or otherwise. 'This is *not* how I wanted to feel today.'

'Some carbs and protein will sort you out,' Jeanie said sagely. 'Come on,' she added, quickly tugging the pillow away. 'Let's have breakfast and then I'll drive you home. Save you having to do the walk of shame in that lion costume.'

It was lunchtime by the time she dropped me off and I still wasn't feeling much brighter − even less so when I opted to have a quick look around the house ahead of shedding the costume and taking a shower in the apartment.

'You've got to be kidding me,' I muttered as a rush of emotions, none of them positive, coursed through me. 'Just as well we didn't see all this yesterday, hey, Tink?'

Had I known the house had been left in such a state, it would have ruined the party.

'What would Nanna and Grandad say if they could see this?' I tutted.

There were only a few requests I made for the guests to fulfil ahead of their departure, but the last visitors had selfishly ignored them all. The beds hadn't been stripped or the bins emptied, and the dishwasher was haphazardly stuffed full of crockery, cutlery, pots and pans with food so firmly welded on that it would doubtless take more than one cycle to come clean. There was what looked like a red wine stain on the sitting room carpet, too, and I was sure I could smell cigarette smoke in the downstairs bedroom.

Tink, I noticed, hadn't ventured far over the threshold, and I couldn't blame her. Having pulled on a pair of rubber gloves, I sorted the dishwasher, turned off the heating and opened all the windows, then headed up to the apartment for strong coffee and the heavy-duty cleaning supplies. The longed-for shower would have to wait, but I did get changed.

'The thing that really pees me off,' said Mum, who had telephoned for a catch-up while I was mid mucking out session, 'is that you can't complain about them.'

'I know,' I huffed.

'They can rate you and the house online,' Mum ranted on, 'but you can't give them a one-star review for being slovenly and disrespectful visitors, can you?'

Having sorted as much as I could, I flopped down on the sofa to carry on with the conversation. I went to run a hand through my curls, but with limited success because it was still full of the product which had transformed it into the Lion's mane.

'Oh, never mind my guests,' I sighed, wanting to change the subject. 'Let's talk about something else. Tell me, how's Alain? How's France?'

Mum had moved across the Channel a while ago. She had initially been lured to look at French property by programmes such as *Escape to the Chateau*, but had soon realized that she had neither the skills nor the exuberance of the Strawbridge family to make a success of a huge renovation project and opted instead to buy a small, but comfortable, house on the edge of a traditional market town, which needed nothing more specialized than cosmetic updating.

I admired my mum immensely. Having been abandoned by my father when I was a baby and then by my wicked stepdad a few years later, she'd thrown herself into work and forged herself a hugely successful career.

For years, she had worked harder than anyone I knew, and

her comfortable retirement and home in France were the much-deserved rewards of her endeavours and the very decent returns on a number of shrewd investments. Retirement had given her a whole new lease of life – and now she had time, men were finally featuring on her radar again. Alain being the latest.

'Oh,' Mum said lightly, 'Alain went back to Provence a few weeks ago. Ask me how Henri is instead.'

'Oh, Mum,' I laughed, thinking that we were peas in a pod when it came to our attitude towards relationships. 'Fleeting but fun' could have been our joint mantra. 'How's Henri?'

'He's very well,' she said, and I could tell she was smiling. 'But France is freezing, so I'm having extra radiators put in and a stove installed in the kitchen to run them off.'

'Is that all happening now?'

'Hopefully within the next couple of weeks,' she said. 'I won't make it back for Christmas, though. Is that all right?'

'You'd already said you wouldn't,' I reminded her. 'And it's fine. I've got so much extra work to do, I'll probably sleep right through Christmas.'

'Oh, Bella,' Mum laughed. 'You couldn't sleep through Christmas if your life depended on it!'

'That's true.' I laughed along with her. 'And that's down to you, isn't it? Well, you, Nanna and Grandad. The three of you always made Christmas so special for me, and I want to continue that feeling, but I do think I'll be yawning through the celebrations this year.'

'It's good that you're busy, though,' Mum said keenly. 'The business is really taking off, isn't it?'

She was proud of my venture, even though the line of work

I was committed to was nothing like hers had been. You didn't tend to find fabric fairies on the corporate ladder.

'It is,' I proudly confirmed. 'And moving back into the house couldn't be better timed.'

'Will you set up a production line for the new range?' Mum asked. She knew all about the new fairies I would be selling on the market and at fairs. 'Make all the bodies first, then paint the faces, add the wings—'

'Of course not,' I cut her off. 'I'm going to carry on making them all one at a time, even though I'm sure your suggestion would be much quicker.'

'But with much less heart,' Mum added kindly. 'I was only teasing. I know you'll carry on making them individually and add that special brand of Bella magic as a result.'

'I certainly will,' I said as my cheeks began to glow. 'You know they're all unique and special to me.'

'And *you're* special to *me*,' Mum said with emphasis. 'And so is Henri,' she added playfully. 'He'll be back from the boulangerie any minute, so I'd better go and get the table set for lunch.'

'Lunch,' I tutted, as my stomach growled. 'It's practically dinnertime.'

'Not for me,' she said contentedly. 'I go slow here.'

'Give this Henri my love,' I said, smiling. 'And save some for yourself, won't you? We'll talk again soon.'

'Yes, my darling. Love you, sweetheart.'

'Love you, too.'

I sat for a few minutes, curled up with Tink on the sofa, and mulled over some of what Mum had said. By the time I had finished thinking and processing, I had made up my mind about the workshop at the café.

'Come on,' I said to Tink as the apartment shower began to call to me. 'It's freezing in here. Let's fire up the heating and move back in properly later when it's warmed up a bit.'

The next morning, I took my time rearranging what had originally been my childhood bedroom and further personalising the whole house with my cushions, throws, paintings and nicknacks – my style was the opposite of minimalist – as well as carrying down the collection of plastic crates which contained everything I needed to create my fairies.

Some were filled with fabric, others with buttons, sequins and lengths of ribbons and tulle. I hoarded anything I was drawn to in the knowledge that it would come into its own at some point. Jeanie often called me a magpie, and it was a fitting description.

It was getting close to midday by the time I'd got everything organized and, with my decision about the workshop filling my head with ideas and my tummy with butterflies, I headed into town to talk to Lizzie and Jemma.

'Bella!' Lizzie called, beaming, when I walked in and set the brass bell above the café door tinkling. 'See, Jemma, she isn't avoiding us.'

Jemma shook her head and blushed.

'I have been a bit,' I confessed. 'But now I've finally made a decision—'

'Please say it's a yes,' Lizzie begged and crossed her fingers.

'It's a yes,' I said, feeling my legs wobble, even though I was certain now that it was the right answer.

It wasn't that I didn't have faith in my work; my former hesitation had been all about the reaction my love of fairies had received during a high school GCSE presentation. When I'd previously put my passion for my winged friends in the public domain, it had been met with teasing, taunts, derision and then, as my confidence completely faltered, a total tech mess-up as the PowerPoint I'd prepared froze and the unsympathetic teacher failed my efforts. Jeanie had stood firmly by me during the fairy fallout (as she'd called it), but the experience had entirely put me off any sort of public speaking.

However, the conversation I'd had with Mum about my fairies being special had got me thinking. The people who signed up to a specific workshop to make them were bound to already be believers, weren't they? They would already be of the opinion that fairies were special, and that would hopefully knock my nerves on the head.

'Oh, thank goodness!' said Jemma, fanning herself with a paper order pad. 'Because we've just had two workshop cancellations and we were really hoping you would agree to fill them.'

'*Two* workshops?' I squeaked as Lizzie guided me to a table.

'I was going to ring you about it this afternoon,' she told me.

'I see.' I swallowed. 'Well, I hope the dates aren't too soon, because—'

'It's this Friday and Saturday.' Lizzie winced, pulling an apologetic face.

'What?' I gasped. 'You're kidding.'

'I wish.' She sighed. 'And I know it's short notice—'

'It's not short notice,' I countered, wondering if I had enough of everything I was going to need. 'It's *no* notice. You haven't even got a week to advertise it.'

'Oh, don't worry about that,' said Jemma, waving my words away. 'We'll fill the spots, no problem. A few of the people who had signed up for the cancelled workshops have already said they'll come along to whatever we can find to run in their place.'

That put paid to my hopes that potentially the attendees would definitely be fairy fans, then.

'You're right that time is of the essence, though, Bella,' Lizzie said, even though I hadn't put it quite like that, 'so email me some pics of what people will be making while you're here, and I'll get some posters made up.'

'Email you now?' I repeated.

'Yes,' Lizzie laughed at my dazed reaction. 'Here's the Wi-Fi code if you can't get a signal.'

I numbly unlocked my phone and sent her images of the simplest fairies I could find, and she rushed off to design the posters and an online ad for the website and Facebook page before I had the chance to say I'd changed my mind.

'Depending on numbers,' Jemma told me, 'we'll either set you up in here or in the gallery next door. Now, what can I get you for lunch? It's on me.'

'Whatever you've got on the specials board, please,' I requested, as it was easier than trying to focus on the menu in my current shocked state. 'The veggie option if there is one.'

Jemma soon returned with a huge vegetarian sausage roll and a hot chocolate that was the size of a sundae. As I began both, I looked at the photos I'd sent Lizzie and mentally broke the fairies down into their component parts. I then ran through their construction and thought of ways I could keep my instructions simple and concise, but still add some magic.

I knew it wasn't half-term that week, so the Friday workshop would be made up of grown-ups, but there might be youngsters coming along on the Saturday. Something else to consider. Tiny fingers might not be as dextrous as mine . . .

'What do you think?' asked Lizzie as she thrust an A4 poster in front of me. 'I'll put one in the window here as well as next door, and it's already up online.'

'It's perfect,' I said, feeling surprised at how well the photos had transferred. I then experienced an unexpected, but most welcome, rush of excitement. 'I wasn't expecting to feel like this, but I think I might actually be looking forward to it.'

Jemma looked delighted by my reaction.

'And so you should be,' Lizzie said, smiling, not knowing the traumatic reason behind why I might not have been. 'I know you're going to be in demand.'

I was amazed to leave the café with a spring in my step and my former annoyance over how the last guests had left the house completely forgotten. This was it. I was going to throw myself into everything I'd somehow managed to manifest and, best of all, I was going to achieve it all while I was home for Christmas.

Chapter 3

I spent the rest of Saturday happily settling back into the house and sorting through potential fabrics, buttons and ribbons for the suddenly imminent workshops, and Sunday thrillingly dawned with the promise of a visit to a home I loved almost as dearly as my own.

I had been invited to Wynthorpe Hall, the family seat of the Connelly clan. The huge and stunning hall was set in the Fenland countryside, and in spite of its size, it still managed to feel cosy, warm and always welcoming, most likely because of the wonderful people who lived there. They might not all have been related by blood, but a few of the residents had been drawn to the hall by some seemingly invisible thread and had settled there to form one very happy household.

Dear Catherine and Angus, the owners of the hall, both felt like family to me. They had been friends with my grandparents and a part of my life for as long as I could remember. They had also helped when I undertook the house conversion, suggesting an architect and builders, and had been on hand from the moment Mum moved abroad to advise and support me if I ever needed a more mature listening ear or the benefit of their combined wisdom – which, on occasion, I had.

That Sunday, I was visiting in a professional capacity, but it didn't make any difference to my reception. I had barely taken a seat at the huge kitchen table before a lunch invitation had been issued and Tink had been absorbed into the eclectic doggy gang which was comprised of a ginormous wolfhound, a miniscule chihuahua and an average-sized spaniel.

'It's roast beef and all the trimmings,' Dorothy, the hugely talented cook, told me as she hung my red wool coat on a peg. 'And you know I always cook for dozens rather than the actual dozen who are likely to descend, so there'll be more than enough to go around.'

'In that case,' I responded, as she opened one of the Aga doors and treated my senses to a wonderfully warm waft of what was already cooking, 'I'd love to stay. Thank you.'

'And there'll be a bowl for Tink, too,' she added with a smile.

My little friend looked delighted.

'Hello, Bella!' Archie, one of the Connelly sons and the partner of Molly, who I had come to see, beamed as he rushed in, red-faced and looking even more like his father than the last time I saw him. 'You're here to see my girls, aren't you?'

'Hello, Archie.' I smiled back. 'Yes, I am.'

'They shouldn't be too much longer,' he told me. 'Demelza slept late, so we're a bit behind this morning.'

'Lucky you,' said Jamie, his brother, as he came in from the other end of the kitchen carrying his son, Alby. 'This little blighter had us up half the night, so I've taken him to give Anna a break. She's feeling all-in thanks to this teething lark. And not to mention the early start Dad kindly gifted us all . . .'

I wondered what that had been about but didn't ask.

'Poor little man,' Dorothy crooned at Alby, who grinned, his cheeks glowing. 'And poor Anna, too. I'll do her a tray if you like. Treat her to a late breakfast in bed.'

'And I'll head over to the cottage, if that's all right, Archie?' I suggested, standing up again and reaching for my coat. 'I can just as easily talk to Molly there.'

It would probably actually be easier now that the Connelly kitchen was filling up.

'Absolutely.' He nodded. 'But watch the courtyard path. The frost is lingering this morning, and it's a bit slippery out there.'

I pulled my coat back on and made my way through the woods to the cottage where Molly, Archie and Demelza lived. It was truly a hidden gingerbread gem. Perfect for someone with white witch heritage, which I knew Molly had. Generations of her female relations had lived in the cottage before her, and I felt a twinge of excitement as I spotted smoke from the chimney curling up into the sky and pushed open the wooden gate, which creaked fittingly.

Molly opened the door even before I had knocked.

'Bella,' she said warmly. 'You looked like Little Red Riding Hood coming through the trees just now.'

'As long as that doesn't make you the wolf, I don't mind that description,' I laughed.

'Absolutely not,' she said, smiling. 'I'm sorry I'm so late. Did Archie tell you we slept in?'

'He did, and it's fine,' I reassured her.

'You don't have anywhere else you need to be?'

'Only seated at the Connelly kitchen table,' I explained as I crossed the threshold into the incense-scented interior and closed the door behind me. 'I've just been invited for lunch, so there's no need for us to rush.'

'Well, thank goodness for that,' she said, scooping up Demelza, who giggled ecstatically. 'I won't have to blame you for Mummy's tardiness after all, my little cub.'

Demelza was identical to Molly. From her red, curly, flyaway hair to the mole on the bottom of her left foot. The cutest clone I'd ever seen. She beamed at the sight of me, and I felt warmed right through as a result.

'So, Molly,' I said, stroking Demelza's chubby little arm. 'Tell me what sort of fairy you have in mind for me to make for this special one.'

I held Demelza while Molly made us warming mugs of spiced cacao, and then we sat in front of the fire, with Demelza between us, as Molly painstakingly described all of the elements she wanted me to include in the keepsake fairy she had asked me to create. She was hoping I would be able to complete it in time to gift it to her daughter at the beginning of Yule.

'And if you can manage it in the few weeks available,' she went on, as I finished scribbling notes and suggesting fabrics I thought might work for the fairy's dress, 'I'd like you to make one for Anna, too.'

'I'm sure I can fit it in,' I said, even though I knew I was committing to working even more hours than were probably available in the run-up to Christmas. 'Is Anna okay?' I asked. 'Archie said that Alby's teething, among other things, was taking its toll on all their sleep.'

My concern for Anna was the reason I had agreed to taking on the extra commission. One of my fairies might be a welcome highlight at such an exhausting time.

'It is,' Molly agreed, discreetly not answering my enquiry about Anna. 'And of course, Alby takes after his grandfather,' she added. 'So he's already creating mayhem up at the hall, in spite of the fact that he's still a babe in arms with sore gums. That similarity is going to be a blessing in the future, but for now, it's heavy going for both Anna and Jamie.'

'I see,' I said, easily imagining that it must be and again hoping Anna was okay.

I knew Angus well. His projects and schemes were either completely over the top or entirely eccentric (or even a combination of both), and he was relentlessly full of energy and exuberance, too. I did love him dearly, mostly in small doses, but I could see how his personality presenting itself in baby form could be . . . challenging.

'An extra special fairy for Anna, then,' I decided, making yet more notes.

'Which I'll add some extra special magic to myself,' Molly added mysteriously.

Back in the hall, we were greeted with an even busier kitchen and, as Dorothy bashed the brass gong, I counted settings at the table for ten adults, one baby and umpteen dogs. The only thing missing was a partridge in a pear tree. And Angus.

'Here he comes,' said Catherine, releasing me from the wonderful hug she'd enveloped me in the moment she saw me. She readjusted her silk shawl, just as a rousing rendition of 'Joy to the World' broke out in the corridor beyond the kitchen.

'The Lord is come!'

Angus charged in, making the adults either smile or roll their eyes and Demelza jump. I thought she might start to cry, but rather than crumple, her little face broke into a smile when she spotted Angus, and he beamed straight back.

'Here we all are, then,' he said, taking his seat at the head of the table. 'Bella!' he then boomed. 'I didn't know you were going to be here.'

'I came to see Molly,' I said, smiling. 'And I didn't expect to be fed—'

'Well, you should have,' said Dorothy as she began doling out vast Yorkshire puddings. 'That's one thing you can always rely on here. I know Anna and Jamie are eating later, but has anyone seen Jude?' she asked, having spotted that the chair next to mine was still empty.

'I think I heard his car heading down the drive a few minutes ago,' said Hayley, the hall housekeeper.

'Well, he might have said,' Dorothy tutted.

'Who's Jude?' I asked, not recognising the name.

I wondered if the hall had collected yet another clan member since the last time I'd visited, but Catherine's subsequent explanation suggested not. Not a full-time clan member, anyway.

'He's the young man Angus has commissioned to write a book for us about the architecture and history of the hall,' she told me.

'Oh wow,' I said, smiling. 'How exciting is that?'

That was bound to make interesting reading.

'He started out as a historical buildings inspector but has turned his hand to writing about properties as well as surveying them,' Angus added. 'And he's a cracking chap. Really knows his stuff. He's already unearthed some fascinating documents from the archive in the loft that we'd never taken much notice of before.'

'Dad's right,' Archie joined in, adding piles of crispy roast potatoes to his and Molly's plates. 'He is a decent chap, but he doesn't seem to hang around here much if he can help it.'

'Is it any wonder?' Dorothy said reasonably as Angus began pulling silly faces to make Demelza laugh.

'He just needs drawing out of himself a bit, that's all,' Angus said when he realized we were all looking at him. 'Then he'll join in a bit more.'

'Perhaps he doesn't want to be drawn out,' Molly said softly. 'Maybe he's happy as he is, keeping himself to himself and quietly getting on with the job he's been employed to do. He might simply need some peace and calm to focus on his work.'

Angus looked astounded at the thought of that.

'He takes himself right off and away when it all gets too noisy for him to handle here,' Catherine continued to elaborate.

'Which, as you can imagine, Bella, is quite often.' Archie winked at me, and I wondered where Jude took himself off to.

'But not usually when one of my dinners is on offer,' Dorothy pointed out.

'No,' Catherine frowned, 'you're right, Dorothy. But he told me earlier that he isn't sure he's going to be able to see the project through. Apparently, the early start you treated us to this morning, Angus, felt like the final straw. He was just about to settle down to start writing the opening of the book when you . . . roused us all.'

I wondered how the household had been woken. I'd bet that Anna and Jamie, already worn out from a night with a fractious Alby, hadn't appreciated whatever had happened.

'I needed to be sure the bugle still worked before I tried to sell it,' Angus said defensively, before Catherine shot him a censorious look.

'Is it really so important that Jude stays on site?' I asked as I helped myself to Dorothy's rich and flavoursome gravy. 'Couldn't he research here and write up what he finds elsewhere if he needs peace and quiet in which to do it?'

Personally, I loved the busyness, fun and mayhem that happened at the hall, but then I didn't have to live and work in it, did I? I could appreciate that those small doses I experienced were all well and good, but living with it all, full-time, when you were trying to concentrate on something important would be a different matter, and it was only going to get even busier in the run-up to Christmas. The Connellys were hosting a fair as well as the Winter Wonderland weekend in December, and preparations for both would begin soon.

'Perhaps he needs a proper bolthole,' I suggested. 'Rather than just some time out in his car. That is, assuming he just drives around for a bit before coming back.'

Catherine turned her gaze to me, and her expression immediately softened.

'It's funny you should suggest that,' she smiled warmly.

'Oh?' I swallowed, for some reason feeling like a rabbit caught in blinding headlights.

'I know you don't generally have guests staying in your house beyond the end of October, Bella, but would you consider putting him up?' she practically pleaded.

I felt my heart sink in my chest.

'Angus would be prepared to pay double what you usually charge,' she quickly added.

'Oh, would he?' Angus laughed. 'That's the first he's heard of it.'

'Given that he's predominantly the reason behind the

problem, I'm sure he'd agree that it's the least he could do,' Catherine said pointedly.

'Well, yes,' he relented, clearing his throat. 'I suppose so.'

'He's meticulously tidy,' Dorothy told me. 'Jude, not Angus. And quiet as a mouse.'

'Again,' Archie laughed, 'Jude, not Dad.'

'You wouldn't even know Jude was there,' Catherine said beseechingly. 'And it's only until the first of December. That's the day he's finishing up and leaving.'

Having only just moved back into the house, I couldn't bear the thought of squeezing into the apartment again, especially when I had so much extra work to do and fairies still to make. Though I supposed there was no reason why I couldn't put Jude in the apartment and keep the house for myself. And if Angus really was offering to pay double my usual fee, it would be a most welcome boost to my bank balance just before Christmas.

'But don't feel obliged to say yes,' Catherine said sincerely when I didn't give an immediate answer. 'I'm sure there must be other places I could try. Is there anywhere you could recommend, Bella?'

I thought of all the times that she and Angus, and even Jamie and Archie, had rushed to help me when I'd needed them, and all the kind words and company Catherine had offered as I became acclimatized to living in the house alone when Mum left for France and I was still getting used to her being so far away. Surely, I could do this simple thing for them in return?

'I can't think of anywhere off the top of my head,' I therefore took pleasure in saying. 'But that doesn't matter, because he can stay with me.'

Catherine dropped her cutlery and clasped her hands together.

'Are you sure?' she gasped.

'Yes.' I nodded. 'I'm sure. I can tell how much seeing this project through means to you, and I'll be fascinated to read whatever Jude writes for myself.'

'But surely you've only just moved back into the house, haven't you?'

This was from Molly.

'Yes,' I said, 'literally this weekend.'

I was just about to explain that I would put Jude in the apartment, but I didn't get the chance.

'And that makes your decision even more generous,' Catherine said. 'There's no way Jude could spread out all the papers, drawings and historical documents he's unearthed and make sense of them in your tiny apartment, Bella, so I truly appreciate you letting him have the run of the house. He'll certainly need the space it will give him.'

I swallowed hard, wondering if I could go back on my promise, but the look of relief on Catherine's face halted the thought and Hayley's next comment further banished it, too.

'And that means I can have my studio back,' she said gratefully, referring to the conservatory the family had adapted for her to draw and paint in. 'Jude commandeered it the other day, and now there's not an inch of empty surface to be seen and I need to get in there to finish my Christmas designs for Jemma and Lizzie. I'm already way behind.'

I knew the hall wasn't short of rooms or space in which Jude could spread out, but guessed that he'd hoped the conservatory, which was a little out of the way, would be quieter.

'So that's settled, then,' said Angus, clapping his hands together. 'Shall we say that Jude can come to yours on Tuesday, Bella? That'll give you time to move back into the apartment again, won't it?'

'Yes,' I squeaked, then cleared my throat. 'Yes,' I repeated a little more clearly. 'Tuesday will be fine.'

Chapter 4

Jeanie hadn't been at all impressed when I'd messaged her and said I wouldn't make our brunch date that Monday. She didn't get much time to socialize thanks to the opening hours of the pub, and therefore our hours enjoying a laid-back brunch with Holly were considered sacrosanct. However, given all the extra things I now had to do, the only sensible option I had was to miss it.

'Don't tell me you said yes, Bella!' Jeanie groaned, when she called later in the day to get to the bottom of why I'd not met her and an equally curious Holly; I had by then explained about Jude's predicament.

'Of course I said yes,' I tutted. 'How could I say no when Catherine and Angus have always been so kind to me and so supportive? I've never given them anything in return, not that they expect me to, but nonetheless this feels like an ideal opportunity for me to do something genuinely helpful for them.'

'Well, when you put it like that,' Jeanie reluctantly relented. 'Jamie was a godsend when that pipe burst last winter and your plumber couldn't come out, wasn't he?'

'Exactly,' I said, shuddering at the memory and thinking that if it hadn't been for Jamie's help, the carnage could have been much worse. 'The kitchen would have been unsalvageable if he hadn't rushed to help.'

'You would have been able to canoe around your kitchen,' Jeanie joked.

'Literally,' I agreed seriously. 'So you can see now why I agreed to letting this guy move in, can't you?'

'Of course,' she responded. 'You've done the right thing, even if the timing is a bit of a nuisance for you.' I considered it more than that but had no intention of refuelling her fire by admitting as much. 'Though I suppose with him staying in the apartment, there isn't enough room for him to make that much of a mess or cause you too much inconvenience, is there?'

I grimaced but didn't comment.

'Bella?'

I'd put her on speakerphone so I could carry on going through my supplies while we talked. With Jude set to arrive the following evening, I was keen to make the most of the space in the sitting room to plan out and organize everything I was going to potentially need for the two fairies Molly had commissioned, as well as all the things for the fairies I needed to make for the fairs *and* the supplies now required for the workshops.

Lizzie had sent me a text earlier telling me that six people had immediately signed up for Friday and ten for Saturday, and I'd messaged her straight back asking her not to book anyone else. Sixteen people to tutor in two days was more than enough for my first post-fairy fallout attempt, especially if I had to convince any of the attendees to truly feel the fairy love.

'Bella?' Jeanie said again, her sharp tone filling the room and making Tink cock her head. 'Are you still there?'

'Yes,' I said, reaching for one of the smaller plastic crates. 'I'm still here.'

'So,' Jeanie demanded, with all the intuition of a life-long friend, 'what aren't you telling me?'

I let out a breath.

'It's nothing, really,' I tried to say convincingly, 'just that Jude isn't going to be staying in the apartment. He's moving into the house.'

'You're kidding?' Jeanie gasped.

'It's the only way,' I sighed. 'Because he needs the space in the house to spread out all the archive papers he'll be bringing with him from the hall.'

'But *you* need the space for your fairy factory,' Jeanie countered.

'It's not a factory,' I tutted.

'You know what I mean,' she huffed.

'I'll manage,' I told her. 'I'm getting organized already, hence the brunch cancellation, and it's only for a month. A little less than a month, actually. He'll be going right at the beginning of December, so I'll be able to get straight back into the house and start decorating as I usually would on the first of the month.'

The thought of getting out the boxes filled with decorations, many of which I'd loved for as long as I could remember, gave my festive spirit a timely nudge.

'You can't tell me you're as happy about that as you're trying to sound,' Jeanie said astutely, and I inwardly cursed her ability to read my mind *and* knock the edge off my festive excitement in one fell swoop.

'Perhaps not,' I admitted, just as someone hammered on the

front door, making me jump and Tink woof, 'but it's all arranged now and I'm not reneging on my promise.'

'You're too kind, Bella,' Jeanie sighed, as if that was a genuine fault. 'You should put yourself first every once in a while.'

'A minute ago, you were agreeing that I'd done the right thing,' I reminded her.

'You know what I mean.'

'Like you, you mean,' I said rather unkindly as I levered myself to my feet and winced because I'd got pins and needles. 'You could be putting yourself first by giving Tim a second chance, couldn't you? He's still the perfect guy for you and he's still available . . .'

'That's different,' Jeanie cut in, sounding hurt and making me feel bad. 'You know I'm committed to staying in Wynbridge now, and Tim and his mates are all pub regulars, so if anything went wrong . . .'

'Why would anything go wrong?'

'You know exactly what I'm getting at,' she shot back, cutting me off, just like I had her. 'If we split up again, it would make life really awkward.'

'Look,' I said as the door was assaulted again, 'I have to go. There's someone at the door and they sound as if they're about to take a sledgehammer to it.'

I ended the call and promised myself I'd ring her back later and smooth things over between us. I hoped I hadn't just reinforced the defences she'd put up against Tim. Especially given that he was so patiently and gently trying to dismantle them. What I'd just said wasn't the worst it could have been, but it was completely out of character for me to be so blunt and I didn't like myself for it.

'I'm coming, I'm coming,' I huffed, feeling rankled as I almost tripped over Tink in my struggle to rush to the door while wearing my huge, fluffy Hallowe'en slippers as my feet slowly came back to life.

Shaped like giant pumpkins, the slippers weren't the safest form of footwear, and I decided it was time they were put away again, especially as I was now going to have to negotiate the narrower staircase in the apartment every day until December.

It was Bonfire Night the next day, so Christmas slippers were just about justified. My favourites had sleigh bells and antlers attached. They were hardly more streamlined than the pumpkins, but maybe I'd risk it. I always reasoned that if you left wearing, reading and watching everything associated with the festive season until December itself, then you'd struggle to fit it all in. Well, I would, anyway, because I had so much to get through!

The door received another blow just as I wrenched it open and before my festive meter spiked again, and I found myself faced with a huge cardboard box and three very full lever arch files precariously balanced on the top of it.

'Did you kick my door?' was the first thing I crossly said, because there really could have been no other knocking option given what was now in front of me. And that supposition would explain the din.

'I *knocked* on your door with my foot,' barked the cardboard box. 'I didn't think you'd take so long to answer. I assume I've got the right house and you're Bella?'

The cheeky sod. He'd done more than knock. I stood on tiptoe but still couldn't see over the top of the pile to find out who had made the impertinent remark.

'Well, please don't knock like that again,' I said haughtily, then instantly regretted that I'd made it sound like a request rather than a command.

'I'm hoping I won't have to,' groaned the box. 'Can I come in? This lot is really heavy, and I'd rather not have to put it all down and pick it back up again.'

'You can't come in until you've told me who you are,' I said, frowning. 'And possibly not even then,' I added in a mutter.

With a heavy sigh, the box and files were lowered onto the porch step, and the man standing behind them straightened. I was somewhat taken aback by the sight of him.

'I'm Jude,' he said, his dark hair falling forward as he looked down at me. 'From Wynthorpe Hall.' His eyes tracked down to my slippers, and he frowned. 'Catherine said you would be expecting me.'

So this was the architectural historian, Jude. He made a lot of noise for someone who was looking for peace and quiet in which to work. And he was at least thirty years younger than I'd unjustifiably presumed he would be, too.

'Not until tomorrow,' I said, feeling my face flush as his blue eyes met mine. 'When I spoke with the family yesterday, we agreed that you could come tomorrow evening.'

Tink, bored of waiting to find out who had been hammering, pushed around me and started sniffing the box.

'He'd better not cock his leg against that,' Jude frowned. 'There's important Connelly history in that box.'

'I'm sure *she* has better manners than that,' I said with emphasis. 'Doubtless she can smell her canine friends from the hall, can't you, Tink?'

Jude and I seemed to have reach an impasse, and I resisted the urge to fold my arms and stick out my chin.

'So,' said Jude, as he looked over my shoulder into the house, apparently unaware that I wasn't impressed with his first impression. 'Can I come in or not? Catherine did say she'd messaged to let you know about the change of plan.'

'Wait there,' I said, going back inside to check my phone.

I knew there was no way Catherine would have sent Jude along without my approval. She would have asked if the change of plan was acceptable, not assumed that it was. Sure enough, there was a message, asking me if it would be all right for Jude to come along a day early. I had missed it landing while I was talking to Jeanie. I supposed it was too late to send Jude packing given that he was already here. I was tempted, though.

'Catherine *has* messaged to ask if it would be all right if you moved in earlier than expected,' I said, briefly flashing my phone at Jude as I went back to the door.

'That's what I said.'

'That's not quite how you put it,' I shot back. 'And I'm certain she wouldn't think you'd have the nerve to just turn up without my having first said you can.'

I felt myself further bristle at the sight of Tink practically sitting on his feet and staring adoringly up at him. She was usually such a good judge of character, but Jude, with his blue eyes and long, dark lashes, had somehow managed to pull the wool over her eyes without so much as a treat or a fuss to make up for his bad manners. I'd have to have words with her later. Remind her what he'd said about her cocking a leg.

'Well, no,' Jude sighed, his shoulders dropping. 'I don't suppose Catherine would be expecting me to do that. I'm sorry. I just assumed you would have spoken to her in the time it took me to pack my car and get here.'

He must have been in a rush.

'And also assumed that I would have said yes,' I pointed out.

'I really am sorry,' he said again. 'I was feeling a bit desperate.'

I supposed his confession did tally with what the others had said about his desire to get away from the hall at lunch the previous day. And if certain family members had been on form again, I further supposed that that had done nothing to temper Jude's desire to escape.

'Well, as you're here now, you'd better come in,' I relented, blocking out the sound of Jeanie's voice telling me to stand my ground and put myself first. 'Let's get the door shut before the heat completely disappears, and then I'll call Catherine and let her know you're here and that it's fine for you to stay.'

'I've got loads more stuff in the car,' Jude said, bending to pick the first load up again and not offering a single word of thanks. 'Shall I bring it all in now?'

'You might as well.' I shrugged resignedly.

While I talked to Catherine and reassured her that Jude was fine to arrive early, I heard him heading in and out multiple times.

'He'll be so relieved,' Catherine said to me as another gust of Wynbridge wind filled the hall. 'He's out somewhere again now, so I know he's definitely had enough of our noise. I'll message and let him know he can come to you today.'

I didn't tell her that he was already with me. I thought I'd leave him to deal with the awkwardness of that. He'd have to tell her he'd expected I would say yes, because he must have already cleared his room and therefore wouldn't be going back today. And if the current toing and froing was any indicator, he'd also removed every document relating to the lengthy and ancient history of the hall, and someone would be bound to notice that.

'There,' he said, putting the last carton down as I went back into the sitting room, having ended the call, 'that's the last of it.'

I looked around the room and wondered at the wisdom of having so recently spent so long tidying the place up again.

'It was pretty full already,' he said, with a nod to all of my fairy boxes, 'but it's almost impossible to move in here now.'

'Don't worry,' I told him, 'I'll move as much of my stuff out again as I can, though a few crates might have to stay down here because there won't be room for them upstairs in the apartment.'

'So where would this lot usually be when you're renting the house out?' he asked, with a nod to the table.

I tried not to bristle again, despite the edge to his tone.

'None of what I need would usually be set out like this,' I told him, feeling defensive. 'So it wouldn't take up as much space. You've landed right at my busiest work time.'

I did obviously make stock throughout the year as well as for Christmas, but given my current extra workload, I had needed to check I had the required number of supplies. Hence the unusually large and detailed stocktake.

'Oh, right,' Jude said, looking around but making no apology for putting me out. Perhaps he hadn't had the chance to process that he had. 'So what exactly is it that you do?'

'I make fairies,' I told him, and he looked astounded. 'My business, Away With The Fairies, specializes mostly in keepsake commissions, which I sell online.'

'I see,' he said, but I could tell he didn't.

Ordinarily, if someone specifically asked, I would have

reached for one of my completed pieces and explained about them, but Jude wasn't exactly giving off an 'I want to know all about it' vibe. I felt belittled as a result, but I wasn't sure if that was the result of his reaction or my interpretation of it. Perhaps the feeling was a hangover from what had happened at school? It had been much on my mind since the workshop offer came along, so I might have been feeling more than usually sensitive, I supposed.

'And what about all this other stuff?' he said, looking at the ephemera I'd only just set out when I restyled the place to my taste again.

'It's not usually so personalized,' I said, feeling a blush frustratingly bloom.

'But you had just set it up to move back in yourself,' he finally twigged, biting his lip. 'Catherine did tell me about your living arrangements . . .'

I thought an apology might be in the offing, but apparently not.

'So are you going to pack all of this lot up again, too?' he asked, sounding hopeful. 'The place is a bit busy for my taste.'

It was just as well he was going to be leaving before I decorated for Christmas, then. He'd never cope with the grotto aesthetic I was already looking forward to recreating.

'If you really want me to,' I said, shrugging. 'I can try to squeeze it into the apartment where I'll be staying for the next month.'

He looked relieved and not at all contrite.

'I'm an out and out fan of maximalism,' I therefore said, playing devil's advocate and making him tense up again, 'but I'm guessing you're more . . .'

'Minimalist,' he said. 'Definitely. I can't see the point of all these dust attractors. Give me an empty table and a clear work surface any day. No offence,' he added, but that didn't take the edge off the fact that he'd now insulted both my taste and my home.

I wondered how many other ways we were going to be polar opposites. With any luck, our paths weren't going to cross often enough for me to find out. I didn't usually take a dislike to anyone on sight, preferring to get to know them before I made up my mind about whether we could be friends or not, but Jude's assumptive arrival and subsequent comments hadn't made that usual exercise necessary.

'Plenty taken,' I muttered.

'Sorry?' he asked, frowning.

'Nothing,' I said. 'Some of these will have to be stacked in the hall,' I told him, reaching for one of my boxes. 'It's not ideal, but there's no other way, I'm afraid. They won't be blocking the door, so they shouldn't pose a risk in the case of a fire, but maybe lay off lighting any candles.'

He looked at me as though I was mad.

'Not a candle fan, either,' I sighed.

'Definitely not when I'm working with documents of such historical value as these,' he said, patting one of his own boxes. 'What the Connelly family had packed in their loft was beyond anything I've had the opportunity to investigate before. It's all fascinating.'

He was totally transformed as he described some of what he'd found, and I was relieved to discover that he was passionate about something. If he could inject even half the enthusiasm with which he talked about the paperwork into the written

words of his manuscript, Catherine and Angus would be thrilled
with the book he was going to create chronicling the creation
of their home.

'Sorry,' Jude said, turning red and running his hands through
his hair when he broke off. 'I got a bit carried away there,
didn't I?'

'It was lovely to hear,' I told him. 'Perhaps some of Angus's
exuberance has rubbed off on you.'

'That man,' he said, shaking his head. 'I'm used to living on
my own and I was an only child, too, so the set-up there has
felt far too full-on for me. Each to their own, of course, but
it's not an environment I can work in, let alone live and work
in.'

That was a shame, really, as I felt the experience might have
added to the tone of the book, but now he'd given me some
context, I could better understand his desire to maintain a little
distance. Perhaps he deserved the benefit of my doubt, after
all.

'I get that,' I therefore said. 'I'm close to the family myself,
but I'm not sure I could live with Angus for any length of time.'

'And the hall is even more cluttered than this place,' he said,
making my fledgling sympathy for him disappear again. 'Shall
we make a start on clearing all your stuff out now?'

'Yes,' I said, resisting the urge to storm off. 'Let's do that.
And you won't forget to let Catherine know you won't be
going back to the hall tonight, will you?'

Chapter 5

Just like Jude with the Connelly family, I was in quite a rush to put some distance between him and me after that initial unsatisfactory conversation and ended up stuffing lots of my fabric into random boxes, which I then had to go through the next day to make sure they didn't end up creased or in the wrong place.

That task took until mid-morning, and it was only afterwards that I remembered I had been going to message Jeanie and apologize for the out of character comment I'd made about her attitude towards Tim. She didn't answer her phone when I called, so I composed a remorseful message and then settled down to carry on selecting pretty pieces for the fairy I was going to make Demelza.

My largest and most intricate fairies took as long to think about as they did to actually create, so I really needed to make that one, and Anna's, a priority over the ones I would be selling at the fairs and on the market, but no matter how hard I tried, I couldn't pull anything together that I was happy with. It was usually such an enjoyable part of the process, and I felt frustrated that right when I needed inspiration to magically strike, all I could think about was my lodger, who seemed to have a gift for saying the wrong thing, even if he didn't realize it.

'Well, in that case, I completely blame that Jude chap for the look on your face,' Holly said loyally when I later bumped into her in town and explained what had occurred the day before. 'You're usually such a ray of sunshine, Bella, but you're definitely not shining today.'

I didn't like the implication of that, not one little bit. A natural propensity to always look on the bright side, a laid-back attitude and a definite Pollyanna predisposition were my go-to and cherished personality traits. I pasted on a smile in an effort to rectify the situation, but Holly looked terrified.

'Don't fake it,' she said, patting my arm, then taking a step away. 'Never fake it.'

I banished the forced smile and shook my head.

'I refuse to let that man zap my Pollyanna power,' I pouted, planting my feet even more firmly on the pavement.

'That's more like it,' Holly laughed. 'Embrace your inner Boudica, and in the meantime, while you're gathering your strength and polishing your shield, let me treat you to lunch in the Cherry Tree Café.'

'Thanks, Holly,' I said, with a nod to the pub, 'but I can't join you today. I really need to talk to Jeanie. I upset her yesterday and I didn't mean to.'

'Crikey,' Holly tutted, knowing I never knowingly upset anyone. 'Jude must have really got to you.'

I didn't tell her that I'd offended Jeanie before he showed up.

'I'll see you tonight, then,' she said, turning towards the café.

'Yes,' I replied, thinking how much I was looking forward

to celebrating the fifth of November with my friends. 'I'll see you tonight.'

It was quiet for once in The Mermaid, so my heartfelt apology, following up the message Jeanie hadn't yet had the opportunity to read, was expressed in the bar while she made me a latte and Tink snoozed at my feet, next to the stool I was perched on.

'I know you're frustrated with me over the Tim situation,' Jeanie said, setting the cup down in front of me, 'but the thing is—'

'It's fine,' I cut in. 'You don't owe me an explanation. I just wanted to say I'm sorry that I upset you and I hope you didn't lose any sleep over it.'

'Oh, don't worry, I didn't.' She smiled, handing me some packets of sugar. 'But I'm guessing you did. You don't look like yourself at all. You should have rung me back last night if you were that worried that you'd upset me.'

'I had planned to,' I told her, 'but I got . . . distracted.'

'Oh?'

'Jude, the guy from the hall, turned up unannounced,' I said succinctly. 'A whole day and a bit earlier than arranged, too.'

'Was that who was hammering on the house door?'

'Um,' I said. 'Hammering with his foot, as it turned out.'

I still wasn't over that. I really should have made a point of checking the paintwork. I hoped he hadn't scuffed it with his size elevens. Or whatever size his feet were. The door had only been repainted in the spring, so it should still have been looking pristine.

'So,' Jeanie said cosily, leaning over the bar and not showing a moment's concern for my door, 'were you good distracted or bad distracted?'

'Bad,' I immediately shot back, refusing to think how lovely Jude's blue eyes looked framed by those long dark lashes. 'Definitely bad. He's a very rude man.'

'Oh dear,' said Jeanie, standing up again and pulling a face. 'No redeeming features at all?'

'As far as I can tell,' I lied, adding more sugar than I'd usually take to my coffee in the hope that it would sweeten my mood, 'not a single one.'

I then went on to tell her how Jude had assumed it wouldn't be an issue if he just turned up, how he'd judged my pumpkin slippers, how Tink had been stupidly charmed by him for no reason at all, how he'd loathed my entire aesthetic *and* how he'd then made a din dragging boxes about until late in the evening.

Jeanie stopped wiping the glass she'd picked up and grinned.

'It almost sounds like the lady doth protest too much,' she laughed.

'Don't you believe that for a second,' I said, hiding behind my cup. 'I'm only telling you the good bits.'

'How old is he?' she asked.

'Not sure,' I said, shrugging and drinking down another rather too hot mouthful.

'Roughly.'

'About our age, I suppose.'

'How tall?'

'Taller than me.'

'Well, that's not hard.'

She didn't say anything else, and I was damned if I was going to fill the silence by mentioning the way Jude's hair fell back into place with Hugh-Grant-circa-Notting-Hill accuracy when he ran his hands through it or his beguiling ocean eyes . . .

'By the way,' I therefore resorted to asking instead, 'did I leave my lion's tail here after the party last week? I can't find it anywhere back at the house or in the apartment.'

Jeanie jerked her thumb over her shoulder towards the other end of the bar.

'Oh, for pity's sake,' I laughed when I spotted it pinned up next to a card filled with bags of peanuts. 'Give it to me. It looks like something Eeyore lost, stuck up there like that.'

She unpinned it and handed it over.

'I'd better get back,' I said, finishing my coffee and stuffing the tail in my coat pocket. 'Will you make it tonight?'

'I can't say for certain, but I'm going to try,' she told me. 'If only to give me the opportunity to further grill you about this Jude guy.'

'Well, you'll be wasting your time,' I said, giving Tink a nudge. 'Because there's really nothing else to say.'

I never liked to turn up at an event I'd been invited to at someone's home empty-handed, but I always struggled when attending a function at Wynthorpe Hall, because they really did seem to have everything. However, their annual bonfire party had provided me with an opportunity to contribute something wonderfully creative, even if it would be ash by the end of the evening. On this occasion, Angus himself had donated some of its component parts, which had made it an even more interesting project.

'Oh, Jude!' I gasped, my hand flying to my chest, when I came around the side of the house and found him locking the front door. 'You made me jump.'

'Sorry,' he said. 'Obviously, I didn't mean to.'

So he was capable of apologising, then. Sort of.

'Have you been home long?' I asked.

'All day,' he said. 'I thought I'd work here today and then have an early, quiet night, but then I remembered the party at the hall.'

I hadn't given a thought to him being invited, too, but of course he had been. That would satisfy Jeanie's curiosity about him, if she did manage to make it. She could suss him out for herself and then I'd really be in for a grilling. She knew I had a weakness for long lashes and would doubtless want to know why I hadn't mentioned them as a redeeming feature during my earlier character assassination.

'I've been working here today, too,' I told him, for want of something to say before an awkward silence descended.

'I know,' he said. 'I could hear your music.'

I managed to stop myself from apologising just in the nick of time. It was an annoying reflex reaction I had, and besides, my music hadn't even been that loud.

'It's a bit early for carols, isn't it?' Jude commented, and I wasn't sure if he was joking or not, but then he didn't know about my Christmas obsession, so he most likely wasn't.

'Not when you want to get in the festive mood,' I told him bluntly, then more kindly added, 'I suppose as we're both heading to the hall, we might as well travel together, mightn't we?'

I didn't particularly want to drive there with him, but it would have been ridiculous to head to the same destination in convoy and then later follow each other back again.

'I suppose so,' he said, sounding about as keen as I was. 'I'll wait out here while you settle your dog. It's Tink, isn't it?'

At the sound of her name, she looked up at him and thumped her tail, but he didn't fuss her.

'It is,' I confirmed, refusing to acknowledge that he'd made the effort to remember. 'And I don't need to settle her, because she's coming with us.'

'But what about the fireworks?' He frowned. 'And come to think of it, what about the other dogs? Aside from the noise, I don't think those so-called silent fireworks are any better than the usual ones, are they? Not for the environment, anyway.'

'The dogs will all be in the kitchen,' I told him, 'and the Connellys don't have fireworks on Bonfire Night.'

'So what's happening at the party, then?' he asked, frowning again.

'You'll see,' I said. 'Come on. Otherwise we'll be late.'

I clicked the key fob to unlock my car, and then it was Jude's turn to jump.

'What the hell is that?' he gasped, catching sight of the person sitting in the passenger seat.

'That's the guy,' I told him, trying not to laugh at seeing him so taken by surprise. 'He's my contribution to the evening. He's wearing some of Angus's cast-offs and he's stuffed with straw, which is why I wouldn't let him in the house.'

Holly had left a trail right through the pub when she'd played her part as the Scarecrow on Hallowe'en, and I had no desire to replicate that up the stairs and in the apartment.

'I was about to suggest we go in my car,' Jude said, 'but not if it's going to end up filled with straw.'

'What's wrong with my car?' I scowled, even though he hadn't actually suggested that anything was. I needed to break the habit of presuming he was criticising me before it took hold.

'Nothing,' he said, his eyes flicking back to me. 'It's just a bit on the . . . snug side.'

'I'll have you know,' I said, drawing myself up and feeling that my assumption – on this occasion, at least – was justified, 'I've had much taller men than you in that front seat.'

'Oh, have you, now?' he laughed, and I felt my cheeks flush. I swallowed hard as his face was entirely transformed. He looked even more attractive. Attractive, I mean. Not *more* attractive because I hadn't so far found him attractive. Not really, anyway. Oh dear.

'You know what I mean,' I said, unable to keep a straight face or look him in the eye.

I couldn't help thinking that it was a relief to know he'd got a sense of humour, even if the first glimpse of it had been at my expense.

'Am I going to have to squeeze in the back, then?' he asked.

'No,' I said, handing him Tink's lead. 'I'll stuff Mr Fawkes in the boot, and you can take his place.'

He was still picking straw out of the footwell by the time I'd clipped Tink into her harness on the back seat.

'Does she mind being strapped in?' Jude asked, glancing over his shoulder at her.

'No,' I said, 'she's used to it, and as it's a legal requirement, she wouldn't have much choice in the matter even if she did object.'

'I didn't know it was the law,' he said, readjusting the passenger seat to accommodate his long legs.

'I'd keep her restrained, even if it wasn't,' I told him. 'Better to be safe than sorry.'

'I agree,' he said, pulling on his seatbelt. 'Safety first.'

There were already a dozen or so cars parked up at the hall by the time we arrived, and Archie dived into the boot of mine almost before I'd applied the handbrake.

'Excellent!' he laughed as he lifted out the guy. 'I was worried it was going to look like we were burning an effigy of Dad after he told us he'd given you some of his tatty old clothes to dress Mr Fawkes in, but this looks nothing like him.'

I had made the face look as much like Guy Fawkes as I possibly could with some felt for his moustache and a beard, and I'd made good use of a marker pen for the rest.

'Well, that's a relief,' I said, unclipping Tink's harness. 'That would have been horrible!'

'Come on, Jude,' Archie said. 'You can help me with this while Bella drops Tink off in the kitchen.'

By the time I'd done that and helped Dorothy carry out trays of toffee apples, baked apples, filled jacket potatoes and hot dogs to where the huge bonfire had been piled up, there was quite a crowd gathered and I couldn't spot Jude among it. My straw-stuffed guy was atop the fire, though, so he must have played his part in helping Archie with that.

'Here you are,' said Holly, coming along and plucking at my sleeve. 'I wondered where you'd got to.'

'I was just helping Dorothy,' I told her. 'Have you seen Jeanie? She said earlier that she was going to try to come, if she could.'

'Not yet,' she said, looking around. 'It's hard to make out who everyone is in the dark, though, isn't it?'

'It'll be easier when the bonfire's lit,' said Anna, also coming to join us.

She had Alby strapped to her front in a sling, and he was sound asleep.

'Hello, Anna,' I said, giving her a hug with Alby between us. 'I was sorry I missed you last weekend.'

'Don't be,' she said with a faint smile. 'I wasn't at my best after endless nights awake with this little man and his terrible teething.'

'How is he now?' Holly asked.

'Better,' Anna nodded. 'Until the next eruption, anyway. And I'm feeling better, too. I've had a referral from my doctor to get some proper support for my "low mood".' She put air quotes around the words. 'This baby business and the adjustment into motherhood isn't anywhere near as straightforward as I thought it was going to be.'

'Well, I think you're doing brilliantly,' I told her, thinking how brave she was to tell us so directly what she was going through and how she was feeling. 'And I admire you for speaking out and saying it hasn't been straightforward,' I therefore added.

'It's taken me a while,' she sighed. 'I was struggling to admit it before, even to myself, and I kept thinking that if Molly had taken to it like a duck to water, then there was no reason why I shouldn't, too.'

I could imagine that having a friend who was contentedly jogging along to compare yourself to had, in some ways, made speaking out even harder.

'Oh, Anna . . .' I swallowed, feeling choked up on her behalf.

'It's okay,' she said, kissing the top of Alby's head, which was covered with a knitted hat in the shape of an acorn. 'Having taken the first steps to getting some help, I already feel better. And of course, Molly has been kindness itself, even when I haven't been particularly lovely to her.'

'She's a wonderful friend,' Holly said and then stopped as the air was filled with feedback from a loudspeaker which Angus was attempting to talk into.

'I hardly think he needs that,' Anna laughed.

Angus handed the ear-offending piece of equipment to Jamie and then began to shout out the running order for the evening.

After he'd said his piece, the fire was lit and the LED glow-stick hunt through part of the woods, which had mostly safe paths, was announced as officially open. Sparklers, food and storytelling were to follow, but as soon as Angus had mentioned the hunt and its environmentally friendly credentials, most people were off, aiming to claim more sticks than everyone else and win the prize. Whatever that turned out to be.

It was a while before I saw Jude, and when I spotted him, he was walking out of the woods next to Jeanie, who was laughing at something he'd said and swinging a bucket positively packed with glowsticks. It looked like they had combined their efforts and actually had a decent chance of coming in first – or close to it, at least.

'I've found your lodger, Bella,' Jeanie said, beaming at me. Jude was smiling, too. 'He's far more interesting than you made out earlier.'

Holly raised her eyebrows at me, and Jude followed suit.

'What's that supposed to mean?' he asked.

'Never mind,' Jeanie laughed, linking her arm through his. 'Let's go and register our tally and see if we've won.'

'Tiny Tim is going to be heartbroken,' said Holly with a sigh as we watched them go.

'Jude's only here for a month,' I reminded her. 'Tim's got nothing to worry about. Shall we go and grab some sparklers?' I suggested, hoping they'd reignite my sparkly mood.

'Food first,' she said. 'I'm starving, aren't you?'

I had been before, but suddenly I didn't have the appetite to eat a thing.

Chapter 6

Ridiculous as it was, given that I barely knew Jude and didn't particularly like him, I had, for some unfathomable reason, felt unaccountably jealous when I'd spotted him and Jeanie walking out of the woods together at the Wynthorpe Hall bonfire party. However, with so much fairy-making to get through and the two workshops to finish planning, I soon forgot all about my uncharacteristic reaction.

Jude and I had barely said a word to each other on the drive back to town, so there had been no further conversation between us for me to subsequently ponder over. And during the days that followed, I focused solely on the work I needed to get done.

By the end of the week, I had settled on colour schemes for both Demelza's and Anna's fairies and had selected the fabrics, tiny charm embellishments and intricate details I would painstakingly include. Demelza's fairy was going to be as light and ethereal as her and her mum, and the colours I picked out were from the soft green, pale cream and silver palette.

By contrast, and somewhat influenced by my conversation with Anna about her current feelings, I decided to make hers feel more grown-up and grounded. Everything about Anna's fairy was strong and bold; her dress would be created in a rich plum velvet, with lots of hand-sewn gold embellishments included, reflecting a true warrior spirit.

I felt that both would complement the magic Molly would imbue them with ahead of passing them on, and they would consequently become even more powerful talismans for and representations of their recipients.

Some might say that was a whimsical way of thinking, but it was an important part of who I was, and you could love me or loathe me for it. Had I had any reason to get to know Jude better, I couldn't help thinking that he would most likely have fallen into the 'loathe me' camp. Or something close to it. Just like some of my school classmates had.

From what I had been able to make out, there was nothing fanciful about Jude. Not that I was supposed to be thinking about him. I had barely glimpsed him during the week, but I had still deciphered enough to know that we had very different characters.

The few times we had bumped into each other, he was either staring at his phone or looking stressed and in a rush. I was obviously far more laid-back than him, even with the pressure of my looming deadlines. A few times, I had heard him taking delivery of meals from local takeaways; each to their own, but I much preferred to settle down to a home-cooked meal at the end of the day and save the takeaway option for an occasional treat.

It was another apparent difference between us, and it was galling to think that Jude was the one with access to the beautiful kitchen my grandad had handcrafted, but he wasn't making use of it beyond boiling the kettle, whereas I was doing my best to cook up a nightly feast in the cramped galley space in the apartment.

I supposed I could have invited Jude up for dinner, so he could see the limitations of what I was working with, but as he didn't strike me as the type to take notice of anything that didn't directly impact him, it would most likely have been a waste of time.

Having immersed myself in fairy-making, the week flew by, and it was with a skittering heart that I loaded the crates I would need for the first Cherry Tree Café workshop into my car. Quite a lot was required, but I was an expert at making things fit in my little Fiat and I wished Jude had been around to witness the amount I easily packed in, even with his seat still pushed back into the position he had fixed it in for the trip to and from the bonfire party.

Having settled Tink in the apartment with the radio playing quietly for company, I drove the short distance to the market square and practised some mindful breathing as I went. I kept reminding myself that what I was about to do was a far cry from the bungled high school presentation and subsequent teasing and taunts I had endured as a result, but it didn't make me feel any better.

'Don't look so nervous,' said Lizzie, when she rushed out to help me carry the boxes in ahead of me going to find a parking space for the car. 'Everyone is going to have a wonderful time.'

'Even me?' I squeaked.

'Even you,' she laughed. 'It's not like you to be anxious, Bella, is it?'

'Not at all,' I agreed. 'You know me, I have a tendency to throw myself into things and I have great faith in my fairies.' As I said that, I realized that Faith would be the perfect name for Anna's fairy. 'But ordinarily, it's just me and them. Me creating them at home and then selling them online or sending one out to an individual client.'

With the recent decision to sell at Christmas fairs and on the market, that was something else that was about to dramatically change, too. Talk about flying by the seat of my pants!

'Having first filled them with your own brand of magical intention, of course,' Lizzie said seriously. 'Don't forget that part.'

It was on the tip of my tongue to fill her in about what had happened at school, but I stopped myself. It was bad enough that I was already thinking about it; I didn't want it to be on Lizzie's mind, too.

'I think that's the part I'm stressing about,' I said instead. 'When it's a commission piece, the magical fairy aspect is all discussed one to one with the client, so I know they get it. Quite often that's the reason why they've picked me to make what they want. But what if everyone here thinks I'm mad when I start talking about adding magic and setting intentions with every stitch?'

Lizzie shook her head.

'I think you need to give the people who have signed up to take part more credit than that,' she gently scolded me. 'For some of them, you might not have been their original workshop choice, but I didn't spot a single non-believer on the list.'

'Well, that's a relief,' I said, smiling.

I did genuinely start to feel better once Lizzie had taken

my concerns to heart, rather than dismiss them, and had kindly tried to allay them.

'Now come on,' she cajoled me. 'Go and park your car, and then you'll have time for something to eat and drink before everyone arrives.'

By the time I'd set the table up for the six attendees and eaten one of Jemma's delicious signature chocolate and cherry cupcakes (which I was certain had a magical ingredient of their own), my nerves had practically taken flight and I was feeling far more confident and settled. I loved the café's homely and cosy aesthetic, and the pretty surroundings had given me a boost right when I needed one.

'I made you this,' said Lizzie, handing me a parcel wrapped in pink tissue paper. 'Everyone who teaches workshops here gets one, but usually a plain one. However, when I spotted this fabric, I couldn't resist putting it to use for you.'

I tore open the paper and inside found a cotton work apron, complete with two patch pockets and wide straps that crossed over at the back, meaning that the apron could simply be lifted over my head with no fastenings.

'Oh, Lizzie,' I said, immediately putting it on and giving her a twirl. It was more like a dress, really, and absolutely ideal. 'It's perfect. Thank you so much.'

'The material is vintage,' Lizzie said as she twizzled me around again, this time to check the fit. 'But it was in great condition, so it should last.'

The fabric was covered in fairies, similar to those created by Cicely Mary Barker. My love of fairies had first been instilled by her beautiful artwork courtesy of a set of seasonal books gifted to me by my grandparents one Christmas. I had never been able to pick a favourite from Cicely's extensive collection, because I loved them all.

'And I've made trays of extra-special fairy cakes for everyone to snack on when you take a break later in the morning,' Jemma said, coming out from behind the counter to tell me. 'That sweet sugar hit should tide you all over until you finish.'

Knowing the generous size of Jemma's cakes, I didn't doubt that. I wholeheartedly appreciated that she and Lizzie had gone to so much trouble to help the Lion character that I had portrayed at Hallowe'en find his courage right when I needed it.

'I can feel the magic in here already,' I sighed happily, and that was just as well because the bell above the door tinkled right at that moment and the first participants arrived.

I didn't feel at all nervous by the time almost everyone had taken a seat and I had run through what we were going to be making, how we could give each fairy a completely different personality and, for those who wanted to, how they could add a wish or intention as they stitched, stuck and embellished.

It turned out that everyone wanted to add something, so Lizzie had been right. There were no non-believers in today's group, and I was delighted about that.

'Sorry I'm late!' panted Holly as she practically burst through the door, making the bell clang loudly rather than softly chime.

'I didn't know you were coming!' I gasped as she dumped her coat into my arms and, completely out of puff, sat down heavily on the only empty seat.

'I wanted to surprise you.' She smiled, once she'd caught her breath. 'And I would have been here ages ago, but I had Jasper issues. Don't ask,' she added darkly.

'I wasn't going to,' I said, grimacing, then set to catching her up on the instructions while everyone else made a start.

The time flew by, and before I knew it, Jemma was beckoning me over to the counter and suggesting that it might be a good time to take a break.

'Oh my goodness,' I laughed, 'it's practically too late for lunch. I had no idea.'

'Well, that's good.' She smiled. 'It shows how much you've been enjoying yourself.'

Everyone else seemed to be enjoying themselves, too. They had all started off chatting together, but when I later reminded them that they could make their fairies even more special by thinking about the person they were gifting them to, or adding a wish for themselves, as they worked, the table had settled into a companionable silence. The arrival of Jemma's perfectly decorated cupcakes soon got them all chatting again, but I could tell the spell hadn't been broken.

'How's it going?' asked Jeanie, who had popped in for a cake on her brief break and offered to make a quick detour to mine and let Tink out into the garden so I didn't have to rush off myself.

'It's been brilliant,' Holly said, before I had a chance to answer. 'Bella's a natural.'

'Well, of course she is,' Jeanie said. 'I don't know why you were getting yourself so worked up,' she added, giving me a nudge and a knowing smile.

'Demons definitely slayed.' I smiled back, feeling flattered by what they had both said.

'Demons?' Holly asked with a frown.

'Story for another day,' I told her.

'In that case,' she said mischievously, 'let's talk about one of the take-aways from the bonfire party, shall we?'

The mention of takeaways annoyingly reminded me of Jude, and Holly's next words put him further at the forefront of my mind.

'Take-aways?' Jeanie frowned.

'You and Jude,' Holly said, eyes twinkling. 'You seemed to be hitting it off with him at the party. Didn't she, Bella?'

'Um,' was all I said.

'Well,' Jeanie said pointedly, her words fired towards me, 'I thought *one* of us should give him a warm welcome.'

Holly laughed at that, and I wondered how warm things had got.

'He seemed lovely to me,' Jeanie continued. 'Even if his arrival at yours did cause a rumpus, Bella.'

'In that case,' said Holly, leaning forward in her seat, 'have you seen any more of him this week, Jeanie?'

So much for her being on Team Tim with me. I had been about to suggest that everyone start working on their fairies again but lingered to hear Jeanie's answer.

'I have,' she said, making me feel something I couldn't pinpoint right when I wanted to feel absolutely nothing. 'But not in a social capacity. He's come into the pub a couple of times when it's quiet in the afternoons but has been so immersed in the work he's brought along with him that he hasn't bothered to chat.'

It said a lot about Wynthorpe Hall that a popular pub in the middle of town was a quieter place to work. Though not as quiet as my house. I supposed Jude could have felt in need of a change of scene when he went to The Mermaid, but it still rankled that he wasn't constantly utilising the space I'd sacrificed for him.

'Well, that's disappointing,' Holly said sulkily.

'Not for Tim,' I hastily pointed out. 'Have you seen anything of him, Jeanie?' I asked meaningfully.

'No,' she said, sounding suddenly so grumpy that I almost got whiplash. 'And there's no need to go bringing him up just because I'm winding you up about Jude.'

'You're not winding me up.' I shrugged, feeling my cheeks turn pink as she gave me a look.

'No?' she said sardonically. 'The thought of me watching him work all afternoon while he's looking studious in his dark-framed glasses doesn't turn you green with envy?'

'Hardly,' I tutted. 'Why on earth would you think that? Brusque, rude men have never been my type. You should know that. Not even for the brief encounters I go in for.'

'Jude hasn't been either brusque or rude to me,' she said mildly.

'Well, he has to me,' I huffed.

'And I also know,' she carried on as if I hadn't said a word, 'that you're a sucker for blue eyes and long, thick lashes on a guy.'

I rolled my own eyes at that.

'Right then, everyone,' I said loudly, mindful that time was moving on and also feeling keen to draw a line under the conversation about my current lodger. 'Gather round, and I'll demonstrate again how to give your fairies their wings.'

'You'd better give Jeanie your apartment key first,' Holly reminded me. 'Then she can go and see to Tink and maybe discover if Jude is in a brusque and rude frame of mind today.'

★

It was a blessing to have had such a positive experience to gently ease me in the day before, because the next workshop was much harder work. Rather than setting me up in the café again, Lizzie had moved me into the gallery next door that she and Jemma ran together, showcasing the work of all kinds of local creatives, which could accommodate the extra numbers. The change of venue also meant that we weren't taking up the tables Jemma needed to accommodate the usual Saturday rush in the café.

'I'm going to be popping in and out,' Lizzie told me while I put the finishing touches to the tables, 'but just message me if you need anything urgently.'

'Like an extra pair of hands?' I suggested. 'I could definitely do with growing those.'

Lizzie laughed at that, but I was being serious.

'How about coffee with an extra shot?' she offered instead. 'That'll keep you going.'

'Yes, please.'

'Have you made arrangements for Tink today?'

The workshop the day before had run to coincide with school hours, but this was a longer session and included a picnic-box-style lunch. That was a great option because it meant we wouldn't have to tidy too much away to make the space for it.

'Yes,' I told Lizzie. 'Holly is going to bring Jasper with her into town and then take him and Tink for a long walk.'

'Perfect,' Lizzie said, smiling, then rushed back to the café next door.

It was perfect, but if fairy workshops became a regular part of my working week, then I would need to make alternative arrangements for Tink. I knew I could rely on my friends, but obviously I didn't want to take advantage. I would have been happy to bring Tink with me to the gallery, but not everyone was a fan of dogs, even impeccably behaved, pretty ones. It was all further food for thought.

'I'm here for the fairy-making workshop,' a nervous voice behind me spoke up just as I was mulling it all over.

'In which case,' I said, turning around with a smile, 'you're in the right place.'

That day passed with the same speed as the workshop the day before, and I was delighted to wave the participants off with a clutch of fairies that ranged from traditional to funky and everything in between. Quickly glancing through the feedback sheets, I was thrilled that they all thought the session was good value for money, that I had provided first-class supplies and guidance and that, in spite of my business name, I wasn't away with the fairies myself. Well, not completely, anyway.

'Don't sit down,' said Lizzie as she bustled in again and caught me about to take a pew, 'and don't even think about taking your shoes off. I know from years of experience that now is the time to power through, pack up, maybe sink a pint in the pub and then, and only then, relax.'

I had to laugh at that. I was still feeling worn out from the day before and even more so now as a result of having to tutor extra participants. I wanted nothing more than to immediately take a load off, but I could see the sense in what Lizzie was saying and bowed to her experience.

'Have you had fun?' asked Holly as she unexpectedly arrived, thankfully without Jasper.

'Do you know what?' I said, looking at the table where

everyone had been so happily settled. 'It was hard work, but I really have.'

'Well, I don't know why you sound so surprised,' Lizzie tutted as she fiddled about with the gallery till. 'We've said for months that you'd be a natural. It's all to do with the passion you feel for your craft, and you've got that by the bucketful.'

'I know you've wanted me to come onboard for a while,' I said, nodding, feeling flattered by her kindness and relieved that I had finally, properly moved on from the mortification over what had happened at school. 'And now I'm delighted that I have.'

'Months!' Lizzie laughed. 'We've waited literally months.'

'Come on, then,' said Holly. 'I'll help you pack up, and there's something I want to talk to you about, Bella. It's actually why I've come back into town after taking Jasper home.'

'Was everything okay with Tink?' I asked.

'Oh yes,' she said, 'she was fine. Sorry, I shouldn't have panicked you like that. She was a joy, as always. Showed Jasper right up when we met some other dog owners who were also out taking a stroll.'

'So what is it you want to talk about?' I asked as Lizzie slipped out again, turning the old-fashioned 'open' sign on the door to 'closed' as she went.

'It's a work thing,' Holly surprised me by saying. 'A potential work thing,' she clarified.

'I'm intrigued,' I said as I began to gather the piles of fabrics together and fold them. 'Tell me.'

'Well,' she began, taking her time to explain, 'I'm wondering if you'd be interested in creating a fairy who I could feature in my *Tall Tales from Small Dogs*.'

'Oh wow!' I gasped.

I hadn't been expecting her to say anything like that.

'I'm not sure of the details yet,' she added, 'but I felt so inspired during the workshop yesterday and fell to thinking that a fairy would be a wonderful addition to Monty and Queenie's world.'

'A fairly fanciful addition,' I laughed.

'Well, as you know,' she reminded me, 'the tales are about two dogs living in a human-free world who travel about together, righting wrongs and championing tolerance and kindness while wearing outlandish outfits. So it's pretty fanciful already.'

'That's true,' I chuckled. 'And you're right, a fairy would be a fun addition. I would be honoured to create one for you. Do you have any ideas about them yet? What their role would be, for example? Or how you might want them to look?'

'None at all.' She frowned. 'Not yet, anyway. I'm sorry to be so vague.'

'From one creative to another,' I said, smiling at her, 'I know how the process works. By which I mean, I know it isn't straightforward or the same for any two projects.'

Sometimes inspiration would strike me lightning bolt-style and on other occasions I had to wait literally weeks for an idea to properly form. As a result, I knew that the art of creation wasn't as simple as just sitting down and getting on with it. There was no rhyme or reason to the process, and one project was rarely like another.

'I'm not sure if the fairy will be someone Monty and Queenie have already helped,' Holly said thoughtfully, 'or if they might be a hero in their own right, waiting to make an appearance.'

'Well,' I told her, 'my fairy kingdom caters for everyone. They're completely inclusive, so take your pick, as well as your time over their development.'

'That's perfect,' she said, nodding, 'and I already know about them being inclusive. The woman who made her fairy with one big wing and one tiny one yesterday told me she felt wonderfully represented as a result of you encouraging her to do that.'

I felt a lump form in my throat when Holly told me that.

'She wrote that on the feedback form, too,' I said huskily. 'I hadn't realized she'd talked to anyone about it.'

'You're doing good work, Bella,' Holly said, pulling me in for a hug. 'And if you really do like the sound of my idea . . .'

'Oh, I do,' I told her keenly as she released me again. 'I love it.'

'In that case, I'll properly get my thinking cap on and give you more details as soon as I come up with them.'

Even though the two days of teaching had worn me out, I was feeling in a wonderful mood after my chat with Holly and didn't even let my smile slip when I arrived home and had to work around Jude to stack my boxes because he was lingering in the hall and taking up most of the space.

'Hello, Jude,' I said brightly, self-consciously aware that my face was flushed from the cold and my hair was most likely an unruly tangle of curls thanks to the Wynbridge winter wind. 'How are you? It feels like I haven't seen you for days. How's the writing coming along?'

'Pretty well,' he said, but he didn't sound particularly thrilled. 'I've finished drafting the introduction now and have just about put into date order all of the documents relating to the initial building and the subsequent changes to the hall.'

'I didn't realize there had been any changes,' I said.

'Just a couple,' he told me. 'And additions, too. But so thoughtfully done that they're barely noticeable to the untrained eye.'

'How interesting.'

I wondered which parts had been added after the initial build. I would take more notice the next time I visited.

'It really is,' he agreed.

'I hope you find a publisher for the book,' I said. 'I'm sure there'd be lots of interest in it, especially locally.'

I'd often thought a camera crew should film both the hall and the Connelly clan. It would be every bit as entertaining as watching the MacCarthy family in *Normal for Norfolk*. I was certain that Angus was even more eccentric than Desmond, who owned Wiveton Hall.

'That would be wonderful,' Jude said wistfully, but then added more seriously, 'but I'd have to get the book finished first.'

'Well, now you've started, I'm sure—'

'Now I've made a start,' he interrupted sharply, 'I need peace and quiet to carry on with it, and that's what I thought I was going to get here.' I guessed his brooding presence in my hallway wasn't to welcome me home.

'I don't understand,' I said, frowning.

I quickly bit my tongue to stop myself saying that the house must at least be quieter than the pub. The last thing I wanted was him knowing he'd been the topic of conversation. I had been about to ask him if he'd like to join me for a drink in The Mermaid, but his change of tone had quickly made the idea take flight – and along with it, some of my earlier excitement about the success of the workshops and what Holly had said.

'Your dog,' Jude said, not using her name even though he knew it, as he knocked yet more wind out of my sails, 'has been barking practically all afternoon.'

'Tink?' I frowned more deeply. 'Tink has been barking?'

I found that highly unlikely but, given that I hadn't been anywhere near the house and that I couldn't ask her, I could hardly refute what Jude was saying.

'Yes,' he said. 'She was fine all morning, but then someone took her out around lunchtime and she hasn't settled since.'

There was no sound from her now.

'And it was the same yesterday,' Jude went on. 'But not as bad as today.'

Tink had never been much of a yapper, but perhaps she hadn't appreciated my absence or being disturbed in the middle of the day. Perhaps I should have just left her on her own, but it would have been a long time to make her wait.

'In that case,' I said, 'I'd better go and check she's all right, and I'll make sure you have an uninterrupted evening.'

I stood on tiptoe and at full stretch to stack the last of the boxes, then made a hasty retreat before I said anything further, because it would most likely be something I'd regret.

Chapter 7

'So tell me, Bella, how are you finding life with that handsome young man you've got shacked up with you?'

It was just as well I'd put the teapot down before Gladys – a resident in the care home, The Laurels, where I had a meeting that Sunday morning – asked me that, otherwise we could have had a major scalding incident on our hands.

'How do you know about him?' I asked her, noting the twinkle in her eyes. 'And we're not *shacked up*,' I hastily corrected her. 'He's a regular guest. He's staying downstairs, and I'm still upstairs in the apartment.' I didn't add that he was a total pain and that practically every conversation I'd so far had with him had put me in a bad mood.

Gladys sucked in a breath.

'I can't imagine you like that arrangement much,' she said astutely, hopefully referring to the time of year I was living in the apartment as opposed to how I felt about Jude and I living apart rather than being 'shacked up' together. 'You're normally well settled back into the house by now, aren't you, my love?'

'Yes,' I said as I carefully set down a cup and saucer on the table next to her and gently lifted Tink off her lap. 'And I almost was settled again, but then . . .'

'Catherine Connelly asked you to do the family a favour, and of course you obliged.'

'I did,' I said, nodding, confirming what she'd said. 'And after everything she and the family have done for me over the years, it was the least I could do.'

Gladys smiled at that.

'Are there really no secrets in Wynbridge?' I sighed, as I realized she already knew the whole of it.

'Not a single one!' said Stanley, winking. He was in the seat next to Gladys, patiently waiting for his turn to fuss my obliging canine companion.

'I suppose I should know that by now, shouldn't I?' I said with a wry smile as I lowered Tink onto his blanket-covered lap. 'Is she too heavy for you, Stanley?'

'Not for a few minutes,' he said, kissing the top of her beautifully dome-shaped head. 'I'll tell you when she gets too much.'

This was always the way at The Laurels. I invariably popped in to do one thing, like coming in today for the meeting about the Christmas fair that was happening the following Saturday, and ended up doing something completely different.

Today it was tea duty and biscuit monitoring. The one thing that never changed, though, was Tink's role. She always accompanied me, and everyone loved to make a fuss of her. She was such a placid little thing. I was still struggling to imagine her yapping for an entire afternoon . . .

'Penny for them,' said Gladys, looking eagerly at me.

'Hmm?'

'You're frowning, Bella. What is it, love? Are you wondering how I found out your lodger is a handsome young man?'

'No,' I told her, neatly changing the subject, 'I'm wondering who swiped the last of the custard creams.'

At the Christmas Fair, I usually helped sell tickets for the raffle and topped up the stallholders' drinks, but as I was going to be a stallholder myself this time, I needed to know about the set-up details and where my table would be. It was going to be my first foray into selling directly to the public, and I had expected to feel nervous about it, but given how well the workshops had been received, I was now rather looking forward to it.

'Would it be an issue if I ended up having to bring Tink with me?' I asked Mandy, the care home manager. Tink's tail swished across my feet in response to hearing her name. 'I probably won't, but I wanted to check, just in case.'

Any other year, I would have left her behind, because as a volunteer helper I wouldn't have been away all day, but this time around I was going to be out of the apartment for far longer – and on top of that, there was the more pressing concern that she might bark again and further disturb Jude if I left her behind.

'No issue at all,' Mandy told me. 'You could put her basket behind your stall.'

'Not that she'll stay in it,' added Helen, her deputy. 'She'll doubtless be barely over the threshold before someone smuggles her into their room.'

'Hmm,' Mandy said thoughtfully. 'Given that it's going to be so busy, perhaps she'd be better off in my office and you can pop in and out to check on her, Bella. At least that way you'll know exactly where she is.'

'Thank you,' I said, but I wasn't sure Tink would be keen to stay put once she realized her octogenarian friends were in the vicinity.

Neither leaving her at the apartment nor bringing her with me felt like the right option, but I'd have to make a decision about what would be best for her soon.

'Right,' said Helen, checking her clipboard once we'd worked through the lengthy itinerary, 'I think that's it. Unless anyone has any further questions?'

There were a few, but it wasn't much longer before I headed off. It was a chilly walk home, and I was just about to turn into the top of my road when I heard heavy footfalls behind me. I turned around and was astonished to see Jude jogging along the pavement. Tink wagged her tail and pulled at her lead to reach him.

'You wouldn't be so keen to see him if you knew what he'd said about you yesterday,' I told her before he came within earshot.

'Hey,' Jude puffed, coming to a stop when he reached us and fiddling about with a device on his wrist.

'Don't stop on our account,' I said. 'You carry on.'

'It's fine,' he said, quickly catching his breath and falling into step with us. 'I'm done for today.'

'I didn't have you down as a runner.'

He must have been pretty fit, though, given how quickly he'd recovered from the exertion. That said, for all I knew he might have only run around the corner.

'I'm not keen on it,' he confessed, wrinkling his nose. 'In fact, I hate it.'

'So why do you do it, then?'

'Heart health,' he said, grimacing, then taking a deep breath and huffing it out again as he wiped his hand across his forehead. 'Looking after my bones. Building muscle.'

Perhaps a bit further than around the corner, then.

'Couldn't you find something you love that will achieve all that?' I asked.

'Maybe.' He shrugged.

'Surely life's too short to spend time doing things you don't enjoy, isn't it?'

'What do you do, then?' he asked. 'To keep yourself fit, I mean.'

'Pilates, meditation, dog walking,' I reeled off.

'Do any of those kick your heart rate up a gear, though?' he asked.

'The dog walking does,' I laughed. 'You should see Tink when she hits her stride.' I immediately regretted drawing attention to her given that he wasn't a fan. 'Are you suggesting I could be in better shape?'

I instantly regretted asking that, too. Who knew how someone with Jude's penchant for plain talking was likely to respond.

'Absolutely not,' he gulped. 'Your shape looks great to me.'

'Oh!' I gasped.

'I mean, you look fit,' he stammered, and I bit my lip. 'Fit and healthy.' He took another breath. 'You look fine,' he said more seriously.

Having so easily caught his breath before, he sounded quite out of puff again.

'Here we are, then,' I said, turning into the drive and feeling grateful that the glacial temperature could account for the colour of my face.

I stole a quick glance at Jude, and he looked rather rosy, too. But then he had been running before he made such a hash of what he'd just said, hadn't he?

He gathered his wits enough to ask, 'Had you been out anywhere nice?' while he fumbled for his key.

'Just to The Laurels,' I told him. 'It's a care home up the road. I'm having a stall at their Christmas fair next weekend, and it was the meeting this morning to go through all the details.'

He shot a glance down at Tink.

'Did you have to take your dog—'

'Tink,' I interrupted, eager to remind him of her name, even though I was sure he hadn't really forgotten it.

'Did you have to take Tink because of what I said about her barking yesterday?' he asked. 'You didn't have to leave her tied up outside, did you?'

I was too appalled that he would even consider I might have done to notice that he had sounded concerned when he asked the question.

'Of course I didn't leave her outside,' I snapped. 'She's welcome at The Laurels,' I added rather sniffily. 'In fact, I always take her along when I volunteer there, so the residents can spend some time with her. It's good for their wellbeing, and she's so well behaved, she's never any bother.'

'I didn't mean—'

'I'll see you around, Jude,' I said, then strode off with Tink at my heels.

It wasn't until I'd slammed the door behind me and had stomped up the stairs that I realized that I'd just behaved in exactly the same way that I was always so cross with Jude about. He'd broken off his run to talk to me and sounded genuinely concerned that Tink had had to come with me to the care home because of what he'd said. If that had been an olive branch, I'd as good as wrenched it out of his grasp and broken it over my knee.

Being mostly holed up in the apartment for the rest of that week creating multiple fairies to sell over Christmas and making great progress with the two that Molly had commissioned, I neither saw nor heard Jude. I heard from Holly and Jeanie, though, and promised I would join them at Cuckoo Cottage on Friday for a catch-up and a dog walk.

I could easily have spent the time I would be with them carrying on with my work and getting a lot more finished as a result, but I'd already missed our last brunch of the year and didn't want to make a habit out of ducking out.

I knew life was all about striking the right balance; when you worked alone and from home, it was even more important to get out, meet friends and go places. Being self-employed meant I could set my own schedule, and I reminded myself that it was vital to my mental health and wellbeing that I didn't become so absorbed in my work, as much as I loved it, that I forgot to ring-fence time for anything else.

And I hadn't forgotten that Holly had gone out of her way to attend one of my workshops *and* that both she and Jeanie had helped out with looking after Tink, too. Friendships required give and take, and I had no intention of being a taker.

Unfortunately, however, my heart sank as I opened the apartment door, ready to lug down a few boxes and then head out to see my friends, because I could hear Jude moving about in the hall below. I supposed I could have waited it out, but really, given that I was the one who had ended our last conversation so abruptly, it was down to me to try to make amends.

'Hey,' I said, when I turned the corner and he came into sight.

He was manhandling a couple of boxes of his own, and the space I'd left for him to move in did suddenly seem ridiculously tight.

'Hey,' he said back, sounding rather less friendly than me. 'We have to do something about all of this, Bella. It's getting out of control. I'm sure there are more here now than there were before.'

'Well, of course there are,' I said, dumping the boxes I'd carried down at my feet. 'These extra boxes are full of stock for me to sell over Christmas.'

'And you're really sure there's nowhere else you can put them?' he asked, also putting his boxes down.

I gritted my teeth.

'Completely sure,' I said, taking a deep breath. 'Unless you're willing for me to put them in the house.'

'But then they'd be even more in my way,' he remarked. 'And you'd have to keep coming in and out to get them.'

That was it. I didn't care how beguiling his blue eyes were or how long his lashes. He was sounding like a whiny brat, and I'd had enough of it.

'In that case,' I vented, 'they'll have to stay where they are, and I'd really appreciate it if you could bear in mind that ordinarily at this time of year, I wouldn't be letting the house out to guests. I'd be living in it myself and I'd have the run of the entire place, and therefore space, or the lack of it, wouldn't be an issue for anyone.'

I stopped to draw breath and wondered how he was going to respond to that. Had it been me, I would have bent over backwards to make sure my presence wasn't an inconvenience to the person who'd so kindly put themselves so far out.

'You know,' he said, looking thoughtful, 'I met a fella earlier this year with the right idea. He lived in a horsebox, and his entire worldly goods were contained within it. Can you imagine reducing your possessions to fit into a space of that size, Bella?'

'Given my line of work,' I snapped, 'definitely not.'

'And your love of cushions, throws and trinkets,' he carried on doggedly, not picking up on my upset at all.

I didn't think I'd ever come across someone so insensitive.

'I like my house to be a home,' I said with dignity. 'Not an empty, soulless box.'

'Or an empty, soulless horsebox,' he said, looking around again and sounding pleased with his wordplay. 'I suppose we'll just have to manage, won't we?'

'Yes,' I said, 'I suppose we will.'

I was still seething when I picked Jeanie up from the pub and set off for Holly's place.

'Hormone alert!' Jeanie quipped to Holly as she climbed out of my car and scooped Jasper up. 'Bella's on a mad one.'

'Oh, you poor love,' Holly sympathized. 'I've got one of those huge slabs of Galaxy hidden away for exactly this sort of emergency. Let's all have a few squares with our coffee.'

'It's not hormones,' I tutted, releasing Tink from her harness and reaching behind my seat for my welly bag. 'Though I won't say no to the chocolate.'

'What is it, then?' Jeanie asked, putting a squirming Jasper back down so he and Tink could caper about.

'Nothing,' I said, shrugging.

'Oh my god, it's Jude,' she laughed. 'That man's getting to you, isn't he?'

'About as much as Tim's getting to you, Jeanie,' Holly said, coming to my rescue and making me wonder if I'd missed something. 'And Bear's getting to me, too.'

'I thought Bear was perfect.' Jeanie frowned.

'Oh, he is, for the most part,' Holly said, shaking her head, 'but a wheel is literally about to fall off his wagon, so he's got to get it fixed before he drives up. And with a stop to see his mum on the way, he reckons he won't be back until late on Saturday now.'

'But at least when he does get here, you'll have him until spring,' I reminded her.

That wouldn't have suited me, but I knew it did her.

'Exactly.' Jeanie grinned. 'Whereas Jude will be gone in . . .'

'Another seventeen days,' I said, checking each one off by counting them up on my fingers.

'I bet she's got a countdown on her phone,' Jeanie said as she and Holly both laughed about the fact that I could so quickly work out exactly the number of days Jude had left under my roof.

'And on my kitchen calendar,' I added, making them laugh all the harder.

'Come on,' said Holly, opening the railway carriage door, 'let's forget the walk and focus on the chocolate.'

'Let's have both,' said Jeanie. 'I need the exercise. My thighs aren't what they once were.'

'And I could do with getting my blood pumping a bit,' I agreed.

'I'm sure Jude has already done that,' Jeanie giggled, pulling me up the steps and into the warm and cosy inside.

Chapter 8

I'd barely finished drinking my first mug of tea when Jude knocked on the apartment door the following morning. I had got up extra early to have one final check that I'd got everything I needed for the Christmas fair at The Laurels because I was now feeling a little jittery about it, and the last thing I needed was to be faced with yet more of my temporary lodger's moaning.

'Jude,' I sighed, 'hey. What can I do for you?'

I'd opened the door just wide enough to acknowledge him, but not far enough to let out Tink, who was trying to nudge her way between my calves.

'I know it's early,' he said, most likely noticing that I was still in my fleecy winter patterned PJs, 'but I wondered if I might just have a word?'

'Okay,' I said, knowing I couldn't really say no. Even though I wanted to. 'Come in.' I opened the door wider and reached for Tink's collar. 'Sorry if Tink makes a fuss. For some reason, she's always excited to see you.'

I hadn't meant for that to sound quite so sarcastic, but I was very much a 'love me, love my dog' kind of person. Unless you had a genuine reason not to be a cute canine fan – and alleged barking aside, Jude didn't.

'She's fine,' he said, coming right in and closing the door behind him. 'Hello there, Tink.'

He bent to give her the attention she'd been hankering for since she'd first laid eyes on him, and then she rolled onto her back in complete submission. She normally only ever did that for me. I tried not to feel affronted.

'Daft dog,' Jude laughed as he gave her soft belly a rub.

'She is that,' I said, feeling myself warm to him a little more than I previously had. I didn't suppose it was his fault that my soft-hearted hound was a pushover where he was concerned. 'Can I offer you a coffee? Or tea? I was just about to pour myself another one.'

'Tea would be great,' he said, straightening up and looking around. 'Thanks.'

He followed me over to the tiny space that was the apartment kitchen and watched as I poured his drink. I felt the weight of his stare. Not in an uncomfortable way, rather more self-conscious. It took all my focus not to overfill his mug.

'A teapot.' He smiled, his tone suggesting it was a rarity. 'I can't remember the last time I was poured tea from a proper pot. I'm not sure I've ever actually used one myself.'

Clearly in his world a teapot was unheard of, whereas in mine, thanks to the influence of my grandparents, it was an everyday piece of kitchen equipment.

'Do you always use it?' he asked interestedly.

'Of course,' I told him, repeating what my nanna used to say. 'If something's worth doing, then it's worth doing properly.'

'Even if that's simply making a cup of tea?'

'*Especially* if that's simply making a cup of tea,' I repeated with emphasis. 'It's like setting the table for breakfast—'

'You set the table for breakfast?' he interrupted, his tone full of wonder.

'Yes,' I said, 'and lunch and dinner. Though not in quite the same way up here in the apartment as I would in the house, because there isn't the space.'

'That's partly what I wanted to talk to you about,' he said, taking the mug I passed him and eschewing the sugar canister.

I glanced at the clock and thought it was a relief that I'd got up so early. If he had a lot he wanted to say, it would soon gobble up the time I'd allowed for checking and double-checking my stock and getting myself and Tink ready.

'It really is a bit of a squeeze up here, isn't it?' he said, looking around again.

Rather than pack away the bits and pieces and cushions and throws I'd put out downstairs ahead of his arrival, I'd added them to the windowsills and the sofa, so everything was even more layered up than usual. All of that, combined with the extra boxes of fairies, made it an almost uncomfortable squeeze. Even for me.

'It's definitely cosy,' I acknowledged. 'Bijou would most likely be how an estate agent would describe it. I can normally keep myself confined up here during the rest of the year, but it's a struggle now I'm dramatically increasing my stock in time for Christmas.'

'Yes,' Jude said, biting his lip and annoyingly looking even more attractive as a result, 'about that. I really am sorry I moaned about those boxes and crates you're having to stack in the hall.'

'I appreciate the apology.' I swallowed as I dragged my eyes away from his lips and graciously accepted his words. Given his previous behaviour, I certainly hadn't been expecting to hear them.

'And I'm also sorry that I didn't really understand the sacrifice you were making in staying holed up up here for longer than you usually would be,' he added.

His heartfelt apology and acknowledgement of his formerly dismissive attitude was quite a turnaround, and I wondered what had prompted it.

'I saw Jeanie in the pub last night,' he continued, providing me with an explanation, 'and she filled me in on a few things.'

I felt a prickle of unease at the back of my neck.

'Oh,' I said, the sound a few octaves higher than I had intended so it came out more like a squeak than a word. 'Did she?' I added, having cleared my throat.

Given some of what had been said during our Galaxy-bar gorging and subsequent dog walk with Holly, I hoped Jeanie hadn't filled him in too much. Our heart to hearts were carried out under the 'what's said between us stays between us' banner, and I hoped Jeanie hadn't forgotten that.

'Yes,' Jude said, 'she did, and it made me realize that I've been so self-absorbed while I got started on the Connelly book that I've been in a sort of sealed bubble and acting like a prat as a result.'

I almost spat my tea out when he said that.

'You obviously agree with that description,' he laughed as I reached for the kitchen roll under the sink.

'Your words, not mine,' I said, smiling as I wiped my mouth.

'But you're not going to refute them.' He grinned.

It felt like the sun came out when he smiled, and the whole

apartment basked in the glow. I reminded myself that Jude now had just sixteen days left under my roof, which was long enough for a liaison should the urge to crank things up come over me. But I also had a whole heap of work to focus on, and the time spent shifting the parameters of our relationship and consequently falling behind with my work would not a merry Christmas make.

'No,' I therefore said lightly as I quickly looked away. 'I'm not.'

'That's fair,' he said, nodding. 'I do know how I can sometimes get when I'm so focused on a project. I have a tendency to block pretty much everything else out. In my defence, I need to, though, in order to make sure I'm getting it all right. And for some reason, this complicated commission and the exasperating Angus who came along with it have got me wanting to get this book even better than right.'

'I see,' I said.

'Hence the extra prat-like behaviour I wouldn't usually succumb quite so intensely to,' he added. 'I really am sorry.'

I was in thrall as he said all that. I could understand him better now, knowing that he was a perfectionist, because I had a tendency to be one, too – where my work was concerned, anyway. I always strove to get my fairies as full of character as I could, and the fact that Jude wanted to do well by Angus, even though he plagued his heart out, made me appreciate his efforts and understand his immersion in the work all the more.

'More tea?' I offered, feeling shocked by the sensation of my heart skittering in my chest. My heart didn't generally go in for skittering, but Jude's passionate words, combined with the earlier lip biting, had made quite an impact.

'There's plenty in the pot,' I added, because I wanted him to stay a bit longer, even though I didn't really have the time to entertain him.

'Do you really always make it in a pot?' he quizzed.

'Yes,' I said again. 'I do, and if you knew me better, you'd know I can make an occasion out of pretty much anything. Especially the everyday things we have a tendency to take for granted.'

'Like making a cup of tea.'

'My nanna always maintained,' I told him, readjusting the skep-shaped cosy the pot was covered with as my heart finally began to settle back down, 'that if you're drinking a cup of tea, then you should take a moment to properly taste it, rather than knock it back while you're on the go and without it touching the sides. And I've been more than happy to carry on with her wonderful way of thinking.'

Jude took a moment to consider that.

'So what other everyday things do you make an occasion of?' he asked.

'Right now, I sadly have nowhere near enough time to tell you,' I laughed, glancing at the clock again.

'Well,' he said, 'now I've apologized for being so rude since I moved in, perhaps there'll be a chance I'll get to know you better and find out before I leave.'

I almost found myself wishing he would be around for Christmas – though not staying in the house, of course – so I could show him what an occasion I made of the festive season.

'Well,' I nodded, as thoughts of mistletoe came to mind, 'perhaps you will, but for now I have to dash, I'm afraid. Which is a shame, given what I've just said about taking time over a cuppa, but I need to get ready to go to the care home fair. Was there anything else?'

'There was, actually,' he said, handing me his now empty mug. 'I think you should leave Tink here today. I'm sure you'll have enough to think about at the fair without worrying if one of the residents who loves her has spirited her away.'

Tink plonked herself on his feet and looked adoringly up at him.

'But if I leave her here,' I said, feeling my heart flutter again as he bent and fondly kissed her silky head, 'and she starts barking, you'll be interrupted. Though you won't be working today, will you?'

'I am actually planning to get some work done,' he told me.

'But it's Saturday, Jude,' I tutted. 'You need to watch that. Work–life balance is every bit as important as making an occasion out of the little things.'

'You're working today,' he pointed out.

'That's different,' I said. 'It makes sense for the fair to happen on a Saturday, and I'll take Monday off to make up for it.'

He nodded approvingly at that.

'You really have got it all figured out, haven't you, Bella?' He smiled again.

'Almost,' I acknowledged.

My feelings for him were now a bit of a muddle after this conversation, but otherwise I generally tended to have a handle on what I was doing.

'Anyway,' he said, 'Tink won't disturb me, if you're happy to go along with what I've got in mind.'

'Which is?'

'That you leave her downstairs with me,' he then completely

surprised me by saying. 'When you're ready, just bring her down and she can spend the day in the house with me for company.'

'Oh,' I said. 'Well . . .'

'That way, you'll know exactly where she is and she'll have someone to feed her at her usual time and let her out into the garden if she needs to go.'

'That's very kind of you,' I began, 'but . . .'

My words trailed off as he sat on the floor to give Tink another fuss and she instantly became putty in his hands. I supposed that settled it, then.

'All right,' I agreed, as I looked at them both. 'I'll leave her with you. Thank you, Jude.'

Given that my head was abuzz with the sudden turnaround in Jude's demeanour, his passionate words about his work, his subsequent apology *and* his generous offer to look after Tink, it was a miracle I didn't forget anything or make a mess of setting up my stall at The Laurels. My darling Tink was my everything, and I had to have complete faith in someone before I handed her over, so that was some measure of how quickly my feelings towards Jude had been transformed.

Trying to shake thoughts of him out of my head, I stood back to look at the layout of my stall.

'Oh, Bella!' Mandy gasped, when she caught sight of me and the pretty tableau I had created. 'This is so beautiful, and you totally look the part, too.'

'The dress felt right for today,' I said, giving her a twirl.

It wasn't the full-on fairy get-up that I loved to wear at home, but it wasn't far off. Thanks to the workshop successes and subsequent release from my mortifying high school experience, I'd made a real effort to look like a fitting salesperson for my fairies. I'd gone for a full-skirted dress with a bolero cardigan that always made me feel good. Jude had said he liked it, too, when I'd dropped Tink off. There he was again, drifting into my thoughts . . .

'There'll be no mistaking who this table belongs to,' Mandy said, again taking me and the stall in.

I set about snapping pictures of the table for my social media accounts and website, and I had to agree. The snowy wonderland theme, with LED-lit twig trees at either end and a blanket of faux snow laid out beneath, was perfect. The fairies hanging on the trees were secured by clear thread and really looked as though they were flying, and the ones sitting in small groups were obviously chatting about all things magical.

I hadn't put out too many, because I didn't want to crowd the space, but I had more stock in boxes under the table, ready to replace any who winged their way to new homes.

'Thank you, Mandy,' I sighed happily. 'I hoped that keeping the backdrop predominantly white would show off the different fabrics I've dressed the fairies in, and I think it works.'

'It really does,' said Mandy, giving my arm a squeeze. 'In fact,' she said, stepping forward and picking up one of the largest fairies, who would look perfect on the top of a small festive tree, 'can I reserve this beauty?'

'Really?' I gasped.

It was one of the most expensive I'd brought along, and to be honest, I hadn't thought it'd sell but would instead give me the opportunity to show visitors what my commission pieces looked like.

'Really,' Mandy said firmly. 'I've had my eye on her right from the moment you unboxed her.'

'Well, that's fantastic!' I beamed. 'I'll pack her away again.'

'No, don't,' she said. 'I can see she's an important part of the display, so pop a reserved sign on her and I'll collect her at the end of the day.'

'Are you sure?'

'Absolutely. Just don't let anyone walk off with her.'

'I won't,' I promised, rushing to rummage through my supplies for a card I could make a reserved sign out of. 'She'll be here waiting for you when it's time to pack up.'

I had a feeling that life with Mandy would mean that this fairy was going to be one of those who didn't get packed away with the rest of the decorations after Christmas. I knew there were quite a lot who stayed unboxed, and it made me so happy to think of them being on display and part of their homes all year round.

'Wonderful,' Mandy said as I carefully placed the small, handwritten sign on the fairy's tulle skirt. 'And the sign might even be good for business,' she suggested. 'Create a bit more demand. Not that I don't think you're going to attract enough.'

'We'll soon find out,' I said, feeling nervous again. 'It's almost time to open the doors.'

'Oh goodness, I'd better get on,' Mandy gasped. 'No Tink today?' she asked before she left.

'No,' I said, hoping my canine friend was okay. 'I left her at home in the end.'

'Probably for the best, because I reckon it's going to be busy.'

There was just enough time for me to do a quick round of the rest of the stalls ahead of the doors being opened, and then a keen influx of rosy-cheeked Wynbridge residents hurried in and we were off.

'Here we go,' Roy, the person set up next to me, said loudly. He had a stunning selection of turned-wood items on offer. 'Good luck, everyone.'

We were all rushed off our feet right from that moment, and at one point I was struggling to keep up with replacing fairies on my ever depleting display. My nerves had no chance of making their presence felt, because I thrillingly didn't have a moment to consider them.

I soon discovered that the peg fairies I'd hung on the tree were the fastest to fly off. As the quickest to make, they were the cheapest, too, and I began to realize just how many more I was going to need over the next few weeks in the run-up to Christmas. I could imagine they'd sell like hotcakes at the school fair. That said, it wasn't only those that sold well – the medium-sized winged beauties were popular, too, and I even had a couple of serious-sounding commission enquiries.

'Here you go, Bella,' said Helen, when I thought the doors had been open for just minutes rather than hours. 'Elevenses.'

'Elevenses?' I frowned as I waved another fairy off. 'Are you sure?'

'Just after half past eleven, actually,' she said apologetically. 'It's taken me a while to get to you.'

I gratefully took the tea she offered and a couple of rich tea biscuits.

'Sorry about the biscuits,' she apologized. 'You know what this place is like. The good ones always go first.'

'I'm actually rather partial to a rich tea,' I told her. 'So these are just what I fancy. Thanks, Helen.'

I didn't have time to chat further, as someone was looking very interested in the fairy that Mandy had reserved. I explained that I had a couple more like it at home and that there were photos of them on my Insta page. Ten minutes later, I had another reservation for one of them, and I was feeling a heady mix of proud, excited and exhilarated. Selling direct was nowhere near as scary as I had previously thought it might be.

There was a brief lull in visitors around lunchtime, and I took the opportunity to telephone the house to ask Jude how he and Tink were getting on. There was no answer the first time I tried. Or the third. Or the seventh. And by that point, I was getting a bit jittery and wondering if I could ask one of the other stallholders to keep an eye on my fairies while I dashed back to the house to make sure all was well.

I had just made up my mind to do that, when Mandy bustled over.

'You've got a visitor,' she told me, looking thrilled to deliver the news.

'A visitor?'

'Two, actually,' she elaborated. 'They're sitting under the pergola. Grab your coat and go and say hello, and I'll watch your stall.'

I pulled on my red coat and wrapped my scarf around my neck before rushing out.

'I'll only be a minute!' I called over my shoulder.

'Take your time!' Mandy called back. 'I would.'

I raced towards the pergola and caught sight of Tink on her lead and wrapped in her warmest coat. She was ecstatic to see me, and I felt myself relax as Jude stood up with a smile on his face.

'We thought we'd bring you some lunch, in case you didn't have time to get anything,' he said kindly.

He looked every inch the Hallmark hero in a dark coat with the collar turned up, and my heart chose that moment to misbehave again.

'You didn't have to do that,' I said, fussing Tink and then taking the cherry-patterned bag Jude held out.

'Well,' he said, grinning, 'it's lunchtime, and someone recently told me that you should make an occasion of everyday things.'

'In that case,' I said, finding myself smiling back, 'thank you very much.'

I opened the bag and looked inside.

'It's the festive veggie sandwich from a place called the Cherry Tree Café,' Jude told me. 'According to the woman behind the counter, who recognized Tink when I poked my head around the door, it's a favourite of yours.'

'It is,' I said as my tummy rumbled in anticipation of eating it. 'That's really thoughtful of you, Jude. Thank you.'

'You're very welcome,' he said. 'And now we've seen you and dropped it off, we'll head home, shall we, Tink?'

She barked at that, and I hoped that was the first noise she'd made.

'How's the work going?' I asked.

He pinned me with another look, and I felt myself go warm in spite of the weather.

'I decided to take the day off,' he said, slowly pulling his gaze away from mine as he stepped out from under the pergola and untangled Tink's lead.

'Not because of Tink, I hope?' I asked.

'Nope,' he said, 'she's been asleep most of the morning. It was because of that person I mentioned before.'

'Oh, I see.' I nodded, trying to stave off another smile.

'They said I needed to be mindful of my work–life balance, so that's what I've been doing. Being mindful.'

'That sounds like some good advice,' I called after him as he moved away.

'That's what I thought!' he called back.

Oh dear, I thought as I watched him walk off with Tink happily melded to his side. If I wasn't careful, I might find myself diverting my attention and falling behind with my work after all.

Chapter 9

The rest of the time at The Laurels fairly flew by, and even though I'd sold so much of my stock, there were still all of the boxes, bags and crates to carry back into the house when I arrived home. Having just repacked it all into my car, and feeling absolutely exhausted, I wasn't much in the mood to take it all out again. So when Jude rushed out of the front door to offer his help the moment I arrived back, I was very willing to accept.

'Thank you so much,' I said gratefully, as he added the last crate to the high stack in the hall. 'You really are a lifesaver.'

'It was no bother,' he said kindly.

'I had planned a trip to the pub tonight,' I yawned, 'but I'm far too tired. All I really want is a hot drink, a long bath and my warm bed.'

'That sounds like the perfect combo.'

'Or it would be,' I remembered, 'if I had a bath. It's just a shower upstairs, unfortunately.'

'Well, I wouldn't object to you soaking in the tub down here,' Jude said casually. 'And I was going to order something in for dinner. Would you like to join me?'

Given how tired I was, I was certain I'd be useless company and was poised to turn him down, but then he mentioned wine and Saturday night TV and my resolve crumbled. What a surprising total turnaround our relationship was suddenly experiencing.

A couple of hours later, I was feeling relaxed and replete, and, with Tink asleep on the sofa between us, Jude looked to be in a similar state himself. I felt a rush of something when I realized that he seemed to be as happy about how things were turning out between us as I was. I tried to work out what that rush of something was, but I was too drowsy to fathom it.

'Would you like me to open you another bottle?' Jude offered, catching my eye.

We'd opted to drink lager in the end to go with the tasty Indian takeaway, and I knew I'd be asleep in seconds if I started drinking another one.

'I'm going to say a very reluctant no,' I told him. 'But thank you, and thank you for a lovely evening, too. It really has been exactly what I needed after such a hectic day.'

'Successful, though, from what you've said,' he reminded me. 'So worth feeling tired out for.'

'Oh, absolutely,' I agreed. 'But now I really do need my bed. Thank you so much for looking after Tink today. It was a weight off my mind, especially when you turned up at lunch-time and she looked so happy. And thanks for the sandwich, too. That was as good as the takeaway.'

I really was in his debt now. Had someone suggested this would be how things were going to work out even just a couple of days ago, I wouldn't have believed them.

'It was my pleasure,' Jude said warmly. 'I feel like I've made amends for being so insensitive when I first arrived. Or at least made a start.'

'You're fine,' I told him, standing up and stretching out my back. Dressed in my cosiest PJs and fluffiest dressing gown, I felt cocooned, safe and settled. 'I forgave you the moment you explained to me how focused you are on telling the Wynthorpe Hall story and how badly you want to get it right.'

'That's still no excuse, though.' He frowned, looking concerned.

'You weren't making excuses,' I pointed out. 'You were explaining your process.'

'Well, that's very generous of you,' he said, switching the frown for a smile.

'And you've been generous today,' I told him. 'You've gone above and beyond, and I'd like to repay your kindness.'

'You don't have to—' he began.

'I haven't told you how yet,' I pointed out.

'Oh, that's true,' he gasped, pretending to wince. 'Go on, then.'

'Don't worry,' I said, laughing at his reaction. 'I was only going to suggest I cooked you Sunday lunch. Unless, of course, you're going to be working and won't be able to stop?'

'On a Sunday?' he tutted, feigning shock. 'Never.'

'In that case, join me upstairs for a roast chicken dinner at one. Assuming I can get the bird in the oven up there,' I added, trying to mentally size the dimensions up.

I'd ordered and frozen the bird on the assumption that I would be cooking it downstairs. I could conjure a few different dishes out of a large chicken from the butcher's in town and always made stock from the bones, which provided the perfect base for soups or a risotto. Nothing went to waste. Or at least it didn't when I had the space to use it. I should have thought about that before I got it out to defrost.

'I'll do that,' said Jude. 'Thank you. Though it might be easier for you to cook it down here if it's that big a bird, mightn't it? I caught sight of your oven in the apartment, and it is a bit of a tiddler.'

'Oh, I couldn't,' I began, thinking that really would be an imposition. 'I've already had a swim in the tub.'

'Of course you can,' Jude insisted. 'It's your house, after all, Bella. Just let yourself in in the morning and make a start. I honestly don't mind at all. In fact, if a roast lunch is on offer, I insist.'

'In that case,' I yielded, thinking of the extra worktop space and room around the table, 'all right. I will.'

By the following morning, the chicken was fully defrosted, and I'd decided to go all out and make an apple crumble to serve with custard after it – or perhaps a little later in the afternoon if we were too stuffed. I thought I'd cook the crumble ahead of starting on the roast, and consequently it was quite early when I carried everything I was going to need down the stairs and let myself into the house.

Even though the rooms weren't currently dressed exactly how I liked them, I still felt at peace the moment I crossed the threshold. The four walls contained my most treasured childhood memories, not all of them set around Christmas, and I loved that I had been able to keep so much of my grandparents' legacy in place.

I might have knocked down walls to make much of the

downstairs open plan, but the elements I loved were all still in situ. The kitchen, for example. I had painted the units soft sage green and replaced the worktops, but they were still the cupboards that Grandad had skilfully built. The Victorian fireplace, complete with patterned tiles, had been a find that Nanna had discovered at a local salvage yard, and my childhood bedroom, with a simple linen and curtain change, could easily be turned back into the room overlooking the garden that I had always loved.

Obviously certain things, such as the high-end bathroom fittings, had to be up to the standard my guests expected, but I hadn't ripped out the things that made the house my home, such as the wonderful reclaimed claw-footed bath.

'Leave him, Tink,' I whispered urgently when I stopped daydreaming and realized that she'd made a beeline for the stairs.

Given how quiet it was, and how early, it was my guess that Jude was still in bed. I dithered for a few seconds, wondering whether to come back later, then decided to just get on with it, albeit without the radio or a podcast for company.

I'd gently softened the apples on the stove with a tablespoon of sugar and was just rubbing the butter into the flour for the crumble topping when I heard the bedroom door fly open, heavy footfalls on the stairs and a rousing chorus of 'Oh, What a Beautiful Mornin'' getting closer with every step. Angus must have been having an impact on Jude, after all.

'I didn't have you down as a showtunes kind of guy,' I said, my eyes still on the bowl.

'Holy hell!' Jude shouted, and my gaze lifted to find him frozen to the spot.

His hair was completely mussed up on one side, and he was

wearing nothing but checked PJ bottoms. His feet were bare, as were his arms, which he immediately folded over his wonderfully toned chest.

'Sorry,' he said, looking embarrassed and very red in the face. 'I had no idea you were here already.'

I suddenly realized I was staring at him and tore my eyes away. I tried to laugh the moment off, but the sound came out as more of a snort and I felt my own entire face flush.

'Well, that evens us up on the mortification front,' Jude laughed, making me blush even deeper. 'Hang on.'

He raced upstairs again with Tink hot on his heels and came back down a few seconds later wearing a long-sleeved T-shirt, with his previously messy hair slightly, but nowhere near completely, flattened. His feet were still bare. They were very nice feet.

'I thought I'd surprise you with an apple crumble,' I said, by way of explaining my earlier than expected presence in the kitchen.

'And in the process provide my cardio workout for the day,' he said, reaching for the kettle. 'Well, at least I won't have to go for a run this morning.'

'I did you a favour, then, really,' I said, checking that I'd created the perfect crumble texture as I played along. 'Because it's icy out there. The near coronary I just caused you might have actually saved you a broken arm or leg.'

'If I broke my arm,' he said, looking genuinely horrified, 'I wouldn't be able to write or type.'

'Or drive,' I pretended to sob, making Tink wander over to find out if anything was really amiss. 'And I'd be stuck with you for even longer.'

'Perish the thought.' Jude pretended to shudder.

While I washed my hands, he made us both tea. I told him how I took mine, and he managed to make it exactly how I liked it. It all felt comfortably companionable, and I wondered – with a fortnight still to go, and in spite of my previous misgivings about my burgeoning workload – if we should squeeze in a brief encounter.

'That looks really great,' said Jude, with a nod to the enamel dish I was spooning the apples into, along with a bowlful of foraged blackberries. 'And it smells amazing, too.'

The dish had belonged to Nanna and was part of a set of half a dozen in all different sizes, which I used all the time. I kept them in the apartment when the house was rented out.

'My nan used to add a handful of oats to the crumble,' Jude told me. 'I think it was her way of trying to get some goodness into me. I was a picky eater when I was a kid.'

'I can do that if you like,' I said. 'I've got oats.'

'No, don't,' he said. 'I want to try yours exactly as you'd usually make it, Bella.'

'Why don't you go and have a shower?' I suggested, feeling warmer than I usually did when he said my name. 'And then we'll have breakfast before I start on the rest of the prep.'

'How very domestic,' he laughed, picking up his mug and heading for the stairs.

'Not really,' I teased. 'I just think you need to do something with your hair.'

When Jude came back down again, he prepped the veg while I got on with roasting the chicken and potatoes and making the stuffing. I also made an extra effort with the table, setting out my favourite napkins from Norwich designer Lottie Day and adding candles alongside the condiments.

'This looks wonderful,' said Jude, when it was all finally ready and served up. 'Far better than a lap tray on the sofa.'

'Nothing wrong with a lap tray if the occasion calls for it,' I said, carrying over the gravy boat. 'But Sunday dinner deserves to be celebrated, in my opinion.'

'I agree,' he said, nodding as he poured us both wine, and I gave him a look. 'All right,' he conceded, 'I agree now that you've reminded me, and my nan would be delighted about that.'

Noises of appreciation aside, we ate mostly in silence, then unanimously agreed that the crumble could come later.

'Leave all that,' Jude insisted, once I'd given Tink a little chicken and gravy in a bowl and was about to start stacking the dishes. 'I'll clear up. Everything can go in the dishwasher, can't it?'

'Everything apart from the carving knife and fork,' I told him.

I'd inherited those bone-handled beauties, and they were handwash only.

'In that case,' he said, 'you set a match to the fire, then find a film for us to watch and I'll tidy up.'

'Don't you have anything you need to be doing?' I asked.

I was surprised he wanted me to stay longer, especially given that he'd left Wynthorpe Hall because he couldn't cope with the hubbub. Though to be fair, Tink and I weren't a patch on the noisy Connelly clan.

'I'm sorry,' Jude said, looking embarrassed. 'I haven't, but you probably have, haven't you? I didn't mean to presume that you'd want to stay.'

'I've actually only got two things I need to do today,' I told him. 'The first is make a few notes about what I need to start restocking from tomorrow, and the second is that I mustn't forget to go to the pub this evening. You're very welcome to join me there, by the way, if you'd like to.'

There was a meeting of Christmas committee volunteers happening in The Mermaid, and of course, being a fully paid-up team member and festive fanatic myself, I simply had to be there. It was the first meeting of the season and long overdue in my opinion, but I supposed we'd soon be organized. We usually were.

'The first of those two things sounds rather like work to me,' Jude teased.

'Very laid-back work, though,' I said, reaching for the remote. 'The sort I can easily do while watching a film.'

'In that case,' he said, opening the dishwasher door, 'I'll let you off.'

Though we were feeling rather full from lunch, we still managed a bowl of crumble and custard apiece for an early dinner before heading off to The Mermaid. It had been a wonderful afternoon, and when we set off on foot into the clear, cold evening and Jude insisted he take Tink's lead and we linked arms, I couldn't deny that my heart skipped yet another beat.

It wasn't a sensation I usually experienced when I was heading into short-lived liaison territory, and that made me start to question what it was that I was actually feeling.

'Well, well, well,' Jeanie said, beaming, when we arrived at the pub, flushed from the chilly air and laughing about something, 'look at you two.'

I quickly took a step away from Jude. Trying to unpick my

feelings as we'd walked along had thrown up a wholly unex-pected explanation.

'Well, well, well,' I batted back, when I realized who she had been leaning across the bar to talk to, 'look at you two.'

Jude looked as confused as Tim.

'Touché,' said Jeanie, taking a step away herself. 'What can I get you both?'

'Do they always talk in riddles?' Jude asked Tim.

'Yep,' he said, 'if you and Bella have hooked up, then you'd better get used to it.'

Jeanie burst out laughing, and I went bright red.

'We haven't,' I said loudly. 'Jude's just staying at the house, Tim. Of course we haven't hooked up. We're not together, as in *together* together . . . we just . . .'

'All right,' said Jude, his hand clutched to his chest. 'I think he gets the idea, Bella. We're not together, and quite clearly the idea of that is abhorrent to you.'

'No,' I said, making even more of a mess of the situation that Jeanie had caused. 'I wouldn't mind us being together – that is, not being a proper couple, because that's not really my . . . Oh, for pity's sake,' I groaned as Jude grinned. 'I know what I meant. We're no more together than you and Jeanie are, Tim.'

'Oh, we're together again,' said Tim, giving Jeanie a look that was so smouldering it would have turned most of the women in Wynbridge weak at the knees.

Jeanie rolled her eyes.

'She just doesn't know it yet,' he added, sounding rather frustrated.

'I'll have a Coke, please,' I said to Jeanie, drawing a line under the conversation.

'Same,' said Jude. He handed me Tink's lead and pulled out his wallet. 'I'll get these.'

'No—'

'I insist,' he said, 'as a thank you for lunch and dinner.'

'Lunch *and* dinner,' Jeanie commented as she filled our glasses.

'I'll grab us a table,' I said, eager to get away before it all kicked off again.

'Don't go too far,' Jeanie called after me. 'The meeting will be starting soon.'

'What meeting's this?' Jude asked when he'd carried our drinks over.

'There's a Christmas committee volunteer meeting happening tonight,' I told him as I shrugged off my coat.

It was warm next to the fire, but that didn't stop Tink lying with her nose practically in the grate.

'Oh god,' Jude groaned, sounding appalled. 'At least I'm not going to be in town long enough to get roped into any of that.'

I looked at him sharply.

'What?' I said, and swallowed, feeling even warmer than I had before, if that was possible.

'Christmas,' he said with a shudder. 'I hate it.'

'You hate Christmas?' I squeaked.

'With a passion,' he practically sneered, sounding even more like Scrooge than Dickens had intended. 'I'd happily bypass the whole of December and skip straight to January if I could. The whole thing is a farce as far as I'm concerned. Something that once had meaning now hijacked by commercialism, and don't even get me started on—'

'Excuse me,' I cut in, leaving him mid-rant.

'What's up?' Jeanie asked when I reached her. She was talking to Tim again but broke off when she spotted me. No doubt troubled by my stricken expression.

'It's Jude,' I told her, with as much pathos as the announcement warranted. '*He hates Christmas.*'

Tim hadn't been able to grasp why that was such an issue, but Jeanie instantly did.

'Oh, Bella!' she gasped. 'Whatever would your grandad say?'

'I know!' I practically sobbed.

Grandad wasn't known for doling out advice, but there were two bits of wisdom he had always been keen to impart. The first was that you should never be friends with someone a dog took a dislike to, and the second was that you should never trust someone who didn't love Christmas. Jude was safe as far as Tink was concerned, but the Grinch thing was a blow.

Of course, there could be a million reasons why a person might not be fond of the season, but as far as Grandad – the only man I had ever completely trusted – was concerned, if Christmas was off the list, then so were they. I might not have taken his insight quite so deeply to heart had my stepdad not happened to hate the festive season.

The scar of his still-unexplained abandonment cut deep, especially as it had taken everything Mum had to put her faith in him after what had happened with my biological father.

'You wouldn't think it to look at him, would you?' Jeanie later whispered as we sat at the opposite end of the pub with everyone else on the committee and Jude stayed with Tink next to the fire.

'No,' I whispered back. 'I might have thought it was a

possibility when he first moved in and was grumpy all the time, but now I know him a bit better—'

'Are you two in agreement about that then?' Jim's stern voice suddenly boomed out.

'Yes, Jim,' I said meekly, having almost leapt off my chair.

'Yes, Uncle Jim,' Jeanie politely added.

I had no idea what we'd potentially just agreed to or signed up for, but I hoped it wasn't to be Santa's elves again, because the outfits were really itchy.

With the festive calendar confirmed and me bowing out of a couple of my usual duties at the switch-on because I was going to be selling my fairies on the Cherry Tree Café market stall, Jim drew the meeting to a close. I was still going to be busy, though, because I'd volunteered to organize and compère the pub's Christmas quiz night. I knew I had truly slayed the public spotlight demons if I was willing to do that. That said, it had already been agreed before I volunteered that, being such a fan of the season, I shouldn't be allowed to take part because I'd doubtless get all the answers right.

'You love Christmas,' Jude numbly stated when I returned to our table.

'Sorry?'

'You love Christmas,' he said again. 'I heard the furore over there when the quiz night came up, and you'd hardly be at the committee meeting and looking happy about helping out if you were a Grinch like me, would you?'

The words spilled out of him in a rush.

'I suppose not,' I said with a tight smile. 'It's true. I *do* love Christmas. As far as I'm concerned, it really is the most wonderful time of the year.'

'And Wynbridge is all set to turn into Christmas Town soon, isn't it?' he said, almost savagely. 'Worthy of a setting in a made-for-TV Christmas movie?'

'Yep,' I said, dropping my hands in my lap. 'You've got it in one.'

'Thank god, I'll be gone by December,' he muttered, and I tried to pretend I hadn't heard him.

'Another drink?' I suggested brightly, as my feelings for him slid back to close to where they had been before his passionate apology and dog-sitting duties.

'Yes, please,' he said, pushing his glass across the table. 'Rum and Coke this time, if that's okay.'

'I'll join you,' I said, because I felt like I needed it as much as he did.

I'd been at the bar no time at all before Holly arrived. She looked rather tired, but happily so, and then I remembered that Bear was finally back.

'Where is he, then?' I asked her. 'Where's that giant of a man who's responsible for your eye bags?'

'Hey!' she tutted, her hands flying to her face.

'Over there,' Jeanie pointed. 'Talking to the man who's broken your heart.'

'What?' gasped Holly, my teasing comment forgotten. 'Jude's done what?'

'Oh, ignore her,' I said, looking crossly at Jeanie and then back at the two men again and narrowing my eyes. 'He's done no such thing. You should know me well enough to know that I don't combine men and my heart.'

I'd told Holly, not all that long after we'd met, about how Mum had been left heartbroken twice when I was a child and how, when I'd grown up, I'd decided to keep all relationships with the opposite sex on the right side of casual as a result.

'Bella!' called Jude, beckoning me over and sounding happier than he had when I'd left him. 'Come and meet Bear. He's the fella I was telling you about who had the right idea about pared-back living.'

That had to be the coincidence of the century – their paths crossing again in Wynbridge. It was almost as unbelievable as me having started to develop a deeper than usual fondness for someone who then declared they hated Christmas. If I found out next that Jude didn't believe in fairies, then I was sending him straight back to the Connellys.

'You seemed to be enjoying my maximalist aesthetic earlier,' I said to him tetchily. 'Hey, Bear,' I added, giving him a smile. 'How's life on the road been treating you?'

'You already know each other?' Jude laughed. 'What are the odds?'

More like, what were the odds of *him* knowing Bear than the other way around. I should have made the connection when Jude previously mentioned someone living in a horsebox. There couldn't be that many people around who did that.

'He's my friend Holly's partner,' I explained.

'It's been treating me really well, but now I'm ready to hibernate with Holly for the winter,' Bear said, answering my question as his voice filled the pub. 'I'm looking forward to moving into the railway carriages—'

'The very packed and colourful carriages,' I couldn't resist adding.

'Until early spring at least,' he finished up.

'Bear!' Holly called him from the bar.

'I'd better get my order in,' he said, patting Jude on the shoulder and knocking a couple of inches off him. 'Let's catch up in the week, yeah? I'd love to know how that project you were working on when we met panned out.'

'Yes,' said Jude, looking a little crestfallen to have discovered that the man he'd thought lived the entire year on the road with minimal possessions was looking forward to staying put and being surrounded by all manner of ephemera for a few months. 'That'd be great.'

'Bella can give you directions,' Bear said, moving off.

Given what Jude had earlier said about Christmas, I was tempted to set his satnav to take him straight to the North Pole.

Chapter 10

'I don't suppose I'll see all that much of you this week, will I?' said Jude on the walk back to the house from the pub.

I had paired him up with Bear again as soon as I had been able in The Mermaid, and as the temperature had risen a little during the evening and the paths weren't anywhere near as slippery as earlier, we hadn't linked arms on the way back home. I had charge of Tink's lead, too, and used her as a buffer to ensure that there were more than a few inches of distance between us as we walked.

'No,' I said, feeling grateful that I had a packed schedule to contend with. 'I'll be keeping my head down and getting on with my work, as well as also planning the quiz now.'

Was it my imagination or did Jude's shoulders tense up a little at the mention of that festive event?

'And I'm going to be working hard, too,' he said, sounding equally keen to tell me about his own unavailability. 'I'll be splitting my time now, writing at the house some days as well as travelling to Wynthorpe to talk to the family about anything further they can tell me about the history of the hall. I really want to get my head down and be properly bedded into writing the book before I leave on the first of December.'

It was still stirring to hear him talk of his commitment to recording the Connellys' knowledge of their home as well as chronicling the building's development and the subsequent use of the hall, but it was nowhere near rousing enough to make me forget what he'd said earlier about loathing Christmas. I could easily imagine the disapproving look and headshake that Grandad would have inflicted on him had he been around to hear Jude's opinion. Goodness knows what he would have made of having the man living in his beloved home.

'As we're both going to be so busy, it's a good thing we made the most of today and took the opportunity to relax,' I said as casually as possible, even though I could already feel the wall between us rebuilding itself.

Clearly, Jude didn't want to become further acquainted with someone who threw themselves into the festive season with as much enthusiasm as Santa himself, and I didn't want to spend my time with someone who went around with 'bah humbug' on their lips. No matter how luscious those lips were or how often their owner had managed to make my heart unexpectedly flutter.

'Here we are, then,' I said as we turned off the pavement and walked up the drive to the house.

'Yes,' said Jude, rocking back on his heels with his hands thrust deep into his coat pockets. 'Here we are.'

With nothing more to say, I fumbled in my bag for the key to unlock the apartment door at the side of the house, while he ducked under the pretty brick-built porch.

'Night, then,' I muttered.

I had to give Tink's lead a bit of a tug, because she looked as though she was expecting to go into the house with Jude.

'Night, Bella,' said Jude. 'Night, Tink. Thank you for today.'

'No problem,' I said. 'Thank you, too. And for helping out yesterday.'

'Any time,' he said, nodding, but I think we both knew that there'd be no helping each other out from then on.

With so much to get on with, there wasn't much opportunity for me to ponder the strange workings of my heart or wonder if Jude was working downstairs or at the hall. However, when I went out to my car on Wednesday afternoon and noticed that his wasn't there, I did consider putting my imminent trip to the hall off on the off-chance that we might run into each other.

Unfortunately, however, when I looked at the diary on my phone, I knew it would be a while before I had an opportunity to see Molly again and decided I just needed to bite the bullet and get on with it.

'Oh, Bella!' Molly gasped gratifyingly as she lifted the lid first on Demelza's fairy and then Anna's. 'These are even more beautiful than I hoped they would be.'

As always when presenting a commission to a client who loved it, I felt a mix of both pride and relief. These feelings were increased tenfold with Molly, because she was such a dear friend rather than someone I'd never met and whom I was Zooming to witness their fairy's unboxing.

'I'm so pleased you like them,' I sighed happily.

'*Love* them,' she corrected as she stroked the skirt of Demelza's fairy. 'And the name "Hope" for Anna's is inspired.'

'Given what she's been going through and how far she's already come, it did feel fitting,' I agreed. 'And I've attached thread to the wings on both of them as you requested, so they're easy to hang,' I pointed out. 'They're both quite heavy, but the thread will easily bear their weight.'

'Perfect,' Molly said, smiling. 'I can't wait to show Catherine. I'm going to give her a sneak preview.'

'I hope she'll love them as much as you do.'

'I'm sure she will,' Molly said, carefully putting the lids back on the boxes and laying her hands lightly on them.

I'd decorated the boxes to match the colours each fairy and their outfits favoured, so they were very pretty, too.

'I told Catherine you'd pop into the hall after you'd seen me,' Molly said, looking at me enquiringly. Given that I'd spotted Jude's car on the drive, that was the last thing I wanted to do, and the expression on Molly's face suggested she knew it.

'Oh dear,' I said, making a great show of checking the time and doing my best to sound disappointed, 'I don't think I can. I've still got so much to do. I'm supposed to be working on the list of questions for the festive pub quiz on Friday night and I've barely started it.'

Unfortunately, Molly was thrilled to hear my excuse.

'In that case, you definitely need to talk to Angus,' she said cleverly. 'He's always in charge of the family quiz night and knows some great websites you can use in the hunt for more challenging questions than you might be able to come up with yourself. He's in the hall.'

Given that I was the fount of all knowledge where Christmas was concerned, I'd already come up with some crackers, but I supposed having a few more to draw on wouldn't hurt.

Therefore I dutifully (although still rather reluctantly) followed Molly back through the woods and into the hall.

'I suppose you could smell these scones warming in the Aga,' Dorothy chuckled, and I realized we'd arrived exactly at tea time.

How anyone managed to eat afternoon tea at the hall on a daily basis and then enjoy Dorothy's delicious dinners a few hours later without piling on the pounds was beyond me. Tink made a beeline for the canine Connelly pack, and I knew then that we were going to be visiting for the duration.

'Cheese, fruit or both?' Dorothy asked, offering me a plate.

'Cheese, please,' I said, taking a seat as everyone else piled in, including Jude.

Anna was carrying Alby, and Jamie had Demelza. The little girl stretched out of her uncle's arms towards her mother, and Molly settled her on her hip and then moved to sit next to Anna.

'So, how are you two getting on?' Catherine asked, looking between me and Jude after she'd said hello.

We both began to answer at the same time and everyone's gaze tracked from one of us to the other. Jamie gave me a wink along with a loaded look which, under the circumstances, I didn't appreciate at all.

'You go,' said Jude, his cheeks burning every bit as brightly as the colour of Dorothy's strawberry jam.

'I was just going to say that we've hardly seen each other.' Given Jamie's wink and knowing look, I wasn't going to share that we'd spent much of the previous weekend together. 'Because we're both so busy.'

'That's true,' Jude agreed. 'That's what I was going to say, too.'

'Well,' said Catherine, 'I'm pleased that you still living in the apartment isn't an issue, Bella.' I hadn't quite put it like that. 'Or interfering with your work. But as you're both living under the same roof, I do hope you'll have time to get to know each other a bit before you head off, Jude.'

'Plenty of time for that yet,' he responded, stirring his tea and keeping his head down.

'Maybe you could go to the pub quiz together,' suggested Jamie, playing devil's advocate whether he knew it or not. 'It's festive-themed on Friday, isn't it?'

'Oh yes,' said Molly. 'Bella wanted to talk to you about that, Angus. She's been put in charge of coming up with the questions.'

He was messily wiping up a blob of jam that had dropped off his scone and slid down the front of his shirt on its short journey from his plate to his mouth.

'What's the theme?' he asked, in spite of the fact that Jamie had just said what the theme was, as he gave up on the shirt and roughly wiped his mouth.

'Christmas,' Jude and I said together but in rather different tones.

'Oh, that will be a fun night,' Angus said, beaming at me. 'Have you picked out your Christmas jumper already?'

'Not yet,' I told him. 'I'm still trying to get the questions together. In fact,' I said, looking pointedly at the clock on the wall, 'that's what I'm supposed to be doing now. I did tell Molly that—'

Angus didn't seem to hear me.

'What about you, Jude?' he asked, talking over me. 'Did you pack a Christmas jumper ahead of your trip here?'

'No,' Jude said rather rudely.

'Well, never mind,' Angus bowled on. 'I don't suppose you thought you were going to need one, did you? You can borrow one of mine.'

'Yes, Angus has at least two dozen now,' said Dorothy, shaking her head.

'Thank you for the offer,' Jude said to Angus, 'but I'll pass.'

'You sure?'

'Yes,' he said, clearing his throat. 'I'm not keen, you see.'

'On Christmas jumpers?' gasped Angus, sounding astonished.

'On Christmas,' Jude and I both said together again.

This admission was met with a stunned silence. Aside from myself, I didn't think there was anyone in Wynbridge who was as festively obsessed as the Connelly clan. The seconds stretched on, and no one said a word. The only sound was the ticking of the clock and light snores from the dog basket.

'I'd better get on,' said Jude, scraping his chair in his haste to stand up and making us all jump. 'Thank you for the tea, Dorothy.'

He took his cup and saucer with him, the cup rattling in his rush to leave.

'Well, I never,' said Angus once Jude had gone. 'I had no idea.'

'About what?' Anna asked.

'His feelings about Christmas, of course.'

'But why should you?' Dorothy shrugged. 'I can't imagine you made it a stipulation that whoever was appointed to write your book about the hall would have to love Christmas? It's hardly relevant to Jude being able to do his job, is it?'

'Well, no . . .' Angus began hesitantly, his words trailing off.

'Poor Bella, though,' said Catherine. 'I never would have

asked you to put him up if I'd known you had such different beliefs.'

Given how she put it, I thought she was joking, but her expression was serious.

'It's fine,' I said, waving her words away. 'It's not as if we're going to go to war over it. As I said earlier, we've hardly seen one another. And besides, he'll be gone soon, won't he?'

'Maybe you could convert him before he leaves?' Jamie grinned.

'I wasn't a fan of Christmas myself when I first arrived here,' Anna said soberly.

'And with good reason,' said Jamie, leaning over and kissing her cheek. 'But I still managed to bring you around.'

'My point is,' Anna tutted, because her best beloved had missed the point, 'that Jude might have a very good reason himself for not liking Christmas, so don't go judging him.'

I had briefly considered that, but it hadn't made me feel any better about his dislike of the season or his venomous and vehement comments about it.

'So,' interjected Molly, the self-appointed keeper of the peace, 'where do you suggest Bella should look for some really challenging questions for the quiz, Angus?'

'Number eight,' I said, the words magnificently amplified by the microphone Jim had handed me when it was obvious my voice wouldn't carry as far as the crowd in The Mermaid stretched that Friday night. 'How many weeks was "I Wish It Could Be Christmas Every Day" by Wizzard number one in the UK charts?'

There was a low hum of chatter as the teams conferred, and I took another sip of mulled wine to clear my throat.

'Don't finish all that,' Jeanie laughed, 'otherwise you'll be slurring the questions.'

She had a point; it was heady stuff. The alcohol definitely hadn't evaporated in the warming process, and this was my third top-up.

'Number nine,' I started, and the familiar requests to have a bit longer came pouring in. 'Number nine,' I said again, determined to stick to the schedule, 'what year was *A Christmas Carol* published? And a bonus point if you can tell me what colour the scarf is that Beaker gifts Mr Scrooge in the Muppets film version of the book?'

After the next question, it was time for a break and the answer sheets were collected in and marked so there could be no sneaky phone-checking. I was having the best time and hadn't felt nervous at all about putting myself in front of the large crowd that had turned out to take part. This lion had definitely found her courage and turned a corner.

'Here,' said Holly as I began quickly setting the sheets out to mark them all at once. 'I'll help.'

Given her request for me to create a fairy for her to incorporate into her next books, Holly was giving the Scarecrow's brain a workout. Adding to her cast of characters was bound to be good for her sales. Assuming I hit the spot with the fairy creation, of course.

'Thank you,' I said, having glanced at Jeanie and wondered if she had yet oiled the cogs in the Tin Man's heart, 'but it'll probably be quicker if I do it myself.'

'I bet you've got the answers memorized, haven't you?' Holly laughed.

'Of course I have,' I said, smiling in response.

It turned out that a couple of the teams were neck and neck, but a few were way behind. I was delighted that the questions were making everyone think.

'Have you thought anymore about our possible collaboration?' I asked Holly once I'd handed the sheets back to Jeanie and had made sure that no one could overhear us.

'Not yet,' she said, grimacing. 'With Bear just back, I've been a bit . . . preoccupied.'

'Of course,' I laughed, clinking my glass against hers. 'You're in the honeymoon phase again, aren't you? I daresay it's the same every time he comes back after a stint away.'

'Something like that,' she laughed along with me, 'but I'll definitely be back to work next week. I was rather hoping you might be enjoying some romance yourself once I'd clocked your lodger, but Jude and you are completely incompatible, aren't you? The difference in Christmas thing is too wide a gap to bridge, even for the briefest winter fling.'

I looked down at the lights flashing on my Christmas jumper and the sleigh bell–embellished boots I'd teamed with my jeans.

'Yep.' I nodded, making the bells adorning my deely bopper headband chime. 'It certainly is an insurmountable gap. I'm just grateful I found out he's a mean old Scrooge McFuck . . . I mean McDuck . . . in time.'

'Who wants another mulled wine?' Jeanie asked.

'Me, please,' I said, pushing my glass across the bar.

'No,' Holly laughed, pushing it back again. 'You've had enough. Let's get a bit of fresh air, and then you can feed her some carbs before it's time for the second half of the quiz, Jeanie, otherwise things could go downhill fast.'

I felt fine after some bracing Wynbridge air and a cranberry and sausage-filled roll, and the quiz continued and the winners were announced without incident or further mispronunciation. So many people told me what a brilliant time they'd had that I was feeling tipsy again by the time they started to clear out, only this time on dopamine rather than wine. At least, I thought it was happy chemicals rather than alcohol units . . .

'That was fantastic,' said Evelyn. She wasn't a woman who was free with her praise, so I appreciated her words all the more. 'Well done, Bella, and thank you. I've just been talking to Jim, and we were wondering if you'd be up for doing another quiz nearer to Christmas.'

'Absolutely!' I said, without even stopping to think about it. 'I would love to.'

'That's settled, then,' Evelyn said happily. 'I'll get Jeanie to run some dates by you next week.'

'Brilliant,' I said, giving her a thumbs-up.

'Are you sure you can fit it in with everything else you've got going on?' Jeanie asked with concern once her aunt had gone.

'Absolutely,' I told her. 'It didn't take me all that long to organize this one, thanks to some direction from Angus, and I've got a back-up sheet with loads of other questions on that I didn't use, so I'll be able to include some of those.'

'Well, that's all right, then,' Jeanie said, nodding. 'How about a weak one for the road and then I'll ask someone to drive you back home.'

'I can walk,' I insisted. 'I'm fine to walk.'

'I don't think so,' Jeanie laughed. 'You'll fall in a bush on the way, and we'll never find you again.'

'I'm merry,' I said soberly, 'not legless.'

'You're still getting a ride home,' she shot back seriously. 'In fact,' she added, her eyes widening as she looked over my shoulder, 'here's the ideal chauffeur for you, if not perfect partner material. I know for a fact that he'll be heading your way.'

'Jude!' I said, sliding off my stool. The wobble in my legs suggested that I wasn't quite as sober as I'd thought. 'Have you been here all evening?'

'Hardly,' he said disparagingly, catching me by the elbow. 'I was just driving through town on my way back from a late night working at the hall and thought I'd see if you were still here and needed a lift home. It's almost closing time, isn't it?'

'It is,' Jeanie confirmed. 'And she would.'

'I can tell him,' I tutted.

'Go on, then.' She nodded.

'Thank you, Jude,' I said graciously. 'You're a true gent, and I would very much appreciate a ride home, even if I can't get to know you better . . . if you know what I mean . . . because you hate Christmas.'

Jeanie shook her head, and Jude looked taken aback.

'What?' I shrugged. 'It's true!'

'Definitely time to go home, Bella,' Jeanie said, still shaking her head. 'Ignore her, Jude. She doesn't usually drink as much as she's had tonight.'

'I *can* hear you,' I tutted, feeling affronted but then immediately forgetting why.

'Right,' said Jude, sounding unamused. 'Let's find your coat, then, Bella.'

'I'll come with you on one condition,' I said as Jeanie passed my coat over the bar and I struggled to put my arms in the right sleeves. Jude took it from me, shook it out and then helped me properly into it. 'I'll only come with you now if you agree to come to the town switch-on tomorrow. That way, I'll be able to work out if you really are a lost cause; we still have a week left, you know.'

Jeanie shook her head again and squeezed her eyes shut.

'What?' I demanded. 'That's a reasonable request, isn't it?'

At that moment, someone cranked the music up and Mariah Carey's impossibly high note painfully filled the bar and our ears.

'Thank goodness Tink isn't here,' I said, looking around. 'Where *is* she?' I panicked, then remembered I'd left her in the apartment. 'I need to get home,' I said, grabbing Jude's arm. 'Come on, we can't hang around in here all night chatting.'

Jeanie began to laugh. And with that, I marched out of the pub, and by the time I was cocooned in Jude's warm car, I had forgotten everything I'd just blurted out, along with the request I'd made. Time would tell whether that was a good thing or not.

Chapter 11

I woke early the next morning. My memories of the night before were muddled, and my head was pounding, which I didn't think was particularly fair, given that I'd gone to so much trouble to make sure everyone enjoyed the quiz.

I seemed to remember that Jude had turned up at the pub at some point, but given that he wasn't a fan of the festive season, I couldn't for the life of me imagine why he'd want to attend a Christmas-themed quiz night . . . Perhaps I'd imagined his presence or dreamt it. Everything to do with and about the entire evening felt a bit . . . hazy now.

My phone buzzed on the bedside table, and I clumsily reached for it. It was a message from Jeanie asking how hungover I was feeling. I replied that I wasn't feeling the worse for wear at all, then grimaced as I groped my way to the bathroom for water and painkillers. I didn't have time to succumb to feeling rough because it was the day the Wynbridge Christmas Market was due to launch and the town switch-on was happening later, too, and nothing was going to ruin either of those annual highlights.

Ordinarily, I would have spent the day swanning about the town and soaking up the atmosphere. Unless it was a year where I'd been roped into wearing an itchy elf outfit, of course. Thankfully, neither Jeanie nor I had unwittingly elected ourselves for that particular role, but my time was still going to be mostly occupied this year.

'Oh, Bella!' Lizzie beamed when I arrived at the gallery to drop off my selection of fairies and show her how I'd wrapped and presented them ahead of setting up the stall. 'What a clever idea.'

'Given that the Wynbridge weather can be a little on the unpredictable side at this time of year,' I said, smiling at her, 'this seemed like the most sensible way to go.'

Each fairy had its own clear bag, tied up with ribbon or string (depending on the fairy's aesthetic), and a handwritten wish. My main aim for packaging them like that was to protect them from any adverse weather, but I'd also realized how wonderfully they would be showcased if pegged to Lizzie's trademark Cherry Tree bunting.

'They're the loveliest addition,' said Lizzie, adding a few to the table she'd already piled with her own stock to work out how it would all look. 'Jemma's biscuits are similarly wrapped, so we'll be able to alternate those and the fairies when we set them out and hang them up.'

'That will be perfect,' I agreed, nodding happily as I looked through her collection of hot-water-bottle covers, snow-scene jars, quilted bags and fabric Christmas decorations.

'Are you going to sell all your stock wrapped like this over Christmas?' she asked.

'No,' I explained. 'Just the fairies for the stall. I don't want to get in the habit of using packaging if I don't need to. Even if they do look lovely.'

They were slightly more expensive bagged, as I'd had to offset the cost, and that was why I'd included handwritten wishes with each one. There wasn't much of a profit to be had, but I knew how much buyers appreciated anything that added value, especially if it was exclusive.

'Which they certainly do,' said Lizzie. 'Can you come back later this afternoon and help me set everything up?'

The main market was already open as usual, but the festive stalls would be launching later in the day.

'Absolutely,' I said, clapping my hands together. 'In fact, I'm raring to go now.'

Lizzie laughed at that.

'After last night,' she chuckled, 'I wondered if you were going to be good for anything today, and I certainly wasn't expecting to see you so early.'

'The quiz turned out to be good fun rather than hard work,' I told her, but I wasn't entirely sure that that was what she was getting at.

'So I heard,' she said, grinning. 'So I heard.'

As I was going to be out for so long later, I decided to have lunch at home and then take Tink for a long walk. Holly had already said she'd drop in to feed her and then bring her into town. She was leaving Jasper at home because he had a tendency to get over-excited when among a lot of people, but Tink took crowds in her stride and enjoyed getting out and seeing everyone. She was an exceptionally sociable little spaniel, and I loved her dearly.

The time flew by, and before I knew it I was dressing in my warmest layers, applying lipstick as bright as my red coat and heading back out the door. There were no lights on in the house, and I wondered if Jude had purposefully headed away from town to avoid the festive fun. Not that I was bothered, but Anna's words about him perhaps having a specific reason for being such a Grinch had popped into my head that day on more than one occasion.

They were soon forgotten, though, as I helped Lizzie set up the Cherry Tree Café stall and tried not to get distracted by everything else going on around me. The stage for the switch-on had now been erected next to what I thought was the biggest tree the town had ever seen, and I knew that tucked away down a side street somewhere would be the horse-drawn sleigh from Wynthorpe Hall and Angus would be donning his Santa suit in anticipation of his annual lap around the Market Square and subsequent gift-giving and time with the children. Knowing him, I wouldn't have been at all surprised if he'd slept in the suit the night before to make sure he was running on time, and I couldn't wait to see him.

'Bella?' said Lizzie, her tone suggesting that it wasn't the first time she'd said my name.

'Sorry,' I gasped, 'I was miles away.'

I took the box of bagged biscuits she was holding out and began pegging them and my fairies on the bunting we had securely draped around the stall and across the front.

'You're as invested in Christmas as Angus Connelly, aren't you?' she said in a teasing but not unkind tone.

'Absolutely,' I was happy to confirm. 'I'm already looking forward to decorating the house. Thankfully Jude will be leaving the day I always set aside for doing that.'

'Which is?'

'The first of December,' I said, rubbing my hands together

in excited anticipation. 'I always make a start at the beginning of the month.'

'That's keen.' Lizzie smiled. 'Obviously, we decorate the café early.' It was looking beautiful already. 'But it's a different story at home.'

'Well, that's me,' I laughed. 'Thanks to the love for the season I inherited from my nanna and grandad, I'm never happier than when I'm decking the halls!'

'And talking of decking the halls,' said Lizzie as she took a step back to admire how the stall was looking, 'I think we're almost done here. We don't want to overcrowd it.'

Knowing how well my slightly pared-back display at The Laurels' Christmas fair had been received, I had to agree with that.

'There's plenty of space for the boxes of stock to be tucked away underneath the stall, so we can put more of everything out as we sell it,' I said, nodding.

'*Hopefully* sell it,' Lizzie amended.

'Oh, we will,' I said confidently, feeling that our mindsets had been momentarily switched. 'I know we will.'

Given the popularity of the evening switch-on and the fabulous stock we'd got, there was no doubt in my mind about that. The café stall was always a hit, and I had every confidence that this year would be no different.

'You're right.' Lizzie smiled. 'We'll be sold out in no time.'

The square began to fill up with local families and visitors from further afield long before the lights were due to be turned on, and by the time the town mayor's voice was booming around the buildings, Lizzie and I had already replenished lots of the stock and she was looking as happy about my prediction being right as I felt.

One of the people who had come along to the café work-shops dropped by to ask if I'd considered selling some of the fairies in kit form, complete with a list of instructions explaining how to put them together. This wasn't something I had consid-ered before, but I thought I might give it a try ahead of the next round of fairs. I could put together a small batch as a sort of trial run, and there'd be nothing lost if they didn't sell because I could always make them up myself.

'Ten, nine, eight . . .'

'Come on!' said Jeanie as she suddenly appeared, grabbed my arm and pulled me further towards the front of the crowd.

'Where's Holly?' I shouted over the countdown.

'Haven't seen her!' Jeanie shrugged. 'Three! Two! One!'

It was a musician who had recently moved to the area who had been roped in to do the honours, and they pressed the big red button with aplomb. The tree suddenly shone as brightly as the rest of the lights which burst into life around the square and beyond, and the speakers loudly pumped out The Jackson Five singing 'Santa Claus is Coming to Town'.

We all cheered, clapped, whooped and sang along, and I thought my heart was in danger of bursting out of my chest. Nanna and Grandad had always brought me to the switch-on, and I felt a sudden hankering to give them both a hug.

'You're not crying, are you?' Jeanie said as she gave me a nudge and pulled me in for a timely hug of her own.

'No,' I said, and swallowed, squeezing her back and knowing that if I explained, then I would be. 'You're crying. I'm just really, really happy.'

And I was even happier a few seconds later as I dried my eyes while Santa and his sleigh arrived in the square, and the children (and admittedly a few of the adults) cheered even more loudly.

'Do you want to go and say hello?' Jeanie asked.

I did, really, but I didn't think it would be fair to take up a little one's place in the queue, and I also needed to get back to the stall. I'd all but abandoned Lizzie.

'No,' I said, rolling my eyes as if it was the last thing I wanted to do. 'I'd better get back. Lizzie will be swamped.'

Jeanie gave me another hug and kissed my cheek.

'You're such a big kid,' she laughed. 'I love you for that. If anyone in this town could convince Jude that Christmas was something to be celebrated, it would be you.'

'Well,' I said, wishing she hadn't mentioned his aversion to the season at such a special moment, 'I don't know about that, but I do know that folk are now pouring into The Mermaid, so you'd better get back to work, too.'

'Oh crikey!' she said and headed off. 'I'll see you later,' she called as she went.

'And if you happen to see Holly,' I shouted after her, 'send her in my direction, would you?'

Jeanie waved and was gone, and I rushed back to help Lizzie, who was – as I had both predicted and hoped – swamped with customers, but happily so.

'All of Jemma's biscuits have gone,' she told me breathlessly.

'Even the bag you'd hidden for me in one of the boxes?'

'Damn,' she said, 'I'd forgotten about those. I could have got double the price, given the demand.'

'Don't you dare!' I told her. 'I've been looking forward to that iced and spiced combo all evening.'

Once the manic post-switch-on rush was over and people

began to drift away – families to their homes and lots of other folk to the pub – I began to feel mindful of the time and even more worried about where Holly had got to.

'Everything okay?' Lizzie asked as she blew on her gloved hands, and I pulled out my phone to see if Holly had sent me a message.

She hadn't. Either that or I hadn't been standing in one of the square's signal hotspots long enough for her message to land.

'I hope so,' I said, biting my lip as I put my phone away again. 'Holly was supposed to be coming along with Tink, but I haven't seen either of them.'

'Well,' said Lizzie, looking over my shoulder, 'I don't know where Holly is, but I can see Tink.'

I spun around so fast that I almost landed back where I'd started.

'Jude?' I frowned, as he walked towards me with Tink on her lead and wearing a different Christmas coat to the one I'd put out for her in the apartment for Holly to find. 'What are you doing here? Is everything okay? Where's Holly?'

He waited while I quickly fussed an ecstatic Tink before answering.

'Bear stopped by the house to walk Tink into town himself, but when he told me why Holly hadn't come, I said I'd bring Tink in so he could get back to her.'

'I see,' I said, but I didn't because I needed more information.

'And given that last night you said you'd only let me drive you home if I came to the switch-on tonight so you could work out if I really was a lost cause,' Jude continued devastatingly, 'I thought it would be wrong of me not to honour my promise.'

Just for a second, the world slipped off its axis.

'I said that?' I swallowed, feeling myself go hot as the brain fog began to clear.

I didn't add that he could have got away with not turning up, as I hadn't remembered what I'd requested.

'Pretty much,' said Jude, scratching his head. 'Or something very much like it. And I'm sorry to disappoint you,' he added, looking around, 'but this isn't my scene at all.'

I was exceedingly grateful that he had assumed that I wanted to work out if he was a lost cause as far as Christmas was concerned, as opposed to deciding if he was someone I wanted to (as Tim had previously put it) hook up with, because in a sudden moment of blinding realization, I remembered exactly what I'd said in the pub and had no doubt that that was what I had meant.

Given what Anna had said about Jude potentially having a personal reason for not liking Christmas, I felt rather bad that I had thrust the switch-on on him and that he had felt obliged to endure it. That said, it was good to know that he was a man of his word.

'Well,' I said, attempting to refocus, 'I appreciate you coming along. What's going on with Holly and Bear?'

Jude looked even more serious than he had before.

'Sadly, there's been a canine emergency,' he told me. 'Bear had dropped Holly and Jasper off at the vets before he came to yours. Apparently, Jasper has eaten something he shouldn't and is about to either undergo surgery or have his system flushed.'

'Oh no,' I said, feeling upset for them all. 'That's awful.'

'Bear looked awful, too,' Jude said sympathetically. 'That's why I offered to bring Tink into town with me.'

'That was very kind of you,' I said, feeling slightly better knowing that his trip to town had been as much about giving Tink a walk as honouring the promise I had forced out of him. 'Thank you.'

'It was no big deal,' he said, giving Tink's head a rub, but given how much he must have hated the evening's entertainment, I knew it must have been, really. 'Here's your spare key, by the way,' he added, pulling it out of his pocket and handing it over.

It was the one I'd given to Holly to use in emergencies or if for any reason she needed to let herself into the apartment when I wasn't there. Such as tonight.

'I hope Jasper's okay.' I swallowed, taking the key as my phone suddenly pinged.

The dog was always getting into scrapes, but I knew Holly loved him just as much as I loved Tink, in spite of his rascally ways. Perhaps a whole winter living under the influence of Bear's bull terrier, Queenie, might calm Jasper down a bit. Queenie was calm, placid and super chilled for a canine who had had a less than lovely start in life.

'It's a message from Holly,' I said, quickly unlocking my phone. 'Two messages, actually.'

That was the thing about Wynbridge: you never quite knew where to stand to get a reliable signal, and it varied depending on which network you were on, what day of the week it was and whether you were standing on one leg. Okay, so that was a bit dramatic, but sometimes it felt like that. To prove the point, Holly's separately sent messages had now ended up arriving at the same time. I read through what she had typed twice to make sure I'd properly got the gist, and then let out a long, relieved breath.

'Jasper's going to be fine,' I told Jude. 'Will, that's the vet, has given him something to make him sick, as he'd only just eaten whatever it was he shouldn't have, and that seems to have cleared it all out of his system. Did Bear say what it was that Jasper had snaffled?'

'No,' said Jude, shaking his head and looking rather green at the thought of Jasper's system being cleared out by making him throw up. 'That never came up. No pun intended.'

I felt a little bilious myself then, and he gave me a wry smile.

'What's going on?' Lizzie asked. 'Is everything okay?'

I quickly explained what had happened while Jude walked Tink around the square and I helped Lizzie start to pack the stall up.

'That was quick,' I said when Jude arrived back. He'd only been gone a few minutes. 'What did you make of the tree?'

'Very nice,' he said, giving it a cursory glance.

I wasn't sure if that was a heartfelt sentiment or not.

'Is there any reason why Tink isn't wearing the coat I set out for her?' I asked, as Lizzie's partner Ben arrived to help carry the few bits of stock we hadn't sold over to the café for safekeeping.

'Well,' said Jude, looking down at Tink, 'we did try that one on, didn't we, love?' She wagged her tail, and I felt taken aback by the ease with which he had called her 'love'. 'But she preferred this one. Is that okay?' he asked me, his brows knitting together in a frown. 'Or does she usually wear certain Christmas coats on certain days?'

'There's no set order,' I said, shrugging, then added, because I was feeling suspicious, 'Is that the truth? Did she really prefer this one?'

'Of course not!' Jude laughed, and I knew I shouldn't have taken him seriously. 'It was the one I preferred, because it was the thickest and it's freezing out here tonight. I had no idea how long we'd be, so I thought I should wrap her up as best as I could.'

'Well,' I said, thinking it was kind of him to consider that, even if he had tricked me into briefly believing that he'd had a whimsical moment, 'I'm sure she appreciates it. And so do I. I'm nearly done here, so I'll take her off your hands in a bit. Unless you want to head back with her now.'

'You can both go, if you like,' said Lizzie, having heard what I had just said to Jude. 'We're practically done here now. It's been a very good night.'

'We've sold loads, haven't we?'

'We have,' she agreed. 'I'll let you know how much sometime tomorrow, if that's all right?'

'Of course,' I said. 'No rush. Are you sure you don't want me to hang on?'

'No,' she said. 'You get off. As Jude said, it is freezing.'

I wouldn't have minded popping my head into the pub, but I didn't for two reasons. Firstly, because Jude had automatically turned in the opposite direction to it when we left the stall, and secondly, remembering now what I'd said at the quiz made me vulnerable to teasing from anyone else who had heard me spouting off.

'Oh damn,' I said, when we were too far from the square to want to walk back again. 'I forgot my biscuits.'

'What biscuits?' Jude asked.

'Jemma makes the most amazing iced and spiced biscuits for Christmas,' I told him. 'We sold out tonight, but I'd kept a bag back and hidden them under the stall.'

'Stallholders' perks,' Jude laughed.

'Exactly,' I said. 'Or it would have been if I'd remembered them.'

'You'll have to get them next week.'

'They'll be long gone by then,' I sighed wistfully. 'I daresay Ben is munching on them right now.'

'Too good to resist, eh?'

'They really are,' I said seriously. 'Did you manage to actually see the switch-on or any of what happened after it?'

'Sadly not,' he said, not sounding sad at all. 'I was late arriving because I was talking to Bear and getting Tink dressed.'

I was tempted to ask him if he'd have come into town at all had it not been for offering to pass on Bear's message. I supposed Jude could have texted me that and not honoured the bargain I'd made with him, but that hadn't been the option he'd taken, had it? I decided not to risk offending him by asking. I realized then that he still had Tink's lead in his hand and that she had rapidly grown on my sometimes grumpy, sometimes Grinchy, but always gorgeous temporary lodger.

And he'd grown on me, too. Had it not been for the Christmas situation, I might have already built on the wonderful time we'd spent together the previous weekend and started something up with him.

I gave him a sidelong look, and my heart again lurched in response. It then became painfully obvious that my feelings for him were still firmly planted in 'deeper than dalliance' territory, so it was actually probably for the best that I hadn't rocked the boat.

He then spoke up, with uncanny timing. 'I know we're poles apart when it comes to celebrating Christmas, but I don't eschew the food and drink the season brings with it, and I happened to pick this up on my whistle-stop tour around the stalls earlier.'

He pulled a small, wax-sealed bottle out of his pocket.

'Christmas pudding gin from the Brambles distillery.' I smiled approvingly. 'If that's as delicious as the rum they sold last year, then you're in for a real treat.'

At least there was something about the season he wasn't averse to.

'I was wondering if you might fancy joining me for a nightcap?' he offered as the top of our road came into sight.

'Oh,' I said, and swallowed.

'If you're feeling embarrassed about what you said in the pub,' he nudged, 'then don't be. We all talk squit when we've had a few.'

Did that mean I'd spoken more rubbish than I realized? Or worse still, had he worked out what I'd really meant?

'Squit?' I said, shaking my head in an attempt to bluff my way through. 'Where did you get that word from?'

'Angus, of course,' Jude chuckled. 'It means a load of rubbish, doesn't it?'

'Yes,' I said, nodding. 'I think it's more a Suffolk and Norfolk word than a Fenland one, but I'm not surprised Angus uses it. Especially given how much of it he talks.'

We'd reached the drive now.

'So,' said Jude, 'do you fancy sampling this with me? Bury the festive hatchet?'

'You know,' I said, taking Tink's lead and avoiding Jude's eye, 'any other night I would have said a definite yes, but it's been a long day.'

'Of course,' he said, putting the bottle back in his pocket and pulling out his house key instead. 'You must be shattered.'

'I am.' I nodded. 'I'm really done in, and I've got loads to do tomorrow. Maybe another night?'

'Absolutely,' he agreed. 'I'm still going to be here for another week, after all. Night, Bella.'

'Night, Jude.'

As tired as I had professed to be, I found it impossible to fall asleep when I went to bed that night. Considering that at the start of Jude's stay I had thought his weeks under my roof were going to drag, I realized now that they had absolutely flown by, and I still wasn't entirely sure if I'd made the most of them or wasted them.

Chapter 12

After a night spent tossing and turning, I was still up early on Sunday morning and determined to make the most of the day. I had turned down Jude's offer of a nightcap the evening before with the excuse of having loads to do, which was completely true, and I had plans to combine them all and make my currently hectic life a little easier. Multi-tasking that day, however, did not turn out to be as productive as I had hoped it would be.

'No!' I screeched, reaching first for the oven gloves and then a kitchen chair. 'No, no, no, no, no!'

I was standing at full stretch on the chair and wafting the gloves under the smoke alarm when Jude came bursting through the apartment door, his momentum almost knocking me for six.

'Is there a fire?' he shouted, looking wildly around.

'No,' I quickly said back. 'It's just a bit of smoke.'

It took a few noisy seconds for the alarm to finally get the message, and when it did, Jude offered me his strong guiding hand to help me climb down.

'Thank you,' I said, moving to open the kitchen window as

wide as it would go ahead of then opening the oven door, which was the source of the still-billowing smoke.

'Oh crikey!' Jude croakily coughed when I pulled out two extremely charred pie trays. 'Oh, Bella, those do *not* look good.'

'Are you sure about that?' I tersely huffed.

He grabbed the tea towel and obligingly wafted the alarm again just to be on the safe side, while I dumped the trays, burnt contents and all, in the sink and further muttered something about his remark being the understatement of the century.

'What happened?' Jude frowned as Tink slunk back out from where she had been hiding in the bedroom. She'd dashed out of the room the second the alarm sounded, as I, in an unusual show of extreme athleticism, had leapt over the back of the sofa.

'It's all right, Tink,' I said soothingly. 'No harm done.'

'I wouldn't say that, exactly,' Jude commented, sounding almost amused as he nodded at the trays. 'Those look unsalvageable to me. Trays and all.'

I had no choice but to agree. 'Um, I think you might be right.'

Not even I could put a positive spin on how this particular situation had turned out, and since I was the queen of doing that, it was an indicator of just how bad it all looked. And how burnt it all smelled, too.

'When I set off for my run, the house smelled amazing,' said Jude, a definite smile starting to play around his lips now he knew there was no danger to him, me, Tink or the house. 'I thought I was getting a waft of a fruitcake or something, but when I came back . . . well . . .'

He nodded at the sink.

'It was good of you to come flying straight up here,' I said, as I thought of how he'd barrelled through the door without a thought for what he might find on the other side of it.

'I could hardly leave you up here alone on the off-chance that you were simply burning your baking as opposed to being overcome by the fumes of something you'd truly set alight, could I?' he pointed out mildly.

'I suppose not,' I told him. 'But even so, thank you.'

'Besides,' he went on, 'I've got all those historical documents from the hall downstairs. I needed to find out if they were genuinely in peril.'

I decided to ignore that, preferring to believe instead that it was concern for my safety that had sent him racing up the stairs in record time.

'Well, as you can see, I haven't been overcome by anything and it was my baking that was burning,' I said, looking again in the sink. 'It's Stir-up Sunday, and I was putting my own spin on the day and celebrating it, as I always do. Or at least, that was what I was supposed to be doing. It's the traditional day in November when people start making their Christmas cake and pudding—' I began to explain.

'I know what Stir-up Sunday is,' Jude cut in, running a hand through his hair.

'Oh, right.'

Given his aversion to the season, that was a surprise.

'But whatever was in that tray doesn't look anything like cake or pudding,' he said, with a laugh he could no longer suppress.

'It's not,' I told him. 'Living on my own, I don't bother

making either of those, but I am partial to a mince pie, so I mark the day by making a few batches. I keep a few out for immediate consumption and then freeze the rest.'

Nanna and I had always had a mammoth fruit-stirring and wish-making session on the last Sunday before Advent when I was growing up, filling her huge Mason Cash bowl to the brim, but I'd pared the day's efforts right down now.

I entertained plenty of visitors throughout the holidays, but had discovered that practically everyone preferred mince pies to a slice of thickly iced cake. Though not the sort of pies currently welded to the tins in the sink, obviously.

'So those were mince pies?' Jude asked.

He was still smiling but sounded doubtful, which, under the circumstances, was fair.

'They were supposed to be,' I confessed. 'Only an assembly job, though. Not made from scratch.'

'A what?'

'You know, using ready-rolled pastry out of the fridge and a jar of mincemeat.'

'Oh, I see,' he laughed. 'Who would have thought something as simple as that could go so horribly wrong?'

'All right,' I huffed, wishing I had inherited even half of Nanna's baking skills. 'I'm not too proud to confess that I'm a pretty rubbish baker, but as with everything in life, I'm always willing to have a go.'

That ethos had served me well in the past. Talking to a group of strangers aside (until very recently, that is), I had always been brave enough to embrace trying new things and not getting too preoccupied about whether or not I was going to be any good at them. I mean, who was an expert at anything from the get-go? No one, I reckoned. We all had to start somewhere, didn't we? My fairies were a case in point. The first ones I'd made and which I kept in my bedroom as a tribute to making a start were pretty scrappy, but I'd gone on to improve my design and technique with each of the ones that followed. It was how I learned. How anyone learned.

'But that crumble you made last week was perfect,' Jude said, frowning.

'And my only real baking accomplishment,' I sighed. 'If you can categorize a crumble as baking, that is,' I pondered. 'Pastry and the like is completely beyond me.'

Nanna, bless her patient soul, had tried on many occasions to help me master making it, among other things, but to no avail.

'As is remembering the time,' Jude teased.

'Hey!' I pouted.

'You need one of those kitchen timers,' he suggested, as his thoughts drifted into his own childhood memories. 'My nan had one shaped like a chicken. I always used to get in trouble for messing about with it and setting it to go off after I'd left. She was never really cross, though . . .'

His wistful words trailed off, and I noticed he looked a little misty-eyed.

'Well,' I said, coming to his rescue because it was obvious that what he had just shared had made him feel either nostalgic or exposed, possibly even both. 'My mince pies wouldn't usually be all that brilliant, even if I did get them out prior to burning them to a crisp, because I have a tendency to overfill them. That said,' I added, biting my lip, 'they wouldn't usually end up anything like this.'

'So what happened today?' Jude asked. 'What's the cause of all this crispy carnage?'

I rolled my eyes at his alliterative, but entirely accurate, description.

'I got distracted,' I confessed, biting my lip again.

'But how did you not smell them?'

'No idea.' I shrugged.

'What was it that distracted you?' he wanted to know.

He sounded genuinely interested, and I pointed over at the coffee table, where I had the makings of a few fairies set out. I hoped the fabrics didn't now smell of smoke.

'A customer at the switch-on yesterday asked if I had considered selling fairies in kit form with a list of accompanying instructions,' I explained. 'And I was trying to figure out if that might work.'

'That sounds like something you needed to be able to properly focus on,' Jude said, stating the obvious.

Even though in my heart I had known that, I'd let my head overrule it. Because I had so much to do, I had let my brain convince me that I could plan and bake simultaneously. Lesson learned. It wasn't often that I ignored my heart, and the current state of the kitchen was proof that that was for a very good reason.

'It certainly was,' I sighed. 'Now I've got no mince pies, a tonne of clearing up to do and a smelly apartment. And I'm no further forward with finding out if the fairy kits are a viable option, either.'

'And as you were working yesterday,' Jude pointed out, 'which was a Saturday, you shouldn't even be so occupied today, should you? Isn't that your usual rule?'

'Yes,' I said, now wishing I hadn't previously mentioned that, 'it is, but like I told you last night, I've got loads to do. *You* might not go in for Christmas, Jude, but it's my busiest time of the year workwise, and I still want to enjoy everything else that comes along with it.'

'Like Stir-up Sunday?'

'Exactly,' I sighed again. 'Just like Stir-up Sunday.'

'And how's that working out for you?' he asked, one eyebrow quirked.

He clearly didn't feel affronted that I'd flagged up his aversion to the season.

'Teasing is not helping,' I said, suppressing a smile as I looked at the welded-on pies and wondered if trying to clean the trays was going to be worth the effort.

It really was time to abandon the multi-tasking. Just for that day, anyway.

'Sorry,' he laughingly apologized. 'Too soon to joke about it?'

'Definitely too soon,' I said, grinning. 'Do you fancy a coffee?'

'I need to get showered, but I'll have one after that, if it's still on offer. In fact,' he said, clicking his fingers, 'why don't I make the coffee after I've freshened up, while you head to town for some supplies?'

'Supplies?' I frowned.

'Yes,' he said, helping himself to a pen and notepad from the worktop. 'I'll write a list of everything you need, and then I'll help you make some proper mince pies from scratch. Apart from using homemade mincemeat, of course. I'll teach you how to make the pastry, just like how my nan showed me.'

'You can bake?' I swallowed, thinking that this was an

unexpected tick in Jude's favour. Though I didn't reckon much for his chances of successfully tutoring me. If Nanna hadn't succeeded during all her years of trying, I didn't think Jude would be able to manage it in one brief session.

'I can,' he said, as he began to write down a list of ingredients off the top of his head. 'What do you think I was learning to do when I was messing about with that kitchen timer?'

By the time I was back from town, Jude had showered, changed and made a cafetière of coffee. I'd left Tink with him, and she was completely relaxed. In fact, when I joined them in the house kitchen, it felt just like it had when the three of us had hung out before. Before I'd known Jude censored Christmas, that is.

I couldn't help wondering how differently the last few days might have turned out had he loved December as much as I did. Would I have pretended that my feelings for him only ran dalliance deep, thrown caution to the wind and kissed him on the porch after the volunteer meeting in the pub, or would I still be avoiding him and ring-fencing my heart from potential hurt?

Being with him again now, I couldn't be sure what I was doing, but it was still a relief that I hadn't kissed him and *then* found out about the festive boycott.

'So,' I said, as I pulled my thoughts back to the task literally in hand as we finished the first part of the pastry-making process, 'tell me why the pastry has to go in the fridge for a while? Why can't we just get straight on and use it?'

I'm sure Nanna would have explained and gone through everything just as patiently as Jude already had, but I was extra eager to throw myself into learning it all over again in the hope that this time around something might actually stick.

'So it can chill out and relax,' Jude told me in terms Nanna would never have used. However, given his tone, I didn't think he was joking. 'It'll be easier to work with in a couple of hours because it will have firmed up, and it won't shrink as much or crack, either.'

'Right,' I said, as I wrapped the ball of pastry that I'd somehow miraculously made with only minimal assistance in cling film, having watched Jude do the same with his.

'And it was your nan who taught you all this?' I further probed, liking the thought of us both having had similar childhood experiences in the kitchen, even if his had been more successful in certain areas.

He had already told me how he'd spent a lot of time with his grandparents when he was growing up and that he had always felt closer to them than to his mum and dad, who had travelled a lot. In turn, I'd told him a bit about my nanna and grandad, too. How they'd gifted me the house and I'd initially struggled to find a way to be able to keep it, until I eventually opted to convert it and rent it out, which then provided me with the freedom to set up my business.

'It was,' he said, nodding in confirmation. 'She was an amazing cook and a very accomplished baker, too.'

'And she put oats in her crumble topping,' I said, remembering what he'd told me the week before.

'Yep,' he said. 'And her steak and ale pie was to die for.'

'Do you have the recipe for that?' I asked keenly.

'Somewhere,' he said thoughtfully. 'The filling was cooked in the slow cooker all day, so it became melt-in-the-mouth delicious.'

'That sounds sublime,' I said, and my own mouth watered just at the thought of it.

'And she added a handful of cheese right at the end to thicken the gravy even more, before encasing it all in buttery puff pastry and finishing it off in the oven.'

'You need to stop,' I told him. 'My tummy is rumbling, and it's a while away from lunch yet.'

'Tell me some more about your family, then,' he said, popping the pastry in the fridge. 'Are you close to your parents? You've told me about your lovely grandparents, but nothing about your mum and dad.'

'Well,' I said, filling our mugs with the last of the coffee and knowing that it was better just to say it straight out. Like ripping a plaster off and hoping the scab had healed underneath, though in this instance I was self-aware enough to know that that wasn't completely the case. 'Dad disappeared when I was just a baby and has never been heard of since, and my stepdad buggered off a few years later and he's never been in touch again, either.'

Jude looked floored.

'In the past, it was hard not to take it personally,' I said, trying to sound blasé even though I didn't feel it. 'I've often wondered if their leaving was because of me.' Jude went to interject, but I quickly carried on. 'Mum, Nanna and Grandad have all insisted that it wasn't, of course, but it still made for some pretty turbulent and tempestuous teenage angst.'

'And what about your mum?' Jude asked quietly. 'How did she cope?'

'All things considered, extremely admirably,' I said proudly. 'She completely shut the door on romantic relationships and threw herself into her work instead, which is why I spent so much time when I was growing up with Nanna and Grandad.

Mum forged herself a hugely successful career and, as a result, is now living in happy retirement in France.'

'Wow.' Jude whistled under his breath.

'I know,' I said. 'She's amazing. I admire her so much.'

'But does that mean that she's had no serious relationships since your stepdad left all those years ago?' Jude asked, then grimaced. 'Sorry, that's a really personal question. You don't have to answer that.'

'It's fine,' I told him. 'Until Mum retired, she didn't have any relationships at all. Nothing serious and nothing fun, either, because she was completely and not surprisingly totally off men. Work and family were what she focused on, but that's changed now. She's having some fun in France and has got to know a few guys since she moved there.'

'But no one special guy?'

'I'm not sure those exist in real life,' I laughed, and Jude frowned. 'And Mum doesn't think they do, either. She and I are very similar in our attitudes towards relationships.'

'What exactly *is* your attitude?'

'We don't get attached,' I told him, forcefully blocking out the thought that my feelings for him had been in an entirely different stratosphere to any I had ever experienced before. 'We don't put our hearts on the line. Just like Mum, I prefer short-term associations.' I swallowed. 'It saves the heartache when the fun stops.'

Jude looked surprised.

'Does the fun always *have* to stop?' he asked.

'In my experience,' I said pointedly, reminding him of what I had shared before, 'yes. Men have a tendency to leave.'

Jude opened and closed his mouth.

'But,' he said, 'just because the father figures in your life—'

'Completely abandoned me,' I said challengingly. Then, because I wanted to turn the emphasis away from me, I added, 'Even you'll be gone in a week.'

'That's hardly relevant,' Jude tutted, 'because we're not in a relationship, but if we were—'

'You'd still be leaving next week,' I cut in.

He looked at me and seemed to be mentally reassessing everything he thought he'd worked out about me.

'I'm not sure how I feel about us not getting together now, Bella,' he said finally, taking me completely by surprise.

'What?' I squeaked, feeling like a rug had been pulled out from under me, leaving me floundering. 'What are you talking about?'

'Well, perhaps it's just been me,' Jude said self-consciously, 'but I've thought a couple of times – since I apologized for being a prat when I first arrived – that there'd been a spark between us, some moments of mutual attraction that could have led somewhere. But I must have misread the signals.'

'What makes you say that?' I asked breathlessly. 'The misread signals bit, I mean.'

I wasn't about to dispute the spark, because I couldn't in all honesty deny it.

'Well,' he said, 'if there really had been some connection between us, given that I now know you're in favour of short-term relationships, I would have thought that would make me the ideal person to . . . get together with.'

'I see,' I said slowly.

'So either you don't fancy me at all,' he said, 'and there's no spark. Or you did, but then you had a change of heart when you found out that I hate Christmas. That's it, isn't it?'

He sounded relieved to have hit upon something to justify my not pouncing on him. Clearly the not fancying him bit couldn't *possibly* be right.

'I suppose it would make you feel better if I said it was the Christmas thing, wouldn't it?' I said coolly while my internal temperature raced up and down the thermostat.

'It would please my ego immensely,' he laughed.

'Well, in that case, we'll go with that,' I said, nodding, thinking that my fibbing might strike me off Santa's nice list, but at least it kept my heart intact and my true feelings for Jude under wraps. 'You're right, I did fancy you, but the whole Christmas embargo buggered it.'

Jude laughed at that, and I wished he wouldn't. My heart couldn't take it.

'I knew you liked me,' he said, reaching for the roll of kitchen towel and anti-bac spray to clean the flour off the table. 'I knew you did.'

'I wouldn't actually have acted on my feelings, though,' I continued, to really hammer the point home and keep things sparklingly clear between us, 'even without the whole Christmas thing.'

'Oh,' he said, looking less happy. 'Why not?'

'Because you're a Connelly employee and a guest here at their behest,' I said seriously. 'It would have been completely inappropriate, wouldn't it?'

Jude wrinkled his nose and gave the table a squirt of cleaner as he processed that.

'When you put it like that,' he said, 'I suppose you're right. It wouldn't really have been the decent way to behave, would it?'

'Not at all,' I said, mentally patting myself on the back for finding a way to properly draw a line under the sparky situation once and for all.

'It was probably just as well I didn't kiss you that night we went to the pub together, then, wasn't it?' he sighed. 'I came so close—'

'Definitely better that you didn't,' I cut in, not wanting to imagine how that might have felt or how I would have reacted. 'And given that your Grinchy attitude has now completely extinguished the spark, I'm hoping you're going to tell me why you hate Christmas so much.'

'I'm going to have to work up to that,' he said, and swallowed. 'Let's bake first.'

A while later, once the perfect, almost professional-looking mince pies had been transferred to the cooling racks, and I had cooed over them in genuine amazement and then let Tink out into the garden, Jude and I sat together at the kitchen table. I was sorry to see that his previously buoyant mood had entirely ebbed away.

'You don't really have to tell me about why you loathe Christmas,' I said, feeling bad as I watched him nurse his mug of coffee and stare worriedly into its depths. 'I was just being nosy.'

'No,' he said, looking up. 'It's okay.'

'It doesn't look like it's okay,' I said softly.

'It's fine,' he said, shrugging, and I waited. As much as I didn't want to further upset him, there was a part of me that was desperate to know. 'You said earlier, Bella, that men have a tendency to leave,' he eventually began.

'I did,' I acknowledged. 'And they do.'

'Well,' he said heavily, 'in my experience, women leave, too.'

I took a moment to consider the implications of that in relation to Jude loathing Christmas.

'You had your heart broken at Christmas, didn't you?' I whispered. 'You've experienced your own fun stopping right at the pinnacle of the year.'

'Indeed,' he said, nodding, then shook his head. 'I did. It's the ultimate cliché, right?'

'It's not an entirely unheard-of situation,' I acknowledged.

My stepfather had made his exit from our lives right at the end of November, but my grandparents had made a gargantuan effort to not let his departure overshadow Christmas that year. As a result, I hadn't lost my love of the season either then or indeed during any year that came after it. I would be forever grateful to them for that.

'It's a classic,' Jude said gruffly. 'The guy running all over town for the right engagement ring.'

My heart fluttered as I processed that he had once loved someone enough to want to marry them. That was a huge deal and way beyond what I thought I was emotionally capable of.

'The house dressed to perfection because he loves Christmas and wants his proposal to be picture perfect—'

'You once *loved* Christmas,' I breathed, interrupting his flow of words as a flame of hope ignited in my heart.

Jude gave me a withering look.

'Sorry,' I said, and swallowed, turning the burner down and picking up my mug.

'He's checking and double-checking every last detail, right up until the moment he has to head out the door to the airport to pick up the woman he hasn't seen for the last four months because she's been working in Hong Kong.'

I began to feel bilious rather than hopeful that Jude could come back to embracing the season then, because there was no doubting that this particular Christmas story was going to have the most horrible ending.

'And then a call comes in. A Zoom call from the woman he's supposed to be rushing off to meet, but how can that be possible when she's supposed to be on the flight and he knows from previous experience that the signal isn't the best for making in-flight video calls?'

'She wasn't on the plane, was she?' I whispered.

'No,' said Jude, sitting back in his chair and drumming his fingers on the table. 'She wasn't on the plane. She was still in Hong Kong, and she was calling to tell me that she was staying there.'

'Oh, Jude, I'm so sorry.'

'Wait, wait,' he said, putting a hand up, 'it gets better. She was staying there with our best friend from uni, who also happened to work for the same bank that she did, who'd joined the Hong Kong office at the same time as her and who mysteriously hadn't been in touch with me for a few weeks prior to her little bombshell.'

'Oh, crap.'

'And they were expecting a baby the following year.'

'Double crap.'

'And getting married in the New Year, so they would have tied the knot before the birth.'

I didn't say anything further but sat quietly waiting to see if there were any more shoes to drop. Jude stared at the table, then looked up at me.

'That's it,' he said. 'I'm done.'

'Just as well,' I said, puffing out my cheeks. 'Cos I'm pretty much all out of crap over here.'

He gave a wry smile.

'But,' he said, 'there was also the huge bonfire I had in the garden with all the new Christmas decorations I'd paid a fortune for, as well as the ones we'd previously picked out together.'

'You burned the Christmas decorations?' I gasped.

'How can you sound as horrified about that as you did about me telling you that my heart had been trampled on and smashed?' he demanded, sounding astonished.

'I'm not,' I said, instantly contrite. 'I just didn't have you down as someone who would react like that. I can't see you as someone who would have such an explosive response to anything.'

'Well,' he said, shrugging, 'it wasn't the sort of hot-headed reaction I'd experienced before or since, and it certainly wasn't a response I was proud of, especially when I realized how badly I'd scorched the lawn.'

I jiffled in my seat, willing the question I desperately wanted to ask to stay in my head.

'What?' Jude frowned, sensing that I wanted to say something further.

'Nothing.' I shrugged.

'No, go on, what?' he insisted. 'I can tell there's something.'

'Was there an angel or fairy on top of the tree?' I blurted out.

'No,' he laughed, which, under the circumstances, was a miracle, 'it was a star.'

'Okay,' I said, nodding and feeling relieved. 'Good. That's good.'

'You're incorrigible,' he said, shaking his head.

'I know,' I acknowledged. 'I'm sorry, but you know how I feel about Christmas. And angels and fairies especially.'

'I do,' he said, standing up. 'And if there had been an angel or fairy on top of the tree, I wouldn't have burned them.'

'Good,' I breathed.

Perhaps he wasn't an entirely lost cause, after all.

'That is, assuming I would have realized before the tree went up in flames,' he continued ponderously, making me yelp. 'I reckon these are cool enough to try now.'

He plated up a couple of the mince pies while I fetched a pot of thick cream I'd spotted in the fridge. The Christmas pudding gin was in there, too.

'I think we need at least one shot of this after what you've just told me,' I said, grabbing glasses and sitting back down again. 'Had you and the woman you were going to propose to been together long?'

I wasn't sure if he wanted to talk more about it, but it didn't feel like the sort of explanation you could give and then instantly move on from without adding a bit more context.

'A few years,' Jude said. 'We met, ironically through our mutual chum, during our first year at uni. It had been long enough for me to believe that marriage was the next step.'

I gave him a look.

'What?' he said, frowning.

'Nothing,' I said, pouring us both generous measures of the gin and thinking that describing the intended proposal as a

next step was hardly romantic. 'I mean, that just sounds a bit
. . . traditional, you know.'

'Oh, it was,' he agreed. 'And it was exactly what was expected
by both sets of parents, too. My mum and dad loved Tabitha.'

'That's a cat's name,' I said, trying to make him laugh again.
He didn't.

'They're still blaming me for not making a success of the
relationship. They reckon it was my fault she went off with
Barny.'

Jude's parents sounded like a hoot, but that wasn't for me
to say.

'And that's a dog's name,' I said instead as I poured the cream.
'With names like that, I don't reckon much for their chances.'

'Funny you should say that,' said Jude, handing me a spoon.
'They split up this summer.'

'Oh,' I said. 'Well, I'm not sorry for them, but it's a shame
for the kid.'

'Atticus.'

'I'm even more sorry for him now.'

'Don't,' said Jude, shaking his head.

'What did you do with the perfect engagement ring?' I
asked, wondering what it had looked like. 'Please don't tell me
that went on the fire, too.'

'No,' he said, with a wry smile, 'that funded my first year
while I made the switch from just blogging about my love of
historical properties to writing about them professionally. It
kept me fed, with a roof over my head, while I was getting
some work under my belt.'

'That must have been quite some rock.' I whistled under
my breath.

'It was,' he said, nodding.

'So before the writing properly took off, you were a histor-ical buildings surveyor, weren't you?'

'That's right,' he confirmed. 'How did you know that?'

'Catherine and Angus told me.'

'Of course they did.' Jude nodded. 'They're such wonderful people. You know, they're actually happier for me than my own parents are.'

'I take it your mum and dad aren't impressed with your change of professional direction, then?' I guessed. Given the little Jude had already told me about them, that had to be the case.

'Correct,' he confirmed. 'They think it's a risky switch from the stable role I had before, but I'm not letting their naysaying put me off. I own my tiny flat outright now, so really I'm as secure as I can be for someone my age. Possibly more secure.'

'Good for you,' I said, knowing it wasn't easy to muster the courage to do something that others felt was unconventional, even if you hankered for it with the whole of your heart. 'But does that make you a complete family outcast or just the odd sheep in the flock?'

'The jury is still out on that one,' Jude laughed. 'I daresay if I'm a huge success, I'll be properly welcomed back into the fold. Either way, I'm not bothered. I'm following my heart whatever the outcome.'

'Shame about Christmas, though,' I said, as my own heart thumped at the thought of Jude's. 'Are you sure you can't come back to it? It was hardly the season's fault that you fell out of love with it.'

'No way,' he said, draining his gin in one. 'That festive ship has definitely sailed.'

'There's a Christmas carol about ships—' I started to say.

'Never mind about that,' he said, firmly cutting me off. 'What do you think of this pastry?'

Chapter 13

Jude and I devoured most of the mince pies and drank almost all of the gin – it was quite a small bottle – before I headed back up to the apartment, and I was grateful to wake the following morning without another alcohol-induced headache, because, in my mind at least, it was a very special day.

'Bella, what are you doing?' groaned Jude when he appeared, sleepy, tussled and delicious-looking, as I hammered up a string of outdoor lights around the stained-glass-panelled front door, which was inside the brick and wood open-fronted porch.

I realized it wasn't a special day to him, but I still couldn't rein my excitement in.

'What does it look like?' I responded, leaning around the side of the step ladder with nary a care for my safety.

'I have no idea,' he grumbled. 'I don't want to properly open my eyes to look, because it's very dark, it's ridiculously early and I'm pretending I'm still asleep.'

'It's not *that* early,' I tutted. 'And besides, don't you have work to do today? It is Monday, after all.'

'I'm not starting work at this hour,' he groaned again, giving a shiver because he was still in his PJs and it was frosty out.

'I'm putting some lights up,' I told him. 'I would usually have put them up yesterday in readiness for today, but the time ran away with me and I was distracted by . . . all that gin.'

I had been distracted by what he'd told me, too, but I wasn't going to bring that up and risk getting his week off to a bad start. In all honesty, given that he'd now only got a few days left in Wynbridge, I didn't think I'd ever mention it again. It was such a horrendous thing to have experienced, and I resented Tabitha and Barny and the fact that their cruelty had blighted Jude's former love for Christmas.

I could well imagine that the trauma had left him reluctant to truly trust another woman again, too. I remembered that he had joshed about being offended that I hadn't made a move on him once I'd told him I only went in for brief affairs, but perhaps he hadn't been joking, after all. Maybe that was as much as he felt able or willing to commit to now, too.

The irony that I had developed unexpectedly deeper feelings for him wasn't lost on me. If I hadn't, and we could have got over the Connelly connection I'd previously cited as a barrier, we might have had a really fun month.

Dismissing that tragic thought, I steered my attention back to the task currently in hand.

'I usually put a few festive lights up inside now, too,' I said, 'but I've got to wait until I've waved you off next week to do that. Unless . . .'

'No,' said Jude, finding his voice again. 'Don't even think about it.'

'In that case,' I laughed, 'you'll just have to put up with a bit of early a.m. hammering out here today, won't you?'

'You still haven't told me what the occasion is,' he grizzled, scratching his head and making even more of a mess of his hair.

'It's the twenty-fifth of November, of course,' I said, my sing-song tone suggesting that he should have known. 'Exactly one month until Christmas Day.'

'And that's a big thing, is it?' he asked, hopping from one cold foot to the other.

'It is in my world,' I declared, jumping off the ladder and stepping out of the porch to see how the lights looked.

It was hard to tell without firing them up, but I thought I'd positioned them pretty much as I usually did with the benefit of the daylight on the twenty-fourth. They went around the door and up and over the tiled roof, then wrapped around the brick pillars right to the ground on either side. The porch was also flanked with two standard clipped box balls in deep red, glossy ceramic frost-resistant pots, and I'd already added tiny lights to those, along with a few all-weather fairies, who were dressed and decorated to match the season.

'Would you care to do the honours?' I asked Jude as I folded the stepladder up, ready to put it back in the garden shed.

'What, now?' He frowned, rubbing his bare arms.

'Yes,' I said, 'it'll be light soon, so we need to get a wriggle on if we want to admire the full effect.'

He looked at me for a moment, and I wondered what he was thinking. Probably what a pain in his butt I was.

'Okay, hang on,' he said surprisingly and disappeared back indoors again.

While he was gone, I put the stepladder away and made sure the other seasonal porch pots, which were filled with red cyclamen and deep-green ivy, were equally spaced and not too exposed to the potentially wet winter weather, which they didn't much like. If the temperature really plummeted or the rain lashed down, I would lift them properly inside the porch, but the effect wasn't as spectacular as when they were arranged as I'd set them up now.

'Perfect,' I sighed happily.

I thought it all looked as pretty as a carefully crafted Insta picture. Or it would when the lights went on.

'Here you go,' said Jude, finally coming back out and looking much more awake.

He was dressed, trainers included, and carrying a tray with two steaming mugs on it.

'It wasn't made in a teapot, I'm afraid,' he smiled, 'because I was trying to be quick, but I thought it might add to the moment and thaw your fingers out a bit. You must be frozen.'

I wriggled my chilly fingers in my snowflake-patterned fingerless gloves.

'I'm okay,' I said, feeling a bit choked that, despite his dislike of the season, he'd decided to play along. He might have just been humouring me, but under the circumstances and given what I now knew about him, I very much appreciated that. 'But the tea is definitely very welcome.'

'Well,' he said, putting the tray back in the porch, 'you know, it's important to make an occasion out of these things.'

I felt even more choked when he said that.

'Even Christmas things,' I said, giving him a nudge, 'and at an uncivilized hour?'

'Just this once,' he said, looking down at me and making something disconcerting happen to my heart again, 'and only because it's you, Bella.'

'In that case,' I said, after a beat had passed and I'd managed to pull my gaze away from his, 'we should definitely fire these lights up, shouldn't we?'

'It would be a waste not to, now that we've gone to so much trouble,' he laughed. 'And I will do the honours if you tell me where the switch is,' he added, handing me his mug. 'Then you can stand back and properly admire the spectacle.'

I didn't tell him that I usually turned the lights on, then felt my way out of the porch and on to the drive with my eyes squeezed shut. He probably already thought I was a bit bonkers, and I didn't want to further confirm his suspicions.

'All right,' I said, gulping down the hot tea, 'but take the mugs with you and leave them in the porch, otherwise I won't be able to clap my hands and jump up and down.'

'That's a necessary part of the proceedings, is it?' he laughed again.

'Yes,' I said seriously. 'It's utterly integral to the proceedings.'

'What are you like?' He rolled his eyes, but still took the mugs from me and strode off.

'The switch is just next to the door,' I called after him.

An electrician friend had set up a double outdoor socket for me a couple of years ago when I realized the natural winter light at the front of the house wasn't strong enough to power solar lights.

'Are you ready?' Jude called.

'Yes,' I said, clasping my hands together, 'go on.'

'Three, two, one . . .' he shouted, properly getting into the swing of it for me.

'Oh, Jude,' I said, clapping and jumping at the same time, 'come and look!'

He came and stood next to me, bringing Tink with him, and then turned around. Rather than keep looking at the lights, I watched him. A slow smile spread across his face, and it grew even wider when he spotted the fairies peeping out of the box balls.

'There's no mistaking who lives here, is there?' he said admiringly. 'It's just as well I'm going next week, Bella, because you'd have me believing in the magic of Christmas again if I was staying much longer, and I'm not sure I'm ready to re-embrace it yet.'

'But you might be one day?' I whispered.

'Perhaps,' he whispered back.

His admission was music to my ears and, without thinking, I reached over and pulled him in for a hug. At least, my initial intention had been to give him a hug. Missing the moment to simply rest my head on his shoulder, I suddenly found my face just an inch in front of his.

'Jude,' I softly whispered as my lips were compulsively drawn to lightly meet his, and he returned the gentle kiss I gave him with a firmer one of his own.

My head had every intention of pulling away, but my heart kept me melded to him. I kissed him again, and he kissed me back. His mouth felt wonderfully warm against mine, and his lips were every bit as soft and full as I had so often imagined they would be.

Neither of us drew away and the moment became deeper, more intense and heading hastily towards hungry as our arms tightened around each other. There was no denying that my feelings for him had surpassed lust and 'brief liaison' territory. The kiss cemented the foundations of a deeper connection that I had already known was beginning to grow, and I wondered if Jude was feeling it, too.

'Sorry,' he suddenly said, letting me go and taking a step away. 'I'm so sorry, Bella.'

Clearly he wasn't feeling any of what I was, and I had less than a second to recover from the disappointment and mortification as the freezing air filled the space he had previously occupied.

'Why are you sorry?' I laughed, somehow managing to look right at him and still pretend that everything was fine. 'I'm not sorry.'

'You're not?' His eyes searched my face.

'No,' I told him. 'Of course I'm not. That was a wonderful way to celebrate the start of the countdown to Christmas, wasn't it?'

'Trust you to make it about Christmas,' he said, looking relieved. 'No mistletoe, though.'

'Says who?' I laughed, pointing at the ball of silk mistletoe hanging under the roof of the porch.

As much as I would have loved to, I never got the real thing, because I always worried that the berries might fall off and that Tink would find them before I did. Or Jasper would, if he was visiting. He'd be the dog most likely to sniff them out and devour them, and that would mean yet another trip for him to the vets.

'I hadn't spotted that.' Jude smiled. 'We should have been under it, shouldn't we?'

Had it been anyone other than Jude, I might have suggested stepping into the porch and having another go, but it *was* Jude, and I knew from how my head and heart had reacted to his lips pressed against mine that I couldn't possibly allow myself to kiss him again. I couldn't recall another time when my actual soul had responded, so the kiss had been a truly unique, as well as unsettling, encounter. Unsettling because Jude was practically on the verge of leaving, and I was now in danger of waving my heart off with him.

'I think we were near enough for it to count,' I therefore said.

I was just about to remind him that we should also veto a rematch because of the Connelly connection we'd previously flagged up, but my phone began to ring, robbing me of the chance.

'Oh, it's Mum,' I said, looking at the screen as I pulled it out of my pocket. She really did have impeccably spooky timing. 'I'd better answer.'

'Of course,' said Jude. 'And I should really make a start on getting ready to head to the hall. Angus phoned last night and said he's found something he wants to show me. I hope it's got something to do with my work and isn't just some random thing that he's found in one of the boxes in the loft.'

'Of course it'll be something random he's found in a box,' I laughed, trying to sound as unaffected by our moment as he obviously was. 'I'll see you later. Merry Christmas.'

'And to you, too,' Jude said, smiling back.

I wondered if he'd purposefully not said the words.

'Hey, Mum,' I said, quickly answering the call before it cut off and watching Jude disappear back into the house, taking the tray and mugs with him. 'How are you?'

'How are you, more like?' she asked. 'What are you smiling about?'

'How do you know I'm smiling?' I laughed.

'I can hear it in your voice,' she explained. 'What's to do? Admiring the lights you doubtless put up around the porch yesterday, or something else?'

'That and possibly something else,' I told her as I ushered Tink around the side of the house to the apartment door.

'Well, now,' she said, 'I'm intrigued. I know it's very early in the day over there, so could it be a gentleman caller? Or even a gentleman over-nighter?'

'Mum!' I tutted.

'Come on,' she said, sensing that she'd either hit or come close to the truth. 'Tell me. It'll make a change for you to make me blush, rather than the other way around.'

Once upstairs, I reached for the kettle and filled it at the sink.

'Okay, okay,' I caved. 'It's the guy I messaged you about – Jude.'

'The chap who the Connellys convinced you to take in for a few weeks?'

'Yes,' I said, 'that's him.'

'Well, what about him? A mild flirtation or a full-on fling?'

'Neither, really,' I said, awkwardly sloshing milk into my mug with one hand while I cradled the phone between my neck and shoulder. I would usually put Mum on speaker, but this was one conversation I definitely didn't want the person currently downstairs to inadvertently overhear.

'Neither?' Mum asked. 'Don't tell me he hasn't fallen head over heels in love with you, Bella, because I won't believe that for a second. You're the hottest ticket in town!'

'Oh, Mum,' I tutted. 'I wouldn't say things have gone anywhere near that far, but I do think there's . . . something.'

'Of course there is,' she said firmly. 'I'm sure he's mad for you.'

'On both sides, actually,' I unguardedly added.

Mum didn't respond for a moment, and I realized that, still feeling heady from the kiss Jude and I had just shared, I'd gone and blurted out a confession I hadn't intended to share with anyone.

'You mean,' Mum finally said, 'that *you* like *him* as well as *him* liking *you*? As in, *properly* liking?'

'I do *quite* like him,' I told her, belatedly reining in my enthusiasm.

'Well,' Mum gasped, 'that's a turn-up for the books.'

'I know,' I said, 'but it isn't going to come to anything, because he'll be gone in a week—'

'Given how much you love short-term romances,' she said, 'that would usually make him a prime candidate, wouldn't it?'

'Usually,' I confirmed, 'yes.'

'So the fact that you're holding back tells me that you more than *quite* like him, Bella.'

'Yes,' I said, because I couldn't deny it, 'I know it does. And the kiss . . .'

'You've *kissed* him?' Mum gasped.

'Just now, on the porch,' I blurted out, cursing the words that kept falling unbidden and unchecked from my mouth. 'To celebrate turning the house lights on.'

'And how was it?' Mum asked. 'The kiss, not the switch-on.'

I closed my eyes and recalled how high my libido had leapt as Jude had pressed his body closer to mine. I also ran a finger over my lips, remembering the soft, then urgent, pressure.

'Absolutely wonderful,' I admitted. 'But under the circumstances, it definitely won't be happening again. I won't be making a habit out of it between now and the first of December.'

Mum tried to say something further, but I insistently said that she didn't need to warn me about heartbreak, because I wasn't going to be setting myself up to experience it, and then I conclusively changed the subject. It took a few attempts to get her to drop the topic, but I managed it in the end.

Holed up in the apartment, focused on making fairies, I didn't see Jude for the rest of the day – or the next couple of days, either. I had slunk away from the house on Wednesday to take my turn selling on the Christmas market stall, and I made sure the coast was clear when I returned home again early that evening.

All the creeping about felt a bit cloak and dagger, but the physical and mental response I'd had to that kiss had made me realize that stealth mode was necessary if I didn't want to put my heart in further jeopardy ahead of the festive season.

'Bella!'

Clearly Jude hadn't got the memo, because he came knocking on my door late on Thursday morning. His sudden hammering made my heart race, but this time because he'd made me jump. I glanced at the calendar. It was the twenty-eighth of November. Still a few more days until he was due to depart, and my avoidance plan was about to lose its initial momentum.

'Come on, open up!' he called. 'I know you're in there.'

I looked at Tink, who was standing with her head cocked to one side, and pressed my finger to my lips. With any luck, Jude might come to the conclusion that I had taken her for a walk and disappear back into the house again.

'Bella!'

Tink began to woof, and I knew the game was up. I gave her a look, and she started to race madly about, barking even more loudly.

'Hold on!' I shouted, moving as far away from the door as I could in the shortest possible time. 'Just a sec.'

I took a moment to gather my thoughts, grabbed my earbuds, then strode purposefully over to the door.

'Hey,' I said, opening it wide with what I hoped was a look of surprise on my face. 'Jude! Sorry, I didn't hear you. I was listening to some music,' I embellished, holding the earbuds up. 'Have you been there long?'

He looked wrong-footed.

'You okay?' I frowned. 'Is something wrong with the house?'

'What? No,' he said, dragging a hand through his hair. 'No, everything's fine. I was just . . .'

'You were just?' I prompted.

'Sorry,' he said. 'Sorry. I think I made a mistake.'

'Oh?'

'I'd got it into my head that you were avoiding me.'

'*Avoiding* you?' I asked, frowning again. 'Why would I be avoiding you?'

'Well—'

'Don't stand out there,' I interrupted, opening the door even wider and playing the hostess. 'Come in. There's tea in the pot.'

With my friendliest smile in place, I poured us both a mug and offered to share my serving of overnight oats, seeds and fruit, which I hadn't got around to eating for breakfast.

'No, thanks,' said Jude, accepting the mug but not the food. 'I'm good.'

I didn't much fancy it myself now, but having made such a show of normality, I had no choice but to tuck in. Tink sat next to Jude with her head on his lap.

'Sorry I cut you off before,' I said, having eventually swallowed a mouthful. 'You were about to tell me why you thought I'd been avoiding you.'

He began to stroke Tink's head and let out a long breath.

'It seems stupid now,' he said, as a slight blush bloomed. 'Especially as I can see how much work you've got on.'

The table in front of the sofa was covered in fairy things, and there were a couple of open crates, too, packed to the brim with bits and pieces, along with a notepad and tablet.

'I am a bit swamped,' I told him, which was true.

As well as the Christmas market stall, Holly and I were sharing a stand at the school fair on Friday, and I still had lots to do ahead of that.

'So,' he said, looking sheepish, 'you're actually working hard, rather than staying out of my way.'

'Of course,' I said, thinking for the second time in recent days that I was looking like a less-than-likely candidate for Santa's nice list that year. 'I've had no reason to avoid you, Jude, have I?'

'I can see that now,' he tutted, 'but I'd got it into my head that after our kiss—'

'Our kiss on the drive?' I asked, blinking at him over my oats.

It was obvious which kiss. We'd only had one.

'After our kiss on the drive,' he carried on, 'I thought you'd been staying out of my way. I was beginning to panic that I was a rubbish kisser,' he said, making an even worse job of making light of the situation than I was.

The truth was, he was a stand-out kisser, not a rubbish one.

'Of course you're not a rubbish kisser,' I laughed as I pushed the jar of oats away. If I ate another mouthful, Jude might end up wearing them. 'Far from it!' I said jollily. 'You're a fabulous kisser.'

A kisser who had made me feel far too much, as it turned out, but he didn't need to be told that as well as how wonderful he was.

'Well, that's all right, then,' he responded equally as heartily. 'Phew!'

'And I haven't been avoiding you at all,' I bluffed. 'As you've now realized, I'm just bonkers busy with work.'

'Good,' he said, slapping his hand on his thigh and only just avoiding Tink's nose. 'Great. Because I'd hate it if that kiss had made things awkward between us again, Bella. It feels to me like we'd only recently got over me being a prat when I arrived.'

'And my shock at you not liking Christmas,' I quipped, then hastily added, 'though with good reason.'

'Exactly,' he said. 'I didn't want that kiss to be the reason we didn't see each other between last Sunday and next.'

'That's not the reason at all,' I reassured him. 'And besides, in my experience, kisses come thick and fast at this time of year.'

'They do?' he faltered.

'Absolutely!' I laughed. 'I can barely get back from a trip to the pub from now until New Year without someone planting a smacker on my lips or a peck on my cheek.'

'Oh.'

'I blame the mistletoe headband,' I quipped. 'I shouldn't wear it, really.'

Poor Jude looked completely confused, but I hoped I'd done a convincing enough job of making him believe that I hadn't been staying out of his way on purpose. The abundant-kisses comment was all made up, but perhaps I should kiss someone else in front of him to really hammer the point home.

And in the spirit of making him believe me . . .

'Let me make it up to you,' I said to him. 'My ill-timed absence, that is. I've had an invitation to the Brambles distillery Christmas party on Saturday night. Why don't we go together? You can be my plus-one. It can be your last hurrah before you leave on Sunday.'

'A Christmas party?'

'Oh, sorry,' I said. 'That's not your thing, is it?'

In truth, I would be relieved if he turned the invitation down. It had been reckless of me to suggest it, prompted by the guilt of lying about avoiding him and the exact opposite of what I knew I should do to protect my heart.

'Not as a rule,' he said with a smile, 'but as it'll be my last night here, and as it's you who's asking, Bella, I suppose I could make an exception.'

'Great!' I choked out, feeling even more grateful that I'd given up on the oats. 'And as festive dress will be expected, you'd better ask Angus if the offer of one of his seasonal sweaters still stands.'

Jude looked as peaky as I felt after I suggested that.

Chapter 14

'You all set, then?' asked Holly when she arrived to pick me up ahead of the school fair on Friday. 'Actually, are you okay, Bella? You look a bit pale.'

'I'm fine,' I said. 'I didn't sleep well last night and I'm feeling it a bit today, that's all. And talking of being a bit off-colour, how's Jasper?'

I had, of course, messaged before to find out, but this was the first time I'd seen Holly in person since the emergency dash to the vets on the night of the switch-on. I hoped shifting focus to her canine calamity would stop Holly worrying about my peaky complexion or asking why I hadn't slept.

'Oh, he's all right,' she told me, but she sounded exasperated. 'Though still feeling a bit sorry for himself, which is hardly surprising. I've left him in Bear's care today.'

'And Queenie's,' I said, naming Bear's placid bull terrier who also featured in Holly's storytelling and illustrations.

'Yes,' Holly nodded, 'and Queenie's. Nothing much gets by her, so they should be all right left to their own devices for a few hours. What about Tink?'

'Oh,' I said lightly, 'she's hanging out with Jude for the afternoon.'

Holly looked at me and raised her eyebrows.

'He offered,' I told her with a shrug, 'and he's going to the hall later, so Tink can go with him and have a play date with her pack mates there. That's got to be better than staying home alone shut up in the apartment, hasn't it?'

'Absolutely,' Holly agreed. 'Heaps better. I do still think it's a shame you and Jude haven't hooked up, though, you know.'

'Oh, don't you start,' I groaned, rolling my eyes. 'You sound like Tim. And besides, how could I possibly get together with someone who doesn't celebrate Christmas? You should know me better than that.'

'Yes,' she said, 'I do, of course I do. I hope Jude at least believes in fairies, though. He does, doesn't he?'

'I've been too scared to ask him,' I grimaced, making her laugh. 'But talking of fairies, I've just realized I've forgotten my wings.'

I'd thought it would be fun to wear the pair I'd made for myself at the school fair. They were bound to go down well with the children, especially as I was wearing regular clothes rather than my beautiful bespoke fairy outfit. Adding wings to a casual Converse-and-jeans outfit would doubtless convince them that I was a real fairy. If I had wings even when I wasn't all dressed up, then it might be assumed – by the youngsters, at least – that they must be anatomically attached.

'Go and grab them, then,' said Holly, her mind successfully taken off Jude, 'and I'll finish packing the car.'

As Holly and I had a combined stall that afternoon and Holly needed extra space to sign the books she was selling, we had the largest table at the fair – and for much of the time, the longest queue, too.

I didn't think we had sold any more than the rest of the stallholders, but some of the pre-school children, and a lot of the adults, wanted to talk to Holly about her *Tall Tales from Small Dogs* and the inspiration behind them, and that slowed movement away from us down a bit. I knew it would be even busier once the school day had ended, and I kept a constant eye on my stock, making sure I replaced every fairy sold in preparation for the post-bell rush.

As well as piles of books, Holly had wonderful banners featuring photos of the real-life Queenie and Monty and lots of her time was spent posing for pics in front of those.

'Are you still up for our collab?' she asked me just as the bell rang to signal the end of the school day and we braced ourselves for the post-pick-up throng.

'Absolutely!' I told her. 'Like I said before, as soon as you've given me a brief, I'll start creating.'

'I thought that's what you were going to say, but I just wanted to be completely sure.'

'Any particular reason why?' I asked, as I set out a couple more fairies and a few of the trial run kits. 'You weren't doubting me, were you?'

I'd produced a laminated sheet to go with the kits, explaining that they were slightly discounted because they were a new product and that anyone who emailed me feedback and pics of their finished results would qualify for money off their next purchase from a certain range of my winged friends. There was also a small extra discount for any images shared online which tagged me, too.

'Absolutely not,' Holly confided, 'but I do have a reason for double-checking with you today.'

'Go on.'

'I was wondering how you'd feel about me dropping a few hints about us teaming up next year to some of the parents. I have it on good authority that the mums' network around here works faster than the best fibre optic broadband.'

'Sounds good to me,' I laughed. 'And I know for a fact that The Laurels care home has an impressive network of info-sharing, too, so if you whisper in a few ears there you'll have pretty much covered the entire community.'

'Brilliant!' Holly beamed as the doors opened and the hall began to fill up with pushchairs, parents and dozens of children, all noisily ecstatic to have the weekend ahead of them.

At least, I initially assumed that that was what the noise was about, but it soon became obvious that there was more of a reason behind the commotion than the fact that it was three-fifteen on a Friday in November.

'May!' Holly gasped as the crowd parted and a striking woman dressed in a vibrant poncho and heeled boots, and with a dachshund tucked under her arm, strode towards us.

'It's May Madison,' I heard a teacher next to me say breath-lessly. 'It's May Madison!'

'And Monty!' squeaked the closest child. 'It's Monty from the books!'

'What on earth are you doing here?' Holly laughed, warmly embracing Bear's mum and kissing Monty's head.

'I thought it might be fun,' May said, a twinkle in her eye. 'I telephoned the headteacher to check it would be okay, and after promising that I wouldn't let Monty lick the pupils to death and would keep him on a tight leash, they agreed.'

'I don't believe it,' Holly said, shaking her head. 'I'm so thrilled to see you. I would have called the local press if I'd known,' she added mischievously.

'All in hand,' May said smoothly, then turned to me. 'Now, who is this delightful winged creature?'

Holly introduced us, but only very quickly, as there were already so many children waiting to meet Monty and adults hoping for an autograph and photos with both May and Holly.

'Right,' May said regally, 'form an orderly queue and we'll make a start, shall we? We've got plenty of time for everyone.'

'Oh, I love your wings!' said a young boy in uniform a few minutes later. He hadn't yet spotted Monty, but I knew that when he did, I'd immediately lose his attention, so I quickly turned to the side so he could see them properly. 'Mum!' he shouted. 'Come and look at this fairy. She's got proper wings!'

His mum turned out to be Kirsty, someone I had gone to school with and someone I knew couldn't keep a secret to herself for more than five seconds. Thankfully she hadn't been part of the fairy fallout fiasco, but she would be the ideal candidate to share my and Holly's exciting news and trigger the word spreading throughout the Fens.

'Hello, Kirsty,' I smiled. The boy looked amazed that I knew her name. 'How are you?'

'I'm good,' she said, as she picked up one of the fairy kits. 'Oh, you're right, Tommy,' she loudly whispered and winked at me. 'She does have wings, so she's definitely a genuine fairy.'

Tommy looked thrilled and began earnestly looking at everything on the stall.

'How about you, Bella?' Kirsty asked me. 'How are you?'

'Great.' I smiled. 'Brilliant, actually, and I'm about to embark on a new venture with someone very special, aren't I, Holly?'

'It's the *Tall Tales* lady!' Tommy hollered. 'Mum, I told you she was going to be here.'

'It's his favourite book,' Kirsty told me, even though I'd already guessed as much. 'He won't go to sleep until I've read at least one story from it.'

Tommy was looking at Holly with just as much admiration as he'd previously bestowed upon me. I had a feeling he was going to be thrilled about our announcement.

'I'm really pleased you like my stories,' Holly said to him, 'and next year, they're going to be even better. Can you guess why?'

Tommy shook his head.

'Because the dogs are going to be joined by one of Bella's fairies!'

'No way!' Tommy gasped, looking between us. 'That's awesome.'

'It is,' Kirsty said with a nod. 'Congratulations, Bella.'

'Thank you,' I said, and smiled, suddenly realising the impact that Holly's collab offer might potentially have on my business.

'And in that case,' said Kirsty, picking up one of the kits as well as a couple of the other fairies, including one Tommy had had his eye on, 'we'd better get in here quick, Tommy, before word gets round and Bella sells out.'

'And when you're sorted here,' Holly took great pleasure in saying, 'there's someone extra special I'd like you to meet, Tommy.'

Just at that moment, a family stepped away from the stall and Tommy spotted Holly's VIP guests.

'Is that *Monty*?' his little voice trembled.

'It is,' Holly said, nodding.

'The real one?'

'The one and only.'

Holly's tactic to share our plan was a good one, and May turning up with no fuss or fanfare proved to be a masterstroke, too. By the end of the afternoon, the whole school was buzzing with our news, folk had come in from town to see May and Monty and our stall was practically empty. Holly only had three books left, which she was planning to donate to the school library, and most of my crates were completely empty.

With the Wynthorpe Hall Festive Fair happening in just over a week, I was going to have another busy few days replenishing my stock. At least, I supposed, that would go some way to taking my mind off Jude not being around anymore. Damn. I'd almost made it through the afternoon without thinking about him.

Once he'd squeezed his way back into my head, I couldn't think of anything or anyone else. I'd been a fool to invite him to be my plus-one at the Brambles party, but it was too late to do anything about that now. Uninviting him might potentially make him resent the season even more, so I wasn't about to do that, and I couldn't feign a bug because it would look like an unbelievably speedy recovery the next day when I got stuck into decorating the house after Jude left. And at least one of my friends would be bound to pick me up on that.

Jeanie definitely would, and she could be like a dog with a bone when it came to sniffing out secrets. It was lucky for me that she'd been able to accept that not even Jude's beautiful blue eyes and long, dark lashes could make up for his lack of festive cheer, making him a brief-fling non-starter. She'd be shocked for life if she could see the genuine truth I currently carried within my heart.

As far as the party was concerned, I supposed my best bet to avoid falling further for Jude in the brief time we'd still got before he left, and which I'd stupidly ensured we'd be spending together, was to get him paired off talking with someone else and avoid all alcohol. And mistletoe. And to simply carry on pretending. How hard could that be? And it would only be for a few hours . . .

'Earth to Bella.'

But it would be hard, even if I only had to maintain the pretence for a few minutes. Perhaps the bug option wasn't such a bad idea. After all, I'd spent the afternoon in a primary school, surrounded by under-twelves, and the air must be full of bugs and germs . . .

'Bella?'

'Sorry,' I said, zoning back in.

'Are you sure you're okay?' Holly frowned, clapping the back of her hand against my forehead. 'You do feel a bit warm, and I said when I picked you up that you looked pale.'

She didn't know it, but she was handing me the excuse to bow out of attending the party on a plate.

'Shall I get you a chair?'

'Here,' May said kindly as she quickly jumped up and put Monty down on the hall floor. 'Have this one.'

All I had to do was pretend just the tiniest bit and the problem would be solved, but when it came to the crunch, I couldn't bring myself to do it. For a start, I'd been looking forward to the party for weeks, and had even picked up a new dress for it. And more importantly than that, Jude had agreed to come. Given that he'd now told me why Christmas was something he struggled with celebrating, that felt like a huge concession. He'd said he'd come because it was me who had asked him, too, so I couldn't really let him down, could I?

'No, no,' I therefore said, waving Holly's kind concern and May's generous offer of a chair away. 'I'm good, but you're both loves for worrying. I'm only feeling hot because it's so warm in here.'

'But you really zoned out there, Bella,' Holly said, still sounding worried, while May nodded in agreement.

'Well, of course I did,' I laughed. 'You know me, I'm always away with the fairies.'

Chapter 15

I'd decided as soon as the Brambles party invitation landed that I was going to go all out and get dressed up to the nines for it, and I had now resolutely decided that just because I was going to attend it with a man I was trying my hardest not to fall in love with and who was leaving the area the very next day, I was not going to change that plan. Not even if it put me at potential risk of experiencing another of his knee-weakening kisses.

Being preoccupied with thoughts of those kisses did nothing for my ability to apply eyeliner with a steady hand, and it took three attempts before I was satisfied with the look I was aiming for. Thankfully, my curls had been easier to tame, and the casual up-do, secured with a diamanté claw and a couple of sparkly clips, was perfect.

I was still scrutinising my reflection in the bedroom mirror when my phone alarm went off, reminding me that it was time to go. I had spent literally hours getting ready and couldn't help wondering if I would have gone to quite so much trouble if I wasn't going to be heading out with Jude. The outfit would have been the same, but I couldn't remember the last time I'd painted my fingernails *and* toenails.

Not that anyone was likely to see my feet that evening, but the head-to-toe treatment I'd treated myself to did make me feel good. A quick spritz from my Jo Malone Velvet Rose and Oud, a kiss on the head for Tink, and I was finally good to go.

I could hear Jude in the hall, so I negotiated the stairs with extra care and resisted the urge to adjust the hem on the sapphire-blue sequin shift dress I'd found in my favourite local charity shop and which I'd teamed with silver heels and a small clutch bag. The bag was second-hand, too, but the shoes were new and, if I was being honest, not all that comfortable.

'I thought we'd take my car—' Jude began.

His words trailed off when he turned around. His mouth fell open, and his eyes widened as he took in what I was wearing. His reaction was comedic, but it didn't make me want to laugh. I was more inclined to throw myself into his arms, which was absolutely not the correct or appropriate response, even if he had made me feel like a million dollars.

'You were saying?' I said, trying my hardest not to look as gratified by his reaction as I felt. I had supposedly dressed for myself, after all, not to please a man. Not even Jude.

'Uh,' he stammered, 'I was going to say we could go to the party in my car, but never mind that for a moment.' He smiled. 'Bella, you look absolutely stunning.'

'Thank you,' I said, smiling back.

I was rubbish at accepting compliments but bit back the usual inclination to shrug it off and start going on about how it was mostly make-do and mend and cheap as chips.

'I mean,' Jude went on, 'that is, you always look lovely, but I've never seen you dressed like this. So smartly, I mean, for a party.'

'I don't think I'd get on very well making fairies in this

outfit,' I said, thinking how wonderful it was to hear him so tongue-tied, even though I knew I shouldn't have allowed myself to feel so thrilled. 'But I'm pleased you like it. As you know, I do love to make an occasion out of things, and especially occasions to do with Christmas.'

Knowing for certain that Jude thought I looked as good as I felt was no help in the not-falling-further-for-him stakes, and I needed to move the conversation on. I couldn't compliment him on his outfit, because he had his coat done up and a scarf around his neck. He did smell very good, though, but I could hardly say that.

'I do know you have a fondness for occasion-making,' he said, smiling again. 'And you're right, that's definitely not a workday dress.'

'I think we'd best get going,' I said, before my head really started to swell. 'And I honestly don't mind driving us there and back, because I'm not planning to drink tonight.'

I would have to change my shoes before I got behind the wheel, though. And knowing me, I'd most likely end up staying in my Converse.

'Funnily enough, I'm not drinking, either,' Jude told me. 'As I'll be driving tomorrow, I'd rather not have anything tonight.'

'You aren't planning to head off that early, though, are you?'

'No,' he said, 'not too early. Though I daresay you'll be itching to get moved into the house as it's the first of December tomorrow, won't you?'

'Don't worry about that,' I told him, reaching around him for my coat, which he then took and held open for me to slip on, 'I have plenty of things I can get on with to celebrate the day without having to be in the house.'

'Why does that not surprise me?' he laughed.

'Because in the month you've been here,' I laughed back, 'and after our rocky start, you've got to know me pretty well, after all.'

In the end, we did take Jude's car, and the heated seats were a revelation. I felt cosily cocooned in the warm interior, and it did feel rather nice to be driven for once as opposed to being the person doing the driving. It was a shame it was dark already, because I would have loved to have admired the landscape as we headed right into the Fens, which was where Brambles was located.

'Here we are,' I said, pointing out the sign for the distillery, even though it would have been impossible for Jude to miss it because it was so brightly lit.

He pulled off the drove road onto the drive, and the sight which met our eyes made my seasonal spirit soar. There were potted Christmas trees lit with tiny warm white lights flanking the door, and I could see the reception area had been transformed with more trees and vast swags all decorated to match the colours of the Brambles branding. It looked like the perfect glittering haven in the dark landscape, and I couldn't wait to get inside.

Jude parked the car in one of the few spaces that were left, then rushed around to open my door.

'Are you sure it's all right that I've come?' he asked, sounding a little nervous. 'I'm not going to know a soul, am I?'

Before I had an opportunity to reassure him, a mud-splattered four-by-four pulled up next to us and Holly and Bear climbed out.

'There you are,' I said to Jude, who was already looking relieved. 'You know two people already.'

'Three,' he nodded, as Bear opened the rear door of Holly's truck and Jeanie inelegantly jumped out.

'You made it!' I called, smiling at her.

'Aunt Evelyn said I deserved a night off.' She grinned, then readjusted her dress, which had ridden up on the drop out of her seat.

'I couldn't agree more,' I replied, nodding. 'Let's get inside. It's freezing out here.'

There were lots of other guests already inside, and the warm air that wafted out to greet us was filled with the traditional pine and cinnamon scents of Christmas, as well as a hearty heated punch, which I knew was going to pack a literal punch. I mentally reaffirmed that I wouldn't be touching that, even though I didn't now have to drive us home.

'Hello, hello!' said Jack, the distillery owner, as he rushed over. 'Thank you all for coming. As you can see, it's almost a full house already, so we're in for a fun night.'

I introduced him to Jude, who he made very welcome, then Tilly, Jack's partner, showed us the room they had set up with racks for everyone to hang their coats on.

'Oh, Bella!' gasped Jeanie as I undid and pulled off my coat. 'That dress is stunning.'

'Wow!' agreed Holly. 'I don't think I've ever seen you so dressed up.'

'Well, you two look gorgeous, too,' I told them, because they did.

'And what about me?' asked Jude, and Jeanie, who could see him over my shoulder, began to laugh. 'Hey!' he objected. 'I'll have you know this was the best of the bunch.'

I spun around to look at him.

'Oh my god!' I laughed, too. 'Where did you find that?'

'Where do you think?' He grinned.

The large jumper he was wearing had a black background, but there was a huge blue, glittery stag on the front and almost every inch that wasn't stag was covered in shimmering silver stars.

'Angus!' Holly and Jeanie said together, and Jude nodded.

'I need sunglasses to even look at it,' I said, making a show of shielding my eyes from the glare as the light caught it.

'Wait,' Jude said. 'You haven't seen the best bit yet.'

He lifted the waistband and fiddled with something underneath, and after a second's delay, the antlers on the stag began to flash madly.

'No way!' squealed Jeanie, clapping her hands together.

'Ah, mate,' said Bear, who was wearing a red checked shirt and black jeans. 'You've shown me right up.'

'Sorry,' Jude laughed.

'But I thought you hated Christmas.' Holly frowned.

'He does,' I whispered.

'I do,' Jude said more loudly. 'But Bella invited me along this evening, and I thought it would have been churlish not to enter into the spirit.'

'I love that you've done this,' I said, then felt my face flame.

'And I love that you've colour-matched,' Jeanie took the greatest pleasure in pointing out. 'You look like a proper pair. You'll have to stick together tonight.'

'Oh yeah,' said Holly, pulling out her phone. 'Let's get a photo of you.'

'Not in here,' I said, keen for that not to happen.

My heart was being stupid again. And having a reminder of

Jude's outfit after he'd left tomorrow and knowing the reason he'd gone to the effort of wearing it was not going to help it settle down or aid my ability to quickly get over him.

'Let's go and join the party and find a festive backdrop,' I suggested, but with the intention of doing nothing of the sort.

Jamie and Angus had just arrived when we all stepped out of the cloakroom, and Angus immediately collared Jude, which gave me the opportunity to slip away and mingle with some of the other guests without feeling guilty about deserting him or missing out on the photo opportunity.

Every aspect of the party was wonderful. The Christmas dinner-themed canapes were utterly moreish, and the mocktails, which were the only drinks that I was determined to taste, were delicious, too. Jack and Tilly were the perfect hosts and introduced me to Fliss, who ran a supper club championing local food and drink on her nearby family farm, which I still hadn't got around to visiting.

'My grandad gifted me one of your fairies for my birthday, Bella,' Fliss told me. 'And I absolutely love it.'

'Oh, thank you,' I said, 'I hope it's bringing you luck.'

'So far, so good,' she said with a wink, just as a guy swooped by and whisked her off to dance.

'This is my partner, Eliot,' she called as she disappeared into the crowd. 'I'll introduce you to him later.'

I gave her a thumbs-up, because there was no way she'd be able to hear me.

'Come on, Bella,' said Owen, suddenly appearing in front of me. He had been the Wicked Witch at the Hallowe'en party in the pub, and I was pleased to see that the green face paint which had given me the creeps had washed off. 'Let's hit the dance floor, shall we?'

'Go on, then,' I said, letting him take my hand and lead me through to a much larger room, which had a DJ set-up and had already attracted quite a crowd.

I never needed asking twice to dance and I certainly didn't need a drink in me before I said yes. I had no idea if I was a good or bad mover, but I was an enthusiastic one, and I'd danced with a few people by the time I noticed Jude standing on the sidelines. He was tapping his foot in time to 'Lola's Theme', which I absolutely loved, but was making no attempt to come and join in, even though he could see me and Jeanie.

'Why isn't Jude dancing?' I bellowed in Jeanie's direction.

'Dunno!' she said, spinning around me. 'I'll go and see if I can grab him, shall I?'

I didn't have time to answer her, because Owen appeared at my side again and, with no preamble at all, planted a whiskery kiss on my cheek.

'Hey!' I protested loudly as the tune began to fade out, taking some of my exuberance with it.

'Not good?' he said, looking shocked that I had so vehemently objected.

'No,' I said. 'Not good.'

'But I'm packing this,' he said, holding up a plastic sprig of mistletoe that had seen better days.

'That doesn't mean you can just go around kissing people, Owen,' I scolded.

'Sorry,' he said, pulling a face. 'I should have asked you first, shouldn't I?'

'Yes,' I said seriously, 'never assume consent.'

He looked chastened, but I wasn't going to tell him not to worry about it. The alcohol units coursing around his system didn't justify his bad behaviour.

'I'm sorry,' he apologized.

'Here, mate,' said Kieran, who had also been at school with us and who I had noticed was watching our exchange with interest, 'let me show you how it's done.'

I wondered what I was in for, and a few guests who were dancing near to us were openly looking at the three of us, too.

'Bella,' Kieran said seriously, 'in the spirit of mistletoe season, may I kiss you, please?'

'That's more like it,' I applauded happily. 'See, Owen? That's how it's done. Yes, Kieran,' I graciously added, 'you may kiss me.'

I had been expecting another chaste peck on the cheek, but Kieran made it a full-on smacker on the lips.

'I meant you may kiss me on the cheek, you twit!' I told him as he stepped away, initially looking thrilled with himself.

'Oh,' he said, his smile vanishing. 'I thought . . .'

'Perhaps we need to be a bit more specific,' suggested Owen to his friend.

'Either that,' I advised, 'or ditch the mistletoe completely and don't go around kissing anyone else.'

They both thought that was a good idea, and we all carried on dancing through the next three songs with their sprigs tucked firmly in their trouser pockets. It wasn't until the DJ started playing Paul McCartney's Christmas classic, which had always been my and Jeanie's favourite, that I realized she wasn't on the dance floor – and she wasn't talking to Jude, either, because they'd both disappeared. I decided I'd go and find them once the song had finished, because it was too good a dancing opportunity to miss. This party, coupled with putting the lights up outside the house, was exactly what I needed to kick my seasonal celebrations off.

'It's a brand-new blend,' I heard Jack telling some other guests in the reception area as he began to pour rich ruby-coloured liquid into shot glasses after I'd left the dance floor. 'Bella, come and try this!' he called when he saw me. 'Jude said earlier that you both enjoyed the gin he picked up on the night of the switch-on.'

Where *was* Jude? I looked around the space, but still couldn't see him.

'I'm not drinking tonight,' I told Jack, as the other guests began to sip and make noises of deep appreciation.

'Driving?' Jack asked.

'No,' I told him.

'These are tiny measures,' he said. 'Sip one, just to get the taste.'

'Oh, go on, then,' I said. 'Just one small sip.'

I didn't stick to the one sip after I'd tasted it, but I did draw the line after my third sample.

'That really is delicious,' I told a gratified Jack.

It had warmed me right to my toes. Not that I was cold, having danced for so long, but there was something almost seductive about an internal warmth sparked from the taste of a rich, thick tipple.

'Another one?' Jack offered.

'No, thanks,' I said, 'but I'm definitely putting it on my Christmas list.'

'I'll get Tilly to bag you up a bottle to take away with you. We've almost sold out.'

'Did Jude like it?'

'He didn't try it,' Jack told me. 'I think he said he's driving tonight.'

'Of course he is,' I laughed, feeling foolish for forgetting. 'He's driving *me*.' Driving me to distraction. I might have spent a lot of the party dancing with other people, but Jude's generous commitment to entering into the festive spirit by wearing one of Angus's most outlandish Christmas jumpers had been at the forefront of my mind for much of that time. 'In that case, make it two bottles if you have enough, and I'll give him one for Christmas.'

I wasn't sure how he felt about festive gifts, but hopefully the drink would be a nice memento of his time in and around Wynbridge, even if he didn't want to associate it with the twenty-fifth of December. I was tempted to check the time then, to work out exactly how much longer in the county he'd got left, but knew that would bring my party mood down, so resisted.

'You haven't seen Jude, have you?' I asked Jack instead.

He shook his head.

'Not for a while now.'

I hoped he hadn't left and forgotten that he was supposed to take me with him.

'I'm going to see if I can find him,' I said, returning my empty glass to the tray Jack was holding.

'Okay,' he said. 'We've put loads of lights up in the gazebo, so if you don't find him in here, then he might have gone for a wander outside to sit under that.'

That did sound likely, given how full-on and festive the party was, and when I'd searched everywhere I could think of inside and checked that Jude's car was still visible through the reception area window, I knew Jack must have guessed right.

With the night so cold and clear, I grabbed my coat from the cloakroom before I slipped out and round the side of the building to where the gazebo was set up. Jack had been right about him and Tilly putting lots of lights in there. It was almost as bright as a summer's day, which turned out to be a blessing, as it saved me from what could have been a mortifying moment.

Having spotted Jude, I had been poised to shout out his name. He was unmistakeable in that jumper, even from the back, but I was relieved I hadn't called out when I realized that there was a woman sitting astride his lap and that they were engrossed in a very passionate clinch.

It was a few seconds before the shock wore off and I could look away. As I stumbled back towards the main building, I realized that Jude must have taken my talk of the abundance of Christmas kisses after our moment in the porch to heart and had decided to dish out a few of his own.

'Hey, Bella!' said a cheery voice. 'What have we missed?'

I looked up a second before I bumped into Jemma, who had just climbed out of a Wynbridge taxi with her husband Tom.

'Quite a lot, as it turns out,' I told her. 'But it's still in full swing.'

'We'd best get in there, then,' laughed Tom.

As they headed towards the party, I ran away from it. I caught the taxi up just before it pulled back onto the drove road and tapped on the window, scaring the poor driver witless.

'Sorry,' I apologized when he opened it. 'I didn't mean to make you jump. Oh, it's you, Nigel. Hello.'

'Bella,' said the man, frowning, who I recognized as school chum Kirsty's dad and Tommy's grandad. 'Are you all right, love?'

'Hey,' I said, trying to smile. 'Yes, I'm good, but I'm feeling all partied out now. Any chance you could run me home if you're heading back to town?'

'Of course,' he said. 'Hop in.'

Chapter 16

Nigel's taxi had barely reached the outskirts of town before I realized that my running away from the party like Cinderella on a bad day (or in this case, night) hadn't been the most mature or sensible response to the situation.

'Jeanie,' I breathed, when she answered my call.

'Bella?' she responded, her tone full of concern. 'Where the hell are you? We were all set to send out a search party.'

'Sorry,' I said. 'I had a killer headache come on all of a sudden, and there was a taxi on the distillery drive that could bring me home, so I took it.'

'But why didn't you say? Jude would have taken you back.'

I was tempted to tell her that I hadn't wanted to disturb him, and why, but I knew that if I said what I'd seen playing out in the gazebo, then she'd do the mental gymnastics and come to the right conclusion: that I'd left because I had been upset.

'The pain got so bad, I wasn't thinking straight,' I said instead. 'But you know where I am now, so no search party necessary. I'll talk to you tomorrow, yeah?'

'Well,' she said hesitantly, 'as long as you're sure you're okay?'

'I am,' I told her. 'I'm just going to get in, wash down some painkillers with a pint of water and go to bed. Will you thank Jack and Tilly for me? Apart from the headache, I had a great time at the party.'

'And I'll tell Jude you're okay, too.'

'Of course.'

'He was worried.'

I was surprised he'd noticed my absence given how occupied he'd been in the gazebo.

'I didn't mean to worry anyone,' I apologized.

'Well,' she said, 'I'm not worried now.'

'Good.'

'And you're not the only person who's disappeared,' she started to say, then swore. 'Shit, my stupid phone's about to die. I'll talk to you tomorrow, Bella, and don't forget—'

The call cut off, but I wasn't worried. I'd told her what I needed to say and, with a headache genuinely starting to develop, I was relieved when Nigel dropped me off at home and, having made a fuss of Tink and let her out and back in again, I could go to bed.

The headache had gone by the time I woke up early the next morning, and as I stared up at the ceiling, I felt a jumble of mixed emotions. The first of December was never usually anything other than a day to celebrate, so I wasn't sure how I felt about there being something other than unadulterated joy lingering about. There were so many lovely traditions that I was about to embrace, and I wanted to enjoy them all, whether I was feeling entirely upbeat or not.

Some of those traditions were of my own making, such as

hanging up the Christmas Day countdown bauble I'd found in a discount store, along with firing up my full-on festive Spotify playlist. Others were the result of years spent enjoying Christmas with Nanna, Grandad and Mum in this very house.

The first of those was putting on display my three advent calendars. They were the old-fashioned sort made from layers of card, and a few of the little doors relied on clear tape to keep them in place now that they'd been opened and closed so many times. This year, I was going to prop them up in the apartment and save creating a tableau around them until I'd moved properly back downstairs.

The same went for my kitchen hot chocolate station. There wasn't room for that in the apartment, what with all the bags of differently shaped marshmallows, the vast range of chocolate flavours and the variety of mugs, so, like the house decorations, its appearance would also be delayed.

Then there was the all-important and always pleasant task of deciding which copy of *A Christmas Carol* I would be reading. I had multiple copies and added to the collection every year. There was one I'd already had my eye on, so I would most likely curl up with that and a mug of simply made hot chocolate later in the day. The evening's entertainment would also be Dickens-themed. No one could match the Muppets when it came to telling the story of Scrooge on screen, but I loved *The Man Who Invented Christmas*, starring Dan Stevens, too, so it might end up being a proper movie marathon.

If I wasn't feeling sleepy after that (I usually would be as a result of the hours spent decking the halls, but this year was different because of Jude's continued presence and my desire to clean once he'd gone and before I got around to the decorating),

I supposed I could break out my beloved Dickensian DVDs. I always tried to watch one episode a day in the run-up to Christmas – as it had originally aired and as a kind of Victorian soap opera – but I never stuck to it because it was such compelling viewing.

When I had been planning this day during November, I had had the feeling that I was going to be keen to embrace anything to take the edge off knowing that Jude had properly gone. I had expected to feel a sharp pang when I thought about him packing up and leaving, but I didn't now, and I was rather taken aback when the sensation didn't land.

I kicked off the duvet and sat up.

It hit me then that even though I had been upset to see Jude kissing someone else in the gazebo, the spectacle had actually done me a favour. It had shifted my thoughts about the sort of guy I had thought he was from one category to another and helped to quell my surprisingly deep feelings for him as a result.

In spite of the fact that he was leaving town today and had previously said he felt something for me, he'd still hooked up with someone else last night. Before I'd seen him going for it in the gazebo, I hadn't seriously had him down as that sort of guy. I had briefly wondered if what had happened with Tabitha and his best friend had meant he could only commit to brief liaisons now but, I hadn't *really* thought that he might be someone who viewed relationships like . . . me. How ironic was that?

If he was the player I now had him pinned as, and if it hadn't been for the unexpected deep feelings I'd developed for him and which had made me back off in an effort to save my heart, then we really could have had some fun . . .

I heard the front door slam and resisted the urge to look out of the window to see if the noise heralded the departure of the woman Jude had been with last night. I supposed it wasn't impossible that he might have invited her back, but I hoped he hadn't. That would have really upset me, and knowing how differently I was already viewing him, I wasn't going to risk pushing the change in my opinion of him even further. I still wanted to like him, even if he was getting ready to head off.

'There's no way he would have asked her back, is there, Tink?' I asked my canine confidante.

She cocked her head and barked.

'No,' I said, nodding. 'Of course he wouldn't have done that.'

My phone buzzed with an incoming message, and I picked it up, assuming it would be Jeanie telling me the rest of what she'd started to say before her battery gave out. However, it wasn't Jeanie, it was Jude. And he was asking if I was alone.

'Yes, I'm alone,' I said aloud as I typed out the words and pressed send.

I then immediately sent another saying that Tink was with me, so I wasn't entirely on my tod. Jude then asked if he could come up, and I told him he could.

'Shall I ask him if he wants to watch the Muppets with us?' I asked Tink as I heard Jude running up the stairs. 'I suppose I could put it on earlier than usual, couldn't I? I could use it as a sort of feelings litmus test.'

That time, she didn't offer an opinion, and I opened the door.

'Hey,' I said.

'Hey,' said Jude.

It could have been my imagination, but he looked different.

I couldn't put my finger on what it was or even if I would have thought that had I not seen him kissing someone else, but I felt it nonetheless.

'Come in,' I said, when he lingered on the threshold. 'I was just about to put the kettle on. Would you like tea? Or a coffee?'

'No,' he declined. 'I'm good. Thanks, though.'

'Did you enjoy the party?'

'Yeah,' he said with a nod. 'Yeah. It was good. Thank you for taking me as your plus-one.'

Last night, on the taxi journey home, I had been regretting that, but now I was pleased I'd done it. It was already feeling easier to be around him and for me not to feel the same way about him as I had before. And he hadn't even left yet.

'So why did you ask me if I was on my own up here in your message?' I questioned, when he didn't say anything further, but just stood there with his hands in his pockets.

Jeanie must have told him that I'd said I'd left the party with a headache.

'Oh,' he said, clearing his throat, 'that guy you were kissing—'

'Which one?'

I had meant it as a joke, but Jude didn't look amused.

'Owen, I think Jeanie said his name was,' he said croakily, his Adam's apple bobbing as he swallowed.

'Owen,' I said and nodded. 'He actually kissed me. I didn't kiss him.'

'Well, whatever,' Jude said more loudly. He sounded completely hacked off, but given that he'd kissed someone else, too, I didn't think that was entirely fair.

'Owen disappeared at the same time as you, and we wondered . . .'

'What did you wonder?' I frowned.

'If you'd left with him.'

'I told Jeanie I had a headache,' I said, a little more waspishly than I meant to.

I was annoyed that any of them thought I'd not been telling the truth, but especially Jude. How dare he – or anyone else, for that matter – make that assumption about me and Owen. I was about to say as much, but then I remembered that I'd told Jude that the only sorts of relationships I went in for were brief dalliances, so of course the fact that Owen and I had disappeared at the same time after he'd kissed me made the prospect of us being together entirely plausible.

'The headache was a real thumper,' I said less harshly. 'And I definitely wasn't with Owen.'

Jude put up his hands.

'I'm not bothered if you were or you weren't, Bella,' he said, which stung a bit, even though it shouldn't have. 'And I wasn't judging you either way. I just wanted to make sure that I wasn't interrupting anything before I came up here.'

'Well, as you can see, you're not,' I said. 'So, what can I do for you?'

I busied myself making calming chamomile tea and wondered how I could get us back on a friendlier footing before I asked if he wanted to watch the Muppets, while he gave Tink, who had plodded over, a fuss. I almost berated myself out loud when it suddenly dawned on me that watching the film was the last thing he'd want to do.

Jude was a man who'd had his heart smashed at Christmas and as a result put as much distance between himself and all things festive as possible. Granted, he'd helped me make mince pies and attended the party last night, but neither of those things were anywhere near as seasonal as Kermit crooning 'One More Sleep'. I decided I wouldn't ask him, after all.

'I've only actually come up to ask you what you want me to do with the house key,' Jude said, as he took it out of his pocket. 'But I suppose I might as well give it to you now, mightn't I?'

'Now?' I echoed.

I looked at the key but didn't take it, and he set it down on the worktop.

'I've stripped the bed, emptied the bin and piled the towels with the rest of what needs washing, per the instructions in the house handbook,' he added gruffly.

I hadn't been expecting him to leave so early. For some reason, I'd got it in my head that he'd still be here for the best part of the day.

'I know the place will need a clean, but it's not too bad,' he went on. 'Nothing worse than a regular housework day, I wouldn't have thought.'

'So you're leaving now?' I said.

'Yes,' he confirmed. 'Well, leaving here, anyway. I'm going to have one last day at Wynthorpe with Catherine and Angus. I want to show them what I've written so far, along with my planning notes for the rest of it, and then I'll be properly off.'

'Right.' I swallowed. 'I see.'

'Oh,' he said, 'I almost forgot this.' He held out a small jute bag I hadn't noticed he'd carried in, with the Brambles logo printed on the side. 'Jack said you wanted two bottles.'

'One was for you,' I dumbly said, as he began to take the

bottles out. 'A memento to take with you. And you can keep the bag, too. I already have one.'

'Thank you,' he said, almost smiling, then returning one of the bottles to the bag. 'I'll look forward to trying it.'

'Maybe you could save it for Christmas Day,' I said quietly. 'Have a small glass and see if it brings back thoughts of me. And Tink,' I added hastily.

I tried to smile, too, but like him, I couldn't quite manage it.

'I might just do that,' he said. 'Though I won't need it to remember you, Bella. I'm not going to forget you in a hurry.'

'Are you not?' I asked, hating the wobble in my voice.

'Of course not,' he said.

He held my gaze for a second, and I willed myself not to cry. Why was I even thinking about crying when my feelings for him had already allegedly shifted away from what they had formerly been? It was a ridiculous reaction and hugely inconvenient, too.

'And I won't forget you, either, Tink,' he said more loudly, making her tail thump.

I took a calming breath while he focused on her, rather than me.

'Right,' he said, as he straightened back up again, 'I better get to the hall. If I get a move on, I might be in time for Dorothy's legendary breakfast.'

'Yes,' I said with a nod, 'I daresay you will be.'

'Thank you for saving my sanity these last few weeks,' he said, as he went to turn away.

'It's been my pleasure,' I told him.

'I know it was a genuine sacrifice for you not to be able to move back into the house when you usually would, and especially when you have so much work to do. But I really do appreciate it.'

'It will be reflected in my bill,' I quipped.

'Make sure it is.' He nodded. 'You take care.'

'You, too,' I said, picking up my cup. 'It's been lovely getting to know you, Jude.'

'Especially after I stopped being such a prat,' he laughed.

I couldn't believe that was going to be the last thing he would say to me, but it was. Because when I looked up again, he'd gone.

Chapter 17

I had discovered that one of the most valuable skills to develop to ensure a life was well lived was fine-tuning the art of processing, by which I meant carefully digesting both the good and the bad. If something joyful happened, then celebrating to mark the occasion would make it even more unforgettable. If something tragic occurred, then leaning into the emotions as they surfaced would pay dividends for well-balanced mental health in the long run.

I wasn't sure which category Jude's departure fell into, but I was determined, after I'd heard him close the house door for the last time, that I was going to be kind to myself when it came to dealing with him flitting back out of my life as speedily as he'd landed in it.

I might have now been able to get back into the house and put the decs up, and I might have been almost convinced that my feelings for Jude had started to ebb away, but I wasn't going to deny that I *had* felt them. Properly felt them, which was something completely unique for me and therefore warranted the time I was willing to allow myself to comprehensively move on. Taking my time over moving back downstairs, as opposed to rushing to do it, was doubtless going to facilitate that, and that was what I decided to do.

'Come on, then, Tink,' I said, once I'd dressed, eaten breakfast and felt ready to face whatever awaited me on the rearranging and cleaning front downstairs. 'Let's tread lightly, with just a little bit of housekeeping to kick things off.'

Just as Jude had said, there was nothing to do beyond what I would usually do on a regular housework day, and he really had followed my requests in the handbook to the letter. I couldn't deny that I felt something stir when I swept up the bed linen and it smelled intensely of him, but I bundled it all into the machine and set it on a hot wash, then opened all of the windows to let the cold winter air rush through and take the last traces of his seductive, masculine scent away with it.

By the end of the day, I'd returned the house to the exact condition it had been in when Jude had rolled up earlier than expected a few weeks ago. It wasn't Christmas-ready, but it was once again back to how I preferred it either side of the seasonal celebration – colourful and just on the right side of full up.

There was now room to manoeuvre in the hall again, too, with my work boxes dotted about the rooms where I wanted them. Looking around, it was as though the last month had never happened. Well, that was what I kept telling myself – and was still telling myself when someone knocked at the front door.

I knew I hadn't quite succeeded in making myself believe it when I rushed to answer the door, immediately thinking (and secretly hoping) that it was Jude coming back for some unfathomable reason. Clearly more processing time was needed.

'I've got a parcel for Bella Bailey,' said a delivery guy I hadn't met before. 'I was going to just leave it in the porch, but I saw the car on the drive and wanted to say how lovely your lights look. I hope you don't mind.'

'Oh,' I said, looking at my and Jude's handiwork and feeling a pang over our one and only kiss, 'no, I don't mind at all. Thank you so much.'

I was truly touched that the guy, who doubtless had a van stuffed full of parcels, had taken the time to tell me that.

'My daughter would love these,' he added, pointing at the fairies. 'She's fairy mad.'

'Actually,' I said proudly, 'I made those myself.'

'You're not "Away with the Fairies" Bella, by any chance, are you?' he surprised me by asking.

'Yes,' I laughed, thinking that that description was currently right in more ways than one. 'That's me.'

He nodded and smiled as he pulled out his phone.

'My little Victoria takes this everywhere with her,' he said, showing me a photo of a little girl dressed in tulle and carrying a fairy I recognized from a collection I'd made earlier in the year. 'She won't believe it when I tell her I've met you. You've made my day.'

'And you've made mine,' I told him. 'Give Victoria my love, won't you?'

'I call her Plum.' He smiled again, this time handing me the parcel I couldn't remember ordering. 'I'll tell her you know her name now, and she'll think that's magic.'

'Thank you!' I called after him, before ushering Tink back inside with the biggest smile on my face.

When I walked back into the house, I realized how cold it was and quickly closed the windows before opening the parcel.

There wasn't so much as a lingering hint of Jude now, and I knew that was for the best. At least, there hadn't been any hint of him until I opened the parcel.

The contents made my heart lurch.

'Saw this and thought of you,' I whispered, swallowing over the lump which had formed in my throat as I opened the novelty kitchen timer and read the accompanying note.

It wasn't a chicken-shaped one like Jude's nan had had, but a plump and very jolly-looking Father Christmas, complete with shiny red nose and big white, bushy beard. It was perfect and I loved it. I set it on the kitchen worktop next to where the hot chocolate station would be going and glanced over at the clock.

I wondered if Jude was still with the Connellys at Wynthorpe Hall. If I set off immediately, I might just be able to catch him and thank him for the timer in person. I lunged for my keys, then realized how ridiculous that would look, chasing after someone when we'd already said goodbye.

'Come on, Tink,' I said, putting the keys down again and attempting to further close the space in my heart that Jude had started to fill, 'let's go and get ready to watch the Muppets.'

It did feel a little strange watching the film and reading *A Christmas Carol* upstairs in the apartment, but I had decided I wouldn't move properly into the house until I'd put the majority of the decorations up the next day. However, when I climbed out of bed on Monday morning, having spent the night tossing and turning, I realized that I wasn't going to enjoy decorating the rooms because of a worry that had landed in my head during the long, dark hours. The Wynthorpe Hall Festive Fair was happening at the weekend, and I was beginning to feel stressed about my stock levels because they were running low again.

Knowing a call from Mum was imminent, I messaged and told her I was going to be working all day so could she ring another time, and I also reassured her that she no longer had to worry about me falling for my temporary lodger and getting my heart broken because nothing further had happened between us and he'd left now anyway.

'Let's have a quick trip around the block,' I said to Tink, who was thrilled with the prospect of an early walk, 'and then it's down to work.'

Having the house to spread out and work in made a huge difference to my output, and even though I was still making one fairy at a time, it meant I could have all of the components lined up and arranged as I needed them, which sped the whole process up considerably. By late afternoon, I could see I was almost back to the fairy numbers I wanted to have, and if I set aside a few hours each day during the rest of the week to make more, I'd soon have enough.

It would have been useful to know the exact size of the stand I was going to be assigned at the weekend and, as Angus still hadn't let me know and because he was hard to pin down on the telephone, I decided that a quick run out to the hall was more than justified. It had absolutely nothing to do with the fact that it was the last place in the area that Jude had been, because that would have been ridiculous.

I'd thought about him a couple of times during the day, but not obsessively. He hadn't responded to the thank you for the timer message I'd sent to his mobile, so I guessed he wasn't obsessing over or missing me, either.

'Oh, Bella,' said Dorothy, an unusual frown etched deeply across her brow when she let me and Tink in via the hall's kitchen door. 'We wondered if you might call in at some point. Come in out of the cold, love.'

Tink scampered ahead and quickly joined her friends in the basket in front of the Aga.

'Can I offer you something to eat?' Dorothy asked, whipping my coat away almost before I'd shrugged it off. 'I daresay you got nothing there, did you?'

I didn't have time to answer before Catherine and Angus came in, and they both looked concerned, too. What was going on?

'Did they let you in?' Catherine asked me, wringing her hands.

'They wouldn't let *me* in,' Angus said grumpily. 'I'm not sure if it was really because I'm not a relative or because I'd previously had a run-in with the—'

'Will you let the girl speak?' Catherine cut in.

Angus looked chastened and sat down.

'How did you find him?' she asked me more gently.

I looked between the three of them, wondering what on earth they were referring to.

'I'm sorry, but I don't know what you're talking about,' I frowned. 'I've just called in to ask Angus what size table he's assigned me for the fair at the weekend.'

'It was listed in the notes I emailed,' he told me.

'I haven't had an email,' I said, shrugging.

'Oh, Angus,' Dorothy tutted.

'As it turns out, I don't think this fiasco is down to Angus,' Catherine responded, taking both Dorothy and me by surprise.

'I absolutely did send them,' he insisted.

'I know you did,' Catherine said with a nod.

'So where has the information got to?' Dorothy asked.

'I've just spoken to Jamie, and he reckons we must have had a Wi-Fi hiatus, which meant some of the emails didn't send,' Catherine carried on. 'Or something like that, anyway. You're not the first stallholder to get in touch, Bella, and I daresay you won't be the last. From what I can gather, potentially half of the list didn't go out. Jamie is going to send the notes to everyone again.'

'But you did pick up the message I left on your phone last night, didn't you?' Angus asked me.

'No,' I said, shaking my head. 'I haven't had a message from you, Angus. Or anyone else, for that matter.'

'On your mobile,' he said more seriously. 'Not the house phone.'

I unlocked my phone and checked my messages, just to be doubly sure.

'No,' I said, 'there's nothing. Why? What's happened?'

I wished they'd hurry up and tell me, because the looks on all of their faces suggested that it wasn't going to be good news.

'You said you'd let Bella know!' said Catherine, snatching Angus's phone up from the table and scrutinising the screen. 'You've messaged Bunty,' she said, almost grinding the words out. 'You messaged *Bunty* instead of *Bella*.'

'Oh dear,' said Angus, plunging a hand into his already messy hair. 'Their names must be next to each other on my contact list. Whyever hasn't Bunty responded?'

'Because she hardly ever looks at her phone,' said Catherine, thrusting Angus's mobile into his hands. 'And she probably couldn't work out how to reply, even if she wanted to.'

Any desire Catherine had previously felt to shift the blame over the unsent emails disappeared in view of this latest blunder, whatever it related to.

'Never mind Bunty,' Dorothy said impatiently. 'Don't you think you'd better tell Bella now?'

'Yes,' I said, pulling out a chair and sitting heavily on it. 'I wish you would. I'm starting to panic. What is it? What's happened?'

'It's Jude.' Catherine swallowed, clasping her hands together again. 'He left here quite late last night and was involved in a car accident.'

My heart suddenly felt like it was going to burst out of my ribcage.

'I thought I'd left you a message explaining what had happened,' said Angus, sounding upset, 'and that you had come here to tell us how you found him at the hospital.'

'Oh my god,' I gasped. 'No, I haven't been to see him, because I had no idea what had happened. Has he been badly hurt?'

'We don't know for sure,' said Catherine, 'but he's in the local hospital rather than King's Lynn or Peterborough, so he can't be that bad.'

'From what we can make out, he'd stopped on the road to let some deer cross,' said Dorothy, furnishing me with the few details they had cobbled together, 'but there was a car either heading towards him or approaching from behind that was going too fast, and it was that that lost control and ploughed into Jude's car.'

'I don't believe it,' I said, feeling both sick and faint as I imagined the scene in all its terrifying detail. 'Whyever didn't you keep ringing until I picked up, Angus?' I demanded.

'I don't know,' he said, sounding desperate. 'I wish I had now.'

'So do I,' said Catherine bluntly.

'So who let you know?' I asked, wondering why no one else had been in touch.

If Tim, or even one of his mates, had been on duty at the fire station, then surely he would have told Jeanie, who would have then called me.

'It was Jake from Skylark Farm,' said Dorothy. 'I don't think it happened all that far from his place, and he got caught up in the rescue traffic on his way home from town. A couple of the deer were injured, too, and sadly had to be . . .'

'I see,' I said shakily as her words trailed off.

I felt desperately sorry for the deer and didn't like the sound of there having been rescue traffic. That hinted at carnage rather than a shunt or slight prang.

'Here,' said Catherine, spooning sugar into a cup, then adding tea. 'Drink this, Bella. Your hands are shaking.'

'I'll make a fresh pot,' said Dorothy, whisking the teapot away. 'That one must be stewed by now.'

'I feel a bit foolish for reacting like this,' I said, looking at my hands as my lip began to tremble.

'Well, you shouldn't,' Angus said softly. 'From what Jude told us, we know you'd grown very fond of each other.'

I wondered what he had told them.

'So,' I said unsteadily, 'he's been in the hospital all night and for the whole of today and had no one with him.'

'I'm afraid so,' said Angus. 'Unless the hospital has managed to track down Jude's family. That is, assuming he has any. We never talked about his private life.'

I didn't think it would be very likely that he'd want his parents there, but then he might not have been in a state to say either way. I wished we knew what injuries he'd sustained and how bad they were.

'I wish I'd lied about being related to the dear boy now when I went to the hospital,' Angus carried on, making a wish of his own as I jumped up. 'I might have actually got on the ward then.'

'Until the ward sister spotted you,' Dorothy said, sniffing. 'Unfortunately, your reputation for hospital hijinks precedes you, Angus.'

'I need to go,' I said, reaching for my coat. 'I'll pretend I'm a relative. They'll have to let me in then.'

Angus shook his head.

'It's too late now,' Catherine said, with a nod to the clock. 'It's gone eight, and that's the cut-off on the wards. They're sticklers for keeping to the visiting hours.'

'And if that ruddy old ward sister is still on shift . . .' Angus muttered, but he was silenced by another stern look from his wife. She usually bore his madcap behaviour and mistakes with good grace, but this had clearly pushed her patience with him to the very end of its limits.

'But these are exceptional circumstances,' I said urgently. 'Poor Jude hasn't had a soul with him for twenty-four hours.'

Dorothy returned the teapot to the table.

'I daresay everyone thinks their circumstances are exceptional, Bella,' she said softly.

She was right, of course.

'What if I telephone the hospital instead?' I suggested eagerly. 'I'll say I'm Jude's partner and that I've only just received the message about the accident.'

'You'll be lucky if you get anyone on the ward to pick up,' Angus pointed out.

'The staff are always rushed off their feet,' Catherine sighed. 'They haven't got time to answer telephone queries from relatives, genuine or otherwise.'

I felt bad for suggesting it.

'In that case,' I said, 'I'll be ready for the start of visiting hours in the morning.'

'It's from ten o'clock, I think,' said Angus.

'I'll be there at nine forty-five, then,' I said firmly.

I couldn't bear the thought of Jude being on his own in the hospital, no matter what state he was in.

'Why don't you leave Tink here tonight?' Catherine suggested kindly. 'That way, you won't have to worry about how long you're going to leave her for at yours. And once you've seen Jude, you can come back here and fill us in and have a meal with us.'

'That's an excellent idea,' Dorothy agreed. 'I'll make it a moveable feast, so it won't matter what time you get here, there'll be something for you to tuck into.'

'And I can come with you to the hospital, if you like,' Angus offered.

Given that he'd already hinted that he'd had cross words with the nursing staff, I didn't think his presence would be any help at all, but it was kind of him to offer.

'Yes, please, to Tink staying,' I said, 'but no to you coming with me, Angus.'

He nodded resignedly.

'As I'm already in town and halfway there, I might as well go in on my own,' I added, trying to make him feel better.

I knew the message he'd muddled would still be playing on his mind and didn't want him feeling bad now that I did finally know what had happened.

'You can help Jamie double-check that all the stallholders have got the notes they need ahead of the fair at the weekend, Angus,' Catherine said decisively. 'That will be a much better use of your time.'

'All right,' he conceded. 'We'll leave Jude to Bella, then. I'm sure he'll be much happier in her capable hands.'

Chapter 18

After a restless night and with no Tink to keep me company in my heightened state of stress, I had whizzed through my morning chores and routine and was ready to set off for the hospital just before eight.

Given that it was only a fifteen-minute drive up the road, I knew it was far too early to arrive and considered trying to telephone the main reception to find out what I could about Jude's injury ahead of my visit. I had the hospital number already keyed into my phone and was just about to call but then changed my mind. Given the state I was in, I might well make a hash of the conversation and that could completely ruin my chances of blagging my way in to see him.

Ordinarily, in a crisis, I'd call Jeanie — and more recently, Holly, too — but the stressed state I was in also put me off contacting either of them. My anxiety and concern for Jude would make it obvious that I had more intense feelings for him than I had previously confessed to, and I didn't think I could deal with my friends knowing and wanting to discuss that on top of everything else.

I couldn't face breakfast and when I tried to settle downstairs to make a fairy or two, I quickly discovered that my shaking hands weren't conducive to doing that, either. I tried reading but couldn't focus on the words, then watching TV but could find nothing to hold my attention, and in the end I settled on moving the Christmas decoration boxes into the rooms they were destined for. The decs would have to go up soon. I was already three days behind my usual December routine, and if I didn't make a start before long, I'd never catch up.

By the time I had finished shifting the boxes, it was time to go, and I left the house wearing my most convincing 'concerned partner' expression, which, given how upset I was, wasn't a stretch at all.

'I'm here to see my partner,' I boldly told the hospital receptionist. 'I've just had a message, which somehow got delayed, telling me that he's been admitted here following a car accident on Sunday evening.'

The words caught in my throat, but that wasn't part of any act because saying them out loud was upsetting.

'I don't know which ward he's on.' I swallowed. 'Is there some way you can help me find him, please?'

'What's his name, my love?' the receptionist asked kindly, as she speedily pressed a few of the keys on her keyboard.

'Jude,' I told her. 'His name is Jude.'

'Jude what?'

'Sorry?'

'What's his surname?'

I felt heat begin to build in my cheeks. I couldn't remember if Jude had ever told me his surname, or if I'd known it and the shock of what had happened had knocked it clean out of my head.

'Oh,' I faltered. 'It's . . .'

'Bella?'

I spun round to find Kirsty standing behind me in a nurse's uniform.

'Oh, Kirsty!' I said, thinking how her dad in his taxi had come to my rescue at the Brambles party and now she might be about to, too. 'Hey.'

'Are you all right?' She frowned. 'You look a bit peaky.'

The blood which had formerly rushed to my face now felt like it had fallen to my feet.

'Yes,' I said with a nod. 'I'm okay. Sort of. I'm just trying to find someone, but I don't know which ward he's on.'

'It's someone called Jude,' the receptionist piped up, and I realized there were three other people waiting behind me to talk to her now.

'Leave it with me, Patsy,' Kirsty said briskly, moving me away. 'Come on, Bella. There aren't that many wards to choose from, so we're bound to find him at some point. He's not on mine, which narrows the search, and I'm early for my shift, so I'll help you look.'

'Are you sure?'

'Absolutely,' she insisted. 'Come on.'

Kirsty hit the jackpot with her second attempt, and while she introduced me to the nurse in charge, my eyes quickly scanned around the beds I could see in the ward opposite the nurse's station.

'There he is!' I said, the words coming out in a loud, strangled sob. 'That's him.'

Lying with his eyes closed in the bed furthest from the door and closest to the window, looking battered, bruised and deathly pale, was Jude.

'Oh my god,' I gasped. 'He looks terrible!'

'You go and sit with him,' the nurse who Kirsty was talking to said to me, 'and when he wakes up, he can fill you in on what happened.'

I'd been so desperate to find him, but in that moment my feet felt rooted to the spot. I didn't know what I had been expecting, but the sight of Jude in the hospital bed and looking so poorly tore my heart in two.

'Bella?' Kirsty said, lightly touching my arm. 'Do you want me to come with you?'

'No,' I said, coming out of my reverie. 'I'll be fine, but thank you. And thank you for helping me find him, too.'

'I'm sure he looks worse than he feels,' she said, smiling. 'Bruising can be like that. Go on. He'll be relieved to see you.'

I walked quietly on to the ward and sat as gently as I could on the chair next to Jude's bed. His hands were resting on top of the sheet, and I fought back the urge to take them in my own because I didn't want to wake him. I could now also see a bruise beginning to bloom on his right shoulder and wondered if that was from the seat belt tightening when the other car ran into his. I was staring at the livid colour of it when his eyelids began to flutter. I looked back at his face just as he let out a long breath and opened his eyes.

'Bella,' he croaked, as he turned his head and slowly focused on my face.

'Hey,' I said, my eyes filling with tears and the lump from before returning to my throat. 'What have you been up to, then?'

He awkwardly inched himself a little higher up in the bed, grimacing and gasping as he did so.

'Just trying to do a good deed.' He smiled weakly, after he'd taken another breath.

'I heard there were deer involved,' I said, leaning further forward in my seat and determinedly blinking my tears away. 'I hope they weren't Santa's.'

I immediately wished I hadn't said that, given the outcome for a couple of them.

'I'm not *that* averse to the season,' Jude said with a smile, then winced.

'Well, that's good to know.' I smiled shakily back. 'So what happened? Can you remember? You don't have to tell me if you don't want to.'

I let out a breath, aware that I was prattling on.

'I can remember,' he said, 'and I don't mind telling you. I'd stopped to let these few deer cross the road in front of me. They were almost away, but then suddenly, from out of nowhere, there was this car.' He swallowed, and I held my breath. 'It was absolutely flying, in spite of the icy conditions. It smacked into the back of me, and that shot my car into the path of a truck which was coming to a stop on the other side of the road.'

It sounded horrendous. I wondered what had happened to the other people involved.

'So you got hit at the front as well as the back?' I choked.

No wonder he looked so beaten up if it was a double impact.

'According to what the hospital staff have told me, I've got off quite lightly.' He shrugged, then groaned because the movement had pained him. 'That said, some of the details about what happened after the event are a bit hazy.'

That was probably no bad thing.

'Oh, Jude,' I said, wanting to give the driver who was going too fast a piece of my mind.

'I'm desperate to find out what's happened to my car,' he went on, sounding stressed, 'because it's got all my work in, my laptop and my luggage. Everything to do with the book I'm writing for the Connellys and all the copies of the documents they gave me. If that's all been lost or gone missing—'

'Hey,' I said, cutting him off, because he was looking even worse than when I first found him. 'Stop. You don't need to be worrying about any of that. I can find out where your car's been taken and get your stuff back for you. In fact,' I said, pulling out my phone, 'I'll get Angus on the case. He's desperate to do something to help.'

Especially now he knew he'd messaged someone else rather than me after the crash, but I didn't tell Jude that. He already found Angus frustrating to deal with, and there would be nothing to be gained from adding to his exasperation.

'The sister who was on duty yesterday said he'd tried to visit, but she wouldn't let him in,' Jude told me, as he struggled to reach for the cup of water on his bedside locker. I jumped up and passed it to him. 'I did appreciate her stopping him,' he told me after he'd slowly drained the cup, 'because I don't think I could have coped with seeing him. Not then, anyway.'

I nodded in understanding and poured more of the water.

'Well,' I told him, 'I don't think she would have let me on the ward, either, but I've blagged my way in thanks to an old school friend – and if anyone asks, I'm your partner.'

'My *partner*,' Jude echoed, raising his eyebrows.

'Yes.' I blushed, as an alarm started to sound. 'I had to say something and was worried it might be relatives or partners only.'

It wasn't until the nurse came over that I realized that the sound was coming from Jude's bed, but as far as I could see, he wasn't hooked up to anything.

'Can you turn that off?' the nurse asked me briskly, sounding cross.

'I haven't got anything to turn off,' I responded, feeling embarrassed and then mortified when I realized that I had. 'Oh, hang on,' I said, grappling in my bag. 'I'm so sorry,' I apologized, as I pulled out the Father Christmas kitchen timer, 'I must have knocked it when I got my phone out.'

I eventually worked out how to shut it down, and the nurse looked at me as if I were mad.

'I don't usually carry it with me,' I told her as my face flushed scarlet.

'Ow!' Jude winced, as he simultaneously laughed and held on to his ribs.

Clearly my discomfiture had amused him.

'Never mind,' said the nurse, holding up her hands. 'I don't need to know. We had that Angus Connelly in here yesterday. One eccentric a week is enough for any hospital ward.'

'I'm not eccentric . . .' I started to object, but she'd already gone.

Jude smiled with an uncomfortable nod to the timer. 'It arrived, then?'

'It did,' I said, holding the jolly chap up for him to see. 'And I love it.'

'Clearly,' he said, 'if you've taken to carrying it around.'

'I wanted to show it to you,' I explained. 'I thought it might break the ice if the conversation was a bit . . . stilted.'

Jude looked upset.

'I'm sorry I was in a bit of a weird mood the morning I left,' he said.

'Doesn't matter now.' I shrugged, knowing that if I considered it too deeply, then I'd find that I probably had been, too. 'And you haven't left, have you? You're still very much here.'

'Yes,' he said, frowning, 'and I've no idea what I'm going to do about that.'

He had a point, because he was in no fit state to carry on with his journey.

'Can you grab my phone?' he asked. 'I think it's in the locker. It was in my jacket pocket the night of the crash, which is how it didn't get lost along with everything else.'

'Nothing will be lost,' I reassured him. 'We'll track it all down in no time.'

'Looks like it's nearly out of battery,' he said once I'd handed the phone over, 'and there's at least two dozen missed calls and messages from the hall.'

'Everyone has been really worried about you,' I told him as I connected his phone to my portable charger before it shut down completely. 'Me included, since I found out what happened. I didn't know until last night, because Angus messaged someone called Bunty rather than me,' I said, letting slip what had happened in spite of my earlier conviction not to. 'Apparently, we're listed next to each other on his contacts list.'

'He has mentioned a Bunty to me.' Jude frowned in re-collection. 'I think she's a distant cousin and, to quote Angus directly, as mad as a box of frogs.'

I rolled my eyes at that. Bunty must have been *really* something if that was Angus's opinion of her.

'Oh crikey,' Jude said as he started to read through the
messages. 'Apparently, I'm not to worry about trying to carry
on with my journey or how I'll look after myself when I'm
discharged, because I'm to go back to the hall, where a downstairs room is being made up for me. To quote Angus again, I
can recuperate with the Connellys.'

He looked at me and pulled a horrified face, and I couldn't
say I was surprised by his reaction. I wasn't sure how much
recuperation he'd be able to do under the hall's roof, even
though everyone living under it had only the very kindest of
intentions.

'I do love the Connellys,' Jude went on, echoing my
thoughts just as a consultant walked on to the ward, 'but
they've got even more family about to descend for the
Christmas holidays, and those who are already there drove
me to distraction when I first moved in. Through no fault of
their own, of course . . .'

Clearly we were on the same wavelength, and he didn't have
to remind me of his reaction to his brief time spent living with
them. That had been the whole reason why he'd ended up
under my roof.

'Good morning, Jude,' the consultant said, smiling as he
strode over. 'How are you feeling this morning?'

'Like I've gone at least seven rounds with Muhammad Ali,'
Jude sighed, putting his phone down.

I wondered how much of that was to do with his injuries
versus the Connellys' kind offer to recuperate at the hall.

'If you'd gone seven rounds with Ali, my friend,' the

consultant laughed, 'you wouldn't be capable of talking to me right now.'

'That's true,' Jude agreed. 'I am still feeling pretty banged up, though.'

'I'm not surprised. You had quite a knock in that crash. Let's see if any more of the bruising is starting to come out.'

'I'll leave you to it,' I said, standing up.

'This is Bella,' said Jude, introducing me. 'My partner.'

There went my heart again. I tried to mentally chant *Jude kissed someone else, and I'm over him*, but it didn't help.

'You can stay, Bella,' said the consultant. 'This is only a quick check-up and examination. It won't take long.'

'No, it's okay,' I said, reaching for my bag. 'I have a call to make, so I'll come back in a minute.'

The Wynbridge winter air felt even colder after the tropical temperature inside the hospital. I wasn't sure if I was shaking because of that or the continued shock of seeing Jude looking so damaged.

He really was in a state, and if what I'd read online about post-car crash trauma the evening before was anything to go by, he was only likely to feel rougher over the next few days, or even weeks, as the bruising and stiffness made its presence felt. There might even be some psychological suffering associated with driving again for him to deal with, too.

'Bunty, is that you?' Angus asked, the second my call connected.

'No,' I tutted. 'It's me, Bella.'

'I know,' he said. 'I could see it was your number, I just thought a little joke . . . but under the circumstances, perhaps not. Have you got in? How is he?'

'Yes,' I said, 'I've got in, and we haven't really had a chance to talk through his injuries yet, but he doesn't look great and he's feeling terrible.'

'The poor boy!' said Angus, as if he were talking about one of his sons rather than an employee. 'I had a horrible feeling he wasn't going to be at his best, but we'll soon get him back on form. I've got loads planned to keep him occupied. I've messaged and told him that he must come here to recuperate. I'm more than happy to help him.'

'But aren't you going to be too busy organising the Festive Fair?' I tried on Jude's behalf. 'It's only a few days away now, after all.'

'There's not all that much to do,' Angus told me, sounding carefree. 'Jamie has it all in hand, and I'm on Winter Wonderland planning duty.'

'I'd forgotten about the Winter Wonderland,' I tried, 'that must take up even more of your time, Angus. Surely you won't have time to—'

'No, it's all easy peasy,' he cut in, sounding entirely unfazed. 'Now it's been running for a few years, it practically organizes itself, so I'll have plenty of time to help Jude.'

There didn't seem to be any way around it, and it hardly felt fair of me to keep pushing to find a reason for Jude not to go to the hall given that Angus was offering to help with his welfare at the forefront of his mind. But it was still an unsatisfactory state of affairs given that Jude had previously tried to live with the family and it hadn't worked out. There had to be another solution.

'You could actually start helping him right now,' I then suggested, remembering the purpose behind my call.

'How so?'

I explained about Jude's concerns regarding what had happened to the contents of his car, and Angus said he'd get straight on the case. He had a pretty good idea of which Wynbridge garage the car had most likely ended up in, and he would contact his local friend on the police force to find out if recovering Jude's work things, suitcase and other belongings would be a possibility.

'And how's Tink?' I asked, after I had thanked him for taking that on.

'I would say she's missing you . . .' Angus chuckled.

'But she hasn't actually noticed I've gone?' I laughed.

'Got it in one,' he confirmed. 'We'll see you later, Bella.'

'Yes,' I said, 'I'll see you all later.'

Jude was sitting with his legs over the side of the bed and one hand resting on his ribs when I returned to the ward. He looked, if it was possible, even paler than before.

'So,' I said, trying to keep my voice even, 'what did the consultant say? Will you live?'

'Apparently,' he said with a smile, 'though I'm going to feel worse before I feel better.'

That tallied with what I'd read online, and if he was going to have Angus buzzing about him – no matter how well intentioned it was – he was going to feel much worse before he felt the tiniest bit better.

'Did you really have to make a call?' Jude asked me.

'Yes,' I said. 'I spoke to Angus, and he's going to track down your car and everything you'd got in it.'

Jude nodded and let out a long breath.

'You're a star to think to do that,' he told me. 'If he comes up trumps, that will be a huge weight off my mind.'

'Oh, he will,' I insisted. 'You know Angus. He's got connections to everyone. I daresay he'll have all of your things and the hall documents arranged in your room before you're even discharged. Have they said when that's likely to be?'

'Tomorrow,' he said, gingerly levering himself into a standing position. 'I'm going to be discharged tomorrow.'

'And what exactly are your injuries?' I asked, feeling the discomfort of every movement as he awkwardly climbed back into the bed.

'Nothing broken, which is a blessing,' he told me, sounding out of breath from the exertion of moving. 'But a lot of bruising. The chest-wall bruising could take up to six weeks to heal.' That put his recovery well beyond Christmas. 'And whiplash, which, believe me, is nowhere near as much fun as I used to think it was when I first came across the word as an innuendo-obsessed tween.'

I was tempted to laugh at that but didn't.

'Shouldn't you have a brace for your neck?' I asked.

'No,' he said, going to shake his head but then thinking better of it. 'And I mustn't keep my head in the same position for too long, either. I need to keep active, well, moderately active, because it will help me heal faster.'

'But you mustn't overdo it,' I insisted.

'Do I look like I could overdo *anything*?'

'No, well,' I concurred, 'I guess not.'

'I think that was your phone.'

'Nothing wrong with your ears, then,' I said, as I checked the screen and saw I'd had a message from Angus.

'I'll probably wish there was once I'm ensconced back in the hall,' Jude said ruefully.

'Well,' I told him, 'at least when you're there, you'll have all your stuff around you.'

'Really?'

'Yep. Angus is going to collect everything you had in your car this afternoon, so you'll have all your belongings back with you as soon as you're discharged.'

'Well, that's something,' he said, resting his head back, then lifting it up again. 'These hospital gowns don't leave much to the imagination, do they? And I missed my electric toothbrush this morning.'

I realized then that other than the clothes he came in wearing and his wallet and phone, which had been placed in the locker, he had nothing.

'I'll pop to the hospital shop and pick you up a few essentials,' I said, checking I'd got my purse.

'You don't have to do that, Bella.'

'I know I don't have to,' I told him, 'but I want to. Just enough bits to tide you over until you're reunited with everything tomorrow.'

He didn't object further, so I knew he didn't really mind, and I headed off to buy a makeshift wash kit and find some snacks that I thought he might fancy. The shop didn't have much, but Jude would be able to freshen up and brush his teeth, and that would be enough until the next day.

He was talking on his phone when I arrived back on the ward, so I waited at the nurse's station until he ended the call.

'Please don't tell me that was Angus giving you the lowdown on all the boardgames he's got lined up to play with you,' I said. Jude looked horrified. 'I'm kidding,' I added quickly, but I wasn't, really.

'No,' he said, 'not Angus. How much do I owe you?'

I handed him the bag.

'Nothing,' I said, 'because they didn't have much.'

'The luxury of brushing my teeth alone has got to be worth at least a tenner,' he said, then started to cough, which caused his complexion to dramatically change colour. 'Damn,' he said, taking a second to catch his breath once the moment had passed. 'That really hurt.'

'I could tell,' I sympathized.

'And knowing it could get worse before it gets better isn't much comfort.'

'No,' I said, biting my lip. 'I can't imagine that it is.'

'It was my mum, by the way,' he said.

'Sorry?'

'On the phone,' he elaborated. 'I was talking to Mum.'

'I'm guessing you told her what's happened.'

'Yes,' he said, 'well, as much as I needed to.'

'Was she upset?'

'Mum doesn't really do upset,' he said, and I wondered what that meant.

'Can she get to see you?'

'No,' he told me. 'She and Dad are travelling abroad until the end of January, so I won't be seeing either of them until I'm completely healed.'

My mum was abroad, too, but if she'd known I'd been in a car accident, she would have rushed straight back to Wynbridge to look after me. I knew it wasn't my place to judge Jude's parents, but I thought it was a bit much that they hadn't at least offered to cut their trip short.

'Which means,' Jude went on, 'that their place in Surrey is currently empty.'

'You're not going to suggest you head there, are you?'

'I had considered it,' he sighed, 'but I don't think I could manage the journey. Even in the roomiest vehicle, I'd be bound to stiffen up even more, and to be honest . . .'

'To be honest, what?'

'Oh, it doesn't matter.'

'No,' I said, 'go on. What were you going to say?'

'Well,' he said, looking embarrassed, 'I'm not sure I want to be in a car at all after what happened, and especially for that amount of time. I suppose that sounds a bit feeble.'

'It doesn't sound feeble at all,' I said, reaching for his hand and giving it a squeeze. 'It must have been terrifying to experience what happened, and you're more than entitled to feel shaken up, Jude. I was knocked off my feet when I heard what had occurred myself.'

'Were you really?' he said, looking straight at me.

'Of course I was,' I told him, squeezing his fingers even tighter.

We were quiet for a second, just staring into each other's eyes, then he let go of my hand and reached into the bag for the Jelly Babies I'd picked up in the shop.

'I'm absolutely dreading the drive to the hall,' he confessed. 'I'm guessing the only way to get there will be to go by the crash site, and I'm not sure I can face that.'

An idea had been slowly forming in my mind, and his admission consolidated it.

'You won't have to face it,' I therefore forthrightly said.

'There's another way?' he asked, struggling to tear into the bag.

'No,' I said, taking it from him, opening it and handing it back, 'there isn't, but I mean that you won't have to travel that way at all.'

'Why not?'

'Because you're coming back to mine,' I said firmly. 'You're coming home with me.'

He looked at me and blinked. My suggestion took a few seconds for him to process.

'No way,' he said eventually. 'I can't possibly do that, Bella. I've already put you behind a whole month, and you've only just got back into the house. There's no way I could manage the stairs up to the apartment, and I'm not turfing you out again.'

A compromise was needed.

'Well,' I said, 'in that case, we'd better come up with a plan, because you can't really go back to the hall, can you?'

Being with the Connellys in the run-up to Christmas would be stressful enough, but getting to the hall ahead of that was too traumatic a thing for Jude to face so soon after the crash. He'd had no processing time at all.

'How about if we share the house?' he asked, after a few moments of thought. 'You have your upstairs bedroom, like you usually would now, and I have the small one downstairs with the shower room attached.'

'Yes,' I said with a nod, pleased that he wasn't putting up a fight or finding reasons for my suggestion not to happen, 'I suppose that does make sense. That way, I'll be on hand if you get into trouble, won't I?'

'I didn't mean that you'd be around to tend to my every need,' he said quickly.

'Neither did I!' I shot back, and he carefully laughed, then groaned. 'You'll have to put up with my decorations, though. I draw the line at not putting them up. I'm already three days late with festooning the place.'

Jude drew in and let out a breath, wincing as he did so and letting out a louder groan.

'All right,' he said finally, offering me his hand to gently shake, 'I will take you up on your extremely generous offer, Bella, but only if you promise not to try and make me fall in love with Christmas.'

That wasn't going to be an issue at all, because I was going to be focused instead on putting all of my energy and effort into not falling back in love with him.

'Deal!' I said, lightly shaking his hand. 'But don't blame me if some of my enthusiasm rubs off on you,' I added. 'Because that will be completely beyond my control.'

'Oh,' he laughed, clutching his ribs again, 'it won't impact on me. Given how I'm feeling, I can say that for certain. I'm going to be more of a Grinch than ever.'

I really hoped he wasn't, otherwise we were both going to be in for a very un-merry Christmas.

Chapter 19

With our minds made up that Jude was going to come back to mine once he'd been discharged the following day, we then spent the rest of the morning working out the finer practical details about how sharing the house was going to work. There wasn't all that much to think about, but it had taken me a while to convince him to get onboard with some of it.

I knew that bundling his washing in with mine, for example, would make more sense than him struggling to wash a separate load, but he had initially been reluctant to agree. It wasn't until I finally pointed out the energy- and water-saving benefits that he finally acquiesced. However, when it came to my suggestion that I could just as easily cook for two as one, he was quicker to approve of that – as long as it didn't involve baking, he said. The cheeky sod.

I left him just as lunch was about to be served on the ward, with everything satisfactorily arranged. And knowing that the consultant had lined up a scan for him in the afternoon, which could take a while, I felt easier in my mind about not going back to see him again later.

'I'll go and pick up Tink and explain about the change of

plan – and assuming that Angus has now got everything, I'll collect your things, too,' I said to Jude. 'And that will give me the rest of the day to make up the downstairs spare room for you and get some extra food in.'

'Are you really sure it's okay?' Jude asked concernedly. 'It's a lot of extra work for you, isn't it?'

I gave him a stern look.

'Hardly any work at all,' I said forcefully. 'It's decided. You're definitely coming home with me.'

Having seen how the colour had drained from his face when he thought about the drive to the hall, there was no way I was going to let him back out of what we'd decided now.

'All right,' he said. 'Thank you, Bella.'

'I'll see you tomorrow,' I said, pulling on my coat. 'Message or call me when they're ready to discharge you, and I'll be straight here.'

'I really appreciate it.'

'I know you do,' I said, smiling. 'Bye, then.'

'The nurse is watching us,' he said in a low voice. 'You'd better give me a kiss goodbye; you're supposed to be my partner.'

I looked at him and raised my eyebrows.

'I don't think we should go there again, do you?' I said quietly, still smiling.

Though perhaps no harm could come from just one tender kiss on the cheek . . .

'Given that you're the ultimate Christmas fairy and I'm the ghost of Christmas past,' Jude sighed, sounding – to my mind, at least – rather regretful, 'I suppose not.'

Not only were we incompatible on the festive front, but good old-fashioned common sense was also telling me that I couldn't possibly allow him to again take up the space in my heart that seeing him kiss someone else had only just booted him out of. I ignored the fact that how my heart had reacted to hearing what had happened to him had been an obvious indicator that I hadn't booted him quite as far away as my head was trying to make out.

I looked at him again and hoped I hadn't made a mistake in inviting him to move back into the house. I was going to have to make sure I did everything possible to ensure that no lines were crossed and no misunderstandings about the param- eters of our relationship flared up. With any luck, my full-on festive spirit would be enough to put him off me again. That was assuming he had ever really been . . . *on* me.

'Would you mind if I kept hold of your phone charger?' Jude requested. 'I have a couple of messages I need to send and people I need to let know what's happened.'

I wondered if one of those might be the person he'd been kissing at the Brambles party. That well-timed thought helped tamp down my feelings for him again.

'Of course,' I said. 'You keep hold of that, and I'll see you tomorrow.'

Jude had been right to be wary about driving by the crash site. There was police tape fluttering around the flattened verge, where I imagined his car had ended up, and skid marks which proved that the driver who had careered into him had barely had any reaction time at all. The sight of it made me feel quite sick, so it wouldn't do Jude any good to see it at all.

'Hello, love,' said Dorothy when I arrived at the hall. 'You're earlier than expected. Is everything all right?'

'Yes,' I said, scooping an ecstatic Tink up. 'All good, but

there's been a bit of a change of plan. Is Angus about, by any chance?'

She looked up at the clock.

'He's gone to collect Jude's stuff from the garage, but he shouldn't be much longer. Have you eaten?'

'Not yet,' I said, and right on cue, my tummy gave the loudest rumble.

'Sit yourself down,' Dorothy commanded, 'and I'll dish you up some soup.'

I wasn't usually so ravenous at lunchtime, but then I remembered that I hadn't eaten any breakfast.

'Leek and potato all right?' she asked.

'Perfect,' I said, as she lifted the lid on the pot and the delicious aroma filled the kitchen. 'Thank you, Dorothy.'

The smell must have wafted further than the kitchen, because within a couple of minutes Archie arrived, along with Jamie and Catherine.

'Anna messaged to say that she and Molly are staying in town for lunch,' Jamie told Dorothy the moment he walked in. 'But they'll be back in time for tea. Hello, Bella. Did you manage to see Jude?'

'You know she did,' said Catherine, sitting next to me, while Archie handed out the soup-filled bowls from Dorothy. 'Your father told you that before he left.'

'Oh yes,' said Jamie. 'Sorry. Baby brain.'

'Jude's very battered and bruised,' I told them all, 'but thankfully, and miraculously, there's nothing broken. He's got a check-up scan this afternoon and then, all being well, he'll be discharged tomorrow.'

'That's when the trouble for him will really start,' Archie

said ruefully. 'Get him here with Dad again, and he'll soon be feeling worse instead of better.'

'Actually,' I said, biting my lip, 'I wanted to talk to you about that.'

'He doesn't want to come back, does he?' Catherine said astutely. 'I did try to tell Angus, but as he was the reason why Jude was so late leaving on the night of the crash, he's going all out to try to make amends.'

'But the accident wasn't Angus's fault,' I said hastily. 'That was down to the moron who was driving too fast for the conditions behind Jude.'

'You try telling Dad that,' Archie said gloomily.

'Well, when I get the chance,' I said keenly, 'I will, but in the meantime, I've said that Jude is welcome to come back and stay with me.'

'Oh my dear—' Catherine began, but I cut her off.

'It's so kind of you to offer to let him recuperate here, but what with the fair at the weekend, and then the Winter Wonderland soon after that, not to mention the influx of extra Christmas visitors, it's going to be so busy.'

'And given that Jude doesn't do Christmas,' Dorothy reminded everyone, 'it's hardly going to be the most relaxing or healing place for him to be, is it?'

'Bella's hardly a subtle celebrator of the season,' Jamie said with a grin, and I gave him a sardonic look. 'But you've both got a point.'

'And I daresay Jude might not be too keen to have to be driven by the site where the crash happened,' Catherine added perceptively with a shudder.

I didn't comment on that. It wasn't my place to tell them

that that was something Jude had said he was worried about. Unless, of course, they objected to him coming to stay with me, in which case I might resort to pulling it out of the bag.

'On balance, then,' Catherine proclaimed, 'I think Jude staying with you will be a better solution, Bella. It's extremely kind of you to offer, given that you'd already put yourself so far out for him.'

'Um,' Archie began with a wink, and Jamie swatted him, 'really kind.'

I felt myself go hot, but pretended I hadn't heard him.

'I'll pick him up tomorrow,' I said to Catherine, 'and take him straight to mine. I daresay, with me being so busy, we won't see all that much of each other, so he'll have some proper peace and quiet in which to recuperate. I only hope Angus won't be offended.'

'You hope Angus won't be offended about what, my dear?' asked the man himself as he walked in, rosy-cheeked and windblown.

'Bella has done the kindest thing, Angus.' Catherine smiled at him and proceeded to explain the proposed change of plan, while he fussed the dogs and then shrugged off his coat.

'That *is* kind,' he agreed once she'd finished telling him. 'And on balance, you are right. It can be a bit busy here over Christmas, can't it?'

That was a huge understatement, but we all let it pass without comment.

'I've got Jude's things in the Land Rover,' he added, graciously accepting the new set-up, 'so we might as well pack them straight into your car, Bella. If that's all right?'

'Yes,' I said, 'perfect.'

'If you give me your keys,' Archie said, 'I'll do it for you now.'

'Don't you want more soup?' Dorothy asked.

'I'll have another bowl when I come in,' he told her, neatly catching the keys I'd tossed him. 'It'll warm me back up again.'

With everything settled, Tink and I went back to the house, and I spent the rest of the day moving the last few things I wanted down from the apartment, stocking the cupboard and fridge and making up the bed in the downstairs spare room. It wasn't the biggest bedroom, but there was a convenient ensuite attached. With everything on one level, it would be easier for Jude to manoeuvre around. Not that I was going to let him sit around all day, even if he felt inclined to. He'd already mentioned that moving about would aid his recovery, and when I was around, that was what I would help him do.

Jude messaged the next morning to say that he could come home as soon as he'd seen the consultant again and to ask me to take him some clothes to wear on the return journey. Having just cleared the house of the smell of him and his aftershave, opening his suitcase immediately topped it back up again.

I resolutely reminded myself of the heartbreak that, in my experience, was tied up with true love and resisted the urge to sniff his chunkiest jumper. While I selected an outfit that would be relatively easy to pull on, I forced myself to think about Mum's relationship losses, the pain she had felt over being abandoned not once, but twice, and how she had been put off relationships for life as a result. And then I pushed myself even more painfully further on and recalled the chest-crushing agony of seeing Grandad struggle alone after Nanna had gone. And then how quickly he had followed her.

I was sunk deep in sad memories when my phone chimed with a video call notification and I jumped.

'Bella!' gasped Jeanie when I answered, as Holly pushed her way into the screen space next to her. 'Oh my god! Have you heard what's happened to Jude?'

'Hey, guys,' I said, sitting at the kitchen table and propping my phone up against the Santa timer, which was still the only festive decoration to be seen. 'I have heard. And I've been meaning to ask you the same thing, but I've been a bit caught up in it all.'

'I just found out literally minutes ago,' Jeanie went on, shaking her head.

'And I only know because I happened to be here when Jeanie found out,' Holly added.

'I can't believe it hasn't been the hottest topic in the pub,' I said, blowing out a breath. 'And even if it wasn't, I thought Tim would have known about it. There must have been a fire crew at the scene.'

'Tim hasn't been to work for a few days,' Holly said when Jeanie didn't comment. 'Has he, Jeanie?' she added meaningfully, giving our mutual friend a nudge with her elbow.

'No,' Jeanie said, blushing, which wasn't an everyday occurrence. 'Tim hasn't been on shift.'

'How come?' I asked with a frown, momentarily distracted from what had happened to Jude.

'Tell her, then!' Holly nudged again.

I'd clearly missed something while I was catching up with chores, making more fairy stock and assisting my returning house guest.

'Tim hasn't been on shift,' Jeanie explained, turning even redder, 'because we went away together for a couple of days.'

'You're back together?' I gasped.

Jeanie nodded.

'Where did you go?' I asked, feeling so happy for her and even happier for Tim, who had loved her for so long.

'To Wynmouth,' Holly said dreamily before Jeanie had a chance. 'To stay in the most romantic former fisherman's brick and flint cottage, located right next to the beach.'

A smile spread across my face as I imagined the romantic coastal getaway.

'Which was freezing,' Jeanie said, obviously trying to play down the shift in her and Tim's relationship, but not really succeeding because she looked radiant.

'Which was the perfect excuse for them not to get out of bed,' Holly added with a grin.

'Oh, Jeanie,' I said, feeling tears start to prickle, 'I'm so pleased for you. For both of you. Goodness knows, Tim has put in the hours trying to win you back.'

'He has,' she agreed, looking unusually misty-eyed herself.

'So,' I sighed happily, 'what else have I missed? How come you and Bear hadn't heard about Jude's crash, Holly?'

'Because *they* haven't been out of bed, either,' Jeanie blurted out, getting her own back on Holly for so eagerly talking on her behalf. 'They've been cosied up in the carriages all week and have only just emerged.'

It was Holly's turn to blush.

'Totally true,' she said, grinning.

It seemed that both of my best friends were making the most of their relationships and had been enjoying some intimate private time. Ordinarily, I would have continued feeling pleased for them both, especially in the case of Jeanie and Tim's rekindled romance, but if I was being completely honest, I suddenly felt, shockingly and wholly unexpectedly, a pang of jealousy that knocked my previously generous feelings off their pedestal.

This new range of emotions I was currently experiencing felt dangerously close to spiralling out of control. First, I'd developed genuine, deep feelings for a man. That was even rarer than Jeanie blushing. And now I was feeling jealous that my friends were both teamed up with their one true loves. Just a few weeks ago, I would have hotly denied that there was one person for everyone, especially me, but now . . .

'What did you mean,' Jeanie began, frowning at me, 'that you've been caught up in it all?'

'What?' I replied, frowning back.

'A minute ago,' she said, 'when I told you I'd only just found out about Jude, you said that you'd been caught up in it all.'

'Oh yes,' said Holly. 'You did say that, Bella.'

'What's going on?' Jeanie asked.

'Oh, that,' I said, trying to sound blasé. 'I just meant that I've been to see him in hospital.'

'I wonder how long he'll be in for?' Holly asked, while Jeanie scrutinized my expression.

'He's being discharged today,' I told them both.

'And going where, I wonder?' Holly mused.

'Yes,' Jeanie said meaningfully. 'Where, I wonder?'

'To mine, actually,' I said quickly. 'He's not fit enough to travel, and the Connellys offered, but there'll be no peace at the hall, so he's coming back here again.'

Holly gawped, and Jeanie looked pretty floored, too.

'But what about Christmas?' she demanded. 'I can't imagine Jude's going to appreciate you in full-on festive mode, Bella!'

Little did she know it, but I was banking on that.

'Well,' I said, 'if he wants somewhere quieter than Wynthorpe Hall to recuperate in, he'll have to put up with me turning into the fairy on the tree, won't he?'

'Well,' Jeanie conceded, 'at least you're not abandoning your seasonal principles for him.'

'Of course I'm not!' I tutted.

'It's really kind of you to take him back,' Holly sighed, sounding dreamy again.

'I daresay we'll hardly see each other.' I shrugged. 'You know how busy I'm going to be during the next few weeks. And by the time I'm finally winding down for the Christmas break, I expect Jude will be well enough to leave.'

'This actually has all the makings of a Christmas channel romance,' Holly said, and it looked for all the world as if Jeanie might be about to agree with her.

'With Jude's aversion to the season,' I hastily reminded them both, 'that's the last thing it's going to be. Anyway,' I rushed on, before Jeanie started to pick at the soft spot I had for Jude and which still hadn't completely healed, 'I'd better go. I've still got stock to make ahead of the fair at the weekend. I'll see you both there.'

'Yes,' said Holly, 'see you there.'

'Hang on—'

'Sorry, Jeanie,' I said, blowing kisses. 'I really have to go.'

I cut the call off, but my phone immediately rang again.

'No,' I groaned, but it wasn't them.

'I've just been given the all-clear,' said Jude. I could hear the pain in his voice and wondered if he'd been prodded and poked during the discharge process to check he really was fit enough to come home. 'Could you come and pick me up, please, Bella?'

'I'm on my way,' I told him, reaching for my keys. 'I'll be there in just a few minutes.'

'Be careful,' he said. 'Don't rush. I'm not going anywhere.'

Jude had stuffed the few things he had, along with the clothes he had been wearing when the crash occurred, into a carrier bag and was looking mortified about the fact that he needed help to get dressed as I slipped a pair of pyjama bottoms over his feet.

'I know PJs won't be the warmest,' I said, while I tried to pretend that I wasn't really helping him to save his blushes, 'but I thought you could just pull them up and then you won't need to get changed again when we get back.'

'That was good thinking,' he replied, grimacing as he stiffly stood up.

I turned away, and when I sensed he was done, bobbed back down and slid on and did up the laces on his trainers.

'Shame you haven't got Velcro shoes,' I said, trying to lighten his mood, but he didn't appreciate the humour and I slipped out of the ineffective and flimsy curtain while he finished up.

'Everything all right?' asked the nurse.

I daresay she thought it was a bit odd that I'd left my partner to struggle alone.

'Yes,' I said, grappling for a reason not to be helping, 'all good. I just wanted to check what sort of painkillers would be best for Jude to take.'

By the time she had told me and given me a few pointers

about how best to support my wonderful faux boyfriend, he was ready to go.

'You stay here,' I said, when we reached the hospital lobby, 'and I'll go and get the car. It'll save you the walk through the car park.'

I hadn't been able to park all that close, and it was freezing cold. Jude was already shaking, and I thought the first thing I'd do when we got back would be to turn the heating up another degree or two.

'Do you want me to help you?' I offered, once I'd pulled into a drop-off space and jumped out again. 'Or would you rather I left you alone to get in?'

'I don't know,' he replied, and swallowed, looking at the low seat in my little Fiat.

'Let me take that bag,' I said, 'and we'll see how you get on.'

He did need help getting the seatbelt on, and once I was back behind the wheel, I promised I would take the quickest, but quietest, route home, and drive the slowest I could get away with without being beeped.

'All right,' he agreed, nodding, and I hoped he wasn't going to be sick.

The journey back happened without incident, but I could see how tense Jude was, constantly checking the side mirror to see how close any cars behind us were pulling up. I tried to make conversation, but he clearly wasn't in the frame of mind to chat.

'Come on,' I said, as I pulled onto the drive. 'Let's get you inside.'

The lights in the porch were twinkling, and home looked wonderfully welcoming, but Jude didn't notice.

'We'll have a cuppa, shall we?' I offered once we were in and I'd nudged the heating thermostat up.

'I think I'm just going to head to bed for a bit,' he said, sounding dog-tired. 'I barely got any sleep in the hospital, and when I did . . .'

His words trailed off and Tink padded over to him, clearly sensing that something was wrong.

'You can come with me if you like,' he said softly.

Thankfully, I was looking at the pair of them at the time and realized he was talking to Tink, not me.

'I'll make you up a hot-water bottle,' I said, reaching for the kettle.

'Thank you, Bella,' Jude replied, nodding. 'That would be great. You really are a star, you know.'

I left him tucked up and already nodding off beneath my weighted blanket, Tink lying on the bed next to him. I tried to usher her out, but she wouldn't budge. I remembered then that she'd had a soft spot for Jude right from the moment she'd met him and in spite of the fact that he'd behaved badly. I should have known that there was more to him than his actions and attitude had suggested the day we'd met and got my heart guard up sooner. I'd never needed one before, so I had no idea how I would have done it, but I wished I'd at least given it a go.

I quietly closed the bedroom door, reminding myself that Jude hated Christmas, came with some hefty former relationship baggage and had also kissed someone at the Brambles party. Of course, in theory I knew that made him fling potential, but ironically it wasn't a fling with Jude that I wanted, was it? *Had* wanted, I amended, immediately but not completely convincingly shifting the tense. I *had* wanted that; now all I wanted was to offer him the space to get patched up and go on his merry way. Didn't I?

It was hours before Jude resurfaced, and when he opened the bedroom door, Tink immediately ran to the back door and I rushed to let her out.

'How are you feeling?' I asked Jude, who looked absolutely no better at all.

'Not too bad,' he said hoarsely, wincing with every step.

'How are you feeling, Jude?' I repeated, ignoring his first answer.

'Like death warmed up,' he said more honestly. 'And in a lot of pain.'

'You slept way beyond the time you should have had your painkillers,' I told him, 'but I didn't like to wake you.'

'I'm pleased you didn't,' he yawned, 'because I really did need the sleep.'

Tink barked to be let back in, and once she was inside, I poured Jude a glass of water and popped a couple of pills out of a packet and into the palm of his hand.

'Are you hungry?' I asked him after he'd taken them.

'Ravenous.'

'Dorothy sent me back with chicken soup and some home-made granary. Do you fancy some of that?'

'I would love that,' he said, going to sit down.

'Don't get comfy yet,' I said bossily, 'I don't think it would hurt if you had a little wander about the place, would it?'

He looked at me and frowned.

'I'm not going to regret moving back in here with you, am I, Bella?' he asked.

'Time will tell,' I said, smiling as I started to warm the soup on the stove. 'Time will tell.'

Jude couldn't deny that he felt better after he'd moved around for a while, and by the time I'd cleared away the fairies I had spent the afternoon working on and we'd eaten the meal Dorothy had so thoughtfully supplied, his spirits had lifted considerably.

'I can tell you enjoyed that,' I said, with a nod to the empty bowl and plate.

'I did,' he said. 'It was just what I needed.'

'It's put you in a brighter mood,' I said, biting my lip, 'and now I'm about to push you back into the pit again. I'm sorry about that.'

'Oh?' He frowned. 'How are you going to do that?'

'Well, the thing is,' I said, reaching for the Santa timer, 'it's the fourth of December today, and this jolly little fella aside, I've got nothing to show for the festive season so far. And if I'm being honest, my Christmas meter is woefully low. My seasonal spirit certainly couldn't lift Santa's sleigh, and that's unheard of.'

I imagined Nanna and Grandad standing in the kitchen and looking thoroughly shocked that there were no decs up and not even a carol playing.

'Oh, Bella.' Jude swallowed. 'I'm so sorry about that . . .'

'It's not your fault,' I quickly went on, because it wasn't my intention to make him feel bad.

'But if it wasn't for my accident—'

'Exactly,' I cut in. 'If it wasn't for the moron who ran into your car, we'd both be carrying on as we'd originally planned. It was *their* fault, not yours,' I said more firmly. 'But it's happened, and now I need to get back on track.'

'And how do you propose to do that?' Jude asked. 'You're not decorating tonight, are you?'

'No,' I said, 'that's going to happen tomorrow. Tonight, I'm planning a festive reset. I'm going back to one of my first of December traditions and watching *The Muppet Christmas Carol* again.'

'You're not expecting me to watch it with you, are you?' Jude grimaced.

'Not if you don't want to.' I shrugged. 'I just wanted to let you know that the film will be this evening's televisual entertainment.'

'In that case,' he said, stacking his bowl on his plate, 'I think I'll have an early night.'

Tink and I were snuggled under a blanket, and I had a bowl of popcorn and a Baileys hot chocolate on the side table, when the door to Jude's room opened and he stepped out.

'I just wanted to top up my water,' he said, as the opening titles appeared on the TV screen and that wonderfully familiar song, which I could never resist humming, started to fill the room.

'You might as well sit down,' I said a few minutes later, when I realized that Jude was still in the kitchen and surreptitiously watching the film from afar.

'I suppose I should stay awake until I take my next dose of meds, shouldn't I?' he said, as he gingerly lowered himself onto the sofa and Tink turned her attention from my lap to his.

I didn't say a word, but I did sneak the odd glance at him as he laughed and sighed in all the right places and barely looked away from the television throughout the entire film.

'I'd forgotten how much I loved that when I was growing

up,' he said rather croakily as the final lyrics were sung and Scrooge found himself destined for a far happier future than the one he'd started out with. 'I watched it every year when I was little.'

'Me, too,' I said, offering him the last of the maple syrup-covered corn. 'And every year since I was a child, of course.'

'I watched it every year, too, until Tabitha . . .'

He looked from the screen to me, and the sadness in his eyes broke me a little.

'Please don't let what she and Barny did taint your childhood memories or the things you loved about Christmas as an adult, Jude,' I said, resisting the urge to reach for his hand. 'You give them far too much power if you continue to allow that to happen.'

'Perhaps you're right,' he said, looking at the scrolling film credits again, 'but it's hard, you know. When you've had your heart broken, you'll do anything to protect it from happening again and go to any lengths to avoid triggers which might make those feelings flare up.'

I hadn't had my heart broken in the romantic sense, but I'd seen the pain of it in my family and friends. It was the reason I was so keen to avoid it, and of course Jude had given my heart one heck of a jolt since he'd arrived, so I could understand a little of what he meant. His disassociation from the festive season was completely justified as a result. The whole of Christmas had become one huge trigger for him, the Muppets included.

'Not that I expect you to understand the heartbreak bit, Bella,' he said. 'I can't imagine, given that you've signed up to a lifetime of brief flings and fleeting dalliances, that you've ever had any reason to factor your heart into your relationships, have you?'

He stated what he thought was true about me without the slightest hint of judgement, and I knew he was only saying what it was that I had led him to believe. Nonetheless, hearing him say it, on the back of seeing Jeanie and Holly so loved up earlier, stung a bit.

'Though I appreciate that your whole relationship ethos did spring from a place of hurt that was all to do with your heart,' he said hastily when I didn't respond. 'It's hardly surprising that you go in for one-offs when your dad and stepdad treated you and your mum so badly, is it?'

'I'd better turn this off,' I said, reaching for the remote.

'I've upset you, haven't I?' Jude said worriedly. 'I didn't mean to.'

'I know you didn't.' I smiled at him. 'And you really haven't, so please don't worry about it. You've actually given me hope.'

'Hope?' Jude frowned. 'Hope for a change in your future relationships, you mean?'

'No.' I swallowed. 'Hope that, having watched your reaction to an evening with the festive Muppets, there might actually be a chance that I can get you a bit back onboard about Christmas before you're fit enough to escape from my festive clutches. Perhaps I might be able to turn some of those negative triggers back into the happy memories they should be.'

'Well, good luck with that.' He smiled and I smiled back.

Chapter 20

I was up extra early the next morning but made sure I didn't make too much noise as I made an extra flock of fairies for the Wynthorpe Hall Festive Fair and was then free to get on with decorating the house, because Jude's bedroom door was closed and there was no sound from within. I was still feeling the sting of what he'd said about my cold, untouched heart. And okay, he might not have put it *quite* as bluntly as that, but that was the implication, wasn't it?

Zero emotional investment in relationships had kept me safe in the past. Having seen how broken Mum, Grandad and even Jeanie had been as a result of whole-heart investment, I had been grateful for that, but now I was teetering dangerously close to questioning whether my way, and Mum's way, was the right way.

What was it that Tennyson had said about it being better to have loved and lost? Why did folk think that was better, I wondered? What was it that was so great about love? It hadn't done Mum any favours, my grandparents had been fine, I supposed . . . but only until the end. And the feelings I'd developed for Jude had stirred up a cauldron of emotions mostly made up of confusion, denial and fear. There was nothing great about that, was there?

But Jeanie's new romance, along with Holly's more established one, made me think about the good things, which I had never experienced – as well as the bad, of which I'd had more than my fair share.

More thinking about Jude and the incredible kiss we'd shared in the porch then ensued, until a thud from his room alerted me to the fact that he was finally awake.

'Bella!' he shouted, his voice muffled. 'Are you out there? Can you give me a hand, please?'

I rushed into his room and found him wrapped up in the T-shirt he must have slept in, which he was trying to pull off.

'I'm stuck!' he said from the depths, his voice muffled by the fabric. 'Can you help me get this damn thing off?'

'Just a sec,' I replied.

'I can't believe I'm aching even more than I was yesterday,' he groaned.

'The staff at the hospital did say that might be a possibility,' I reminded him, as I focused on the twisted fabric rather than the clearly defined muscles in his arms and the breadth of his chest. 'You're bound to hit the pain peak soon.'

'I bloody hope so,' he said, as I gently released him from the material and his shoulders relaxed.

Lust, I then remembered. That was another emotion that had come along with those other feelings I'd previously been having about him and that I was now experiencing a libido-lifting dose of again, in spite of the fact that poor Jude was feeling so uncomfortable and was making no effort to look appealing. His bruises were extensive and livid in colour.

Lust was a fling-induced feeling, too, I reminded myself as I looked away. I could actually tick that box with nothing more involved than a well-timed brief encounter.

'How about I get you some fresh water to drink with your first meds of the day?' I suggested brightly, pulling my thoughts back to where they should be, 'and then I'll get the shower warmed up for you.'

'You don't have to do that,' he said, sounding forlorn. 'I really don't expect you to do anything further for me, Bella. It's enough that you've let me move back in here again.'

'You're feeling really rough this morning, aren't you?' I said, looking right at him.

'Um,' he said, nodding, and I didn't think it would take much for him to shed a tear or two.

'In that case,' I said more softly, 'let me help you, okay? By the time your meds have kicked in and your muscles have loosened up a bit in the shower, I could have a bacon roll on the table with your name on it and a fresh pot of tea to go with it. I was about to make both for myself anyway,' I added quickly before he had time to object.

'All right,' he relented with a grateful smile. 'That does sound good. Thank you.'

'And then you can help me unpack the boxes of decorations,' I said, making for the ensuite, 'or at least point me in the direction of where you think I should unpack them.'

'So,' said Jude a couple of hours later as he stood holding the ladder, while I set about festooning the sitting room ceiling with Christmas hanging paper decorations in the shape of snowflakes, hearts and stars, while my seasonal Spotify playlist quietly but enthusiastically serenaded us, 'you put everything up now, other than the tree.'

'That's right,' I told him. 'And I always start with these going up on the ceiling, and then work my way down.'

That was how we'd always done it when I was growing up. Grandad would be up the ladder with Nanna steadying it, and then I'd get involved as we worked our way down to a level that was more accessible for me. I had wanted to hang the ceiling decs when I was old enough to reach and Grandad was getting a little frail, but he wouldn't hear of it. Every year, we followed the same pattern and routine, and I was enthusiastically continuing it. Everything went up in the same place, and the memories of the four of us happily celebrating Christmas all together and with no time pressure came thick and fast.

'And you have decorations in all the rooms?' Jude asked.

'Of course,' I nodded, as if that was obvious. 'Even the bathroom.'

'So why no tree?' He frowned, not commenting on the bathroom decs.

'Because the Wynbridge tree and greenery auction doesn't happen until the second Saturday in December,' I explained, 'and I like to buy my tree from there.'

'Oh, I see,' Jude said, stepping aside as I climbed back down the ladder and shifted it along a bit.

'I had planned to rent a potted tree from the place that supplies the cut ones for the auction from this year on,' I went on, 'but time and events ran away with me and so I've got it in the diary to organize for next year now.'

'You can rent a Christmas tree?' He sounded incredulous. 'A real one?'

'Yes,' I explained, 'you get the same tree for a few years running, and for the rest of the year, it's looked after by the rental company, which, for me and a lot of other locals around here, will be Wynter's Trees on the Norfolk coast near Wynmouth.'

Jude looked amazed that such a place existed.

'Some people even name their trees,' I told him, and he looked even more astounded.

'And you will, of course.'

'Of course,' I confirmed.

'What are you going to call it?' he asked, quirking a brow, and I knew he was taking the mickey.

I stopped and put my hands on my hips.

'How can I answer that?' I tutted, playing along. 'I haven't been introduced to it yet. I can't pick out the name until I've actually seen the tree, can I?'

Jude put his hands up in surrender and attempted to laugh.

'I apologize,' he said. 'My mistake.'

He closed his eyes for a second and then grabbed hold of the ladder to steady himself.

'I think you'd better sit down for a bit,' I told him as I steered him towards a chair. 'You've spent ages holding that ladder and looking up. Take a minute to regain your equilibrium, and I'll make us another drink. Then you can just watch me for a bit, rather than participate.'

'All this festive exposure is tantamount to abuse to someone like me,' he pouted, but there was humour in his tone.

'It's not abuse!' I objected.

'Immersion therapy, then,' he amended.

'Yes,' I said, smiling, 'that's more like it. If I completely cocoon you in my kind of Christmas, you'll be so over-exposed by the New Year that you won't object to it anymore and you'll be able to go back to enjoying it again.'

'I don't expect I'll be here by the New Year,' he said rather glumly. 'I'll be out of your hair long before then.'

'Perhaps you will,' I said, wondering how I was going to cope with our second parting in as many months, 'but for now, let's just take things one day at a time, shall we?'

By lunchtime the next day, the house was suitably bedecked and there was barely an inch of space anywhere that wasn't covered in twinkling fairy lights, something glittery in its own right or a festive fairy that was part of my private collection. It might all have happened slightly later than the first of December, but I was thrilled with the results and surprisingly Jude hadn't objected to any of it.

Whether he genuinely didn't mind it or was keeping his real thoughts about it all to himself because of my willingness to let him move back into the house after the car crash, I couldn't be sure, but he was certainly making the most of one of the decorative touches.

'If I transfer some funds into your bank, Bella,' he said, as I was getting ready to head to Wynthorpe Hall to start setting up my stall ahead of the fair the next day, 'could you pick up some more squirty cream and marshmallows?'

The kitchen hot chocolate station was a definite hit.

'You can't have got through the first lot already,' I gasped, looking around him at the depleted Kilner jars.

'Not quite,' he said, squirting a copious amount of cream onto the top of the largest reindeer mug I owned, 'but it won't take long. These flavour combos are all so delicious.'

I looked at him and raised my eyebrows.

'And this isn't completely Christmas-themed,' he added hastily, thinking I'd caught him out.

'Yes, it is,' I batted back. 'The station is only up in December, so that makes it a completely festive treat in my book.'

Despite what I'd said, he didn't look inclined to abandon it.

'I think you're already coming back around to my way of thinking about the season, aren't you?' I teased, as I realized that I didn't actually need to doubt how he was feeling about it all and that he wasn't simply playing along because he was back under my roof. 'First you enjoyed the Muppets,' I reeled off, 'then you helped with the decorating—'

'Watched the decorating,' he amended.

I didn't remind him that he'd directed and curated the set-up of the mantlepiece *and* a couple of the bookcase shelves. The usual pieces were on display, but this year in the arrangement Jude had configured.

'And now you're maxing out on sugary treats before you've even got your mitts on a selection box,' I pointed out.

'And don't forget I showed you how to make the perfect mince pies a while back,' he then reminded me. '*And* I opened the door on one of the advent calendars this morning, too,' he confessed, as his eyes widened and I laughed.

'Exactly!' I said. I had noticed the calendar but had decided not to make a thing of it. 'So have you fallen in love again?'

He looked at me and opened his mouth as wide as his eyes, but no sound came out.

'With Christmas,' I rushed to add. 'Have you fallen back in love with Christmas?'

'I wouldn't go that far,' he said finally, 'but I'm not feeling quite so inclined to badmouth it as I was before.'

'Yes!' I said, punching the air as I remembered his rant in The Mermaid on the night of the volunteer meeting and happily considered how far away from that attitude he'd been able to move. His slagging off the season had been one of the things that had put me off him, though, and if he was now backing down about that . . .

'Spending time with you is helping me disconnect Christmas from what happened with Tabitha. And I'm genuinely redis-covering some of the joy associated with the season, again,' he said, smiling and scooping up some of the cream from his mug with a long-handled spoon.

'That's music to my ears,' I told him, endeavouring to push my previous thoughts aside for fear they'd take me down the path I was still trying not to tread.

'As well as adding to my waistline,' he added as he patted his tummy.

'You look just fine to me,' I told him, 'but if you keep knocking back the hot chocolate at your current rate, you'll be as round as Santa by the big day.'

'Well,' he said with a shrug, then took a breath because the action had been uncomfortable, 'it wouldn't be the season without the addition of a little holiday weight, would it?'

'I guess not,' I laughed as I checked the time and realized that I really needed to get on. 'And now this fairy has to fly.'

Having loaded Tink and the majority of the crates I needed for the fair into my car, I set off into the Fens, feeling thrilled about Jude's change in attitude insofar as it was going to be good for him to enjoy Christmas again, not because it had the potential to make my feelings for him reignite.

Jude might have come back to me again, but his second stay under my roof was a fluke, not fate, and his presence in my life still had an expiration date. Even though that made him fabulous fling fodder (had he been up to flinging), I had sense enough to remember that I had shockingly worked out that that had never been where I had wanted to head with him.

My heart thumped as I realized that if I'd managed to reach that depth of feeling with Jude, then surely I would be able to replicate it with someone less likely to leave town. Not that geographical proximity was any guarantee that someone would stick around – my father and stepfather were proof enough of that – but surely if I was actually considering embarking on a real-relationship maiden voyage with someone, then someone who lived a little closer to home and who I could see on a regular basis would be a good choice. That was assuming that there was any such thing as choice when it came to matters of the heart.

I remembered then that Jeanie had once said that my attitude towards love and relationships didn't marry up with my whimsical work and Pollyanna ethos, but she had relented when I justified it with a reminder of my tumultuous parental past. But had she been on to something?

Was it time for me to align my love life with the rest of my idyllic life? And if I decided it was, then who was the man I was going to make the switch with? Not one who was set to leave town before the needles had fallen off my Christmas tree, that was for sure.

As I turned off the road and on to the bumpy Wynthorpe

Hall drive, I decided my potential manhunt could wait. The only thing I needed to focus on this side of the New Year was enjoying my work and helping Jude fall for all things festive rather than me falling for him again.

Us both being home for Christmas was a great start, but where Jude's continued change of attitude was concerned, bruised ribs or no bruised ribs, it was time for me to further up the ante.

Chapter 21

In my determination to ensure that Jude wasn't going to fall back into his former Grinchy ways once he left Wynbridge, I went further to work on him as soon as I arrived back from setting up at the hall. I graciously said that he could continue to open the doors on the advent calendar that he had already been tempted by, and then filled him up on a dinner of mini pigs in blankets, brussels sprouts, apples, cranberries and crusty bread, all dipped into a rich and creamy baked Camembert.

'Oh, Bella,' he groaned, once the last of the soft, warm cheese had been mopped up with the thickly buttered bread, 'that was obscenely good.'

'I know,' I agreed, checking that we hadn't missed even the tiniest bit of the cheese. 'It's one of my favourite meals to eat in the winter, but I don't have it all that often.'

'Why not, if you like it so much?' he asked, sounding surprised. 'I thought you were all for embracing what you love.'

'Oh, I am,' I nodded vehemently, 'but a Camembert just for me isn't a good idea.'

'Too much waste?'

'Nope,' I laughed, as I began to pile the dishes together.

'Zero waste, and that would be the problem. I could quite easily eat the entire thing, but then it wouldn't be just you who was destined to carry a truly excessive amount of Christmas weight.'

'But then I could be Santa and you could be Mrs Claus.' He smiled impishly.

I rather liked the thought of that. The pair of us rosy-cheeked and replete as a result of a Christmas well spent would be wonderful. On second thoughts, perhaps I was a little too keen on the idea.

'Why don't you go and pick a film for us to watch?' I suggested, rather than confirming that Jude's suggestion was a wonderful one. 'I'll stack all this lot in the dishwasher and let the machine take care of it.'

Jude chose *Last Christmas* starring Emilia Clarke, which I adored and which he had never seen before, for us to watch, and we sat close together on the sofa under a blanket with just the width of Tink between us, and we laughed and sighed in all the right places. It felt wonderfully cosy, which was perfect for further fuelling Jude's festive feelings, but I knew I was going to have to keep an eye on my own feelings, because those I had for him had further ramped up as the evening went on, too.

'Right,' I said the second the credits started to roll, and not only because I needed to put some distance between us. 'I'm off to bed. Do you need help with anything?'

Jude looked at the clock.

'It's still early yet,' he said. 'Are you sure you don't want to watch something else?'

'It is early,' I agreed, 'but Tink and I will be heading to the hall first thing for the fair, and it's going to be a super busy weekend, so I need all the rest I can get.'

'Of course,' he said. 'And Tink can stay with me tomorrow, if you like? If that would be easier.'

'Thanks,' I said, smiling, 'but I'll take her with me. She'd never forgive me if I made her miss out on two days of socialising and snoozing with her friends at the hall.'

'I hadn't thought of that.' He smiled ruefully.

'But thanks for the offer,' I responded gratefully.

'Well,' he said, 'as you're turning in, I might as well head to bed, too. I don't think I need help with anything. Maybe a hand in the morning, though, if I'm still struggling to get dressed. It really hurts when I have to lift my arms up.'

'I can do that,' I said with a nod, feeling relieved that he was wearing a shirt he could unbutton without assistance.

For the sake of my libido, I was going to have to trawl through his wardrobe to find a few more things that he would be able to manage to get on and off unaided. A few more shirts, if he had some, should hopefully do the trick.

It was still dark when I loaded the last of the things I was going to need into my car the following morning, and the temperature had plummeted. The stars were shining, and there was a thick frost covering everything. I knew it was going to take a few minutes to defrost my little Fiat and was pleased I'd allowed myself plenty of time to get organized.

The drive to the hall might be a bit dicey and take longer than usual, too, as the roads around it wouldn't have been treated, but the grounds would look spectacular and hopefully get the visitors even more in the mood to stock up on Christmas gifts. A potentially lucrative couple of days stretched ahead, which would help to keep the home fires burning.

'Jude?' I said quietly, as I knocked on his bedroom door. 'Are you awake?'

I didn't want to rush him, but as I was going to be setting off a little earlier than originally planned as a result of the weather, I needed to stay ahead. If he needed my help getting dressed, it was very much a 'now or never' scenario.

'Yes,' he said, 'I'm awake. You can come in.'

He was sitting on the bed and looked as surprised by the sight of what I was wearing as I was to see him already dressed.

'You managed!' I smiled, torn between relief and disappointment, which was entirely inappropriate.

'Just about,' he said, nodding. 'I don't feel in any less pain, but I'm determined to keep moving like the consultant said I should.'

'Don't overdo it, though,' I urged, not wanting him to push himself too far and do further damage to his already bruised body.

'You're a fine one to talk.' He smiled, looking me up and down.

'Well,' I said, giving him a curtsy, 'you know me, I like to overdo everything if I can.'

I was wearing my favourite fairy outfit, which included a full tulle layered skirt and a silk fitted bodice with full length sleeves in soft green and pale cream.

'There's a mistletoe crown and a pair of wings to go with it, but obviously I can't drive in those,' I told him.

'Obviously,' said Jude, looking amused.

'I had planned to get changed at the hall, but the change in weather means it might take me longer than planned to get there.'

'It isn't still raining, is it?'

'No,' I said, 'the rain stopped, but then the temperature must have plummeted. It's really icy, but it's going to look beautiful. Perfect Festive Fair weather.'

Jude didn't look anywhere near as thrilled about that as I was.

'Will you be all right driving in it?' He frowned.

'Yes,' I said airily, 'I'm used to the frosty Fenland drove roads.'

Given what he'd so recently experienced, I shouldn't have mentioned it and was therefore determined to make light of it.

'I am going to set off rather earlier than planned, though,' I told him. 'In fact, as you don't need me, I think I'll get the car thawed out and go now.'

Jude made me promise to message him when I arrived at the hall, which I did the second I'd got parked up. The roads had been even trickier to traverse than I had been expecting, but I didn't mention that. And I had barely sent the message before my mobile began to ring.

'You made it all right, then,' Jude said the moment I answered.

'Yes,' I said, repeating again what I'd just typed out. 'I'm here now and about to head inside to finish setting up.'

'Well, that's good,' he said, sounding relieved. 'You've had a phone call here at the house,' he then told me. 'Someone called Ruby, just wanting to make sure you hadn't forgotten about the film night that's happening in town tonight.'

'Oh, damn,' I said, screwing my eyes up and letting out a breath. 'I had forgotten, actually. I'm supposed to be helping serve the snacks and drinks during the interval. There was a meeting about it last night.'

I had been so focused on Jude and upping his Christmas spirit that I'd completely forgotten I was supposed to attend.

'I'll ring Ruby now and tell her I'll be there,' I told him. 'Thanks for letting me know.'

'No problem,' he said. 'I suppose this will be a *festive* film night?' he asked with emphasis.

'Of course,' I said, smiling, as Holly pulled up in the space next to mine and waved. 'In fact, you can come with me.'

Jude was quiet for a moment.

'I don't think so,' he said, attempting to turn my invitation down. 'I'm still feeling pretty banged up, and I'm not sure I'll be able to sit through an entire film.'

'You managed last night,' I reminded him.

'Yeah,' he said, 'on a comfy sofa. I don't think a cinema seat will be quite so accommodating.'

'There aren't cinema seats,' I told him. 'You'll see. I'd better go. I'll fill you in about it properly when I get back.'

I hung up before he could talk himself further out of it and indicated to Holly that I had another call to make. Then, with Ruby reassured that I wasn't going to be a no-show, I released Tink from her car restraint and climbed out of the car.

'Hey, you,' said Holly, giving me a hug. 'Everything okay?'

'Yes,' I said, as she fussed Tink, 'I just needed to let Ruby know I'd be there tonight.'

'I spoke to Jeanie late last night, and she said she'd confirmed at the meeting that you would be,' Holly told me, and I wished Jeanie had messaged to tell me that.

I'd hardly heard from her since she'd succumbed to Tim's advances, but then I was just as bad. I'd barely been in touch with her for days, either, though not because of a romantic entanglement, of course. My radio silence was purely down to my festive workload. Wasn't it? I supposed some of it might have been down to my preoccupation with looking out for Jude, but I didn't want to admit that. Not even to myself.

'I guess Ruby just needed to double-check,' Holly continued. 'I daresay she's having to make absolutely sure she's got enough volunteers. You're just helping out at the evening performance, aren't you?'

'Yes,' I said, 'I didn't want anyone covering my stall here this afternoon, and Ruby had told me a while ago that they'd had enough offers to support the afternoon film.'

'It's going to be a good day for a Christmas fair,' Holly said, opening the boot of her car. 'I've got loads of extra stock. Oh, and this,' she added, handing me a large envelope from the top of one of the many boxes of books. 'There's no rush to let me know what you think this side of Christmas, especially as you've got your hands even more full over the festive season now. Tell me, how is Jude?'

'Bruised and battered,' I said succinctly.

'Not up to flinging, then?' she asked, wrinkling her nose.

'No,' I said mock-sternly. 'Definitely not up to flinging. And even if he was, I wouldn't.'

She didn't look inclined to believe that.

'So what is this?' I asked, looking at the blank envelope.

I had a good idea but wanted to change the subject.

'My initial thoughts on your fairy character,' Holly said, smiling, mercifully distracted. 'She's a total powerhouse.'

'I like the sound of her already,' I laughed, going to open the envelope.

'Leave it for later,' Holly said with a nod to the hall. 'I can see Angus by the door waving at us, so we'd better get our butts in gear.'

'You're right,' I said, as I began to shiver. 'And it's too cold to stand about out here for long.'

'Especially dressed as a fairy!' Holly laughed.

As my stall set-up at The Laurels care home had been such a success, I'd gone with a similar arrangement and again had as much stock packed under the stall as I had on display. Once my crown and wings were in place, I walked around the entire stand to make sure I had enough clearance and wasn't in danger of knocking anything or anyone else out of kilter. My outfit had already been met with a variety of expressions from some of the other stallholders, not all of them approving, but the Connelly clan were impressed without exception.

'Well, now, Bella,' said Angus, stopping by as he did the rounds and spoke to everyone ahead of the time ticking down to when the doors would be officially opened. 'Don't you look the part?'

'I hope so,' I said with a smile.

'I'm almost tempted to pull on the old Santa suit,' he said thoughtfully. 'It's a shame it only gets the odd airing every year.'

'No time for that, my dear,' said Catherine, sounding relieved that he'd left it too late to change. 'There's a huge queue on the drive, and it's freezing out there. I think we need to open the doors now, don't you?'

It wasn't freezing inside, with blazing fires lit at either end of the great hall, but it might well be a different story once the doors were flung open and people started to pour in, bringing the frosty air with them.

'Right you are, my dear,' said Angus, sounding thrilled at

the prospect of so many members of the public being about to descend on his home.

'I hope Tink's behaving herself,' I said to Catherine, just as they were about to walk away.

'Always, my dear,' Catherine said fondly. 'She's one of the family, just like you.'

I felt such a warm glow as a result of her kind words that no Wynbridge winter chill could have cut through it.

'How are you getting on?' Dorothy asked me later, as she and Anna wove their way among the stallholders, doling out sandwiches and hot drinks.

'Wonderfully,' I said, looking at my stall, which I had already restocked. 'I can't imagine there are many people in Wynbridge now who haven't got at least one of my fairies living with them.'

I would think more about growing my business online in the New Year and possibly travelling to sell at some fairs further afield, too. Though I daresay there wouldn't be many that were as well catered as this one. Food and drink hadn't been part of the stand price, a large percentage of which was going to the charity that Anna and Jamie ran from the converted hall's stable block, but that was Dorothy for you. If you stood still long enough, she was bound to cram you full of cake and other tasty delights.

'And Angus said you've had loads of photos taken, too,' Anna added, coming over with an empty tray tucked under her arm.

'I have,' I said, readjusting my wings. 'I'm so pleased I got properly dressed up now.'

'It wouldn't surprise me if "hashtag away with the fairies" is trending online,' Anna said, beaming, putting air quotes around the words.

I hoped she was right.

'Right, come on, Anna,' said Dorothy. 'Let's get that urn filled up again.'

I was properly pooped by the end of the day, and having collected Tink and resisted the temptation to open Holly's envelope when I returned to my car, I hoped that a quick soak in a hot bath would put the life back in my legs ahead of the festive film night in town.

'I might see you later,' Holly called as she headed off. 'I'll see how I feel.'

I had no idea how she had the strength in her right arm to drive, because her signing pen had been in full swing for hours. I wouldn't blame her if she decided to give the film a miss. Living out of town would make it more of an excursion for her.

'Oh, Jude!' I gasped when I opened the house door and found the table set for dinner, festive tunes playing and him grappling with the corkscrew in a bottle of wine. 'You didn't have to do all this!'

'To be fair,' he said, giving up on the wine, 'I haven't done much. I had dinner delivered and, as you can see, I've failed to let the wine breathe, so all I've really done is turned the music on. How have you got on?'

'Brilliantly,' I told him, slipping out of my shoes and taking off the crown I'd forgotten I was still wearing. 'I'm not sure where I'll find the energy to do it all again tomorrow, but fingers crossed for a decent night's sleep. How have you got on?'

'I've had a pretty productive day, too,' he told me, sounding very happy about it. 'I set my laptop back up earlier and read through the start of the book and the notes I'd made at the hall the day I was supposed to leave. It felt good to get back into it a bit, though my neck and shoulders ached too much to type for many minutes.'

'Well, I'm pleased you've not been bored,' I said, washing my hands at the kitchen sink. 'And tonight should be fun.'

'Now, about that . . .' he started.

'There are no cinema seats,' I told him, cutting him off quickly. 'It's all sofas and comfy chairs at the town hall, and I'll take extra cushions to make sure you're properly supported.'

'I was just going to say that I'd googled it and seen some photos from previous years, so I knew the set-up should be okay.'

'So you'll come, then?' I asked, showing him my crossed fingers and feeling thrilled that he had felt inclined to look.

'I'll come,' he announced.

'Yes!' I said, uncrossing my fingers and then ecstatically punching the air.

'There's actually someone I'm hoping I might see there,' he then added devastatingly.

My heart sank as I realized that that was most likely the person I'd seen him kissing under the gazebo at the Brambles party.

'That's perfect, then,' I said hoarsely as the very last dregs of any energy I'd conserved for the evening's outing upped and left.

'I asked for Maltesers and M&Ms,' huffed a disgruntled voice. 'And you've given me two bags of Maltesers.'

'Oh, sorry,' I said, taking back one of the packets and switching it for the requested confectionery instead. 'There you go.'

The huffy customer moved along the line to pay, and I tried to focus on who was next.

'You all right?' Ruby, who was in charge of the cashbox and card reader, asked when there was a lull. 'You don't seem yourself tonight, Bella.'

'I'm sorry,' I apologized. 'The Wynthorpe Hall fair was full-on today, and I'm more tired than I thought I'd be, even after a hot salt bath.'

My still-aching feet actually had nothing to do with me being unusually distracted. My lack of focus on the queue was all down to me being too focused on Jude, but I could hardly tell Ruby that.

I had secured him the biggest chair, where he could sit safe from the threat of getting knocked into or squished against, but now he was on his feet and milling about on the periphery of where everyone else was standing. I knew he was supposed to keep moving, so that was fine, and I wasn't too preoccupied with him getting walked into because there wasn't anyone all that close to him at the moment. I was more interested to see who he might end up talking to. So far, however, he hadn't talked to anyone. I hadn't taken my eyes off him – hence the confectionery muddle – so I was certain of that.

'You can leave me to it, if you like,' Ruby offered kindly, in spite of the fact that the queue was still snaking halfway around the town hall.

'No,' I said, pulling myself together, 'I'm fine. Let's get these folks fed and watered, and then we can get the film back on.'

For the next few minutes, I did what I had signed up to do and completely lost track of Jude as a result. With the film about to start again, I realized he wasn't back in his chair. That had now been filled by a canoodling teen couple, and after I'd rescued my cushions, I finally found Jude standing in the shadows right at the back of the hall, looking pained.

'Are you all right?' I asked, as Kevin McCallister began planning his assault on the two dastardly crooks who were determined to ransack his family home.

'No,' Jude said, grimacing. 'I'm uncomfortable.'

'Perhaps walking into town wasn't the best idea, after all.'

We hadn't drunk any of the wine that Jude had been trying to open, but as the frost had completely thawed, we'd thought the fresh air might invigorate us both. And it had, for a while, but Jude was understandably flagging now.

'I can call you a taxi if you like,' I suggested.

'No,' he said, 'it's okay. I've already got someone coming to pick me up.'

'Is that the person you were hoping to see here?'

I hated myself for asking but had done it anyway.

'Yeah,' he said, looking over my shoulder towards the door. 'Can I take your key for the house?'

We'd only come out with one, because we had been expecting to go home together. Or at least, I had.

'Of course,' I said, pulling it out of my pocket and handing it over. 'Here you go. If you could let Tink out when you get back, that'd be great.'

'No problem,' he said, shifting from one foot to the other. 'And then I might call it a night.'

'I don't blame you,' I said. 'I'm sorry if this has been too much. I shouldn't have suggested it.'

'It's fine,' he said. 'To be honest, it's probably done me good to get out. I think I'll go and wait outside.'

'Do you want me to come with you?'

'No,' he said, as he stiffly levered himself away from the wall. 'You stay here. I'll be fine. They'll be here in a minute.'

I watched him walk away, and with him went my chance to find out who it was that he had called on to come to his rescue. I was aware that it shouldn't have bothered me that it wasn't me, but it did. And for the first time ever, I watched the end of *Home Alone* and took no pleasure at all in seeing the aptly named Wet Bandits get their comeuppance.

Chapter 22

Jude was up with the lark and in a wonderful mood the next morning, which perversely made mine plummet. Whoever he'd spent some of the previous evening with seemed to have worked wonders on his state of mind, and I had to bite my tongue more than once to stop myself from asking who that was.

'If you've got room for me,' he said, as he whipped up his first hot chocolate of the day, 'I'd love to come to the hall with you this morning.'

'Oh,' I said, taken aback.

'But no worries, if not,' he said, most likely assuming I hadn't got space for him because of my response. 'I daresay you've got tonnes to take again, haven't you?'

'No,' I said, 'pretty much everything I need is still at the hall, so I can easily squeeze you in. I'm just surprised you want to come.'

'I don't think I'll manage to visit the fair itself,' he admitted. 'The last thing I want is to get bumped into by hordes of Christmas shoppers, but I wouldn't mind seeing the family.'

'You've changed your tune,' I commented. 'It wasn't that many weeks ago that you couldn't wait to get away from them.'

'I know,' he laughed. 'But then, quite a lot has changed in those last few weeks, hasn't it, Bella?'

He wasn't wrong, and not all of it for the good, but I didn't have time to succumb to thinking about the details of all that.

'You might have to get someone else to run you back, though,' I said instead. 'Assuming I've got stock to bring home. Because it might be too much of a squash to get you in with all of the boxes, even with the seats down.'

'I'm sure Jamie or Archie will oblige,' he said, 'or even Bear if he's there with Holly.'

I swallowed down the question of whether it was one of those who had escorted him home from the film night or whether it had been the mystery woman from the party.

'In that case,' I said, determined not to get distracted, 'let's get going.'

The fair had been busy on Saturday, but it was nothing compared to the number of people who turned out on the Sunday. I didn't see anything of Archie or Jamie at all, as they were both on car parking duty along with Mick, the hall handyman, and Gabe, who was Hayley's partner. I didn't see much of Angus, either, but I certainly heard his laughter echoing around the hall. He really could give Santa a run for his money when it came to ho-ho-ho-ing.

There was a brief lull in visitor numbers around lunchtime, and it was then that Jude put in an unexpected appearance. He carefully made his way around the hall, and I was intrigued to see that he picked up and paid for a few things, although I couldn't see what they were.

'Oh, Bella,' he said, beaming, when he eventually made it to me, 'this looks stunning!'

The stall was still holding up well. There were a couple of gaps I couldn't refill because I didn't have more stock, but I had strategically manoeuvred the sets of lights to cover those.

'It is pretty, isn't it?' said a woman who had a child in each hand. They were twins, I quickly realized. 'My two had to come and say hello once they'd had their copies of *Tall Tales* signed by Holly. Didn't you, guys?'

'Yes!' they both rushed to say at once.

'Well, I'm very pleased to see you both,' I said with a smile.

They were silent for a second and then both began talking at once.

'Is it true that you're making a fairy that will be in the next book?' asked one.

'What's it going to be called?' asked the other.

'Will they have superpowers?' asked the first, picking up the baton while the second caught their breath.

'Are those real wings?'

'Yes, can you fly?'

Jude looked at me with the biggest smile on his face and, caught out by the sight of his wholly happy expression, I felt my heart lurch. Tabitha had been a total idiot to break Jude's heart, especially for someone who then hadn't gone the distance.

'Most of that is top secret information,' I whispered to the excited duo, when I could finally get a word in.

'Of course it is,' they gasped, giving each other a look. 'We shouldn't have asked.'

'As you can't share the secret details of what's in the pipeline,' said their accompanying adult with a wink, 'maybe we could have a photo with you instead?'

'Oh yes!' the twins squealed, clapping, then bouncing up

and down and shoving their books into her hands. 'And you have to be in it, too, Mum. Come on!'

Jude kindly took at least a dozen photos with the woman's phone, then waited to carry on our conversation while the pair picked out their favourite fairies. Their mum very firmly said that the chosen fairies would be fluttering away until Christmas, and they accepted that with almost good grace. I let out a breath once they'd gone, feeling thrilled to have made such an impact and extremely grateful that Holly had suggested our collab.

Given the success of her debut book, our joining forces had the potential to send my sales soaring even higher! I could imagine I was going to end up making a lot of fairies to accompany the book, but I wouldn't compromise on the way they were made, and if demand outstripped supply, then I'd put people on a waiting list.

'My goodness, Bella,' Jude laughed, 'you're a total hit.'

'Oh,' I said self-deprecatingly, 'it's not me, it's my fairy persona. The wings make all the difference.'

I made them flutter to prove the point. They looked so pretty when they caught the light, and not for the first time I wished I could wear them all the time.

'I don't think it is,' Jude said seriously. 'The outfit might add a certain something, but actually the good stuff that comes along with them is all you.'

'I don't think—'

'Well,' he cut in, 'I'm telling you. Look how you've started to bring me back around to celebrating Christmas for a start. No one else in the world could have done that.'

I couldn't deny that I was thrilled about that and secretly

very happy to take the credit for turning his frown upside down every time Noddy Holder's dulcet tones rang out, which, in December, was a lot.

'And you've also kickstarted my . . .' he then began to say, intriguingly.

His words trailed off and I looked at him intently, willing him to finish that sentence. My heart was beating a tattoo, so I knew full well what it was that I wanted the next words to be, but my head didn't think it was particularly likely that they would be the ones to fall out of Jude's mouth.

'What have I kickstarted?' I asked softly when he didn't say anything further.

His eyes searched mine, and I felt myself drawn to him by some invisible magnetic pull. The hall seemed to fall silent in spite of the number of people still in it, and it was just me and him again. Just like it had been on the drive before we kissed.

'My passion for baking,' he said, as I was about to take a step towards him. 'You've got me in the mood to put my pinny back on and dig out all of my nan's favourite recipes.'

Was that *really* what he had been going to say before he took a beat? I didn't suppose I would ever find out, but I couldn't help wishing that what he'd originally been poised to say were the words I had been hoping to hear.

Was it perhaps possible that Jude was still feeling something for me, in spite of the fact that he was convinced my being in favour of brief flings rendered me incapable of feeling anything where love and romance were concerned?

I would have dearly loved to delve deeper into that conversation and maybe even find the courage to tell him that, where he was concerned, a fling wasn't what I wanted, but it wasn't the time or the place. I was just about to suggest that we should continue to talk when we got home, knowing that by then I could have plucked up the courage to ask him who he'd kissed at the party, when Bear appeared and, forgetting the bruised state Jude was in, clapped him hard on the back.

'Hello, mate!' he boomed.

Jude looked at me with watering eyes and gritted his teeth.

'Oh shit!' Bear then immediately apologized as I moved to steady Jude, who looked poised to pass out. 'I forgot. I'm so sorry.'

'It's fine,' Jude said, trying to sound blasé. 'No worries. You just set my recovery back about a fortnight, but that's fine.'

'Does that mean you'll be two extra weeks under my roof now, then?' I quipped, also trying to lighten the moment.

'You wouldn't mind that, would you, Bella?' Bear grinned knowingly, and I wondered what Holly might have surmised and said.

'If I throw up in your truck because of the pain, Bear, you only have yourself to blame,' said Jude, as some of the colour returned to his cheeks, while mine flushed bright crimson.

I was relieved he hadn't made anything of Bear's teasing comment.

'Are you heading home, then?' I asked, my voice sounding rather squeaky.

We'd both brought door keys with us on the off-chance.

'I am,' said Jude. 'Bear's driving me back, but first we're going to the garage to check out the state of my car.'

'Are you sure you want to see it?' I asked, stepping back around the stall as a couple wandered up and began looking through the few fairies I had left.

'That's what I said,' said Bear. 'There's no need to see it, because the insurance company will just write it off and deal with it.'

'Have you got one like this in silver?' asked one of the browsers.

'I don't think so,' I told them, 'but I can certainly check for you.'

'Yes, please.'

It was impossible to carry on the conversation with Jude and Bear then.

'I'll see you later,' Jude said to me.

'Sorry,' Bear apologized to the couple. 'We're taking up far too much space. See you later, Bella.'

By the time I'd found the couple the perfect fairy, the guys had gone. I hoped Jude wasn't going to regret seeing the wreck his car had ended up as, especially as he had been in the driving seat when it had been wrecked. That could be really triggering for him.

Visitor numbers picked up again in the afternoon, and by the end of the day, my stall was definitely displaying more lights and decorations than fairy folk. It was thrilling to think that so many of my fairy friends were heading off to new homes, and I hoped they would bring cheer to everyone they were destined for. As I tiredly packed the last few away, along with all my other bits and pieces, I told them not to feel sad. When their perfect person came along, they'd be ready to embrace them.

I didn't say any of that out loud, of course, because the other stallholders, who were also packing up their depleted stock, would think I was even further away with the fairies than they had already guessed!

I realized there was a bit of a lump in my throat as I stacked my boxes next to the now empty table. My perfect person had come along, but I hadn't found the courage to embrace him, and as a result I still didn't know if he felt the same way about me.

'You are staying for the buffet and debrief, aren't you, Bella?' Anna asked, as she began gathering together the chairs behind each of the tables. 'Dorothy has created a spread big enough to feed every visitor as well as every stallholder.'

'In that case,' I said, because I had previously put my name down and could hardly duck out now even though I wasn't in the mood, 'how can I resist?'

It was impossible to believe that when I'd signed up for the post-fair food and chat with the family about how the weekend had gone, I hadn't even known Jude existed, let alone fallen for him, talked myself out of falling for him and tripped back into him again. He'd only been in my life for about five weeks, but in that time he'd got me more emotionally stirred up than I'd been in the whole of my adult life.

So where did that leave me now?

More muddled than ever. I had thought I could handle having him living back in the house, but the look on his face earlier and the words he'd hinted at but hadn't spoken had thrown me into the maelstrom again . . .

'Bella!'

The tone of voice which accompanied my name being called suggested that it wasn't the first time it had been uttered.

'Coming!' I responded, as I realized I was the last person left in the hall and that I was developing a bit of a habit of tuning out. 'I'll just take my wings off and I'll be right with you.'

It was time I got a grip and rejoined the real world, even if it was currently confusing the heck out of me.

It was unanimously agreed that the Wynthorpe Hall Festive Fair had been a huge success, and the Connelly clan – not just Angus – very kindly agreed that it should become a permanent feature in the Wynbridge winter calendar.

Everyone who had a stall put their names forward to be invited back the following year, and not for the first time I thought that I had never known a family who gave so much and yet asked for so little in return. The extended Connelly family didn't get only a little in return, of course, because everyone thought the world of them and were always willing to come to their aid should the need arise. Though in reality, it was often the other way around.

I knew Jude was home when I eventually arrived back, stuffed full of fabulous food and with a bulging bag of leftovers packed by Dorothy for him, because his coat and boots were in the hall, but his bedroom door was firmly closed, and I assumed he must be sleeping off the exertions of the day. At least, that was what I was hoping he was doing, rather than fretting over the state he'd found his formerly lovely car in.

I had planned to spend the evening looking over the ideas Holly had given me for the fairy destined to join her doggy duo, but by the time I'd had a shower and then sat on the bed for a moment, I knew the only thing I was really good for was a few hours of undisturbed sleep. With Tink similarly worn out from her time at the hall, but for different reasons, we dozed off together and I don't think either of us moved during the entire night.

It was quite possible that I could have overslept the next morning, not that it would have mattered, because I was gifting myself a couple of lazier days after the long working hours over the weekend, but clattering from the kitchen roused me just before seven.

'Need a hand with that?' I yawned from the foot of the stairs.

'Shit, Bella,' Jude groaned. 'I'm sorry. I didn't mean to wake you.'

'It's okay.' I shrugged. 'I should have been up by now anyway,' I added generously, because he did look genuinely remorseful.

'Rubbish,' he shot back. 'I know for a fact that you were going to sleep until you woke this morning, because you told me so the other night.'

'Well, in that case,' I said with a smile, as I came further into the room, then realized Tink was waiting to be let out, 'what the heck are you doing banging about in my kitchen?'

'Looking for something that will take my mind off the crumpled state of my car,' he said gruffly. 'I mean, my old car.'

'I knew you shouldn't have gone to look at it . . .' I started to say, but the look on his face was indication enough that the last thing he needed from me, or anyone, was an 'I told you so' moment.

He delved further into the cupboard. Well, as far as he could with his still-stiff gait and aching chest.

'What about waffles?' I suggested. 'Do you fancy making me waffles for breakfast? I have streaky bacon and maple syrup, so we could go all-out.'

'Why not?' he said, shrugging, sounding less enthused than I would have liked.

We'd barely sat down to eat when his phone pinged, and when he read whatever it was that had landed, a dazzling smile immediately replaced his frown.

'Good news?' I asked with a nod to the phone as I piled more bacon onto my plate, even though I wasn't now sure that I wanted it.

'Hopefully,' he said, putting the phone down again. 'I'm going to head out in a bit.'

'Will you need a lift?'

'No, thanks,' he said, but frustratingly he again didn't elaborate.

'Just as well.' I smiled tightly. 'Because I'm really too tired to drive anywhere today.'

Chapter 23

Having helped clear the breakfast dishes as best he could, Jude then headed off to shower, and by the time I came down from getting dressed, he'd gone out. He hadn't given any clue as to where he was going or who he was going with, which was perfectly proper, and I knew I had absolutely no right to be put out by his absence but annoyingly I was.

The only good thing that came from the sudden surge in Jude's social life was that it put pay to me being tempted to have the in-depth conversation with him that I'd been thinking about at the fair the day before. Baring my feelings, my never-before experienced feelings, to a man who had actually gone off the boil would have been mortifying, especially as I was currently living with him.

Having taken Tink for a long walk around the block and caught up with Mum on the phone while I did so, purposefully avoiding all talk of relationships and focusing instead on how successful the fairs and market stall had so far been, I then made myself a hot chocolate from the depleted station and settled down to look at Holly's notes.

As I tore open the envelope, I felt a pang of guilt that I

hadn't filled Mum in about Jude's accident and the fact that he had moved back into the house, or that this time I was sharing the downstairs space with him, but, as was always the way where fairies were concerned, the moment I fell into their winged world, I forgot the rest of the world existed. Even the real reason why I hadn't further mentioned Jude to Mum was soon forgotten.

It wasn't until my tummy gave the loudest rumble that I realized how late in the day it was. Ordinarily, Tink would have alerted me to the passing of time, but she was still worn out from a weekend spent socialising and hadn't moved from her spot in front of the fire. It was currently unlit, but she had a vivid imagination and, as usual, snoozed with her nose practically in the grate, no doubt dreaming of the warming embers and bright, licking flames.

'Ow,' I said, wincing as I sat back in the chair and stretched my neck from side to side.

It took a few seconds for the feeling to come back and the blood to start properly circulating again. It was no wonder that the hospital staff had advised Jude to keep on the move. Not that I wanted to be thinking about Jude. The fact that he had been out all day was proof enough that he was capable of thinking for himself and also now well enough to fend for himself, too. Never mind the New Year; at this rate, he might be gone before Christmas.

'What do you think, Tink?' I asked loudly as I held up one of the sketches I'd been immersed in creating.

The notes Holly had supplied me with, along with a very basic drawing of her own – she had kept it simple so I could get the gist but not be too guided by her visual idea – had inspired me to create a fairy who I felt would fit the bill perfectly.

I wasn't sure how easy she would be to translate from paper to reality, but I was going to enjoy the process. And with only the Cherry Tree Café market stall now to keep stocked, along with a stand at the Wynthorpe Hall Winter Wonderland, which I wasn't responsible for manning, and a steadying trickle of online orders, I'd have time to immerse myself in it, which was no bad thing. A creative distraction was exactly what I needed.

Tink dutifully opened her eyes, then stood, stretched and came to loyally lean against my legs.

'You approve?' I asked, and her tail thumped. 'Come on,' I said, as a reward for giving me the seal of approval, 'let's have another walk, shall we?'

I had an early night, and there was still no sign of Jude when I went to bed. His bedroom door was closed the next morning, but his coat and boots were back, so I guessed he had come home at some point. The sudden distance between us, after the closeness I'd felt at the fair, felt a little strange, but then I could have been making too much of it.

I thankfully didn't have an excess of time to obsess over it, as I was responsible for setting up and running the market stall that morning. Having fed Tink, I wrapped up in my warmest layers, left Jude a note explaining I'd be back to see to her later and headed off.

'How are you getting on?' asked Jemma, not long after I'd finished setting up and had made the first couple of sales of the day.

'Not bad considering it's a Tuesday morning and freezing cold to boot. I smiled, rubbing my gloved hands together. 'I've already sold one of Lizzie's quilted hot-water-bottle covers, so the weather is helpfully playing its part.'

'She'll be thrilled,' Jemma said, smiling back. 'I've made you a coffee,' she added, handing it over. 'And I've got some extra iced and spiced bagged biscuits for the stall, too.'

'Thanks, Jemma,' I said, warming my hands around the insulated cup. 'I'll have a bag of biscuits myself. Cold weather always gives me an appetite, and I missed out on the last lot.'

'I can bring you out a bacon roll, if you like?' she offered kindly.

I put the cup down and paid for the biscuits, before opening the cellophane bag and releasing the deliciously festive aroma.

'Thank you, but I'd better not,' I said to her. 'I had bacon yesterday. These biscuits will more than keep me going.'

'*I'll* have a bacon roll if you're offering,' said Chris, who ran the fruit and veg stall and had obviously been listening in.

'Nothing wrong with your hearing, is there, Chris?' Jemma laughed.

'He's not allowed one, Jemma,' chimed in Steve, Chris's son, who worked alongside him. 'He's been told he's got to cut a few things out of his diet. Bacon's one of them.'

Chris looked furious.

'Good to know,' said Jemma with a nod. 'So I take it he shouldn't have had a bacon roll yesterday, then?'

'Dad!' Steve admonished him.

'You'd better tell me what else he's not allowed, Steve,' Jemma said, while I bit my lip to stop myself laughing at Chris's outraged expression.

'I'll give you a list,' Steve said, and Chris began to darkly mutter.

'How much is this bunting with the Christmas trees on?' a customer asked me, and I turned my attention back to what I was there to do.

The next few hours seemed to take an age to pass. Tuesdays weren't known for being busy, but I was gratefully kept amused for some of the time listening to the banter happening among the sacks of spuds and stalks of sprouts on the stall next door. It was well after midday when Lizzie came out to take over.

'I'm so sorry I'm so late,' she apologized. 'We had a rush on in the café. I didn't think there were enough people about for it to get busy, but everyone in town seemed to pile in for a while.'

'I'm not surprised about that,' I told her, handing over the money belt, 'it's bitter out here today, so no wonder everyone wanted to be inside when their bellies started rumbling.'

'Are you going to grab some lunch?'

'No,' I said regretfully, 'I need to get off home to see to Tink, but first I'll run you through what I've sold this morning.'

I wasn't going to rely on Jude to let Tink out, which was just as well, because when I got back, there was no sign of him again. He hadn't repaid the courtesy of leaving me a note, like I had for him, but then he had no real need to, had he?

'Where are you, Tink?' I called, as I unravelled my scarf and shrugged off my coat.

I found her curled up on Jude's bed.

'Come on,' I said, 'you shouldn't be in here.'

I ushered her out and closed the door, not quite shutting away the smell of Jude's aftershave.

'Let's get some lunch, shall we?'

It was late in the afternoon when I heard the front door open. I'd again become immersed in the fairy sketches and had also put together a mood board and some fabrics that I knew I could easily get lots more of and that I thought would be a great jumping-off point to show Holly. I'd sent her a message asking if she'd be about the next day, and she'd replied saying that she was coming into town so we could meet in the pub.

I more than happily agreed to that because it felt like ages since I'd seen her and Jeanie together. I hadn't hinted to Holly just how far I'd got with my plans, so I hoped she would be surprised by the amount of work I had to show her.

I cleared everything away while Jude swore in the hall, no doubt struggling to take off his shoes, and then I began getting out everything I would need for an evening of further fairy-making. So much for taking it a bit easier now I allegedly had less to do!

'Hey, Bella,' said Jude, when he finally came in.

'Hey, yourself,' I responded rather coolly.

It seemed to be taking him an age to get across the room, and when I looked at him, his face was ashen.

'Are you all right?' I asked even though I could see he wasn't.

'Not really,' he groaned. 'I think going out two days in a row has been a bit much.'

'Well,' I said, the words escaping before I could stop them, 'I hope it was worth it.'

'It was.' He smiled through the pain as he took a deep breath.

'Look,' I said, further losing control of both my mouth and my common sense, 'I know it's none of my business . . .'

'Go on.'

My head was screaming at me not to do it, but my heart really, really still wanted to know.

'What's none of your business, Bella?' Jude asked.

'I was just wondering,' I said, trying to make my tone suggest that I truly didn't care either way, although it must have been extremely obvious that I did, 'if you'd been out yesterday and again today with a certain person you kissed at the Brambles party.'

Jude was still making slow progress across the room, but my words stopped him in his tracks entirely.

'If I was what?' He frowned, his brow tightly knitted.

'I know I wasn't the only one under this roof who had a festive kiss that night, Jude,' I said, laughing. 'And I'm not referring to Tink.'

He looked genuinely confused, but I knew what I'd seen. That crazy light-up Christmas jumper he'd borrowed from Angus made him the most identifiable guy in the room. Or in this case, the gazebo.

'Bella,' he said, sounding flummoxed, 'I have absolutely no idea what you're talking about. I didn't kiss anyone that night. I haven't kissed anyone since our moment on the drive when we put the lights up—'

'It's fine,' I cut in. 'You don't need to make out nothing's going on. I saw you in the gazebo with someone that night and I just wondered if that's who you've been with today. And yesterday. I'm not bothered if you were,' I added, no doubt sounding like a total twit.

'Why ask, then?' he said crossly.

That was a perfectly reasonable question, and one I didn't have an answer for. Not one I was prepared to give him, anyway.

'Not that I was kissing anyone at the party,' Jude continued. 'That was solely *your* thing that night. But why ask this now? Why didn't you bring it up before?'

I was already wishing I hadn't brought it up at all.

'I was being kissed, rather than doing the kissing,' I reminded him, 'and I suppose I'm mentioning it now because I'm being nosy. Forget I said anything.'

'You're not asking because you might be feeling a bit jealous?'

'Of course not,' I snapped back, embarrassed to have been seen through, 'don't be so absurd. We've already established that we aren't right for each other, so why would I be jealous? You have a justifiable dislike of my favourite time of the year—'

'Had,' Jude automatically corrected me. 'And you're only interested in relationships with a three-week shelf life.'

I don't know where he'd plucked that timescale from. In the past, I would have considered three weeks about a week too long, but that wasn't the case where Jude was concerned, was it? My feelings for him had opened my heart to the potential of something far longer, but at the end of the day, he was still going to leave Wynbridge at some point. And when he did, I'd most likely be left broken-hearted, so there was absolutely nothing to be gained from telling him that.

'What's your point?' I huffed, wishing I could turn back time and bite my tongue.

'My point is,' he said, beginning to sound amused rather than annoyed, 'that as you've experienced my kissing technique first-hand, you might now be feeling jealous that I'm bestowing it upon someone else. Even though I'm not.'

The arrogant sod!

'I know what I saw,' I muttered, scooping up the fairy components I'd just started to set out, 'and believe me, I'm not jealous.' Liar, liar, pants on fire. 'Just like me, you're a free agent. You can kiss and spend time with whoever you like. I just didn't have you down as that kind of guy, that's all. I mean, why start something up now, when you're getting ready to leave town?'

'I'm not that kind of guy,' he said through gritted teeth. 'Never have been, never will be, but I haven't got the energy to try to convince you otherwise. And quite frankly, given that I haven't so much as looked at another woman since I met you, I don't see why I should.'

He walked off to his room, looking very much the worse for wear.

'Well,' I said to Tink, 'that went well, didn't it?'

'Oh my goodness, Bella!' Holly gasped, within seconds of me handing over my ideas for our fairy collab, 'you've totally nailed it. This is exactly the kind of aesthetic I was imagining.'

'Really?' I said, letting out a long breath.

'Really,' she repeated, looking more closely at it all. 'This is perfect. It's like you've looked inside my head and pulled out exactly the character I was imagining.'

'Well, thank goodness I've got something right this week.' I swallowed.

It was a huge relief that she was so thrilled with what I'd come up with, because I was in even more need of something to keep me occupied between now and Jude's still-to-be-determined leaving day. Ordinarily, Christmas would be taking up all of the space in my brain from now until New Year, but this year it was filled with my crazy feelings for a man I was only just really getting to know and my mortification at having potentially screwed things up with him. We hadn't spoken at all since I'd fluffed asking him the question about the mystery party kiss the day before.

'What have you got wrong?' Holly said with a frown, looking concerned, as she realized what I'd just said.

'What's all this?' Jeanie asked, pointing at my sketches as she came to join us.

The pub hadn't been open long and, aside from a couple of other customers drinking coffee rather than beer, we were the only people in there. Hence Jeanie's opportunity to take a quick break and join us.

'It's a secret,' said Holly, quickly but carefully putting everything back in the box file I'd transported it in and firmly closing the lid. 'You'll find out soon enough.'

Jeanie pouted, and I grinned at her predictable reaction. She hated not being in the know.

'Bella was just about to tell me about the balls-up she's made this week,' Holly went on to distract her, but in the process dropped me in it and banished my smile.

'What have you done, Bells?' Jeanie nudged. 'Slept with that juicy Jude you've still got staying under your roof.'

'No, I have not,' I said primly.

'I bet it's something to do with him, though, isn't it?' Holly asked shrewdly. 'I know you like him more than you're willing to let on.'

'I do like him,' I confessed, 'but there's no point, because he'll be taking off as soon as he's able.'

'Which has always made a guy the perfect prospect for you in the past,' Jeanie nudged again. 'Unless, of course, you've really fallen for him—'

'No,' I swiftly interrupted, before she mined my mind too deeply. 'I have not fallen for him. I'm just not willing to hook up with someone who I know has already got someone else on the go. There are limits, and that's mine.'

'Jude hasn't got anyone else on the go,' tutted Holly.

'Not anyone from around here, anyway,' added Jeanie.

'That's where you're both wrong,' I said, deciding to tell them what I'd seen and how Jude had denied it. 'I saw him kissing someone at the Brambles party, and I reckon that's who he's been spending so much time with during the last couple of days.'

'No way!' said Jeanie, her eyes like saucers.

'Yep,' I said, 'I saw him with my own eyes, and he's been getting messages on his phone since the accident and then disappearing for hours.'

'That is pretty damning evidence,' Holly sighed. 'What a shame. I really thought the two of you would make a good match.'

'So who was he kissing?' Jeanie asked interestedly.

'No idea,' I said, shrugging. 'I wasn't close enough to the gazebo to see, but it was definitely him.'

'The gazebo?' Jeanie squeaked.

'Yep,' I said with a nod, 'and wearing that crazy flashing jumper from Angus, there's no way he can deny it. Identity definitely and unequivocally confirmed.'

Jeanie looked at Holly, whose mouth had fallen open.

'What?' I said, looking between them.

'Is that jumper the only evidence you've got that it was Jude kissing someone in the gazebo?' Holly asked.

'Isn't that enough?' I laughed.

'Not really,' said Jeanie, biting her lip, 'because Tim turned up late for the party and was wearing exactly the same one.'

It was my turn to look wide-eyed then.

'He did not,' I gasped, feeling sick all of a sudden.

'And we snuck out and made up for the lost time in the gazebo,' Jeanie devastatingly added. 'Which was right around the time you disappeared from the party, Bella.'

Chapter 24

'I need to go,' I said urgently, as I jumped up and gathered my things. 'I have to apologize.'

Now Jeanie had enlightened me that it was she and Tim who had been kissing in the gazebo at the Brambles party, she thought the situation was highly amusing, but Holly was more sympathetic and mortified on my behalf.

'Don't forget all these messages you mentioned he's been getting and the trips out,' she hastily reminded me. 'There must be something he isn't telling you.'

'He's perfectly entitled not to tell her anything,' Jeanie said, standing up so I could get around her. 'Bella's just his landlady, and as she hasn't fallen for him,' she wryly continued, 'this is all of no real consequence anyway.'

'Let us know how you get on!' Holly called after me as I rushed off with the box file tucked under my arm and my face aflame with embarrassment and shame.

'Jude!' I called, the second I was in the door and had shrugged off my coat. 'Are you here?'

'Yes,' he said grumpily, as I found him sitting in a sort of supporting nest of cushions on the sofa. I noticed he had my favourite Christmas film channel on but turned it off the second I appeared.

'What are you going to accuse me of now?' He frowned. 'Stealing Rudolph's red nose? Bricking up the chimney? Scoffing the last of the mince pies?'

Actually, he *had* scoffed the last of the mince pies, but that was currently of no concern to me at all.

'I'm not going to accuse you of anything,' I said, sitting on the arm of the chair so I was facing him. 'I'm going to apologize.'

'Apologize?' he repeated, his eyebrows rising in surprise.

I took a deep breath, then said, 'Yes. I'm sorry for being such a prat.'

'Hey,' he tutted. 'That's my line.'

'Well, I'm borrowing it,' I told him. 'I've just seen Jeanie in the pub, and she told me that Tim was wearing the same jumper as you at the Brambles party. Not that I can really believe there's more than one of those in the world, but still . . .'

'Well, I could have told you that,' Jude huffed.

'So why didn't you, then?'

'Because you were hellbent on believing what you *thought* you saw, rather than what you *actually* saw,' he sensibly pointed out.

'That's fair,' I sighed, knowing I couldn't dispute it.

'I know it is.'

'I'm sorry,' I apologized again.

'I know that, too,' he said, sounding less put-out. 'I meant what I said about not having looked at another woman since I met you, Bella,' he added, making my heart go berserk.

Did he mean he hadn't looked at another woman because

– and the thought made my stomach swoop – he only had eyes for me, or was it that he hadn't had the chance to go anywhere recently where there were other women to look at? I had to concede that he had spent most of his time (up until the accident, anyway) either in the house or at the hall, and everyone at the hall was already taken. Whatever he meant, I could feel myself being navigated towards yet more turbulent waters and started to desperately paddle my canoe back out of the current.

'Well,' I said, as I quickly stood up again, 'that's sorted, then. I hope you really can forgive me for jumping to conclusions.'

'I do forgive you,' he said generously, then added, 'I admire you, actually.'

'Admire me?'

'Yes,' he said, 'you've obviously come straight here from finding out that you were wrong and have apologized without pause. A lot of people would have either put it off or found a way to gloss over the situation without having to say sorry. But then,' he said, smiling, 'you're not most people, are you, Bella?'

I did love the way he said my name.

'Nope,' I briskly gabbled. 'I can't abide putting things off or procrastinating over what needs to be done. If there's something to be dealt with, I get on with it. Whether that's doing the washing up or setting something straight. In my experience, it's always better to come clean and carry on.'

Funny that I hadn't applied that ethos to making it clear to Jude that the last thing I wanted to do with him was have a fling. Had I got my head around my feelings for him far sooner and then found the courage to tell him, it might have been us who had ended up kissing in the gazebo, rather than Jeanie and Tim.

I supposed I could have said something then, given that we'd cleared the air, but every minute that ticked by was a minute closer to him heading off, so it wasn't a situation I could get myself into now. I would have to consign his kiss to the memory bank, labelled *best kiss ever*, and carry on.

'Is that right?' Jude asked, and I wondered if he'd just read my thoughts. 'Come clean and carry on,' he repeated, mantra-like.

'Yep,' I said, as I quickly pulled my gaze away from his. 'Now, why don't you turn the TV back on, and I'll make us a drink. I'm certain you were watching that *Snow Globe Christmas* film when I came in, and I've only seen it half a dozen times.'

Jude rolled his eyes but picked up the remote, and I headed to the kitchen to cool off. Fingers crossed, that was the end of that and we were back on an even keel.

The air might have been cleared, but we were still skirting around each other the next day. I knew why I was avoiding anything deep and meaningful, but I wasn't sure why Jude was. That said, when I checked the calendar at lunchtime and realized I had fallen behind with yet another thing on my festive schedule, worrying about what was going on in Jude's head went completely out of mine.

'Oh, bugger and balls,' I muttered, letting out a frustrated groan.

'A double swear,' said Jude, looking and sounding amused. 'What's up?'

'Oh,' I said, 'sorry, I didn't realize you were there.'

'Evidently,' he laughed.

'The swears were justified,' I said, defending my rude

language. 'I'd forgotten I was supposed to be making something to enter into the Wynbridge bake sale at the weekend and I haven't given it a moment's thought.'

'I thought it was the Christmas tree and greenery auction.' Jude frowned.

'Oh, it is,' I told him, 'but there's a bake sale, too, and cookie-making and decorating workshops happening in the town hall at the same time.'

'Of course there are.' Jude grinned, and I remembered how he had, not all that long ago, commented about Wynbridge turning into a Christmas town worthy of a Christmas film. He'd been scathing then, but he didn't seem to mind now. At least when he did leave, I would be able to wave him off, feeling proud that, if nothing else, I'd restored some of his faith in the season. That was quite an accomplishment given his reasons for losing the love for it in the first place.

'I suppose I could make some more mince pies,' I said, opening and closing cupboards to check I'd got enough ingredients.

'What do people usually take?'

'All sorts,' I told him. 'The gingerbread house competition classes are the most popular, but they're the most competitively fought for, too.'

Jude's face lit up at the mention of gingerbread.

'Obviously that's way beyond my skill set,' I said quickly in the face of his wholly unexpected reaction.

'But not mine,' he batted back confidently. 'If you make the gingerbread today and let it rest, we could make the house and decorate it tomorrow, ready to take to the town hall first thing on Saturday.'

He sounded remarkably enthusiastic and very much as though he'd shrugged off the last remaining trace of lingering awkwardness. There was no skirting around each other now.

'But I'm sure I haven't got a single thing here that we'd need to do that,' I pointed out, in spite of his unexpected eagerness. 'The mince pies will be far easier.'

He fixed me with a look.

'And also far less fun,' he said in a sing-song tone. 'Where's your Christmas spirit, Bella?'

'You're right,' I said with a nod, deciding to wholeheartedly embrace his seasonal change of heart, even if it might put my own heart in further jeopardy. 'If you're offering to help, then this might be the only opportunity I get to do this and not make a total fool of myself.'

'You don't strike me as the sort of woman who worries about making a fool of herself.' Jude grinned.

Was that a dig about my misplaced kissing accusation?

'Surely you're someone who throws themselves in at the deep end and has a go at something without worrying too much about the outcome, aren't you?' he went on.

He wasn't teasing me, then; actually, he'd pretty much summed me up.

'You're right,' I agreed. 'If we didn't make mistakes, we wouldn't learn, improve and refine, would we? The way my fairies have changed during the time since I started making them is proof enough of that.'

'So we're making a gingerbread palace, then?'

That was definitely a residential upgrade!

'Let's start with a gingerbread house and go from there,' I suggested.

'In that case, I'll start writing a list of everything we're going to need,' Jude said enthusiastically.

He reached for my notepad and pen and then groaned because he'd overstretched.

'And I'll go out and get it all,' I told him sternly, 'but only if you don't get carried away and set your recovery back.'

'Someone's keen to get rid of me,' he laughed, then started writing.

I looked at the top of his bent head and resisted the sudden urge to kiss it. If only he knew . . .

It took Jude almost as long to write the list as it took me to buy everything. Stocks of ingredients were running low everywhere in town, and I guessed the competition was going to be even stiffer than usual. I had no luck finding boiled sweets in any of the shops, but Jemma came up trumps and weighed me out a few from the café's supplies.

'No prizes for guessing what you're doing today.' She smiled as she handed the bag over.

'And tomorrow,' I said. 'Apparently, it's a lengthy process.'

'But a fun one.'

'I'll let you be the judge of that when we submit our efforts at the town hall on Saturday morning.'

'You and Jude are baking together, then,' she said, having picked up on the 'we', and her gaze softened. 'How romantic is that?'

'It's purely practical,' I said succinctly, putting a stop to her train of thought and refusing to jump on it myself. 'I have no idea what I'm doing, but he does.'

As it turned out, Jude was an expert gingerbread-maker, and by the end of the day the fridge was packed with clingfilm-wrapped balls of the stuff. Between us, we'd drawn up a sketch of what we were hoping to achieve. I thought it looked rather ambitious, but Jude was convinced we'd manage it. Time would tell.

What we ended up with was far better than what I'd imagined we would be able to create, and Jude had been right – a lot of it came down to the finishing touches and decorations. It was fairy-themed, of course, and one of my favourite components were the bright-red fly agaric toadstools that flanked the door. They had a festive connection, too, which I had taken great delight in explaining to Jude as I set to work with the piping bag.

'I love the lights you've put inside,' he said, sitting down once the house was completely finished so he could take it all in at eye level.

I'd had to remind him to be careful on more than one occasion, because he had got so carried away that his injuries had pulled him up short when he'd rushed about and forgotten that he was still very bruised.

'I don't think putting two inside is too much, do you?' I asked, bobbing down to check the effect myself.

I'd made sure the door was wide enough to very carefully slide in two battery-operated tea lights, which lit the stained glass-effect windows up.

'No, it's perfect,' Jude confirmed. 'I daresay it will be light in the hall, so you needed two to make the windows really shine.'

'That's what I thought,' I agreed.

We looked at each other and smiled. We'd worked as a perfectly synchronized team throughout the entire process. My unwarranted accusation had been forgotten, Jude had been completely present the whole time – with no more mystery messages landing, as far as I could tell – and I had thoroughly enjoyed both the process of making the fairy house and Jude's company.

We'd laughed and chatted and even sung along to my festive playlist, which had been serenading us in the background, and even though this wasn't anything like my usual run-up to Christmas, I was having a wonderful time and I knew Jude was, too, because he'd told me as much on more than one occasion.

'Have you checked the forecast for tomorrow?' Jude asked, his eyes still focused on mine.

I quickly stood straight again and pulled my phone out of my jeans pocket.

'I have,' I said, as I unlocked the screen, 'but I'm going to see if it's changed.'

'I hope it won't rain,' Jude said, crossing his fingers. 'It would be such a shame if it did.'

'It wouldn't dare,' I said seriously. 'Not for the switch-on or the tree auction and bake sale. Or the Winter Wonderland, for that matter,' I added, so as not to jinx it. 'No, look.' I turned my phone around and showed him what had popped up.

'Snow!' he gasped.

'Only a potential light dusting,' I said, 'but even that would be wonderful.'

'For the most wonderful time of the year,' Jude said ecstatically, pointing at my speaker, because that song had literally just started playing.

We began to sing along, and Jude reached for my hand and

very carefully waltzed us around the kitchen. I didn't know what to do or where to look, but one thing I did know was that my mind was finally made up.

At some point during the next twenty-four hours, I was going to tell him how I felt about him. I was going to say that if he was game and we could make long distance work, then, for the first time in my life, I was up for a whole lot more than flinging with him.

Chapter 25

Jude and I were both up with the lark the next morning, and I was relieved to see that our beautiful gingerbread fairy house hadn't collapsed overnight. When I said as much to him, he theatrically rolled his eyes.

'I told you it wouldn't,' he reminded me. 'Have at least a little faith, Bella.'

If the day panned out as I was hoping it would, I was going to need all of the faith I could lay my hands on. I had spent much of the night thinking about my decision to tell Jude I was ready for more than a fling, and it still felt like the right thing to do.

I wondered what Mum was going to make of it, but I wouldn't ask her ahead of me putting my plan into action, for fear that she'd try to talk me out of it. Given our traumatic history where my father figures were concerned and the fact that she'd never had a serious relationship since, I felt she would have been bound to and I wouldn't have blamed her.

'I do have faith,' I said to Jude, with a nod to our clever creation. He raised his eyebrows. 'Now I've seen it's still in one piece,' I added with a smile.

He laughed at that, but his expression changed as his phone buzzed with an incoming message. My heart stopped skipping so abruptly that I almost tripped over it.

'Tea, coffee or hot chocolate?' I offered as he picked it up.

I hoped he wasn't about to announce that he was heading off again. That had been the outcome following the flurries of phone messages he'd received before. I would be so disappointed if our day didn't have the chance to develop as I had hoped it might. He didn't answer my question, and when I turned around, I found him frowning at the screen.

'Tea, coffee—' I started to say again.

'Sorry,' he cut in. 'Coffee, please. Coffee would be great. A strong one.'

I wondered if there was a reason why he needed it made strong and was about to offer breakfast options when his phone started to ring loudly.

'Are you going to answer that?' I asked, when he didn't.

'No,' he said gruffly, turning the volume down a bit. 'It can wait.'

It eventually stopped, but then immediately started again.

'You know,' I said, because I didn't want him ignoring it if it was important and he was only doing so because he felt an obligation to stay with me, 'you really don't have to come to town with me today if you're needed elsewhere.'

'What do you mean?' he asked, turning his frown on me.

'Well, the last time you had a phone influx, you had to head off,' I said lightly. 'So if there's a change of plan today, I honestly don't—'

'There's no change of plan,' he said with a smile that didn't quite reach his eyes. 'This isn't the person who got in touch before.'

He didn't say who it was this time around, but clearly he'd rather not have heard from them. Given that he wasn't about to dash off, I hoped that their mysterious intrusion wasn't going to tarnish what had previously had the potential to be such a perfect day.

'One coffee,' I said, setting the festive-themed mug down on the table. 'A strong one.'

'Thank you,' he said, looking a little more like himself again. 'Something tells me I'm going to need a few of these to keep up with what's happening in town today.'

'No, you're not,' I protested, and he gave me a look. 'Oh, all right,' I relented. 'Maybe just a couple.'

Lizzie had already kindly said that I could park behind the café, which was a weight off my mind because the parking spaces always filled up fast ahead of the tree auction and bake sale, and Jude and I couldn't walk into town because we needed to carefully transport the gingerbread fairy house.

Dressed in a long, woollen winter dress, boots, hat, scarf, gloves and my bright red coat, I hoped I was going to be warm enough. I was just considering adding another layer, when Jude appeared in a chunky jumper and smelling as well as looking delicious, and I realized my internal temperature was going to keep me cosy enough.

'You look absolutely lovely, Bella,' he said, as I readjusted my hat.

It was impossible to keep my curls trapped underneath it, so I had left them loose and they cascaded almost halfway down my back.

'Thank you,' I said, warming up even more as a result of the compliment. 'And I love your jumper.'

'It's not quite a Christmas jumper,' he said, looking down at it, 'but I think it'll pass muster, don't you?'

The red of it was an almost-perfect match for my coat.

'Definitely,' I agreed. Then added to stop myself from staring, 'We'd better get going, otherwise we'll miss out on the best trees.'

Having promised Tink I'd be back as soon as I could be, we left her snoozing in her bed and set steadily off into town. Jude had carefully lowered himself into the passenger seat and awkwardly pulled on his belt, before I set the box containing the gingerbread house lightly on his lap.

'Are you sure it's not too heavy?' I asked, biting my lip.

'It won't get the chance to be if you stop fretting and get on with driving, Bella,' he said, with a smile. 'The sooner we get there, the sooner you can take it from me again.'

Just as I had known it would be, the little market town was already heaving. As I squeezed my car into the tiny parking space and rushed to open Jude's door, a few snowflakes began to fall. I took it as a sign that romance was going to be guaranteed, and the feeling increased tenfold when I leaned in and Jude softly kissed my cheek.

'Thank you for giving me the love of this back,' he said, when we reached the packed square, which was full of greenery and trees, the scent of pine hanging heavy in the air. 'Just a short while ago, I would have done anything to avoid a scene like this.'

I felt my heart swell with pride. If I didn't give Jude anything else for Christmas – though I planned to, of course – the sight before us and his accompanying words would be enough.

'I'm not sure I can take all of the credit—' I started to say, but he cut me off.

'Oh, you can,' he nodded. 'You definitely can.'

Whereas the market square had smelled of pine, foliage and fresh air, the air inside the town hall was all cinnamon, spice and very much warmer.

'No way!' Jude laughed, when he looked towards the back of the building, where the gingerbread entries were being lined up.

'Careful,' I said, as someone nearly walked into him.

I was mindful of his bruised ribs, even if he seemed to have forgotten momentarily about them.

'What is it?' I asked, trying to look around him. 'I can't see.'

He was a few inches taller than me and was bravely standing in front to put a buffer between himself and the box in case we got jostled among the crowd. Though now I realized that that might not have been the best plan under the circumstances.

'There, look,' he said, stepping aside as we reached the dais, where the trestle tables positively groaned under the weight of so many gingerbread creations.

On a table in the middle of them was the best and most magnificent one of all.

'No way!' I gasped, echoing Jude's reaction. 'It can't be real.'

'Oh, it is,' said a voice next to me. 'And I don't want to even begin totting up the hours it has taken me to get it finished in time. You can guess whose idea it was, can't you?'

'Dorothy,' I said, 'it's a total triumph! You must be thrilled with it, really.'

'Angus's idea?' Jude asked.

'Who else?' Dorothy laughed.

'Where on earth did you make it?' I asked her. 'It must have been impossible to keep it hidden.'

Sitting proudly on a table all of its own was a gingerbread construction much bigger than the average doll's house and an exact replica of Wynthorpe Hall. There were countless windows and chimneys, and even a tiny figure of Angus, wearing a Christmas jumper and waving from the front door.

'I made one of the rooms behind the kitchen out of bounds,' Dorothy explained, 'and worked on it when I could. It's not turned out too bad, I suppose.'

I wondered how on earth they'd transported it.

'Not too bad,' Jude laughed. 'It's magnificent, Dorothy.'

She looked well pleased.

'It's for decoration only,' she said, with a smile. 'It isn't being judged.'

'Because you know no one else would stand a chance of winning if it was,' I said, and she blushed.

'So what have you got in there, Bella?' she asked, with a nod to the box I was still holding. 'If it's a gingerbread house for the competition, then you'd better register it quick. The entry time is almost up.'

I left her and Jude and rushed over to a woman called Kathleen, who was holding a clipboard and was efficiently in charge.

Once our entry had been registered and squeezed onto an already packed table, I took dozens of photos from all angles and then heard the bell ringing outside, which signalled the start of the tree and greenery auction.

'Come on,' I said to Jude, automatically reaching for his hand as we wove our way through the crowds and back outside again.

It was snowing a little harder and everyone had rosy cheeks, bright eyes and happy smiles. It was turning out to be, just as I had hoped it would, an idyllic festive day.

'You can't be serious,' Jude said in my ear when I finally began to bid on a tree. 'You'll never get it in the house. It'll touch the ceiling.'

'Trust me,' I said, raising my hand again. 'This is our tree.'

'How are you going to get it home?' he asked, sounding amused.

'Holly said she'll deliver whatever I buy in her new truck.'

I focused on the bidding, and when the gavel went down, I punched the air in triumph.

'Just as well Holly offered transport,' Jude laughed. 'It's a whopper.'

'Right,' I said determinedly, with a nod to the other side of the square, 'now we need the holly and ivy.'

I was on a mission.

'No mistletoe?' Jude asked, following close behind as I rushed off.

There seemed so much of it this year, and what was on sale was all full of beautiful creamy-coloured berries. I always wished I could fill the house with it, but with dear Tink likely to tuck into any fallen berries, I simply couldn't risk it.

'The berries are poisonous, remember?' I reminded Jude as I began looking through the bunches of ivy and bright, red-berried holly.

'Oh yes,' he said. 'And you have got loads of lovely silk stuff, haven't you?'

The silk mistletoe was very lovely, and although not the same, it was the safest option.

'More than enough,' I agreed.

'But can you ever have too much mistletoe, Bella?' Jude whispered in my ear, and I felt myself shiver, though not with the cold.

'How many bunches, love?' asked the man selling the holly, as I held up both huge plain and variegated bunches.

'Two of each, please,' I replied rather breathlessly.

Once I had explained to the vendors who would be collecting both the tree and the greenery I'd gone for, it was time for lunch. That day, there were more options than usual to choose from, because lots of vendors flocked to the town safe in the knowledge that they would be able to swell their pre-Christmas coffers.

'How's your mac and cheese?' I asked Jude, as I tucked into my raclette and made a mess of my serviette in the process. We'd both picked the German food stall for our first course.

'Delicious,' Jude said, through a mouthful. 'You've got a rogue bit of cheese,' he added, pointing at my chin.

'Don't worry,' I said before taking another bite, 'I'll tidy myself up when I've finished the whole thing.'

It took a while to devour the lot, and as we ate, we walked among the stalls, keen to see what else was on offer along with all of the green stuff. The snow hadn't completely stopped falling, and it was a genuinely picture-perfect scene.

'Hey, Bella,' said Lizzie, who was currently manning the Cherry Tree stall. 'Hi, Jude. Having fun?'

'So much fun,' I told her as I wiped my face again, and Jude handed me another bundle of serviettes. 'I can thoroughly recommend the raclette.'

'You look like you enjoyed it,' she laughed.

'Am I still wearing it?' I asked.

'No,' said Jude, with a grin so I wasn't sure if I believed him or not. 'You're good.'

'Are you sure you've got enough people to cover the stall?' I felt obliged to ask Lizzie after I'd given myself another wipe around. A few of my fairies were still for sale, after all.

'More than enough,' Lizzie said. 'I might need to call on you next week if you're going to be about, but for now, we're covered.'

'I'll be happy to help,' I told her. 'The only thing I've got planned for next week, aside from getting more ready for Christmas, of course, is making more stock and then running the pub quiz on Friday night.'

Since I'd got in a muddle over a couple of things in my diary recently, I'd been checking it much more regularly.

'In that case, I'll be in touch.' Lizzie smiled, then turned her attention to a customer who was keen to stock up on Jemma's biscuits.

'How are you holding up?' I asked Jude, as we walked away.

'I'm having a great time,' he told me. 'But I wouldn't mind a bit of a sit-down. Do you fancy heading to the pub? Or I can head to the pub and rejoin you in a bit, if you want to carry on.'

'No,' I said, 'pub sounds good, and I'd rather stick with you.'

'Perfect,' he said, smiling.

'Perfect,' I agreed.

It wasn't too busy in The Mermaid, because everyone was still milling about outside or in the town hall. I knew the gingerbread judging would be happening soon, but I wasn't expecting us to be placed. The taking part had been more than enough of an achievement for me, and a fun one at that.

'What can I get you?' Jeanie asked Jude with a grin.

'A pint of Winter Warmer, please,' he said, naming a local brew.

'Bella?'

'I'd love the same, but I'd better not as we came into town in the car.'

'You could leave it and pick it up tomorrow,' she suggested, grinning even more mischievously.

'I can't do that,' I told her. 'I've got a gingerbread house to transport.'

'We could leave that in the car, too,' Jude suggested. 'I don't think one night would do it much harm.'

'Did you hear that, Bella?' Jeanie winked. 'No harm can come from just one night.'

I gave her a tight-lipped look. Had I filled her in on the fact that I was going to tell Jude that I wanted to go for it with him, and for much longer than one night, she wouldn't have said anything like that. She would have been too shocked to say anything.

'In that case,' I said, ignoring her innuendo and refusing to meet her eye, 'I'll have a pint, too.'

'Take a seat,' Jeanie said, 'and I'll bring them over.'

She didn't usually offer table service.

'No, it's okay,' said Jude, as a noisy crowd came through the door. 'I can carry a couple of pints. Why don't you bag that table next to the fire, Bella? I have a feeling it's about to get busy in here.'

He wasn't wrong: within the next couple of minutes, I watched the place fill up, and I also watched Jude talking intently to Jeanie. Whatever he was saying, she was rapt. When she had eventually pulled our pints and Jude had paid for them, she gave me the biggest thumbs-up behind his back as he walked over.

'Everything all right?' I asked, wondering what had got her so excited.

'Yes,' he said, setting the glasses down. 'I'm really starting to feel better now.'

That hadn't been what I meant, but I raised my glass to his improving health and ignored my friend, who was doing some sort of stupid happy dance behind the bar.

'Fancy another?' Jude asked, once we'd both finished our first pints.

When we'd arrived, I had been considering telling Jude how I felt about him while cocooned in the warm, fireside sanctuary of the pub, but it had got so busy and so noisy since our arrival that it was impossible to have a conversation without raising your voice, and I just knew that the moment I blurted out what I wanted to say, the pub would fall miraculously silent.

'Not for me,' I said, 'but thank you. Are you having another one?'

'No,' he said, looking around, 'I don't think I will. It's got a bit loud in here, hasn't it? Shall we head out again?'

'I'd love that,' I practically had to shout, 'but only if you're really feeling up to it.'

I was mindful now that we would end up walking home and didn't want him overdoing it, especially as I had designs on tiring him out in a different way to walking around Wynbridge. One pint wouldn't have put me over the limit to drive, of course, but I never got behind the wheel after any amount of alcohol. It was a rule I lived by.

'I'm good,' Jude told me. 'Come on, let's go.'

When we stepped outside again, it had stopped snowing and I thought the temperature had dropped, but that could have been because it had been so warm inside the pub.

'Look,' I said, pointing at the town hall. 'The door is open again, so the judging must have finished.'

'Let's go and see if your fairy house has been awarded a prize,' Jude said keenly.

'*Our* fairy house,' I corrected him, linking my arm though his.

Our effort hadn't been placed, but I didn't feel disappointed at all, especially when I looked at those that had. There were all sorts of categories and the under-twelves was my favourite. The Spice Girls concert stage tableau was a masterpiece, and Jude loved the most lopsided little house, which made me love him all the more.

'Do you mind if I disappear for a minute?' he asked me, once we'd finished looking around and I'd purchased a couple of bags of cookies. 'There's something I need to pick up from the market.'

'No,' I said, thinking how fortuitous his timing was, 'of course not. I was actually going to ask you the same thing. There's something I want to do, too.'

'In that case,' Jude suggested, 'let's meet next to the Christmas tree in half an hour. Assuming that gives you enough time?'

'More than enough.' I nodded. Along with making a small purchase, I was going to be running through the speech I'd been formulating, and any longer than that would crank my nerves up way too far. 'I'll see you there.'

A makeshift and very festive floral display had been set up

around the tree courtesy of a local garden centre, along with a few ornate benches, and as I approached at the end of the thirty minutes (which had seen me talking to myself and geeing myself up), I saw that Jude had bought the same thing that I had picked up.

'Great minds,' I said tentatively, shakily holding aloft the small sprig of mistletoe I had sought out and planned to use to embellish my speech.

Jude smiled and nodded, his cheeks turning endearingly even pinker.

'Great minds indeed,' he said with a smile. 'Let's sit down, shall we?'

'Yes,' I said, taking a breath. My legs had begun to shake as I realized we were potentially on the same track, so taking the weight off them would be most welcome. 'Let's do that.'

There was no one else making use of the thankfully dry benches, and I led us to one that was almost hidden from the view of the still-bustling market behind the huge, lit tree and afforded us the privacy I felt the moment was going to require.

'So,' said Jude, sounding appealingly unsure.

'So,' I echoed, hoping that he really had picked up his sprig of mistletoe for the same reason that I'd purchased mine. Surely there could only be one. 'Jude,' I therefore bravely said, 'I have something important that I need to tell you.'

'And I have something important that I need to tell you, too,' he said straight back to me.

'In that case,' I said, taking a breath, 'you go first.'

'No,' he said, shaking his head. 'You first.'

I opened my mouth to tell him, but when the moment came, I felt unbearably nervous and just couldn't do it.

'Please don't make me go first,' I ended up saying instead.

In the end, Rock, Paper, Scissors settled it, and I held my breath, waiting to hopefully hear Jude's version of what I had been planning to say.

'Okay.' He swallowed. 'I'm just going to come out with it, because I've been rehearsing this for a few days now, and I'm still not sure I've found the right words.'

'If it's any consolation,' I told him, feeling slightly better, 'that's exactly how my part in this exchange is going to start.'

His shoulders dropped a little, and his eyes sought out mine.

'The thing is,' he continued, briefly looking at my lips and then into my eyes again, 'I haven't been able to put that kiss on the porch out of my mind, Bella, and the better I've got to know you, the more I've thought about it and the more I've wanted to do it again.'

This was going exactly the way I had hoped it would. We were going to say slightly different versions of the same thing and secure ourselves a very merry Christmas as a result. That was, as long as my galloping heart didn't make me pass out.

'Since my accident,' Jude went on, 'we've spent so much more time together in the house, and it's made me realize . . .'

'It's made you realize what?' I asked, feeling fit to burst.

'It's made me realize that it's time to pick up the relationship reins again,' he said in a rush.

'Oh, Jude,' I gasped, inching closer as my heart made a further bid to beat its way out of my chest.

'I know,' he said, also shifting along the bench towards me, 'that you're not looking for anything long term, but I want to be with you, Bella, even if that is just for the duration of my stay in Wynbridge.'

My heart suddenly wasn't sure that our versions of what we had been gearing up to say were going to be quite so in tandem.

'So you're saying . . .' I swallowed.

'I'm saying that I'm willing to fling with you, if you'll have me,' Jude laughed, his eyes lighting up further with the words. 'If all we can have is a brief encounter before I move on, then let's go for it and enjoy being with each other while we can. It isn't the sort of relationship I've gone in for before, but I know you have, so—'

'Well,' I cut in, as my stomach rolled and I rushed to put Jude straight about what it was that I wanted from him, how my desire for fleeting flings had completely waned since he'd come into my life and my home, 'that would be great. So great, but the thing is—'

'Having given it some truly deep consideration,' he then devastatingly interrupted me, 'given what happened with Tabitha and the fact that I haven't had any sort of a relationship since then, I think a short-term thing would be best for me right now – and as that's what you're into, it's a win for both of us. Right?'

There was no way I could inflict my 'I've fallen for you, hook, line and sinker' sentence on Jude now, so I did the only other thing I could think of. I held aloft my mistletoe sprig, kissed the lips off him and hoped my heart would one day forgive me.

Chapter 26

There must have been a hundred moments between Jude telling me what he wanted – a quick fling – and us arriving home (having stowed the gingerbread fairy house in the car for safe-keeping overnight) that I could have told him what I had *really* been going to say on the bench in the square, but I didn't capitalize on any of them.

As we slowly paced the pavements back towards the house, I played over what Jude had said and tried to convince myself that having a fling with him, which was all he could under-standably currently commit to, was better than having nothing with him. By the time I put my key in the house lock, breath-less with the feel of his hand on the small of my back, I had completely recategorized him as 'dynamite dalliance' material. In my head, at least.

'So,' I said, having let Tink, who was ecstatic to have us back, out into the garden.

'So,' Jude responded, his eyes trained on mine.

'Are you hungry?' I asked.

'For you,' he said huskily, then rolled his eyes. 'That was bad, wasn't it?'

'So bad,' I agreed, then added, playing my part, 'but as you're only going to be a part-time partner, I suppose your dire chat-up lines are of no consequence.'

'Well, that's a relief,' he exhaled, 'because I'm really out of practice.'

If, a few hours later, anyone had asked me if Jude had been out of practice, I would have hotly denied it. 'Hot' being the most appropriate word. Sitting astride him in my bed, with my hair cascading onto his broad chest and my breath coming in short gasps, as another wave of pleasure pulsated through me, I was certainly far from thinking he was out of practice.

'Bella,' he gasped, gripping my thighs as I moved to arch my back and he came to another shuddering climax of his own.

He'd said my name so many times, I was in no danger of forgetting it. He loosened his grip a little, and I looked down at his face.

'Are you sure you haven't been practising?' I asked him breathlessly, as his hands moved to cup my face and draw my lips down to his.

'I honestly haven't,' he whispered between kisses. 'You just have this talent for bringing out the best in me.'

'Likewise,' I said as I kissed him back. I found myself thinking that if Jude had been in the market for a relationship and this had been the sex I would have lived with for the rest of my life, I would have been the happiest woman alive. And the most satiated, too.

'You're amazing,' he said as I sat back and tried to banish the thought that I was warming him up for someone else he would meet further down the line.

'Thank you.' I smiled, determined to halt my thoughts in their march towards a darker place. It would be so much better to stay in the moment, which had been more than magnificent. 'You're amazing, too,' I told him. 'You aren't too stiff, though, are you?'

'Jeez!' Jude laughed, and I felt him tense inside me. 'Give me a minute, would you?'

'I meant,' I giggled, nimbly climbing off him and lying down next to him, 'from your injuries.'

He turned to face me and quirked a brow.

'Are you sure about that?'

'No,' I laughed. 'But given that you are still recuperating, I will generously give you the minute you require.'

'So kind,' he said, tickling me.

Having missed dinner, we ate supper in bed, then made love again during the night. I woke in the early hours and found Jude looking at me, his head propped up on his hand.

'Are you okay?' I asked sleepily.

'Yes,' he said, softly kissing me. 'Go back to sleep.'

When I woke the next morning, I realized he hadn't been okay. And the reason I knew that was because he was gone.

I slept late, and it was the sound of a truck horn that woke me. I stretched out in the bed and groaned. My body ached, but in a wonderful way, and I turned over to reach for Jude, but found the side of the bed where he'd previously been sleeping was stone cold. My eyes sprang open. He wasn't there.

The truck horn sounded again, and I pulled on my dressing gown and went to the window. Tink was barking downstairs, but until that moment, I hadn't heard her.

'You all right?' Holly frowned as I opened the window and leaned out. 'We did say a ten o'clock drop-off, didn't we?'

'Ten!' I gasped. 'Is it really?'

She checked her phone.

'As good as,' she said, shrugging, then her eyes widened. 'Are you *entertaining*?' she whispered theatrically, making a rude gesture with her hands that I would have thought Jeanie capable of, but not Holly. 'Is Jude up there with you? Shall I come back later?'

'No,' I said, 'Jude is not up here.' I had no idea where Jude currently was. 'I've just overslept. Give me five minutes and I'll be down.'

I rushed to pull on joggers and a hoodie and tied my curls up in a scarf, before dashing down the stairs. Jude's bedroom door was open, and his room was empty and as neat as a pin. The only thing out of place was an envelope with my name on, sitting on the bed. I felt suddenly sick as I pulled the door shut, tripped over Tink and went to let Holly in.

By the time I'd opened the front door, she'd unloaded the bundles of holly and ivy and stacked them in the porch.

'Are you sure you need all this?' she said, giving the greenery a nod.

'Yes,' I said, moving it to one side and trying to sound as though everything was fine, even though it was anything but. 'I'll easily use it all and might even need more.'

My head was spinning, but I wasn't going to let it show. I wanted to assess the situation before jumping to conclusions and knew if I told Holly what had happened, then there'd be no opportunity to fathom things for myself, undisturbed. She'd mean well, better than Jeanie, who would rant and rave before she knew even half of the facts, but I needed to process what had or hadn't happened in peace.

'Now for the tree,' Holly said, looking at it with her head on one side. 'You'd better get Jude out here. I don't think we can manage it between just the two of us.'

'Of course we can,' I said, shoving my feet into my trainers and hoping Holly wouldn't notice the absence of Jude's outdoor wear from the hall. 'He's still asleep,' I fibbed. Though he might have been, just not under my roof. 'And he was knackered after yesterday,' I added, which was definitely true. 'I don't want him further damaging his ribs moving my Christmas tree, do I?'

'I suppose not,' Holly said, thankfully accepting what I had said. 'Come on, then. Have you got a stand for it?'

'Yes,' I said, 'that's all set up, so hopefully, between us, we'll find a way to get it in there.'

We were both scratched to pieces by the time we were done, and the hall paintwork had borne the brunt of our struggle, too, but when the tree was finally in situ, straight and secure, it did look magnificent.

'It's huge, Bells!' Holly laughed, as she stood back to admire it and I filled the stand with water. 'Why on earth did you go for one this size?'

'I always have a big tree.' I shrugged.

The real reason, of course, was that I had wanted to pull out all of the stops and indulgently decorate it with Jude. I'd had plans for an entire day filled with festive music, seasonal snacks and plenty of mulled wine. His neat and tidy room suggested I wouldn't be doing any of that now, though. Not with him, anyway.

'I can't believe our toing and froing hasn't woken Jude,' Holly further laughed. 'What exactly did you do to tire him out yesterday?'

I was saved from having to reply by her mobile, which started to ring.

'Oh yes,' she said, when she answered it. 'I had forgotten. I'll go back for it.'

'Do you fancy a coffee?' I asked her, when she ended the call.

I felt rather bad that the only reason I'd offered was because her side of the phone conversation had suggested she'd say no.

'No, but thanks for the offer,' she said regretfully. 'I'd better get off. I need to pick up a prescription from the vets for Jasper.'

'Another one?'

'I know,' she huffed.

'And on a Sunday?' I frowned. 'That'll cost you.'

'Don't,' she said, making for the door. 'We're such regular customers now that Will has cut us a deal. We've got a hotline to him 24/7.'

'Oh dear,' I said, glancing over at Tink, who was sniffing at the tree but making no effort to wreck it, which I knew Jasper would have.

'I need to keep writing about dogs to pay for my dog,' Holly quipped, and I admired her for seeing the funny side. 'I'll see you in the pub on Friday for the quiz, if not before,' she said, giving me a hug. 'Bye, Jude!' she then mischievously shouted, but of course there was no reply.

'Yes,' I said, looking at the thankfully closed bedroom door. 'See you on Friday, and thank you for delivering Christmas. I couldn't have had that tree without your help.'

'And that would have been a tragedy.' She grinned.

Once she'd gone, I considered my options. I certainly wasn't in the mood for dressing the tree, but I wasn't sure I was ready to face whatever was in the envelope Jude had left on his bed, either. I fed Tink, made myself a coffee, then had a long, hot shower and got dressed.

I checked and rechecked my phone, although there were no missed calls or messages, and then tried to eat some breakfast, but it didn't matter how many times I chewed each mouthful – they were almost impossible to swallow.

'Right,' I said, abandoning the cereal bowl and rushing to Jude's room, where I snatched up the envelope and returned to the sofa.

I opened it with shaking hands and pulled out what looked like a hastily written letter.

'Darling, Bella,' I read aloud. 'I know that my sudden and silent departure after the hours we have just spent together will make you think the very worst of me, so I have left these words to try and explain why you will have woken this morning and found me gone.'

I drew in and let out a shaky breath, then curled my legs under me on the sofa.

'Come on, Tink,' I said, patting the cushions.

She obligingly jumped up, and I nestled close to her as I continued to read the rest of what Jude had written, this time in my head.

As you may recall, I didn't answer my phone yesterday morning before we headed to town, and that was because I knew it was Tabitha who was ringing.

I felt nauseous then, assuming that Jude had returned to the woman who had previously broken his heart as well as snatched away his enjoyment of the festive season, but I couldn't have been more wrong.

She's been messaging me for a few days, but something she sent last night when I made a trip to the kitchen after you'd fallen asleep made me realize just how deeply I have fallen in love with you, Bella.

I let out a shocked gasp, which made Tink jump.

Tabitha was begging me to forgive her and go back to her in time for Christmas, and it was the moment I read those words about being together for the holiday season that I realized the only person I ever want to be with at Christmas is you. My feelings for you surpass everything I have ever felt for anyone else, and especially Tabitha.

'Oh, Jude!' I choked, letting out a strangled sob.

I only ever agreed to have a fling with you because I know that's the extent of your relationship remit and I couldn't bear not to be with you, even if it was only ever going to be for the shortest time. But that was a mistake. Last night was like nothing I have ever experienced before, and I am broken-hearted to know that I'll never experience it again. I don't expect you to forgive me for taking off without a spoken word, but I hope, having read this, you will perhaps understand why I have done it. I love you, Bella, with the whole of my heart, and I always will.
Jude x

I dropped the letter, pulled Tink closer and sobbed so hard I thought my heart was going to tear in two. If only I had spoken first in town the day before. If only I had told Jude that I had fallen in love with him and that I wanted to have so much more than a stupid fling with him, then neither of us would now be nursing a broken heart.

I had felt bereft the first time I'd thought I had lost him, but I had been given a second chance courtesy of his terrible crash, and I had now stupidly squandered that, too. I had wasted the opportunity to confess my true feelings, and now I was left with a shattered heart, which ached with longing and regret.

Chapter 27

After a day and most of the night spent curled up on the sofa, trying to decide what to do next, I remembered that my car was still parked behind the Cherry Tree Café and if I didn't hurry up and collect it, Lizzie and Jemma would be in touch to check up on me. I knew their enquiry would be kindly meant, but for the time being, I didn't feel up to hearing from or facing anyone.

Therefore, close to dawn on Monday morning, I snuck to town in the dark on foot and returned with my car and the partially collapsed gingerbread house, which I then completely dismantled and reluctantly threw away, uneaten.

The process of doing that felt entirely symbolic and gave me the courage to ring Jude's mobile with the intention of telling him the truth about what I had been planning to say and how I wished I had been brave enough to talk first during our bare-all conversation on Saturday.

I didn't want our relationship to be as unsalvageable as the gingerbread confection we'd so lovingly crafted, but my determination went unrewarded because the call didn't connect. I briefly considered sending him a message, but as the phone was turned off, I knew he wouldn't read it. Besides, I could hardly declare undying love via a text, could I?

And involving the Connellys by asking if they had a forwarding address for Jude was definitely out. For now, at least. I would only go to them if I couldn't come up with a better plan, because I knew my enquiry would raise questions . . .

Lizzie rang the house early on Tuesday to ask me to cover the market stall, and that meant there was only one thing for it. I had to paste on a smile and put my best foot forward. There was no reason for me to have to talk to anyone about my former housemate, and I hoped no one had designs on talking about him to me, either. I also hoped that if I wasn't sat at home obsessing over the situation, then I might start to feel at least a little better about it and perhaps even come up with a solution.

'Hey, stranger!' said Jeanie, when she spotted me rearranging the stall and adding a few extra festive fairies from one of the crates I'd rummaged through at the house. 'Where have you been hiding yourself?'

'Hey, yourself,' I said, giving her an extra-bright smile. 'I haven't been hiding anywhere. I've just been busy. I'm all set for the quiz on Friday, though. It's going to be even more seasonal than the last one.'

'Oh, right,' she said, looking at me quizzically, and I wondered if I'd overdone it on the Tigger-like behaviour. 'Well, that sounds great.'

'How's Tim?' I asked, hoping to distract her, while keeping my eyes trained on the stall.

I knew I had dark circles under my eyes as a result of the torrent of tears and lack of sleep that Jude's departure had instigated, and that no amount of concealer could disguise them or stop Jeanie noticing them.

'I haven't seen much of him because of his current shift pattern, but he's more present than Jude,' she then unfortunately said. 'Why didn't you tell me he'd left?'

It was my turn to look puzzled then. Or at least attempt to.

'I didn't realize you'd be interested.' I shrugged. 'It was no big deal and always part of the plan, wasn't it? He was feeling better, so it was time for him to head off.'

I realized then that I had no idea who he had called to pick him up. I didn't think it could have been anyone I knew, because Jeanie would have just mentioned it. A moonlight flit would definitely have been commented on, and even though I had been keeping my head down, she would doubtless have heard the details of that from someone in the pub and quizzed me sooner than this.

'Who told you he'd gone?' I asked breezily as I picked up a packet of hand-printed cards and put them down again in the exact same spot.

'It was Pete from the garage,' she told me. 'He said Jude had been in touch about his car yesterday and told him that he was no longer in the area. So where's he gone, then?'

'I don't know,' I laughed, still none the wiser as to who had assisted him in his clandestine departure. 'I'm not his keeper.'

A young couple then fortuitously stopped at the stall and started looking through what was on offer.

'Fair enough,' Jeanie said, shrugging, sounding a bit put out. 'I'd better get back to the pub. I'll see you later.'

'Friday,' I said. 'I probably won't make it in before the quiz.'

'Friday, then,' she said back. 'See you then.'

I knew I'd only just got away with trying to blag my way through the conversation, and I felt bad for being so offhand with her. It wasn't her fault that I'd made such a mess of things, but the last thing I wanted was to have to talk it all out. That is, with anyone other than Jude, who was now goodness knew where and not using his phone.

I still hadn't decorated the gargantuan tree that I'd secured at the auction, and having it centre stage and unadorned was doing nothing to lift my seasonal spirits. What I needed to do was put my 'best foot forward' ethos into practice at home, as well as while I was out and trying to convince my friends that Jude's departure hadn't impacted me.

I also needed to get a grip behind closed doors before my continued low mood tarnished my happy decorating memories and rubbed off on Tink. I could tell she was missing the housemate she'd always been smitten with, so she didn't need me being down in the mouth, too.

'Right, Tink,' I said cheerily when I arrived home after another freezing cold day working on the stall. I was now determined to stop telephoning Jude's turned-off mobile. He clearly didn't want to hear from me. I had to accept that we'd missed our opportunity to honestly come together, and therefore I was going to put him right out of my head in time for Christmas, starting now.

'Let's get the tree dressed, shall we?' I said with a clap.

Tink had no idea what I was saying, but barked in approval and skipped around my feet as I lugged boxes and bags and then began to set everything out. Hopefully my upbeat tone would be enough to reassure her that I was feeling more enamoured with life again, even though that was as yet far from the truth.

'This is going to take a while!' I said, looking at the vast collection.

I immersed myself in my childhood memories of decorating the tree with my grandparents as I found the perfect place for each treasured ornament and strand of tinsel, and I refused to think about how romantic the scene would have been if my original decorating idea, the one that had been created around Jude's presence, had gone according to plan.

'Three, two, one!' I counted down, once I'd finally finished primping.

I'd already checked that the long cables of fairy lights were working before I'd hung them and then again when they were in place, so I could scrutinize their arrangement and make any adjustments ahead of putting everything else on the tree, but this was the big reveal.

'What do you think?' I asked Tink as the warm white lights began to gently twinkle.

She woofed again.

'I agree,' I said. 'Utterly perfect. Now, let's just add a few more things, shall we?'

I did feel a little better once the tree was dressed. The plethora of treasures from my childhood and the more recent past were all artfully hung, and I lingered over each of them, admiring their details and remembering the story behind how they had come to be in the collection and the precious remembrances associated with them.

The handcrafted and handsewn felt Christmas puddings and stars made with Nanna were firm favourites and still looked good. Conversely, my kindergarten angels were beginning to show a little wear and tear, but that didn't matter. They still had pride of place on the top of the tree, just like they had when my grandparents were alive, and the very first few fairies I had attempted to make were in prominent positions, too.

When I was completely happy with the result, I sent a few snaps to Mum.

'Now,' I said to Tink as I gave her a fuss and tried to keep the wobble out of my voice, 'I don't know about you, but I reckon some warmed wine would slip down a treat right now.'

I was just filling my glass a second time when my mobile rang. I snatched it up, hoping it was Jude, but it wasn't.

'Hey, Mum,' I said, belatedly realising that she had set up a video call.

'Hey, yourself,' she said, smiling. 'What's with the photos? I always get a video tour of the decs. Is everything okay?' She frowned, peering closer.

'Yes,' I said, carrying my wine over to the sofa and sitting down heavily. 'The photos were a preview. I thought we could have a tour another day.'

'I see,' she said, drawing the words out as I propped up my phone.

I took a sip of the wine, then put the glass down on the coffee table next to my mobile.

'You look tired, Bella.' Mum frowned.

'Just what every woman wants to hear,' I joked. 'And of course I do. You know I've been working flat-out.'

Mum shook her head.

'I do know that,' she stated, 'but you don't look work tired.

What's going on? And do *not*,' she warned as I opened my mouth, 'try to fob me off.'

I sucked in a breath and released it, puffing out my cheeks.

'I've fallen in love with the guy who was staying in the house,' I blurted out with no preamble, taking myself completely by surprise. It must have been the tongue-loosening strength of the wine I'd drunk on an empty stomach. 'I didn't tell you, but he had a bit of a car accident and ended up staying here longer than planned. And as a result, I realized I had fallen completely in love with him.'

'Oh, my darling,' Mum said, beaming and looking delighted. 'No wonder you look so worn out. That's wonderful!'

'Well,' I went on, 'it would be if . . . wait, what?'

'I said that's wonderful,' Mum said again, louder this time on the assumption that the signal had cut out. 'I was beginning to think you were never going to find the one.'

I didn't tell her that the one had left before I'd found the nerve to tell him that he was the one, or before he'd told me that I was the one for him.

'You never thought I was going to . . .' I said weakly, the words trailing off as my world fell completely off its axis. 'I can't believe you thought I'd ever be in the market for love, Mum. Not after what happened to you. You've only ever gone in for flings since the two despicable dads did a bunk, and I'm exactly the same. Brief encounters only.'

Mum's eyes widened, and her expression changed to stricken.

'That's not how it is, Bella,' she told me, sounding shocked. 'That's never been how it is.'

'But you didn't find anyone else after they left,' I stammered. 'Not for years anyway, and then only fleetingly.'

She vehemently shook her head.

'I never had more serious relationships when you were growing up,' she rushed to say, 'because I was scared of the damage it would do to you if they came to an end. I could have coped, but I didn't think you could. I hadn't fallen out of love with love, I was just trying to protect you from further hurt.'

I took a moment to try to process the seismic shock she had just delivered. It was nowhere near long enough.

'But I genuinely thought you were through with love, Mum.'

'No,' she said. 'Never. And it was never my intention to put you off romance, either.'

I looked at her and blinked as my brain tried to recalibrate.

'So if the right guy came along now—'

'I'd grab him with both hands,' she cut in. 'In fact, I think he has.'

'But what about Nanna and Grandad?' I numbly reminded her. 'They were dead within weeks of each other.'

'After a lifetime of happiness,' Mum said succinctly. 'Neither of them would have had it any other way.'

'But I thought your career was everything to you,' I said, tracking back to the rest of what I had believed about her. 'Work became your everything because love had let you down.'

'No.' Mum swallowed. '*You* were always my everything, Bella,' she said forcefully. 'You and Mum and Dad, and then work. I worked the hours I did to secure the life I have now, not because I had sworn off love. And I did date sometimes, but I never introduced you to any of the men in my life, because I wanted to protect you when the relationships ended. That way, I always hoped, your understanding of love wouldn't get further skewed.'

'So you did still date?' I whispered, the words barely audible.

'But I can see now,' Mum went on, 'that I got that completely wrong. It was never my intention to put you off falling for someone, Bella. I thought your penchant for flings was a choice you'd made because it worked for you. I assumed it was a way of life that suited you, rather than something adopted because of what had happened in our collective past.'

'My preference for flings was based purely on my belief that all serious and involved relationships would end in heartbreak,' I told her. 'Having seen what you went through, Mum,' I added, as a rush of horrible memories from the time when my stepdad left washed over me, 'I didn't want to risk that ever happening to me.'

Mum's face crumpled.

'I'm sorry,' I apologized.

'No,' she sniffed. 'I'm sorry, my darling, and now I want you to listen to me, Bella. Listen and believe.'

I nodded, feeling close to tears myself.

'Love is worth the risk,' Mum said, emphasising every word.

Her declaration left me floundering. It was completely at odds with everything I had clung to.

I swallowed. 'You can't really think that?'

It had been hard enough to hear, but her request that I should believe it felt insurmountable.

'I do,' she said seriously. 'Love is worth the risk, my darling.'

'It is?' I squeaked, feeling heavy tears starting to build. 'You really think it is?'

If that was the case, then I definitely shouldn't have let Jude slip through my fingers. If only Mum and I had had this conversation just a few days ago.

'Yes,' she added fervently. 'I do. And now you've fallen in love with this guy—'

'Jude,' I interrupted, choking the words out. 'His name is Jude and he's gone, Mum. Gone before I told him how I felt, and gone before he'd told me that he loved me.'

'Oh, my darling.'

'I only know how he felt, because he left me a letter,' I sobbed. 'Such a beautiful letter.'

The tears that had threatened finally began to spill over.

'In that case,' Mum burst out, 'you have to contact him! Ring him—'

'I've tried,' I said desperately. 'His phone's turned off. It has been for days.'

'Find him, then,' she said insistently. 'You *have* to do this, Bella. Ask everyone who has got to know him where they think he might have gone. Do *not*,' she said forcefully, 'let this chance of true love pass you by.'

'I don't know . . .' I started to say.

Having only just made up my mind to put Jude out of it, could I really do another about-turn? I was in danger of meeting myself coming backwards.

'Well, I do,' Mum said, her face filling the screen. 'I know. You get out there and find him, or I'm going to come and look for him myself!'

I felt utterly exhausted. My entire relationship ethos had just been smashed to smithereens by the person who had most influenced it.

Though to be fair, Mum had never said that I shouldn't form attachments. I supposed I had just assumed that would be her opinion because, as far as I was concerned, she'd never dated since the dads had left. She'd mentioned a few men since she'd moved to France, but that was doubtless because I was distanced from the impact of any potential resulting fallout. Though hadn't she now hinted that she'd found someone who could be her one?

I tiredly ended the call after promising to do my best, but not really knowing what I was going to do next. One thing I was certain of, though, was that my Christmas now had the potential to become a complete calamity.

Reeling from Mum's revelation about her attitude to relationships, by the time Friday night rolled around and it was time for the festive quiz in the pub, I still hadn't made up my mind about tracking Jude down. It felt like only seconds ago that I had been trying to convince myself to forget all about him. In theory, the 'I love him, he loves me, Mum's all for it' mantra sounded pretty straightforward, but I was a jumbled mess of emotions and wasn't sure any good would come of rushing into acting just because Mum had said I should.

One thing I did know, though, was that I had no desire to draw parallels with the previous quiz night, so not a drop of inhibition-evicting alcohol passed my lips. I wholeheartedly adopted my very best Pollyanna persona and flitted about in full-on festive mode, wearing my brightest smile and my flashing Mrs Claus hat and telling all my very best cracker jokes.

In fact, I did such a convincing job that there wasn't a single soul present who wouldn't have been shocked to their very core to have suddenly become privy to the tumultuous and tortuous feelings battling it out in my heart.

'Question number seven,' I said loudly, my voice further

amplified by the microphone, 'in the popular carol "The Twelve Days of Christmas", how many pipers were piping?'

The din this question created was deafening. No one, it seemed, could hold a note.

'Question number eight—'

'Hang on!' more than one voice called.

'I'm only up to maids a-milking!' shouted someone else.

'Question number eight,' I firmly repeated, 'what year was *Die Hard* released?'

I ignored the comments that Bruce Willis in a vest didn't qualify as festive and ploughed, smilingly, on.

'Are you okay?' Jeanie asked, when we reached the halfway point and had a brief intermission.

'Yes,' I said, rubbing my temples, 'just trying to keep track. It's busier than last time, isn't it?'

'Yes,' she said with a nod, while deftly pulling pints. 'Definitely busier, but that's not what I meant.'

I knew exactly what she meant.

'I must have done a decent job before,' I laughed, 'to get so many extra punters in tonight.'

'Are you sure you don't want a drink?' she asked me.

'Yes, I'm sure,' I said decisively, though I was almost tempted. 'It's the Winter Wonderland tomorrow and Molly's solstice celebration, too, and I don't want to miss either of those because I can't drive there because I'm still over the limit.'

'I was only suggesting one drink,' Jeanie said, grinning, 'not a vat like last time!'

I refused to think further about last time. Or indeed any time that included Jude.

'I'll stick to the mocktails.' I winked as I raised my glass and hoped she'd believe I was just 'busy' stressed, as opposed to 'wrestling with feelings for the love of my life' stressed.

I knew I'd pulled out all the cheery stops, but Jeanie and I had been friends forever and if anyone could read between my lines, it would be her.

'Are you going to the Winter Wonderland tomorrow, Bella?' said a voice next to me.

'Oh, hey, Bear,' I said, turning around and looking up. He seemed even taller close to and especially in the confined space of the packed bar. 'Yes, I wouldn't miss it for the world.'

Any opportunity to pet a reindeer and ride in a horse-drawn sleigh was unmissable as far as I was concerned, even if I was going to be doing both on my own.

'Are you going?' I asked, when Bear didn't say anything further.

'Yep,' he said. 'Holly's all for it. She reckons there'll be reindeer.'

'Oh, there will be,' I confirmed keenly. 'Though not pulling the sleigh. The Wynthorpe ponies have that honour. You'll need to get there early if you want a parking space that's not a million miles away from the action.'

'Duly noted,' he said with a nod. 'You know, Bella—'

'Time's up,' Jeanie interrupted, as she pulled at my sleeve and pointed at the clock.

'What is it?' I asked Bear.

'Never mind.' He sighed as Jeanie rang the bar bell.

He picked up the microphone, which screeched as he handed it to me.

'Right, then,' I said, clearing my throat. 'Duty calls.'

The second half of the quiz proved to be as controversial

for some as the first, thanks to a question about Alan Rickman's character in *Love Actually*, and when it was time to tally up the totals and announce the winners, there was some careful checking and rechecking required. Everything was eventually settled, and I was exhausted by the time I'd handed out awards to the top three teams and thanked everyone for coming along.

'And this is for you,' said Evelyn, handing me the exact bottle of the new blend from Brambles distillery that I'd picked up for me and Jude on the night of their party. 'To say thank you for all the trouble you've gone to to make the quizzes so memorable.'

I could feel a lump forming in my throat, and my eyes were prickling with tears, too. I couldn't let myself down now, not after doing so well all evening.

'Thank you,' I said. 'I need this after what some of you have put me through tonight!'

I held the bottle aloft, and everyone clapped and cheered. I couldn't look at Jeanie.

'Are you okay?' Holly asked later, echoing what Jeanie had said earlier.

'I am,' I told her. 'Just a bit knackered.'

'She's doubtless getting too excited for Christmas,' Jeanie chimed in. 'There'll be tears before bedtime. You mark my words.'

She was probably going to be right, but I wasn't about to explain why.

'Back in a sec,' I said, leaving the Brambles bottle on the bar. 'I just need to nip to the loo.'

Bear was coming out of the door that led to the restrooms just as I went to walk through it, and he held it open for me. I was the other side of it before he said anything.

'Bella?' he said loudly, making me jump.

'Yes?'

'Are you going to the solstice thing as well as the Winter Wonderland tomorrow?'

'I am,' I confirmed.

'Great,' he said, nodding.

'Are you?'

'Yeah, we've been invited.'

'Bear!' Holly called. 'Are you coming or what?'

She couldn't see me, so it doubtless looked like he was standing there holding the door open for no reason.

'On my way!' he shouted back. 'I'm only asking because Holly mentioned she was going to talk to you about it,' he said, with a nod in her direction. 'I bet she's forgotten, hasn't she?'

'Yes,' I laughed, 'she hasn't mentioned it.'

'We'll see you there, then.' Bear smiled, moving off.

'See you tomorrow,' I responded, not giving the conversation another thought.

Chapter 28

I spent another night tossing and turning and mulling everything over. I had been looking forward to making the most of the most magical weekend in the local festive calendar, but when I got up that Saturday morning, my head was frustratingly more preoccupied with concerns about facing the Connelly clan than petting reindeer.

I had no idea if the family were aware that Jude had left the area, because I hadn't been in touch with any of them since he'd gone, and that weighed heavily on my mind because they were bound to ask after him. Another worry making its presence felt was the misguided promise I'd made to Mum that I was on track to talk to Jude, in response to a message she'd left on my phone while I was compèring the pub quiz.

The day hadn't even got going, and I was already feeling worn out. I was supposed to be feeling sick with excitement and festive-ready by now, but my mood that morning was more akin to the misery felt by someone who suffered with the January blues.

'Come on, Tink,' I said, as I rattled her lead and refused to further tie myself up in knots over it all. 'Let's go for a walk. A really long one.'

The extra-long walk benefitted us both. It gave Tink enough exercise to keep her worn out while I was away for the day (it was going to be too busy at the hall to leave her in the Wynthorpe kitchen), and given how icy the pavements were, it gave me something to focus on that wasn't my horribly heavy heart.

'I'll see you later,' I said to my faithful companion once I'd forced down the little breakfast that I could manage. 'Don't do anything I wouldn't do.'

I piled on the layers as it was so cold, and rather than wearing my red wool coat, I opted for what I considered a more coun-trified outfit, complete with waxed coat and warm Dubarry boots. With the heating in the car on full blast, I was rosy-cheeked by the time I arrived and parked. The stunning sight of the grounds so beautifully dressed for the Winter Wonderland lifted my spirits a little and made me glow all the brighter.

'Mum said could you head round to the kitchen when you've got a minute, Bella,' Archie, who was directing the already steady stream of cars, requested as soon as I had turned off the car engine.

'Did she say why?' I asked, feeling my mood plummet again.

I had been hoping to avoid talking to the family until at least the solstice celebration, which was happening in the afternoon, but my plan to keep my head down had been scuppered even before I'd got out of the car.

'Probably,' Archie said, grinning, 'but I can't remember now.'

'If you're not careful, Archie Connelly,' I tutted, 'you're going to end up as distracted as your father.'

'He's halfway there already,' Jamie chimed in. 'Come on, Arch. I'm not parking all this lot on my own.'

'I'll see you later,' I said to them both.

'Are you staying for the solstice celebration?' Archie asked before I set off.

'Yes,' I told him.

'Excellent!' Archie said with a nod, looking delighted.

'Why?' I asked, feeling justifiably suspicious.

'Because the more people that attend,' he told me, 'the less chance there'll be that Molly will rope me in to doing something as part of the performance.'

'*Performance?*' I squeaked.

I hadn't attended the ritual before, so hadn't known there would be a performance.

'Archie!' Jamie shouted.

'You know,' Archie said vaguely as he headed towards his brother, 'the Oak King and the Holly King battle and all that malarkey.'

'Right,' I said, biting my lip and feeling none the wiser. 'Of course.'

With my conscience still pricking, and not wanting to feel worse about it, I did head to the kitchen door as Catherine had requested. However, I didn't knock particularly loudly and when no one immediately answered, I sloped off again, keen to have a wander around the Wonderland before it got too busy.

'Did you know,' the guy looking after the reindeers told the assembled crowd, 'that the reindeers pulling Santa's sleigh are actually all girls?'

There was a collective gasp among the younger onlookers

and a few suspicious frowns from the adults accompanying them. I gave a smile and a nod, already aware that it was the female reindeer that kept their antlers during the winter, and therefore it was the gals who provided the horsepower. Reindeer power. Whatever.

I lingered and listened to the explanation I'd already heard, and then, as the crowd dispersed, I stepped forward to take a few close-up photographs before more admirers arrived. One reindeer among the little herd was particularly photogenic and very friendly.

'Loki loves all the attention,' the guy told me, as another group of people began to quickly gather around. 'He'll pose all day.'

'Does he live up to his name?' I asked, as the reindeer gave my phone a closer look. The photo I snapped was endearingly all nose.

'Sort of,' the guy said, nodding. 'He's definitely a trickster, though not cunning with it.'

'It's their noses that I love most,' I said, tucking my phone away and looking properly at Loki's furry snout. 'They look so . . . cute. Does that sound a bit pathetic?' I grimaced.

'Not at all.' The guy grinned. 'I think cute pretty much sums it up. Were you here last year?'

'I was,' I confirmed.

'I thought I recognized you.'

I looked at him properly. He was a handsome chap and clearly a bit of a charmer. I knew the odds were stacked in his favour if he was asking all the women who were attending on their own if they'd been at the Winter Wonderland before, because practically every local had. Consequently, I wasn't flattered by his suggestion of recognition and went to move out of the way for the next round of reindeer admirers.

'You're the woman who makes the fairies, aren't you?' he then surprised me by saying. 'You had a stand here last year and you were wearing wings. I picked one up for my nephew, and he loved it. Still loves it, actually.'

I felt myself turn warm. Not particularly because I had assumed he had been trying a line and felt guilty that he hadn't, but because his nephew loved the fairy friend I had created.

'I'm delighted to hear it.' I smiled. 'And I still have my wings, of course. They're tucked under my coat as it's so chilly.'

'Of course,' he laughed. 'Can I buy you a hot chocolate later?'

'I'm not sure I'll be here later,' I said, taking another step away. 'But thanks for the offer. And do give my regards to your nephew.'

Before I'd met Jude, I would have said a definite yes to an offer like that, but given that my heart and emotions were still a tangled mass of confusion, I felt no inclination to acquiesce and moved on.

I spent the rest of the morning walking around the woodland trail, stamping my card when I found the landmarks and highlights marked on the paper map that Hayley the housekeeper, who was an accomplished artist, had drawn up. I wondered how the Connellys kept coming up with fresh ideas every year. I didn't claim my prize when I reached the end, though, because I could see that Anna was doling out the stickers and festive treats and I still wasn't in the mood to chat.

A while after my delicious lunch, which was made up of mini pigs in blankets in a plum and cranberry chutney-topped bread roll, I made my way through the woods to the very edge of the hall's boundary, where I knew Molly was going to be setting up for the solstice celebration.

Ordinarily, she had told me the day I dropped her fairies off, the fire and ceremony would be held right in the middle of the woods, but with the date falling on the same day as the Winter Wonderland, she had changed the location so as not to draw too much attention and to keep it a more intimate occasion.

I was looking forward to finding out what the ritual entailed, even if Archie's earlier words about getting roped in to feature in it had made me feel a little apprehensive.

'Bella!' Molly called with a smile when she spotted me.

She looked stunning in a full length, dark-green velvet hooded cloak and with her red hair framing her beautiful face.

'Am I too early?' I asked, looking around.

There was no one else in sight.

'Not at all.' She smiled, holding out a hand. 'You arrived at exactly the moment you were meant to.'

That was just the sort of thing she always said, and I supposed she was right.

'Are you all right?' she asked, her smile switching out for a frown as I took the hand she offered. 'You look a little pale.'

I had thought I was still rosy-cheeked, but perhaps she could see beyond my complexion.

'I'm okay,' I said, and swallowed. 'Just feeling a little tired.'

'And missing Jude?' she ventured, giving my fingers a gentle squeeze before letting them go.

So his departure was known about, then.

'A little,' was as much as I was willing to confess. 'I've never actually shared the main part of the house with a guest before, so it does feel a bit strange now he's gone . . .'

My words trailed off when I realized how intently Molly was looking at me.

'A guest,' she echoed ethereally.

'Um,' I said, and swallowed, 'but I suppose I'll soon get used to it.'

Molly didn't say anything further, and I knew she was waiting for me to fill the silence, but I wasn't going to fall for that tactic. Her approach wasn't witchcraft, just clever psychology. She let out a long and steady breath, released me from her gaze and took a slow anticlockwise turn around the bonfire.

'I just wish he hadn't left without talking to me!' I suddenly blurted out. 'I got up last Sunday to find him gone. If only he'd talked to me . . .'

Okay, so perhaps a little witchcraft had been involved. I had felt adamant that I wasn't going to say anything more and suddenly I'd shared far more than I probably should.

'That sounds to me,' Molly began, smiling serenely as the sound of feet and voices coming through the trees towards us began to get louder, 'like a wish you should take to the Wishing Tree.'

The vast hawthorn tree wasn't all that far from where we were standing. In a clearing, it stood like a beacon and was visited by anyone who had a wish to make or a hurt they needed help to heal from.

Some visitors even tied tokens to the branches to accompany the wishes and help the wind carry them off and away. I'd never made a wish there myself, but I had dropped fairies off from time to time for visitors to take, and I knew that there had been a recent change in the tokens people were being asked to leave behind to make the process as environmentally friendly as possible.

'I think it's too late for wishful thinking,' I whispered, willing myself not to cry.

'It's never too late,' Molly said insistently. 'Go after the ceremony and say the words you've just said to me directly to the tree.'

There was no time to talk with her further, because everyone else who had been invited to the celebration stepped into the clearing at that moment and Molly quickly began directing them to where she wanted them to sit. Archie and Jamie were then long-sufferingly dressed up as the Oak and Holly Kings, and their seasonal battle commenced.

Their duelling was occasionally a little too boisterous but, accompanied by Molly's mellifluous voice and explanation, the ritual sent my already emotional state soaring even higher, and when she began to talk about the returning light and slowly lengthening days and the joy that both could offer us, I had to blink long and hard to stop the tears I could feel building starting to flow.

As the Oak King was finally crowned and everyone rejoiced in the rebirth of the sun, which had been stubbornly absent all day, Molly caught my eye and nodded in the direction of the Wishing Tree. I took that as my cue to leave, slowly stood up and silently slipped away.

The laughter and cheers of the others gradually lessened, and as I stumbled over a tree root, I realized it would soon be dark and I needed to make my way quickly, otherwise I could end up lost in the woods for hours. I wasn't sure what good saying a few words to the ancient tree was really going to do, but if there was even the slightest chance it might help clarify my thoughts, I was willing to give it a go.

Completely alone, I made no attempt to check the tears which traced a path down my cheeks and stung my face in the icy breeze. What a Christmas this was turning out to be. Ordinarily, my festive spirit could barely be contained by now, but this year I wouldn't know where to look to find it.

Blinded by my tears and not paying proper attention to where I placed my feet, my boot caught again, only this time I went flying. With a heavy thud, I fell into the tree clearing. I made no immediate attempt to get up, neither caring that the ground was cold and hard nor thinking that I should probably check I hadn't done myself a mischief.

'I thought Elton said you should "Step into Christmas",' a voice somewhere near the tree said, and my heart rate rocketed. 'Not fall headlong into it.'

It was a voice I would have recognized anywhere.

'Are you hurt?' it came again, this time much closer.

'Jude!' I sobbed, his name catching in my throat as he gently helped me to my feet and then let me go.

'Bella,' he said back, his eyes searching my tear-stained and probably grubby face.

'What are you doing here?' I asked, roughly wiping my cheeks on the sleeve of my coat.

'Someone told me about the tree, and I felt drawn to come here and make a wish,' he explained, sounding surprised to find himself in the clearing. 'What about you?'

His explanation gave nothing away as to where he'd been staying or how he'd got to the tree.

'What about you, Bella?' he asked again softly.

'I came to make a wish, too,' I said shakily.

'Was it to erase me from your memory?' he asked with a grimace.

'No,' I told him. 'It was more of the time-turning variety.'

'Oh?' He frowned. 'Let me guess. You wanted to go back to the time of Catherine's request to put me up and turn her down?'

'No,' I said, although there had recently been conflicting moments when that might have been a tempting option. 'I was going to wish to go back to when we'd been sitting on that bench in town and you told me that you wanted to have a fling with me.'

'Fascinating,' he breathed, taking a step closer and looking deep into my eyes. 'That's the time I was going to wish I could go back to, too.'

'Why?' I asked tentatively.

'You know why if you read my letter.'

'Tell me anyway,' I whispered.

'Because telling you I wanted a short-term fling was a huge mistake,' he began. 'I realized that the night we spent making love.'

Those words on his lips, and the memory of that night, made my breath catch.

'I wanted more from you, Bella,' he continued. 'So much more. And knowing you couldn't commit to anything deeper, I left. I couldn't bear the thought of waking up with you and having to pretend.'

'I see.' I swallowed.

'I'm so sorry,' he apologized. 'I know I shouldn't have done that, but for the sake of my sanity and my heart, I didn't know what else I could do. I tried to convince myself that since you're someone who only goes in for short-term relationships, you wouldn't mind, but . . .'

His words trailed off and I shook my head, unwilling to let him shoulder the blame for the mess that we'd made of everything between us. I was every bit as guilty as he was for the muddle and misunderstanding.

'I'm sorry, too,' I said, reaching for his hand and holding on to it.

'But what are you sorry for?' Jude asked with a frown, looking at our entwined hands. 'I'm the one who—'

I took another step, so I was just inches from him, and put a finger to his lips.

'I'm sorry,' I said breathlessly, 'because the truth is, I didn't want to have a brief encounter with you. I never did.'

I felt a huge weight lift from my shoulders as I finally said the words and imagined the new version of Mum I was beginning to understand breathing a sigh of relief somewhere.

'What?' Jude asked, looking at me again. 'What are you saying?'

'I'm saying,' I reiterated, 'that I never wanted to have a short-term thing with you. I've had feelings for you, proper feelings, for weeks, but I had no idea what to do with them because I'd never experienced them before. And then,' I sighed, 'literally just as I'd decided I was going to go for it and tell you that I wanted something long-lasting with you, I let you speak first. And what you said you wanted from me was the exact opposite.'

'I don't believe it!' Jude gasped, reaching for my other hand.

'Oh, please do,' I groaned.

Jude smiled at that.

'I mean, I can't believe we've done this,' he said, shaking his head as his gaze flicked to my lips and then back to my eyes. 'We've both been second-guessing the other and getting it completely wrong. We've been so stupid, haven't we?'

'Yes,' I agreed. 'We've both been pretty useless. But now we know the truth, don't we?'

'Yes,' he said, echoing my assertion and completely closing the gap between us. 'But just to be sure, will you spell it out for me? Tell me *exactly* what it is that you want, Bella.'

His lips were so close to mine, I could feel his warm breath as he said the words.

'I want you to come home, Jude,' I said as I softly kissed him. 'I want you to come home for Christmas.'

Chapter 29

It was almost dark by the time Jude and I had finished kissing and making up in the Wishing Tree clearing and we were able to sneak away from the hall and back to the house, unseen. Having only just found our way back to each other, we weren't ready to go public quite yet, but there was one person Jude needed to let know how the day had turned out.

'So, how did you find it, staying in a converted horsebox?' I asked him as he sent Bear a message, having explained to me that that's where he'd been holed up while he tried to get his head and heart straight and his injuries further healed.

'Now, don't make too much of this,' Jude said, grinning, as I negotiated the drove roads back to town, paying particular attention as we passed the spot of his crash. He didn't comment on the location, and neither did I.

'Go on,' I encouraged him. 'Tell me.'

'I actually found it a bit lacking on the décor front,' he admitted.

My mouth opened and closed, but no words came out.

'I know,' Jude laughed at my response, or lack of it, as his phone loudly pinged. 'You've maximized me, Bella! I prefer a full house now to a spartan one. It feels so much cosier and more lived in.'

'Well,' I said, finally finding my voice, 'at least I've done something right since you've been here, then.'

'Oh,' he said, 'you've done loads right. We both have.'

He was correct, of course. It was only our previous miscommunication about our true feelings for each other that had made a mess of things, and that was all very happily untangled now.

'We have,' I therefore agreed, feeling my festive spirit suddenly soar as I realized that we were both in for a fabulous Christmas. 'And now everything's all right.'

'One hundred per cent all right. Better than all right, in fact.' Jude grinned, and I smiled back. 'Bear says he can drop my stuff at the hall tomorrow for us to pick up,' he read off his phone screen. 'I take it you were planning to go back again?'

'Yes,' I said, 'I always visit the Winter Wonderland on both the days that it's running.'

'Why does that not surprise me?' Jude chuckled. 'And actually, I'd like a look at it all, too, because I mostly stayed out of sight today, trying to pluck up the courage to talk to you if I saw you and not get spotted by the Connellys.'

'Now I think about it,' I said thoughtfully, thinking more about Bear, 'when I saw Bear in the pub, he was keen to ask if I was going to be at the hall today.'

I wondered if Molly had had an inkling that something was afoot, too.

'We actually have a lot to thank Bear for.' Jude smiled. 'Not only did he move the horsebox away from Cuckoo Cottage so I could stay in it without Holly seeing me, but he also gave me a good talking to about telling you the truth about how I really feel. He's become a firm friend. And a straight-talking one, too.'

'In that case,' I responded, thinking that the two men had got to know each other far better than I had realized, 'we really *do* have a lot to thank him for.'

'And then there's the book, of course,' Jude said.

'The book?' I asked as we neared the sanctuary of home. 'The Connelly one, you mean?'

'No,' he said mysteriously. 'Not that one.'

'There's another?'

'There is now,' he said, rubbing his hands together.

'Tell me!' I insisted.

'Bear has put me in touch with a family that wants me to write about the history of their historical home, just like I'm doing for Catherine and Angus,' he explained excitedly. 'He was talking to the owners about the idea a while ago, while restoring a part of their garden. He didn't think he knew anyone who could do it at the time, but then he met me again and heard more about my change of direction and put me forward for it.'

'Oh wow,' I gasped. 'That's fantastic! How wonderful to have your next project lined up before you've finished the current one. That's a great position to be in.'

'It is,' said Jude, rubbing his hands together again. 'We sorted it all out in the first few days following the crash,' he said. 'We got together to talk it through and then had a few Zoom meetings with the family to firm up the details.'

'So that's where you kept disappearing to.'

That made total sense.

'Yes,' Jude said, nodding. 'I didn't want to tell you about it until everything was signed and sealed.'

'And is it now?'

'It is,' he said happily.

'Is the house you're going to be writing about very far away?'

I didn't like the thought of him disappearing so soon after we'd got together.

'Just over the county line in Norfolk.' He grinned.

'So does that mean you're planning to hang around Wynbridge for a while?' I asked, feeling my stomach swoop with further excitement at the thought.

'Absolutely. You won't be getting rid of me in a hurry.'

'It's just as well I didn't let your room out when you disappeared, then, isn't it?' I responded mischievously, feeling even happier. We both knew I wouldn't have done that, but it was fun to tease him.

'Actually,' he then said more seriously. 'I wanted to talk to you about the room.'

'Go on,' I said, as I turned the car onto the drive.

The porch was perfectly lit, and I couldn't wait to show Jude the tree inside.

'Well,' he said, 'I would love to stay at the house, if you're happy for me to. But I was wondering if I could move into the apartment, so you could have the run of the rest of the place as you usually would at this time of year. I don't want to put our relationship under any pressure, and I know how much you love living in the house during the closed season.'

'Are you sure you'll be able to manage the stairs?'

'Absolutely.'

Given his previous athleticism in the bedroom, a single flight of stairs should prove to be no problem now, and I felt my cheeks colour at the memory.

'All right,' I agreed, thinking his suggestion was a good one. 'That sounds perfect. I haven't actually taken any early bookings for the house yet, and I can block out a bit more time to give us longer into next year to enjoy some peace and privacy. We can decide what to do after that when the spring reservations start rolling in.'

Jude didn't say anything, and I felt my stomach lurch.

'I mean,' I started, and swallowed, trying to backtrack in case he thought I was looking too far ahead, 'that is, if you think that would work. I don't want you panicking that I'm expecting you to stay for the duration . . .'

Jude's sudden smile made the words die in my throat.

'I think it's an amazing idea,' he said. 'I just can't believe that it's coming from the woman I love, who I thought was super-glued to brief relationship encounters and all set to permanently ring-fence her heart.'

He was right. It was quite a turnaround, but I wasn't focused on that.

'The woman you *what*?' I squeaked.

I watched Jude's expression as he played over what he had just said.

'The woman I love,' he repeated, guessing which words I'd honed in on. He clearly wasn't afraid of saying them again, either. 'But don't panic, I don't expect you to say it back.'

'But I *do* love you, Jude,' I said, without a pause. 'I've loved you for quite some time.'

'Well, how about that?' he said, leaning across to kiss me again.

'How about that indeed?' I laughed when we pulled apart.

★

Just as she had always been, Tink was ecstatic to see Jude. And just as I had known he wouldn't, he didn't make it up to the apartment or into his bed in the spare room that night.

'Do we *really* have to go back to Wynthorpe today?' he asked me early the next morning as I carried a tray up to the bedroom, loaded with tea and toast.

While I had been making us breakfast, I'd tried to call Mum and give her the thrilling news that Jude and I were together, but she hadn't answered her mobile. Given what I now knew she really felt about love and that she had wanted me to track Jude down, I couldn't wait to tell her how everything had turned out, but my announcement would have to go unspoken a bit longer. Hopefully, she'd spot my missed call and ring back soon.

'I'd much rather stay holed up here with you, Tink and that fabulous tree,' Jude continued.

He loved the way I had decorated the tree and eventually said he forgave me for doing it without him. Given that he had disappeared with no hint that he was ever coming back, there wasn't anything to forgive there, but I was delighted that he felt miffed to have missed taking part.

The Jude who had turned up with his Christmas ill-wishes just a few weeks ago wouldn't have given a damn, but he wasn't that man now. He'd worked through his former relationship trauma and the impact it had had on his relationship with Christmas – and I certainly wasn't the woman he'd first met, either.

We'd both been on the receiving end of a Christmas miracle, and we were still three days away from the big day yet. And I had no intention of wasting a single second of them. Not that time spent in bed with Jude was wasted, but you know what I mean.

'As tempting as that sounds,' I therefore told him as I carefully set down the tray and encouraged Tink to get off the bed, so there was room for me to get back into it, 'today is the twenty-second of December. And you may not realize this, but I have a whole lot of Christmas catching-up to do.'

'Such as?' Jude asked with interest, inching himself up in the bed and wincing a little in the process.

Given the stamina and strength he had again shown overnight, his discomfort was no surprise, but we'd have to be more careful going forward if we didn't want to hinder his post-crash recovery.

'Well,' I said, bracing myself to reel everything off, 'I have presents to deliver, more baking to do, the house to clean, a Christmas shop to undertake—'

'You don't have it delivered?'

'No,' I told him. 'I prefer to shop local and that's just as well, isn't it, because I daresay the butcher, baker and—'

'Candlestick-maker?' Jude butted in.

'Oh,' I said, reaching to make a note on my phone, 'candles . . .'

'Go on,' he nudged me, making everything on the tray wobble.

'And Chris on the fruit and veg stall, I was going to say,' I corrected him, 'will be able to provide everything I'm going to need more easily than a supermarket with limited stock this close to the twenty-fifth and with a million online orders to try to honour.'

'Surely you won't need that much more just because I'm back?'

I gave him a look.

'Fair enough,' he said, grinning. 'There's something missing from your list, though.'

'There is?' I gasped, looking down it again. 'What?'

'A party, of course,' he said, as if that should have been obvious. 'With your hosting skills, I'm sure a festive drinks and nibbles soirée here would be wonderful.'

'Maybe next December,' I said, my mind already filling up with ideas for décor and dishes and the image of us hosting it together. 'I think I've got enough to contend with for now, and it would be a bit short notice.'

'True,' Jude agreed.

'I feel like I'm going to cram the twelve days of Christmas into far less than half that time this year,' I laughed, looking again at my lengthy to-do list.

'And I can't tell you,' Jude said, beaming, 'how thrilled I am to be here doing it all with you.'

I was extremely happy about that, too.

We were nowhere near as early in setting off for the hall as I had been the day before, and as a result, we had to park quite a distance away from where everything was set up.

'Well, I never,' Archie said with a grin, as he directed me to a space and spotted who leant over and kissed my cheek as I applied the handbrake. 'Together at last!'

I rolled my eyes at that. It didn't turn out to be the only time we heard the comment that day, either.

'Bella!' shouted Holly, from her place with Bear in the queue for a sleigh ride.

Jude and I walked over to join them, and Bear had the

biggest grin on his face. Holly biffed him on the arm when she noticed it.

'I had absolutely no idea!' was the first thing she said to me. 'Had I known you'd genuinely fallen for each other and had an inkling that Jude was staying in the horsebox, I would have been straight on the phone to you.'

'Which is exactly why I didn't want you finding out,' Bear teased, and tickled her side. 'I was more than capable of match-making. Or tying up the loose ends, at least.'

'Well,' Holly pouted, 'I would have liked to take some of the credit.'

'No way,' said Bear. 'This was all me. Or at least, a bit me.'

'So you're properly together, then?' Holly asked me, biting her lip.

'We are,' I said, as Jeanie came rushing up with Tim in hot pursuit and weighed down with bags, which told us that our friend had been catching up with her Christmas shopping.

'A little Connelly bird,' she said, beaming and pulling me in for a hug, 'has just told me that you two are an item. A *proper* item. I can't believe it! I'm so pleased for you, Bella. And Jude,' she said, turning her attention to my beau, 'you must be quite a guy to have cracked the lock on Bella's heart.'

'Oh, I am,' he said nonchalantly, which made us all laugh. 'And she's quite a gal, to have helped me through some difficult stuff during these last few weeks, too.'

'No more hating on Christmas?' Jeanie asked in her usual blunt manner.

'Definitely not,' Jude confirmed.

'So,' said Tim, 'are we all queueing up for a sleigh ride, then?'

We watched the sleigh return. It looked like a bit of a bumpy ride.

'I know it looks romantic,' Jude said to me, 'but I think I'm going to sit it out. I'm not sure my ribs can take it, after . . .'

His words trailed off, and I felt a blush blooming because I knew exactly what he was referring to. Unfortunately, so did everyone else. Once the whoops and teasing had died down, Tim said he had a thirst on him and would take Jude for a drink, and Bear then suggested that he could tag along with them, too. I gave Jude the keys to my car so Bear could shift Jude's stuff from the truck to my Fiat, and that left Jeanie, Holly and I to take a turn in the sleigh together.

'We can go later,' Bear told Holly, 'and I can promise it will be far more romantic without this lot looking on.'

'All right,' she relented, standing on tiptoe to kiss him. 'Come on, girls. My treat.'

Sitting in the shiny red sleigh between my two best friends, with a vast, warming blanket stretched across all our knees, I filled them in on what had most recently happened between Jude and me. Even though Holly already knew some of it, she was keen to know all the details. Well, nearly all of them.

'So you really have fallen for him, then?' Jeanie asked, once I'd finished my explanation and as we whizzed along, our eyes watering because of the chilly breeze.

'I really have,' I said, still amazed to hear myself saying the words out loud.

'And he's fallen for you, too,' Holly dreamily added.

'How amazing is this?' Jeanie laughed. 'We're all of us loved up for Christmas! Well done us! What does your mum make of it, though, Bella?' she asked. 'I bet she's a bit shocked, isn't she?'

'I haven't managed to get hold of her yet,' I said, pulling out my phone and checking it again. 'But she might not be quite as shocked as you are no doubt thinking.'

'Oh?' Jeanie frowned. 'Why's that, then?'

It was my turn to shock them then.

'So,' said Holly, once I'd finished telling them about Mum's real thoughts relating to matters of the heart and what she had wanted me to do about Jude. 'It turns out she's not down on love, after all.'

'Nope,' I confirmed. 'And now neither am I!'

For once, Jeanie looked completely flabbergasted.

Jude loved the Wynthorpe Hall Winter Wonderland experience as much as I did, and we spent hours there. We were just getting ready to go, as I was mindful that Tink was home alone, when Angus finally caught up with us.

'I hear congratulations are in order!' he boomed loud enough for everyone on the entire estate to hear. 'Jamie tells me you're together at last.'

The day before, I had predicted that Archie was turning into his father, but now I realized a fair bit of the wonderful man's genes, generosity and love of a good gossip had rubbed off on Jamie, too.

'We are,' Jude and I said together, and he squeezed my fingers even tighter.

'I had a feeling this might happen,' Angus said, beaming, looking at our entwined hands. 'And I'm thrilled for you both. I hope you won't have to leave the area too soon, Jude?'

Jude then told Angus a little of what he had lined up to do after he'd finished writing the Wynthorpe Hall book, and his current employer looked thrilled.

'And I'd very much like to show you the chapter outlines for your book after Christmas, Angus,' Jude added, and Angus looked even more elated.

'I can't wait to see them,' he said, nodding. 'And I know you found us a lot to live with,' he said, clapping poor Jude heartily on the back, 'but I always felt that, deep down, you were already one of us.'

In spite of his rattling ribs, Jude looked delighted to hear him say that.

'Why don't you come into the hall,' Angus then suggested, 'and we'll find the others and open a bottle or four to celebrate?'

'I'm sorry, Angus,' I apologized. 'I really need to get back for Tink, and I need to call Mum, too. I've been trying to contact her all day, but she hasn't been answering her phone.'

'Doesn't she know about you two yet?' Angus asked with a grimace.

'No,' I said. 'Not yet, but fear not. Her reaction isn't going to be what you might expect.'

'Oh?'

'I'll fill you in another time,' I told him.

'What's going on?' Jude asked as we went off to search for my car.

On the journey home, I filled him in on how Mum's opinions about love were actually completely at odds with what I had always assumed she felt.

'Oh my goodness,' he said, letting out a breath as I finally drew one in. 'Clearly we weren't the only ones with crossed wires in the heart department, then.'

'I know,' I said, shaking my head as my phone began to

chime. 'The fact that they're all now uncrossed is the best Christmas present ever.'

'That's your mum,' said Jude, looking at the screen. 'You'd better ring her back as soon as we get in. I'll see to Tink.'

My boots were barely off before my phone rang again, and that time I was able to answer. Mum's face filled the screen.

'Mum!' I said, as I headed up to my room and Jude let Tink into the garden. 'I've been trying to get hold of you all day.'

'I've just realized,' she said, looking rather flushed. 'I was . . . preoccupied. So,' she then urged me, 'tell me.'

'I found Jude!' I said happily. 'Or rather we found each other. At the Wishing Tree, of all places . . .'

'And?' Mum asked impatiently.

'We're together.' I grinned. 'We're a couple.'

My own cheeks flushed as brightly as Mum's when I said that.

'Oh, my darling girl,' she said, her eyes filling with joyful tears. 'I'm so happy for you!'

'I'm happy for me, too,' I laughed, propping up my phone and shrugging off my coat.

'I can see that.' Mum nodded. 'And I'm happy for *me*, too,' she added intriguingly.

'Any particular reason?'

I wondered if the 'preoccupation' she had mentioned was connected to her flushed complexion.

'There is one,' she said with a smile.

'Go on.'

'I'm in love, too,' she blurted out. 'I think Henri and I are going to go the distance!'

Chapter 30

Needless to say, I was thrilled for Mum and her partner, Henri, and in turn she was delighted for me and Jude. I couldn't help but laugh about the fact that we then spent ages chatting about the men in our lives and both enthusiastically championing love, when just a few days ago I would have expected the exact opposite to happen.

That could have been the festive highlight of the year, but the next two days were in contention for the crown, as they were as idyllic as the days depicted in the many Christmas romance novels I borrowed from the library every winter.

'Are you cold, Bella?' Jude asked when he and Tink came to meet me in town on the afternoon of Christmas Eve.

'Freezing!' I said, as I stamped my feet and blew on my fingers, which still felt numb even though I was wearing thick gloves.

It had been a good idea to keep the Cherry Tree Café stall running for the morning, as between us, Lizzie and I had made the most of the last-minute, slightly wide-eyed and panicked Christmas shoppers, but it was bitterly cold. By the time Jude arrived, I really had had enough.

'Was everything all right at the butcher's?' I asked him, as I stamped my feet again.

We'd walked into town together early, and then Jude had gone on to collect the meat order and a few extras to see us through the next few days. We'd done a big local shop the morning before and then spent the afternoon baking together, so we were pretty well stocked up. But as I'd told so many people to just drop in if they happened to be passing, I wanted to make sure I had something to offer them. We had considered making another gingerbread house, but with the time counting down, it would have been stressful trying to squeeze it in, and neither of us wanted that.

'Yes,' Jude said with a nod, then bent down to smooth down Tink's coat, which had slipped as a result of her having a good shake. 'The queue had snaked practically right around the building by the time I got there, but everything on your list was in the bags.'

'And you carried it home all right?' I winced, only then realising just how much there must have been to manhandle. Knowing how big just the turkey was, it must have been a nightmare. I should have thought of that and asked Jude to look after the stall while I collected the order in the car.

'I didn't have to carry it,' he told me, and I felt relieved. 'Bear was in the queue, too, and he gave me a lift back to the house.'

'That was just as well,' I laughed, now I knew he hadn't had to walk. 'Your arms would have reached the floor by the time you got back.'

'I fail to see how that would have been funny,' he pretended to pout.

I reached for the front of his coat, pulled him towards me and planted a kiss firmly on his luscious lips. The moment quickly deepened and even more quickly started to thaw me out and warm me up.

'That'll do, you two!' shouted Lizzie, as she pulled the café door closed behind her and came over to join us. 'You'll put the customers off.'

I let Jude go with a very contented sigh and then looked around.

'I don't think there will be any more customers now,' I said, taking in the deserted square. 'Everyone's got more sense than to still be out here in subzero temperatures.'

'The café's emptying fast, too,' Lizzie told us. 'Jemma's getting ready to close up, and then we're heading to the pub. Will you be going over? It'll only take a minute to pack up here, as there's practically nothing left, so you might as well.'

'That sounds good to me,' said Jude keenly.

'Well,' I said, checking the time on my phone, 'I was planning to clean the house this afternoon . . .'

'You're going to do housework on Christmas Eve?' Lizzie gaped.

'I usually do,' I told her. 'I like the place looking perfect for when I get up on Christmas morning.'

I could feel another sudden rush of excitement bubbling up inside me when I thought about Christmas Day and the traditions it entailed. I wondered what Jude would make of my continuing the custom of putting out a mince pie and whisky for Santa and a carrot for the reindeer. Given that I'd now whipped him up into a festive frenzy strong enough to rival my own, I hoped that he'd be all for it.

'And then you spend the morning opening presents and creating dust,' Lizzie said wisely. 'I'd leave the vacuuming, if I were you, and come to the pub instead.'

She made a very good point, and it was hardly as if the house was in disarray. I'd given everywhere a thorough clean when I'd finished decorating the tree, and Jude and I had been pretty much confined to the bedroom since his return.

'What do you think, then, Jude?' Lizzie asked him as between us we made short work of packing up the stall. 'Pub or chores?'

'I think it's up to Bella,' he said diplomatically. 'I know how much her Christmas traditions mean to her.'

'Well?' Lizzie said, turning to me.

'I think this is one tradition I can forgo in favour of the pub,' I said willingly. Everything else I'd reeled off to Jude just a day or so ago had been ticked off my to-do list, so now it was time for some festive fun with friends. 'And as we walked into town this morning, I can indulge in a few glasses of Jeanie's mulled wine to warm me up, can't I?'

Jude laughed when I said that, and I remembered what had happened after the first quiz night.

'Maybe just the one glass,' I then quickly amended that to, and he laughed all the harder.

Was it really only a month ago that I had been battling with my feelings for him? It was impossible to believe I'd ever questioned them now, because they felt so natural and so right. Flings had been fine until the real deal came along, and Jude was every inch that.

'Come on, then,' Lizzie nudged me, pulling me out of my momentary reminiscing. 'Let's get this oilcloth folded and us all out of the cold. I reckon it's going to snow.'

'A white Christmas,' said Jude, his face lighting up with the biggest smile. 'How perfect would that be?'

'So perfect,' I said dreamily, and Lizzie rolled her eyes.

'You won't be saying that when it turns to slush,' she teased.

'Don't spoil it!' I tutted. 'I'm imagining opening the curtains in the morning and looking out on a winter wonderland of my own. And I know Tink would love that, too, wouldn't you, girl?'

As always, she woofed on cue, and I bent down and kissed the top of her beautiful silky dome-shaped head. She felt lovely and warm in her fleece-lined coat.

'Have you got more of those kisses to spare for me?' Jude asked, and I straightened again and kissed him, too.

'Right,' said Lizzie. 'That's the lot, and here's Ben. He can help me carry the crates to the café, so you two can go straight over to The Mermaid—'

Before she had a chance to ask her partner for his assistance, he presented her with a sprig of mistletoe from his pocket and pulled her into his arms.

'This Christmas kisses lark is catching,' I laughed, but neither of them heard me, and Jude, Tink and I stole away and into the pub.

The warmth inside felt like a welcoming balm. I wasn't sure if it was a result of the roaring log fire or the number of people still propping up the bar. I didn't think I'd ever seen the pub so busy, but the place had become even more popular since Jeanie had arrived back in town, so I shouldn't have been surprised.

'Merry Christmas, you two!' shouted Archie, who was just pulling on his coat.

'Merry Christmas to you, too,' we said back.

'Are you all leaving now?' I asked.

'Afraid so,' said Molly, who didn't usually come to the pub. 'We've left Angus in charge of the little ones, so . . .'

'Oh, right,' I said, pulling a face. 'In that case, I wonder who will be running rings around whom.'

'Our boys are helping him, too,' said Christopher, another Connelly brother. He and his wife, Cass, and their two sons lived quite a distance away, but mostly came to stay for Christmas.

'So there are a couple of steadying influences looking out for Alby and Demelza,' Anna said, hiccupping tipsily.

'Mum said if we saw you two, we were to ask if you'd come to the hall on New Year's Day,' Jamie said, addressing both Jude and me, then looking puzzled. 'She'll have to text you what time, though, because I've completely forgotten.'

I would have loved to have said yes to any time, but knowing that the entire clan would still be in situ, I didn't think Jude would be up for it. But I was wrong.

'I think that would be wonderful, Bella, don't you?' he said, before I'd had the opportunity to graciously decline. 'A wonderful way to start the New Year.'

'It's going to be quite a houseful,' Archie said.

'Hall full,' Molly quietly amended.

'So the more the merrier.'

'Perfect,' I said.

'Perfect,' Jude echoed.

It took a while for the six of them to do the rounds before they left, and from what I could make out, Archie was issuing New Year invitations left, right and centre. I knew Catherine and Angus wouldn't mind, though, and Dorothy certainly wouldn't be fazed. She was always ready to serve up a feast at a moment's notice.

The pub was only quiet for a few seconds when they all finally left, because Holly, Bear and Tim arrived almost immediately after. Holly had Jasper with her on a tight lead, while Bear had his docile bull terrier Queenie by his side without any restraint at all.

'It takes the dogs longer to say hello to each other than it does us,' said Holly, who had already got Jasper's lead in a tangle with Tink's.

'You guys go and find us all a seat,' suggested Bear, because the scene had the potential to descend into canine chaos, 'and I'll get the drinks in.'

'I'll give you a hand,' offered Tim. 'You can spare Jeanie for a while, can't you, Jim?'

'I don't see why not,' her affable uncle agreed.

Once the six of us, or nine if you included the dogs, were sat around a table and all enjoying whatever drink we'd opted for – my mulled wine was certainly hitting the coldest spots – I looked around our little group and felt a warm glow of contentment.

Holly and Bear had arrived in town as a couple, but Jeanie and I, even just a few short weeks ago at the pub Hallowe'en party, had been flying solo. And there was nothing wrong with that, of course, but seeing us now with our perfectly matched partners felt so special, and that wasn't the wine talking. Well, not yet anyway.

'Who fancies a singalong?' Jeanie suggested once we'd all shared our plans for Christmas and had more drinks.

'Me!' said Tim, immediately jumping up. 'You know I can do a cracking Mariah when the mood takes me.'

'Oh crikey,' Bear said with a grimace. 'Please don't say the mood's taken him.'

The impromptu party was still in full swing when Jude and I looked at one another and both silently agreed that it was time for us to make a discreet exit. Tim's dulcet (if you could call them that) tones followed us outside and into the square, where it had obviously been snowing for a while. Arm in arm, Jude and I slowly walked home, with Tink snuffling ahead and occasionally stopping to try to catch a slowly falling flake or two.

As always, the house felt like a comforting embrace when we stepped into it, and I was pleased that I had turned the heating up a degree or two. While I lit the fire and some candles, Jude went around and turned on all the fairy lights.

'Is it too early for PJs?' I asked him as he headed to the hot chocolate station.

'It's never too early for PJs,' he said seriously. 'Especially on Christmas Eve.'

'I was hoping we were going to agree about that,' I said, smiling, and ran up the stairs with him in hot pursuit.

A little while later, we were snuggled under a thick fleecy blanket in front of the well-stoked fire and tucking into the cheese, crackers and grapes I had definitely overstocked us with. *Carols from King's* was on the television in the background, and with the curtains open, I could see it was still snowing. I let out a contented sigh, and Jude turned to face me.

'Happy?' he asked, looking into my eyes in a way that made me feel as though I was not only the most important person in the room, but in the entire world.

'*So* happy,' it was easy to tell him. 'You?'

'Yes,' he nodded. 'Blissful. Not only have you gifted me back my love of Christmas, Bella, but you've healed my heart, too.'

'And you've opened mine,' I told him, feeling a wonderful excess of happiness and contentment welling up as he took our plates and put them to one side so we could snuggle up. 'Being home for Christmas with you means everything to me, Jude.'

He drew me closer still and kissed me softly on the lips.

'And for me, Bella,' he said breathlessly, 'being with you feels like coming home.'

He kissed me again, and I felt myself falling fathoms deeper in love with him. A part of me had always been away with the fairies, but now I was heading off on a brand-new adventure and I couldn't wait to see where it took me.

Acknowledgements

Merry Christmas everyone!

I've just had a look at the bookcase in my writing room and worked out that *Home for Christmas* is the sixth title set in Wynbridge that celebrates the winter holiday season. Can you believe it?

No wonder writing this one has felt like a genuine homecoming and the scenes set in the town and at Wynthorpe Hall the loveliest to create. I hope you have enjoyed being in Wynbridge as much as I have, whether this has been your first festive trip with me to the Fens or your sixth.

As always, there are a whole host of folk to thank for their part in helping me turn the seed of an idea into a beautiful bloom. A poinsettia perhaps, given the time of year . . .

Heartfelt thanks to my wonderful agent, Amanda Preston, and world-class editor, Clare Hey. Thanks also to Judith Long, Harriett Collins, Amy Fulwood, Sara-Jade Virtue and the entire Books and the City team!

A huge hug for my Famous Five – Ian Wilfred, Jenni Keer, Clare Marchant and Rosie Hendry – your friendship and words of wisdom are a constant comfort.

Thank you, too, to Sue Baker (my soul sister), Claire Howard (who gets the medal for longest serving confidante), Jenny, Lucy and my wonderful mum for listening to me talk at you for endless hours about imminent deadlines, plot twists and the pain of picking a title!

Thanks also to the hugely supportive blogging community, the reviewers, librarians, event organisers, social media chums and book buyers who continue to champion my words. Your enthusiasm for my fictional worlds keeps me doing the job I love! Thank you.

And last, but never ever least, thank you so much to every reader who joins me on the coach to Wynbridge and beyond. It's a pleasure to keep booking you a seat on the bus.

Wishing you all a very happy and healthy Christmas and New Year and, until the next time we meet, may your book-shelves – be they virtual or real – be filled with fabulous fiction!

H x

About the Author

Heidi Swain lives in Norfolk. She is passionate about gardening and the countryside, and collects vintage paraphernalia. *Home for Christmas* is her nineteenth novel. You can follow Heidi on X or Instagram @Heidi_Swain or visit her website: heidiswain.co.uk

That Festive Feeling

Holly has the place to herself this Christmas, house-sitting for friends who live on Nightingale Square. Newly single and finding herself unsure about next steps for her career, she plans to hunker down and make some life decisions.

On early morning walks around a nearby lake she bumps into May, who is also new to the area, and her dapper dachshund Monty. Quickly, a firm friendship blossoms. Then when Holly meets Bear, a rather large and rather attractive man, and his rescue dog Queenie, her stay suddenly feels even more appealing.

As the community comes together for the season's festivities, Holly must start thinking about where life will take her next. But distractions close to home make thinking about the future more tricky than ever ...

Will she get that festive feeling this Christmas?

AVAILABLE IN PAPERBACK AND EBOOK NOW

A
Christmas
Celebration

When Paige turns up unannounced at Wynthorpe
Hall, she discovers the place she knew when she was
growing up has changed beyond all recognition.

One night while driving home after delivering library
books and shopping to residents she stumbles across
an isolated cottage and meets Albert, its elderly and
rather grumpy owner. She quickly realises there's
more to Albert than meets the eye and the same
can be said for the other man she can't seem to help
running into, handsome but brooding Brodie.

Each of them has a secret and a desire to hide away
from the world, but with Christmas on the horizon, is
that really the best way to celebrate the season?

AVAILABLE IN PAPERBACK AND EBOOK NOW

The Holiday Escape

Ally and her dad, Geoff, run a creative retreat from their home, Hollyhock Cottage. They give their guests their dream coastal break, but Ally hankers after something different.

Ally's survival strategy is to escape out of season and pretend to be the person she always imagined she would be. She meets Logan while she's away in Barcelona and he turns out to be *exactly* the kind of distraction she's looking for.

With her spirits restored, Ally returns home, picks up the reins again and sets her sights on another successful season. But when Logan unexpectedly arrives on the scene, she soon realises she's in for a summer that's going to be far from straightforward . . .

AVAILABLE IN PAPERBACK AND EBOOK NOW

The Book-Lovers' Retreat

Novel *Hope Falls* is friends Emily, Rachel and
Tori's favourite book. So, when they get the
chance to spend summer at the cottage in Lakeside
where the film adaptation was located, they know
it is going to be the holiday of a lifetime.

Six weeks away will give them a chance to
re-evaluate their life choices. For Emily to make
career plans and for Rachel to decide whether to
move in with her partner Jeremy. Then Tori has
to drop out at the last moment, and her space is
offered to another *Hope Falls* afficionado, Alex.

Alex turns out not to be who they expected. But as the
summer develops, so does their friendship. Could this
be where their lives will change course forever . . . ?

AVAILABLE IN PAPERBACK AND EBOOK NOW

booksandthecity.co.uk
the home of female fiction

NEWS & EVENTS | BOOKS | FEATURES | COMPETITIONS

Follow us online to be the first to hear from
your favourite authors

booksandthecity.co.uk   **@TeamBATC**

Join our mailing list for the latest news, events and
exclusive competitions

Sign up at
booksandthecity.co.uk